TRACKS

By Elaine Bailey

Pompadour and Pearls:
a Patchwork of Poetry

Buttermilk Clouds

Explosion in Villa Rica

TRACKS

A novel by

Elaine Bailey

Tracks

Cover: Thanks to Cameron Tibbets, Sueann Smith, photographer, and Rick Smith of RS Creative Services Inc.

ISBN: 978-0-9628023-8-6

⚜ Lillium Press

This book is dedicated to

Franklin and Lila Berkshire,

who never gave up on their son,

Brad.

Contents

Part III—Losing Myself, Finding Myself

TRACKS

This book is a composite of a real life story, telling real events. Name changes, omissions, and imaginative additions cause this story to be classified as fiction.

Prologue

Oakdale, Georgia

As I drove, I thought back to the events which changed me from an innocent kid into a teen who was like a mad dog that had been fed gunpowder. I eased my SUV over to the Oakdale exit of I-285, west of Atlanta. Looming ahead, so familiar yet so surprisingly old looking, was the tall electric power plant smokestack. I had seen this smokestack tower earlier today from the tenth story of a building in the city ten miles away and knew I had to revisit there. This smokestack tower marked my youth—and it had drawn me back. I had not been back here in years and had not wanted to come back until today. There were too many memories here—some good but many bad that I had wanted to forget. With the success I finally had in my life, I felt an overwhelming desire to take a look back—to face the past.

After a few more miles, I drove slowly down the parking lot of the new mall that stretched out in front of me. Surveying the area, I looked for anything I could recognize. I turned my head and saw, way down the main street, what used to be the elementary school, and the old, worn building where Pac-a-Sac Groceries had been.

The parking lot began a gradual slope downward for about half a mile. At the bottom of the incline I found the narrow, winding creek where I had played so many times as a child.

Then I parked my SUV and got out. I took off my suit coat and tie and left them on the seat beside my briefcase and went to find the old plank bridge—a few worn boards that extended over the almost dried up creek. Some of these boards looked rotten. I decided not to trust this old bridge to my six foot two inch, two hundred eighty pound frame, so I jumped the creek as I had so many times in my youth. I recognized everything on the other side of the creek and memories came flooding back like the sounds of several small boys joking and clowning around playing in the creek on spring days all those years ago.

The small, white board house in front of me looked vacant. When I found the front door unlocked, I walked through the rooms. Even after thirty-five years, the house stood strong and still in good shape, but I doubted it would ever be occupied again as it sat practically in the back parking lot of the mall. As I walked through the rooms, I ached with a longing for the good times I spent here with my family.

In the backyard, weeds touched my elbows as I walked through them. I looked up to the bluff on the right side of the house and noticed several people walking there on the railroad track. The thoughts of happy times I spent on these tracks as a youth came back to me, but were quickly overshadowed by the thoughts of pain and tragedy as I surveyed the area.

From the center of the backyard, I looked toward the tiny dilapidated barn to my immediate left then up to the huge shopping center looming just behind. The contrast was staggering. Just as staggering, in contrast, were the memories of where I used to be and where my successful life had taken me in the last few years. I walked toward the railroad bridge on a high bluff over the creek and then over the general area for almost an hour trying to find landmarks I recognized.

My growing up years were spent here, practically in the shadow of the Atlanta skyline, where a small grid of streets ran out from a cluster of oak trees nestled in a curve of the Chattahoochee River. On a clear day you could see an inch or two of gleaming city buildings above the horizon. You could always hear the gentle roll of the Chattahoochee and even smell its musky, brown waters after a rain. As a child I fished in this river, rode the boxcars of the Southern Railroad tracks, and walked up and down the main road, Atlanta Road, that all ran parallel to each other.

This tiny town of my youth deserved the name Oakdale because of the main street's abundant oak trees towering over every shop with huge limbs that reached out and touched the limbs of the next tree to form a canopy. In the deep South of thirty-five years ago, the frequent rains and the rivers meandering throughout the countryside kept everything moist and green. Kudzu covered the rolling hills and climbed, possessed, and took the shape of the oak and pine trees and everything else in its path, even junk cars and dilapidated farmhouses.

In the South then, each spring brought a riot of color beginning with pink and white dogwoods in March giving way to runners of wisteria sprouting in April. The honeysuckles tangled their fragrance with the seven-sister, running rosebush blooming in the summer. Geraniums didn't die until the first frost in early November when red maple leaves covered the dry, brown grass. The mild winters caused you to search way back into the closet for a coat if the temperature ever fell below thirty, or if there were one of those rare winter days when everyone got excited because the one-inch-of-snow-every-five-years had fallen.

When I lived here, every family including my own devoted a tremendous amount of time and energy in the springtime to planting a crop. Then they spent most of the summer harvesting and preserving fruits and vegetables. My mother and the local women found their true self-worth in how many quarts of green beans they could "put up" and how many pints of peaches they had in the freezer at the end of the summer.

The heart of the Bible Belt ran smack through this northwest Georgia town as white, steepled churches dotted the Oakdale landscape. I looked toward my Dad's old country church and smiled to myself as I remembered the highlight event of dinner-on-the-ground which was held several times a year. Unsteady tables, made of a few boards, placed under the oak trees outside the church held a mouth watering feast. Each church lady prepared her specialty. There was fried chicken, baked ham, potato salad, butter beans, and fried okra, crowder peas, and corn-bread. Banana pudding and yellow layer cake with homemade chocolate fudge icing were the desserts. In the summertime, old men fussed over salt and ice and hand cranked ice cream freezers and stirred in a pint or two of last years peaches from the freezer into homemade ice cream.

Mom and Dad brought me up to be afraid if I didn't go to church, sin would take me over. I became afraid that God would strike me down dead if I missed the Sunday or Wednesday night service. If one did, you became known as a backslider. But if you attended these three functions the next week, you were not a backslider any more until you missed service again. If you happened to go fishing on Sunday or missed several weeks then you became known as sinner.

Oakdale had its ruffians too—backsliders that just kept sliding back into real meanness. My Aunt Lilly, Momma's twin sister, and a few church ladies referred to these lost souls as "heathen." Older, blue-haired, "proper" women and soft spoken, judgmental, gentlemen deacons looked down their noses and scurried away from heathens as if they could be contaminated just by looking at them. The heathens drank alcohol, smoked, went drag racing, and, God forbid, hung out at honky-tonks on Saturday night.

The wives who had the misfortune of being married to a heathen husband just couldn't do any better. We gave these families our hand-me-downs at Christmas and Thanksgiving.

My family certainly could not be called heathen but far from it as they were from good pioneer stock. Daddy said my great granddaddy, Cornelius Elijah Berkshire, came down from the Appalachian Mountains and settled a hundred acres in the area around Oakdale, but the family had long since sold most of the land since no one in the family farmed and didn't need that much land. Cornelius Berkshire also helped establish the Oakdale Primitive Baptist Church as a charter member. With great pride, my family told his story and pointed to the pictures of him that hung on the wall at home.

My parents, Lila and Frank Berkshire, followed in the footsteps of ol' Cornelius, as a founding father, seeing that the Oakdale Church of God, and the Riverside Church, were in existence partly due to their efforts. My sister, Kay, sang in the choir and was a member of the Young People's Endeavor.

In the South, the way the mild climate lulls you summer and winter, the way fireflies twinkle on a summer night, the way the kudzu climbs slowly, and the way southern fried chicken gravy flows into the bowl at Sunday's dinner, you sometimes have a false reassurance of a smooth, idyllic kind of life. The way everything else in your surroundings is beautiful, peaceful, and laid back fools you into thinking that the whole of life should be the same way. Eventually you expect a life without problems. Until my generation came along, kids usually followed their parents in habits, culture, work ethics, and morality. "Raise up a child in the way he should go and he will not depart from it when he is old." My parents expected this of me.

As I left the area, I eased my SUV over to the sidewalk and looked down. I found what I searched for—my name and the date crudely carved in the concrete sidewalk: BRAD 1966. Laughing to myself I thought, Well I left my tracks here. Prints of the knobby tires of my bicycle were left in the cement beside my name and the date. I remembered riding my bike through the wet cement in spite of the city worker hollering for me to not go through the freshly poured sidewalk. I came back later to write my name and the date. This, my first conscious act of rebellion, started my unraveling so gradually, I didn't know just how destructive I had become to myself until I had traveled so far down a wayward path.

I've turned out to be a sort of a pioneer. I helped bring changes to this area—a gradual change like a shadow over my young friends, but no one really noticed until young lives were ruined, families disrupted, and within a decade, our community became the "bad part of town." My destiny seemed to be that I become both a backslider and a ruffian. My Aunt Lilly said I traveled that hell-bent road. I guess I proved that to be true. But at the time, I felt like an innocent kid trying to have a good time. Troubled times came, and I got caught up in the undertow of the trouble and became a part of it—even causing some of it.

Part I—Bradley Boy

1.
My Short Childhood

When I came as a late-in-life sickly baby to a mother with health problems, I made my way like a slow wind that no one saw as a potential tornado that picked up speed, and brought turmoil and potential destruction to all in its path until you looked back and saw the wide swath of people left in its wake. I cannot say a single person came out better for knowing me unless knowing me made them stronger by testing their patience, their capacity to love, and even improving their prayer life. Like the aftermath of a tornado, we all look back and marvel at those who survived.

My parents, Lila and Frank Berkshire, had been married twenty-three years and had a daughter, Kay, age eighteen when I came, unplanned, into this world. Lila, age forty-two, and Frank, age fifty-seven, added to their small family, five pound, nineteen inch, Bradley Elijah Berkshire. They met this challenge head on like they had with all else life had thrown their way.

As I grew, Dad taught me about the outdoors, but Mom became fearfully overprotective of me. She let me play in the yard but warned, "Don't cross that bridge," referring to the small plank bridge which crossed the creek beside our house joining our yard to Hill Street. She felt she could protect her family in this small framed white house that she loved. It stood close to the railroad tracks running on top of a bluff to the right of the house. A huge field blocked an acre in front of the house. A small offshoot creek —coming off the Chattahoochee ran the length of our land to the left of our house and crossed to the back under the railroad bridge. At night when we were in bed and left the windows raised, we were close enough to hear the swirling brown water.

When Daddy built this house as a rental house, Mom had to have it even though Dad had told her "No." He said they could not afford to keep the house as they needed the rental money as income. This house was closer to town than where they lived and only three doors down from Aunt Lilly, Mom's twin sister. Mom just had to have it. She hated the drafty old house they lived in next to her parents on Pine Street, one block parallel behind the new house. So one day, she waited until Dad left for work, and she began to move into the new house. My sister, Kay, helped her move as Grandaddy and Grandmother O'Neal—her parents, sat on their front porch watching with disapproval.

When Dad came home, he ran from room to room in dismay as he found each room empty. Then he ran over to Mom's parents. "What happened? Why's the house empty? Where's Lila and Kay?" Grandpa O'Neal told him where to find them. Then he sped into the yard at the new house and slammed the truck door. "Lila! Have you lost your mind! I built this house to rent! We can't afford to live here."

"Oh Honey. I can go back to my nursing job." Lila sweet-talked him into letting her have her way. The move back to the old house would have been too much trouble. This new house had acreage that backed up to Lila's parent's land, and she could see their rooftop from her new house. This is the house where they lived when they brought me home from the hospital.

As I grew Mom didn't know how to handle me. All the boyish or mischievous things I did made Momma uneasy. When I was three, I got down in the floor of her car when she drove. Once I leaned over and pressed the gas pedal down further under her foot. I loved the sound of the motor and wanted to hear it go louder. Mom hollered at me to stop and pushed me back to my side of the car. When we got home, she cut a small limb off a bush by the front door. She skinned the "hickory switch," grabbed me by my arm, and started whipping me. I went out as far away from her as I could and ran in a circle around her legs. As she hit me across the backside, I could time it just right and jump a little and go up on my tiptoes, but it really didn't make the sharpness of the hickory stick any less on my backside.

"I won't do it anymore. I won't do it anymore. I promise," I cried. I know she loved me, but I got the feeling as I grew that she became frustrated and did not know what to do. This showed by the way she treated me at nighttime.

When she couldn't get me to stay in bed at night, she told me, "The boogie man will get you. He lives under the bed and if you try to get up he will grab you by the leg."

I lay afraid all night and of course, I didn't dare get up. The next morning, I dared to look under the bed. When the boogie man wasn't there, I believed he had already gone and would come only at dark again, each night.

As a young child, I was small and anemic. Every morning, my entire childhood, Mom gave me a terribly strong tasting iron tonic. She tried to get me to eat more. She loaded my plate with roast beef, salad, and smashed potatoes. Smashed potatoes were part mashed potatoes and part whipped potatoes all blended together with melted yellow butter floating in the middle. She chased me around the rooms in the house trying to get me to come to the table and eat.

I became the center of Mom's attention during most of her waking moments. As I grew, I began to understand why Mom tried to protect her family from the world. Some of her fears could have been brought on because the train-car wreck Kay had been in before my birth. I heard Mom, Dad, and Kay many times talking about this wreck I knew nothing about, and when I came into the room, they changed the subject. They never told me why a wheelchair hung in the barn.

When I was about four, I questioned Dad about the wheelchair and he told me what had happened. Before I was born, my sister, Kay, had been in a serious train-car accident. Kay, who was sixteen at the time, rode with a boyfriend who drove his car onto the crossing in Oakdale in front of the Silver Comet passenger train coming down the tracks at sixty miles an hour. The train broad-sided the car, dragging it down the tracks on the bluff passed our house. The car was caught underneath the train with her hanging out of the right side of the car.

"Son, Kay had severe cuts from that wreck and she's had many reconstructive surgeries on her face, leg, and right foot. Glass is still working its way up to the surface of her side. That wheelchair in the barn—she used it for a year. The doctors said she would never walk, but after many surgeries and a year of practicing she can walk." I had noticed my sister walked with a limp.

As I played out in front of my house, I noticed some mornings when the train went by, the conductor slowed the train, waved, blew the train whistle, and threw the newspaper down into the front yard. I always waved back to him. My dad unrolled the newspaper and inside the Atlanta Journal and Constitution he always found a pack of lifesavers.

"Daddy?" I asked. "Why does the trainman leave the paper instead of the mailman?"

Dad told me Mr. Long had been the conductor when the train hit the car in which Kay was riding. Mr. Long came to see Kay when she was in the hospital and had remained a long-time friend. The newspaper with the lifesavers continued. I knew Mr. Long often came to visit Kay after the wreck, when she still lived at home before she went to college and then married.

As a small child, I felt very close to Mom when she felt good and everything went her way. Those first six years there with her were especially good. Stately-built, Mom stood out as a beautiful woman with long, brown curly hair and blue eyes that sparkled when she was happy. I fell in love with Mom as many little boys do with their mother. I sat on the floor, at age four, at the end of her bed watching her. She sat at her vanity in front of the big, oval mirror brushing her long, curly hair. I liked the smell of the powder from the compact when she took the powder puff and powdered her face. The compact had three dimensional gold roses down the center and each rose held a rhinestone of a different color.

I watched her as she carefully applied her red lipstick. Then she took a Kleenex and kissed it, to blot her lipstick.

"Why did you kiss that Kleenex? Are you in love with it?" I joked.

She turned, surprised I had been watching her. I don't think she even knew I was in the room.

She held out her arms, and I ran to be embraced. "Bradley, I'm in love with you." She put a red kiss shape on my cheek and laughed at me looking in the mirror, trying to wipe it off with my fist making a big red smudge on my cheek.

Dad had always wanted to be a man's man, but since he wasn't, that's what he wanted me to become. He started me young to be an outdoors, adventuresome boy. He took me on the railroad tracks walking with him on the bluff above our house, making up stories. Down past our house, we named the section of track that ran on top of a long bridge, Church Road Bridge. The dirt logging road became Dead Horse Road. We named a nearby creek, Split Rock Creek, where a huge granite rock stood in a creek and the water ran through a crevice in the rock. Further down, we found an old log cabin which Dad said had stood for three generations.

The dirt path that led to it became Log Cabin Road.

"Tough—be tough." I heard this even as young as six years old when Dad sent me up a tree at dusk dark to fetch a roosting, chicken for Sunday dinner while he shined a light to temporarily blind it so I could get my fingers around its legs. He laughed at me but he didn't know I cried trying to reach that scratching ol' chicken as it kept jumping to a higher branch. He didn't see the scratch marks on my wrist, and I didn't show him or let him know I blinked back tears.

By the time I turned seven, Dad and I took Blue, his Bluetick hounddog, hunting for squirrel and rabbit. When he let me shoot his gun, I accidentally shot Blue in the foot, but he survived. Dad and I decided to let Mom think Dad had shot Blue. She would have had a fit if she had known Dad let me shoot a 22 rifle.

Dad worked hard to make a cushion of a life for his family, to make the good things happen and to ease the difficult times. Dad almost never sat down. From six in the morning until after supper he stayed on the go. He worked at Southern Railway, and then every afternoon he did the chores around the house, taking care of the farm animals. In the spring and summer he grew a garden and a large crop of corn. His crew that built the rental houses reported to him every night, and every Saturday he went on site to check on the progress and work alongside them. Each night before bed time, he took his Bible down from the mantle in the living room, sat in front of the fireplace in his big blue corduroy recliner, and read for half an hour. Many times he fell asleep there. Once when he awoke, he remarked, "Sleeping in a recliner is some of the best sleep you can ever have."

Being a neat, handsome man, Dad dressed with great care. Mom liked to take his picture down from the mantle and tease him about being her "debonair catch." The photograph showed him—as a younger man, wearing his Sunday felt hat and a scarf thrown around his neck.

Like every kid, I looked forward to going to school. In the first grade, I learned my letters and a few words. I got along with all the kids, but before the end of the year, I got a hint I wasn't as smart as some of the others. I couldn't read as well as the other first graders.

In the second grade, I went into a low reading group because I had trouble reading sentences. That is when I first knew I had a problem learning to read. I figured out I liked being at home on the farm more than I liked being at school, except for recess and lunch and walking to town after school. Those things were pretty fun.

The summer after the second grade, Dad told Mom to take me for swimming lessons for two weeks. "It won't be anytime until he is wanting to go in the swimming hole." He referred to where the creek widened large enough and deep enough to swim—down at the edge of our land in the back underneath the railroad bridge. Dad never allowed me to go there without him.

After two weeks of swimming lessons, Mom took me to a nearby lake. I couldn't wait to get into the water. I ran as hard as I could in the water, splashing water clear up past my head. When Mom wasn't looking, I took off swimming to the dock. I heard her calling from the shore, "Don't do that. You might not be able to swim that far."

I ignored her and dove off the dock and swam to the bottom. The water turned from warm to cold as I went downward. I stayed down as long as I could —at the bottom. Several times I came up under the dock and stayed in a space between the surface of the water and the underside of the dock. I hid there. I stayed a few minutes watching the fish swim around me. I knew Mom watched from the shore waiting for me to come back up above the waterline. I knew it drove her crazy. But I couldn't help myself. I just loved swimming and that's where I wanted to be, in the deep water.

I got tired of hiding and started swimming back toward our towel where Mom waited. She met me with a towel and suntan lotion. "Bradley, you nearly scared me to death. When I wiggled my feet down into the sand until they disappeared, she slapped the fool out of me. “I told you to stand still.” I knew she felt angry with me for scaring her.

This summer before my third grade, Mom spent time with me taking me to the movies and shopping for school clothes. In Marietta at the Strand Theater, we saw the Saturday matinees, usually a rip roaring Clint Eastwood movie. We went to Belmont Hills Shopping Center and bought jeans and plaid shirts for school and even the black cowboy boots I wanted.

Just about the time I started third grade, I noticed Mom changing. I noticed the dark circles under her eyes and how pale she had become. She stopped carrying me to the movies on Saturday and many days she came home from work early, and when I got home from school, she would be lying on the sofa. She didn’t talk to me or play games with me. I knew she had some sort of problem. Dad began to do some housework and help with the dishes.

As Mom’s health declined, she became someone I didn’t know as my Mom. I heard Dad and her talk about an inoperable tumor, but I didn’t know what that meant.

2.
Bullies

I first heard about bullies up in Oakdale when I started third grade. I learned that these bullies harassed and beat-up on little kids just for the sport of it, so I knew I really had to get a grip.

My time to face them came too soon. One day after school, I sat on a high rock wall in front of Fitzgerald Elementary School swinging my legs and eating jawbreakers and Red Hots with two of my friends, Rooster Roberts and Tophat Taylor.

Rooster came off as an ordinary kid. He was a little bigger than me and had brown hair, but he tried things he knew better than to try and became somewhat of a daredevil. His real name—Dusty Roberts—became just Rooster, a nickname that fit because when he did something that scared us, he bragged and strutted around like our bantam rooster strutting in the yard.

No one knew Tophat by any other name since his name fit him so well. His kinky-curly hair grew out over his forehead as far as it could go before gravity took over and curled it under. His thick, reddish hair had the look of a weird cap. As he got older, Tophat grew taller than Rooster or me and became kinda skinny. I think Tophat came from a poor family. I'm not sure, but he always wore the same old jeans, and he had only two shirts, a blue one with lines on it and a brown one with checks. I liked

Tophat. Not only did he look different, but he said crazy things that were funny—things no one else would think to say.

When we had eaten all our candy, we wanted to go into town for more, but we had heard there were big guys hanging out in town who just loved to shove and harass any little kid who came down the street.

"Brad, should we risk getting beaten up? Is a trip to Pac-A-Sac worth the risk if we're spotted?" asked Tophat. "Should we go?" He looked at me then at Rooster.

"Yeah, we're faster, and we can out run them and hide," Rooster said.

"We can't let a couple of bullies scare us," I replied.

We jumped from the wall and headed down the street. I walked out front, faster than either Tophat or Rooster, acting confident, but my heart started to pound. We went to Pac-a-Sac Groceries located about midway of town. So when we got close to Pac-a-Sac, we ran inside quickly before any of those bullies who hung out there spotted us.

As we came out of the store, there they were—a couple of tough high school guys coming down the street, walking fast, toward us. We took off running in the opposite direction as fast as we could. We ran past Daniel's Drug Store, Ace Hardware, Dave's Pizza Parlor, and Murdock's Service Station. Not once did we look back, but we could hear them running behind us yelling, "Hey, you little whimps!"

We ran toward the taxi stand—a two car business with a lean-to on the sidewalk where taxies were routed by a retarded man nicknamed, Mayor Mortimer. He saw the big boys coming after us and motioned to us that he had a hiding place for us. We ran and hid behind the tall desk where Mayor Mortimer sat on a high stool taking calls all day. The tough guys ran up to the taxi stand and looked around then walked on down the street still looking for us.

We scrunched down and listened to Mayor Mortimer answer

the phone. "Oakdale City Cab," he should have said, but he spoke with a lisp, so it came out, "Oakda Silly Cab." We tried to be quiet as we were afraid the guys would find us there, but when we heard Mayor Mortimer speaking, we broke into smothered giggles.

Mortimer hurried out to a waiting cab. "Hurre, Ms J'nes ne'ds to go to tha' doc t'day."

We stayed under the tall desk and watched Mortimer which I think was his first name. Everyone called him Mayor Mortimer as a joke since he seemed to be slow, but yet he acted so important in everything he did. His eyebrows arched over his eyes as they were supposed to, but then they ran together in the middle over his nose. It looked like he had one long eyebrow reaching clear across his forehead. His brown hair lay flat and oily but was combed slick. His eyes bugged out a little, and his mouth hung open when he wasn't talking. He always wore a white button-up-the-front long-sleeved shirt, red suspenders, checked pants, and polished-to-a-shine, black boots. He turned to us and said, "They gonn'. You come out now."

We took off running. As we ran we heard the racing of a hot rod engine. The bullies had been watching for us.

They jumped out of the hot rod and pursued us as we ran. Tophat, Rooster, and I ran as fast as we could. When these tough guys caught up with us, Tophat and Rooster got away. I tripped on a root, of a huge oak tree, growing up through the sidewalk. One of the big boys, Mike Blackmon, grabbed me and threw me to the ground, then straddled me.

He sneered to the other guys, "Hey! You think Brad Berkshire needs a hair cut?" I heard laughter from the other boys and the click of a switch blade. I thought he planned to stab me with that switchblade. I thrashed around trying to break his hold on me. I tried to holler, but I couldn't. Fear grabbed my throat and with this guy sitting on my chest, my holler came out as a muffled moan. Before I knew it, Blackmon had cut my hair which grew a little long just to the collar of my plaid shirt.

Tophat and Rooster came back yelling, "Let him go." A few of the store owners and patrons came out to the sidewalk to see who was causing all the racket. I kicked and quickly glanced around then saw a half empty quart beer bottle laying on the sidewalk. Blackmon laughed and looked at the rednecks who were with him as he held up the piece of my hair he had cut. He relaxed his hold just enough so that I got my hand around the bottle then swung it, clobbering him right across the bridge of the nose. The bottle shattered and he let out a yell, grabbing his eyes, and, at the same time, letting go of me. Not only did the beer go into his eyes but some of the glass did also. He hollered and danced around like a scalded hyena as we made our escape.

Tophat, Rooster, and I were pretty shook up as we headed back to the school, got on our bikes, and went the one mile down Hill Street toward my house. Every afternoon the three of us usually raced down Hill Street—a long gradual downward slope that dead-ended into the plank bridge that led into my yard. We usually slammed on our brakes to see who could make the longest black mark on the pavement, but not today. We rode right on over the plank bridge that jolted under the force of our three bikes hitting it at the same time. We rode right over the worn spot in the grass where cars had always turned around. We were off our bikes and as we propped them up, I glanced down the long rows of the one acre cornfield in front of the house. I searched for my dad to tell him what had happened. I didn't see him.

We sat on the front porch stewing over what had just happened. Tophat lay in the porch swing, Rooster swung his legs off the side of the porch, and I sat on the front of the steps thinking about what had happened.

I noticed both Dad's truck and Momma's car parked in the driveway though neither of them should have been in from work yet. Something must have happened. When Mom had a day off from her nursing job, she usually worked in the flower bed out front where she had planted Gerbera Daisies and Old Maids along the sidewalk. She must have worked today and came home early for some reason. I also didn't understand why Dad had come home early.

While we sat there a train came barreling down the tracks toward our house. The tracks ran on a high bluff above the top of our house. We just sat there watching it. The power and speed of the train vibrated our entire house and vibrated us sitting there on the porch. The Mimosa trees which were in full bloom making a canopy of blossoms over the house now stirred like they were in a small hurricane. As the train passed above us, it seemed as if the train literally went through the tallest oak trees that grew in the grove on the side of the bank and seemed to disappear into the summer foliage. "Should we tell our parents what happened?" Tophat's question brought me back from my thinking. "Nothing this bad has ever happened to the three of us before."

"We've known the bullies were bad news," Rooster said. "We've known it had to happen sooner or later."

"We're buddies and have to stick together," I said "Tophat, maybe we should tell Dad about the bullies chasing us."

Tophat replied, "Yeah, one day we won't get away—we'll get cut with a switchblade. Maybe we should tell."

Rooster said, "Naw, we can outrun them. We're getting bigger and will learn to run really fast."

The big boys had no motive for picking on us little kids except for the sport of it. This is just what they did after school—find some little kids to terrorize, and today they had picked us.

"Dad wants me to be tough," I said. "He might think we're sissies if we go running to him scared. Anyway, what can he do?" We three agreed not to tell Dad.

"Hey Brad, how about your hair? How are you going to keep your parents from seeing your hair?" Tophat asked.

"Come on. I've got an idea."

As we walked quietly into the house, I saw Mom lying on the sofa with her eyes closed. Lately, she lay there almost all the time that she wasn't at work. She looked sickly and too pale.

As we tried to get past her and to my room without waking her, she opened her eyes and exclaimed, "Bradley, what is that I smell? What are you three tracking on the floor? Go back outside and clean off your shoes." Quickly we hurried out before she could see my hair.

We had picked up the rotten mimosa blossoms onto the soles of our shoes when we had walked in the yard earlier. Now we hurried out without answering. I guess Mom went back to sleep. More likely, she got up and cleaned the green slimy tracks off the hardwood floor.

Later, Rooster and Tophat went to my room while I went into Mom's bedroom and got her sewing basket which contained the scissors. Back in my room, Rooster cut the other side of my hair in the back as short as Blackmon had so my parents wouldn't notice. Then I put the scissors back in the sewing basket, put the sewing basket back in Mom's bedroom, put on a straw hat, and we went out the kitchen door to the backyard to hang out for a while.

As we went into the backyard, I smelled food cooking. I waved to Dad who stood by the grill preparing hamburgers and hotdogs for supper. When I had started to school, Mom had gone back to her nursing job at the hospital. She had not worked since I was born. Today, Dad said she had come home from work early and she had called him to come home as she did not feel well.

Across the creek, Dad had built a barn large enough for our two cows and four horses. Our pasture, behind the barn, joined to the back of my Grandfather and Grandmother O'Neal's land making a total of thirty acres. Their old home faced Pine Street that ran parallel to our street, only one block away.

Dad called me in for supper, and Tophat and Rooster left for home. In the kitchen, I washed up, took off my straw hat, and sat down to eat at the yellow formica and chrome trimmed table right in front of the big bay-window which overlooked the backyard. I knew it would just be a matter of minutes until my parents noticed my hair.

As I worried about how scared I had been this afternoon when the bullies chased us, I tried not to make eye contact with either of my parents as we started eating.

I glanced at Mom who rubbed her forehead and took deep sighs. Then I took a quick look at Dad who seemed pretty interested in stacking up his hamburger with a slice of onion, tomato, cheese, and mustard and ketchup.

"Bradley Boy, you're mighty quiet tonight," Dad said.

I just shrugged, and stared at my plate, thinking, what will happen if the bullies caught us little kids again. I had felt really scared when Blackmon clicked that switch blade. He might cut one of us next time. I wanted to talk to Dad, but what could I say?

I helped myself to a hamburger. Finally I asked, "Dad, do you know what a bully is?"

"Oh, yes. Son, there's always one around trying to show off. People just have to ignore a bully. That's usually a tough guy wannabe."

The phone rang suddenly, and Dad got up to answer it. A guy in his building crew called to discuss business for a couple of minutes. After he hung up and sat back down, we ate in silence, and I didn't bring up the subject of the bullies again.

Sure enough just as I helped myself to homemade french fries, Mom exclaimed, "Bradley Elijah Berkshire, what have you done to your hair?!" She startled me so much that I dropped the french fries, right into the bowl of turnip greens.

Curious, Dad looked up. I glanced from one of them to the other. I didn't know what to say. So I told the truth, well part of it anyway. "Rooster, cut my hair."

"Well, Son, why did he do that?" Dad began to smile.

"It touched my collar and bothered me," I replied as I studied Mom. Sure enough, I saw her soften somewhat.

"Bradley, I'm just flabbergasted," she said. "Tell me next time it's bothering you and I'll take you to the barbershop like I've always done." She emphasized, "like I've always done."

Now Dad really smiled, "Son, tell me, what did Rooster use to cut your hair, my hedge trimmers?" With this he let out one of his big, booming laughs. Friends said you could find Frank Berkshire without seeing him—just listen for a few minutes, and if he were nearby, you would hear him laugh sooner or later. He had to throw back his head to get all the laughter out.

"Mom's scissors," I said in a very small voice.

She leaned forward as though she couldn't hear me. "Did you say my scissors? You went into my sewing box?" I watched her getting riled.

I nodded.

"Simmer down, Lila. Give the boy a break. I'm sure he had a reason to get Rooster to cut his hair. And it's such a bad haircut." He smiled even broader. I wondered if Dad knew about Blackmon cutting my hair. It found it hard not to tell, but Tophat and Rooster and I had already decided to keep this a secret. So I concentrated on eating and watching my parents when they weren't looking at me wondering if I should tell them. We ate the rest of our supper in silence.

I knew Dad understood me. I knew him as a patient, kind, generous man, spending a great deal of time with me at night and on the weekends.

Mom brought me back to the present from my thinking, "Bradley do you want desert?" I nodded and answered, "Yes Ma'am." She served me a slice of homemade apple pie and looked at me curiously. I ate slowly remembering what happened today. I finished my apple pie and asked, "May I be excused?" Mom and Dad looked at each other and back at me. Dad asked, "Bradley Boy, is anything wrong? You look so serious tonight."

"No sir. Everything is fine."

Just as I got up to leave the table, my Aunt Lilly, Mom's twin sister, came in without knocking. "Hey, got any supper left?" Mom cut her a piece of apple pie and they began to talk. You never knew what would happen when they were together. Lila and Lilly were born rivals and the rivalry had never let up. They were so jealous of each other that they almost hated each other. Sibling rivalry probably began in their mother's womb when they pushed and shoved each other for space.

Their parents—Granddaddy and Grandmother O'Neal, had a large family of boys before they had the twin girls. When the twins were born, everyone made over the Lila and Lilly so much they became so spoiled that eventually all that attention affected their individual personalities and even their relationship with each other. When Lilly showed up at a church Christmas party wearing a long, glittering gold dress, everyone ooh-ed and ahh-ed over how beautiful she looked. Well, she hadn't told Lila about her beautiful new dress. No one noticed that Lila had a new outfit. She became so enraged at Lilly for getting all the attention that she went over and stomped Lilly's toe and left the party in a huff.

As Mom and Aunt Lilly talked, I went to my room and lay on the bed wondering about what the bullies would do to us next and if I should talk to Dad. That night I dreamed the bullies chased me again.

3.
Bradley Worries

I had always liked going to church with my parents, but something happened on Sunday that terrified me. My family went to church on Sunday morning and Wednesday night and my Dad talked about keeping the commandments. I often saw him reading his Bible at the picnic table by the big granite rock that jutted up in the middle of our backyard. Dad trusted in God and when things were beyond his control, he prayed. No matter what the circumstance, he prayed.

Everybody thought of my Dad as being as great a man as I did. When we went to church he greeted almost everyone he met with, "How you doing old buddy? How's everything going today? "

I once heard a man say, "If Frank Berkshire had only two dollars, and you asked him to borrow a dollar, he'd give it to you."

The Sunday after we were chased by the bullies, we had a guest preacher, Clyde Heath, a man who weighed close to four hundred pounds, Dad said. Preacher Heath, shouted, "Sinners go to hell. All have sinned and fallen short of the glory of the Lord."

When he said, "All have sinned," he hit the podium so hard with his fist that a corner of it broke off and flew out into the congregation and landed on the floor. Everyone sat stunned for a moment. I felt scared when I glanced down at the piece of wood laying there in the aisle close to me. Then everyone laughed, including Preacher Heath. When everyone laughed, I felt better. I think the laughter took some of the thunder out of his sermon.

He continued to preach, "You don't know tonight when you leave this church and walk out across the road if you will get killed by a car and wake up in hell, burning forever. Oh, it won't be a little fire like you burn your hand on the stove. It will be a fire seven times hotter than anything here on earth." I saw the sweat rolling down his face and onto the collar of his Sunday suit. I noticed he had a little, white spittle in the corners of his mouth.

"There will be weeping and gnashing of teeth and wailing and casting out into outer darkness, and it will be just awful," he hollered. His face grew red and he rocked back and forth on his feet from his toes to his heels. "Jesus is coming back. Jesus is coming back." I guess that meant the world would end. I felt scared to death. Preacher Heath asked, "Who wants to be saved."

I thought about the fire. Well, I could not imagine how something could be seven times hotter than the stove. I raised my hand. He said, "If you want to be saved from eternal damnation, come down to the altar." He nodded at me to come down front. I joined him at the altar, but I didn't know what it meant. My chin quivered. I felt all worked-up—I guess from pure emotion. I had been saved and did not understand what this meant.

While I stood up front with Preacher Heath's hand on my shoulder, I looked around at the congregation. Preacher Heath said we are all sinners and that sinners go to hell. If "All have fallen short of the Glory of God," and all are sinners, I guess sooner or later that meant I would be a sinner, too. After the service he told the deacons that he would repair the podium. They told him not to worry about it as they would repair it.

Dad was the first to come down to the front of the church after the service and shake my hand, "Son, I'm glad you made this decision on your own." Mom and Dad stood on each side of me as the entire congregation lined up and filed by me one at a time shaking my hand and congratulating me on "getting saved" and on the fact that I would be baptized at the next Baptismal Service.

I worried about the preacher's words and as we rode home, I asked Dad, "How could you be in a fire seven times hotter than the stove and not be burnt up?"

"Well now, Son, you don't have to worry about that now. You have accepted Him as your Savior and that means everything will be okay." I put this out of my mind and when we got home we had our usual big Sunday dinner where all the relatives came.

When I walked into the house, I could smell the roast in the oven that had been baking, slowly, since we had left for church that morning. Aromas and people filled the house. Aunt Lilly and her husband, James placed their food on the long dining room table. My sister, Kay, and her husband, George Lee, whom she'd married last year, came into the living room. A feast filled the long table. It seemed as though Lila and Lilly had a cook-off to see who could outdo the other. We not only had roast, but fried chicken, squash casserole, deviled eggs, turnip greens, corn on the cob, fresh sliced tomatoes out of the garden, and hot biscuits with chicken gravy. For dessert, we always had coconut cake.

After every Sunday dinner, the family gathered around the piano and sang hymns for hours. Mom played the piano at church and sang in two choir groups. She could play any tune she heard once. She said she played "by heart." When she picked up an accordion for the first time, in just a few minutes she could play it as well as she could her piano. The house filled with hymns such as J*ust a Closer Walk with Thee, Peace in the Valley*, *How Great Thou Art,* and *Where Could I go But to the Lord.*

Kay had tears in her eyes all during the meal, and George kept his head down except when he glimpsed over at Dad. Two days ago, George had accidentally set the house he and Kay lived in on fire—one of Dad's rental houses. Dad said he couldn't be mad because he knew accidents happen. Even though Dad had insurance on the house, he took a big loss.

Last Friday with Kay at work, George had stayed home, and happened to be smoking, sitting up in bed. He fell asleep and caught the mattress on fire. The mattress smoldered, flamed up, and caught the curtains on the window beside the bed on fire. As the room filled with smoke, George began to cough and wake up. Before a fire truck could get there, the house had gone up in a blaze. All of Kay's new things from her bridal shower were gone.

When everybody left, I asked Dad, "How can you not be mad at George? He burned your good house down. And all of Kay's gifts are gone. She is really upset."

"Well Son, I am upset, but what good would it do to get all mad and get everybody upset? We can't do anything about it now. I know George didn't do it on purpose. We just have to forgive him." I knew my Dad was a good man and went to bed thinking about this.

That night I had a very strange dream. There were two ladders coming down from heaven, straight down from the sky. I looked up at the one ladder and couldn't see the end because of the clouds around the top. I went over to the other ladder and looked up. At the top, the clouds surrounding it opened up and I saw blue sky in the opening.

God came right down that ladder, through the opening, carrying a very large ball and He started playing ball with me in the front yard. He looked like George Washington but all bright, like aluminum foil covered him. Well, God smiled at me. When He spoke, he had a strong voice but spoke to me gently. The large ball looked shiny and bright like it had lots of crumpled up pieces of aluminum foil pressed together covering it. We tossed the light ball back and forth for a long time. God showed me patience and kindness. He showed me several times how to pitch straight to Him. We had a nice time playing ball then He went back up the ladder to heaven and took the ball with Him.

The next morning at the breakfast table when Mom served bacon and hot pancakes with strawberry jelly she said, “Brad, why are you so quiet today? Are you sick?”

I just shook my head and slowly spread the jelly over the pancakes. I didn’t look at her. I just pretended to be very interested in the way the red jelly melted on the hot pancakes and slid into the melted yellow butter. I puzzled over the dream. It made me feel good that God came down the ladder to my yard and even played ball with me, but I remained confused. I had been told that He would burn me in a fire seven times hotter than the stove. But he had been kind and loving. When I played ball in the dream, I didn’t feel the fear that I felt in church when the preacher talked about going to hell for sinning. Did everyone have the wrong idea about God being so mean and scary? I wondered, Does God love me or will he burn me to a “crispy critter” in hell?

When Mom set a glass of orange juice in front of me, she leaned down and felt my forehead. She looked concerned when she found I didn’t have a fever. “I’m confused,” I said. Is God nice or does he burn you up?” My mother looked shocked then she seemed quiet like she didn’t quite know how to answer. “God is a good and forgiving God. He wants us to follow him and everything will be alright.” She seemed to be talking to herself.

I rubbed my forehead trying to think. “But yesterday Preacher Heath said we were all sinners and that sinners go to hell.”

“Son you’re just too young to worry about sinning and going to hell. You just go to church with Frank and me and be a good boy and mind us and you will be fine.” She gave me a weak smile.

As I rode my bike up Hill Street to school, I thought about what

Mom had said, and then I remembered Reverend Heath's sermon about Jesus coming back and wondered if that meant the world would come to an end. I guess that meant people would die. I went into the classroom hoping this would not be the day we would all die. I liked being a kid and wanted to do good. My Mom told me if I minded her and Dad and went to church everything would turn out fine.

In school with my new third grade teacher, pretty and sweet Mrs. Richards, I had hopes that I would do better than I had in the first and second grade. In my first two years of school, I always felt unprepared for the work and never did a good job in writing or reading my letters. Mrs. Richards gave us our books and our instructions. At the end of the day, she put a star by our names if we did our work and behaved. I tried my best to listen and follow the instructions, but so far I had not gotten a single star beside my name on the poster on the wall by the blackboard.

One morning the second week of school, us kids were at recess playing on the playground. I picked up a rock, ready to throw it toward the wooded area just for the fun of throwing then I heard Mrs. Richards call out to me, "No, Brad, you're not allowed to throw rocks." I looked up the hill at her where she stood watching us play, and I just let the rock drop.

When we got back into the classroom, she put a black X by my name. I felt the black mark deep as if she had put it on me instead of the poster board on the classroom wall. If I had known of the things to come, I would have taken the black X as a sign. In my innocent youth, I didn't suspect anything at the time.

I couldn't always understand Mrs. Richards when she explained things. She talked too fast. "Boys and girls, get into your reading groups. Take out your books. Begin reading where we left off yesterday. I will be over to read with each one of you at your table. Start reading now."

When she said now, I sat with my blackbird reading group. We had reading groups: the bluebirds, the redbirds, the thrashers. I didn't think some of the kids in the blackbird group could read too well; neither could I. I looked at all the pictures and tried to find the place where we had read yesterday. Mrs. Richards came over to my group and listened to each child read one paragraph. When my time came to read, I thought about my dream of God instead of what Spot and Dick and Jane were doing. I stammered *"Then"* and the teacher corrected.

"Brad, the word is *They*."

Next I said, *"They ran to stop."*

Mrs. Richards took a deep breath and said "The word is *Spot*, Brad, *Spot. They ran to Spot."* I heard the kids in my blackbird group snicker because I missed these words. Two of the girls were whispering, and I heard them say "can't read." I didn't understand why I couldn't learn like the other children. This year had started out to be the same as the first and second grade had been. I stayed behind everyone else.

I wanted to be like the other kids. I wanted to be able to read and do my work and not have everyone snickering and whispering when I couldn't understand what I tried to read. I began to feel inferior.

4.
Danger

After school, Rooster, Tophat and I went into Oakdale again. We wanted to find out if I had blinded the big Blackmon boy. We went inside the Pac-a-sac and got our candy. The cashier looked at me with a knowing look but didn't say anything. We looked out the door of the store before we left and started down the sidewalk. A cluster of the high school guys hung out on the sidewalk.

"Hey there's the kid that hurt Mike Blackmon," one of the guys called out and pointed toward us. We ran back into the Pac-a-sac and out the back door and hid in the woods. We waited for about a half hour and then went behind the stores to our school, got our bikes, and went home not knowing how badly the Blackmon boy had gotten hurt.

When we got to my house, Dad met us in the front yard. "Son, I've got something for you out in the barn." The three of us boys took off to the barn. I went to the barn expecting anything but what Dad had for me.

In the past, Dad had traded in Oakdale for animals to bring home. Many times he brought home a large burlap sack with something alive thrashing around inside. Once it held a Bluetick, hounddog puppy. He had long ears and the saddest big ol' eyes. His coloring of gray with black and white altogether made his coat look bluish. I knew right off that I would name him Blue. Dad kept Blue as his hunting dog. Another time a tiny scared-looking kitten crept slowly out of the sack. After the kitten got over being scared and started racing all around the barnyard, we named it Harley. Then Dad brought home a little bantam rooster, we just called "Banny-Rooster."

This time when we got to the barn, I could not believe my eyes. A small black pony stood in the stall. Dad had a saddle and while he put it on the pony we decided on a name, Thunder. We took turns riding for a while. Thunder tried to bite me, then he bucked me off, then he tried to stomp on me. If I managed to stay on, he tried to catch my knee on the side of the house and rip me off his back.

I did a "Hi-ho Silver!" I imitated the Lone Ranger I watched on television. Thunder reared up, and pawed the air, but then he came straight back. I fell off, and Thunder fell on my left leg. Rooster and Tophat both tried to get Thunder up off me.

"Rooster, you and Tophat pull the reins, while I push on his rump with my foot," I groaned. They pulled and I pushed. Nothing happened except Thunder struggled, hurting me more. "I'm the strongest," Rooster bragged. "Let's see if I can lift a horse." Rooster—always the show-off, I thought. Rooster got up under Thunder's front leg to push.

"Once more," I said. "All together now." I took my free foot and put it right on Thunder's behind and in one motion we got the pony up and off my leg. I glanced toward Dad, in front of the barn, just in time to see him look away pretending not to watch. But I saw him smile. I knew he would have come over to help if we had really needed him. But he let me do things whenever he thought I could handle the situation.

I limped around for a while and noticed Rooster had pushed out his chest and strutted around, "Well, I guess I just lifted that horse right off Brad," he said. Tophat and I looked at each other and shook our heads.

Just then our Banny-Rooster strutted by. "We nicknamed you right," I said and we all laughed.

For the rest of the week, I forgot about not being able to read and did fun things with Rooster and Tophat. We led Thunder down to the swimming hole and put him in the water up to his belly. He liked it so much that the next time, I rode him into the water. We continued to ride Thunder after school and on the weekends, and we continued to play in the creek but found another fun thing to do on the railroad tracks.

With the train tracks on a bluff the same height as the roof of our house, the tracks and the trains were always a big part of my life. About every two hours, a freight train or a passenger train barreled down those tracks above our rooftop. The tremendous force of it shook the house, until you thought you could feel the vibrations in your bones. The roar and clatter of it drowned out any other sound. This noise was as common to us as the music on the radio or the alarm clock going off in the morning. If I watched television, and the train came through, I just leaned forward and turned up the volume for a few minutes until the train passed.

That next Saturday Rooster, Tophat, and I did some dangerous things when we went to the railroad bridge and threw rocks into a big pool of water fifty feet below, for hours. When we got tired of throwing rocks, we decided to put pennies on the railroad track. We lined them up on the track then we stood back in the edge of the woods as the train came pounding and shrieking through. After the train passed us, we ran out to see some pennies were squashed and some were even hot to the touch. Most had stuck to the wheels of the passing train so we never got our pennies back.

"Wow," said Tophat. "Look at this hot, squashed penny. It's not even round any more. Abe Lincoln doesn't know what hit him."

"Let's lay something else on the tracks," Rooster said.

The next train was due to come by two hours later, so we decided to put big rocks all up and down the tracks. When we were finished, we waited up on the hill above the tracks. This time a passenger train came by going really fast. I'm glad we were way back from the tracks and up on the hill because the train wheels crushed the rocks flinging chunks to the sides like a baseball going sixty miles per hour.

We decided to find dead tree limbs and small fallen trees and put them across the tracks. This time when we finished a very long freight train came by. The three of us waited anxiously up on the hill above the tracks to see what happened. The really long trains had to have another engine in the middle of the box and oil cars to help pull. When the last car finally passed, we slid down the sharp hill to find on each side of the track short pieces of broken trees. In the middle between the rails, powdery fine sawdust piled up and there were big splinters between the rails.

"Wow," said Rooster. "Can you believe that? I wonder what would happen if we put a crosstie on the tracks?" Tophat and I looked at each other.

"We can't put a crosstie on the tracks. It too big," I said. "It might wreck the train or something," I said slowly and apprehensively because I knew we were going to do that very thing.

"You're crazy," Rooster replied excitedly. "Nothing will stop the train. I know where to get a crosstie. You know, down by the railroad bridge. There's one laying down the side of the bank."

We walked to the bridge. It took the three of us a long time to struggle with the crosstie to get it up to the track. We were further down the track from the hill we had sat on that morning. The track was located in the middle of where a sharp hill fell off on each side. When we got the crosstie almost to the top of the hill, we heard the train coming. It was a passenger train, and it was coming fast, blowing a shrill whistle.

I think the conductor saw us in the distance and that's why he wouldn't let up on the whistle. We struggled and almost had it there when

I screamed over the tremendous noise of the oncoming train, "It's too late. Let's give up," I shouted as loudly as I could. But Rooster kept pulling. Tophat and I gave the crosstie one last big shove and fell back down the steep hill to the right side of the passing train. When the front of the train hit the crosstie, a "crack" sounded like a gun shot as it was cut in half, each half shooting out at an angle from the sides of the track. I had no idea if Rooster had gotten safely to the other side before the train passed between us. We only heard the tremendous noise and rush of power as the train raced on down the tracks.

My heart pounded in my chest, and I had never been so afraid. Tophat and I crawled back up to where we were eye level to the wheels of the train. We could see between the wheels, but the noise on the tracks was deafening. I thought I saw something red. I remembered Rooster had on a new red shirt. I hoped I saw the red shirt and not Rooster's blood. I feared Rooster might have been killed.

It took the passenger train only two or three minutes to go passed us. As the last train car cleared, Tophat and I were back on the tracks. Rooster lay on the other side at an angle like he had slid down the hill.

"Oh! My arm! Ohhh!" I didn't see any blood, but my heart pounded hard. Rooster held his arm, groaning. He managed to say, "When the train hit the crosstie, I had just turned loose, but not quite. I heard my arm pop. I know it's broken."

"You're lucky you're not as flat as Abe Lincoln was on the penny yesterday," Tophat said. I grabbed Rooster around the waist putting his left arm—his good arm over my shoulder. Tophat pushed on his back, and we got him up the hill. It took us a while walking slowly to get him home.

When the three of us went into Rooster's house, his mom gasped, horrified. Rooster told her he had fallen at the railroad bridge, and that was not entirely a lie. Rooster's mom took him to the doctor, and he had to wear a cast on his broken arm for the next two months.

The next morning we saw several white pickup trucks with the Southern Railway insignia on the side door descend on Oakdale. Officials went to every house asking questions about three boys doing dangerous things out on the tracks. We took cover and were never caught. Rooster wore a cast on his arm until Thanksgiving and that slowed our adventures down for a while.

5.
Butted by a Goat

On Monday after Rooster's accident, I dreaded going to school. Last Friday, I had missed quite a few words. Sure enough when reading class started and I went to my Blackbird reading group, I struggled with every word. I could not remember the work I had done on Friday. Mrs. Richards sent a note home to my mom. The next afternoon after school, my mom met with my teacher and came home with books to help me.

At home when Mom helped me, she said, "You're not reading this correctly. Read it again." She read for me, but she read so fast I could not keep up with her. "Jane and Dick went to the big park to have a picnic," she read.

I tried to read what she had read but stammered, "Jane and Dick when to the big picnic. I guessed **when** for **went** because both words started with the letter w. I guessed **picnic** for **park** because both words started with p. I missed the word picnic.

Mom got a belt and hit me on the backside about ten times. "You're just not paying attention. You've got to try harder, she kept saying as she hit me. My backside hurt, and my feelings inside hurt too. I tried, but I just could not get it right. The whipping didn't help. I still could not read any better when the whipping was over. I told her I would try harder. She stormed out of the room. I sat on the side of my bed and cried, not so much because of the whipping but because I did not know what to do to read better. I went to bed, still crying, feeling frustrated. I lay there thinking about school. I dreaded going back.

At school the next day, I was supposed to follow the words in the reader as each of the other children took turns reading out loud. Mrs. Richards said, "Brad, you're not even on the right page."

She showed me the right page and when my turn came, I tried to read but struggled. I just didn't know the words. I felt so glad when the bell rang and I could leave.

At home that night, my dad came in late. I lay on my bed waiting for him then I heard his pickup coming across the plank bridge. I came off the bed, ran out the door, and into the yard to see him. He waited for me out by the barn. "Son we've got to go see Mr. Goodson at the new Busy Bee General Store."

When I was around my dad, I became his shadow, always ready for a new adventure, and I was right there when he needed me. We were in Oakdale in no time. Mr. Goodson, the manager of the new Busy Bee General Store, planned a grand opening and needed a goat to be a draw for a crowd.

Mr. Goodson stood slightly taller than my daddy but was skinny. He had a lump on the front of his neck that bobbed up and down when he talked. Mr. Goodson told my dad, "Frank, I'll give fifty dollars for the biggest, meanest goat you can find." I stood there looking up, watching that knot on his neck. I looked to see what happened to the knot when he wasn't talking. It just stayed still until he talked again then the knot bobbed up and down again as long as he talked. "I will give a prize for anyone who can put the forehead of the goat to the ground for one second."

On Saturday, Dad and I went out in the pickup truck looking for a goat farm. My Dad knew where it was located, so we went to Lithia Springs near Sweetwater Creek looking for the farm. I felt like we were on an adventure. We were on a dirt road when all of a sudden I saw a pasture full of goats. The farmer greeted us when we drove up to the barn, then he went into the barn and came out pulling on a rope.

He pulled hard on the rope and brought out a goat that looked as big as a calf. The goat's horns twisted around on each side of its head in a circle and looked just like the hood ornament on my daddy's truck.

When I saw the goat, I jumped behind Dad. When the farmer said we could carry the goat home, he helped Dad load the big goat into the back of the truck. Dad tied the "Billy Goat" where he would not jump out, putting two ropes around its neck, tying one rope to the right side of the truck and one rope to the left side. The goat's head was where Dad could glance back and check on him to make sure he was secure.

As we drove home in the pickup, I sat in the seat next to Dad, and I kept looking back through the rear window at the big curly-horned goat. We were eye to eye, with the truck window glass between us. I made faces and stuck out my tongue at him just because I could, all the way home. The goat just looked at me eye to eye, starring back at me.

On the day of the grand opening, it came time to take the goat to Mr. Goodson. Dad said, "Bradley Boy, it's time to load up Billy Goat. Go get him."

I went out to where the Billy Goat was staked on a chain near the fence by the barn. When I approached, the goat gave me a funny look, by turning its head sideways. Then it hit me—with its rolled up horns —right in the chest, knocking me on the ground. The thud when its forehead hit my chest sounded like a cantaloupe dropping on the ground. I stood up and ran back to Dad.

"Son, where's the goat?"

"He butted me down."

My chest hurt, and I wanted to cry, but I didn't.

"Well, my goodness alive. You can't get a little, old goat?" he said.

I went back. The goat gave me that funny, sideways look again, and hit me right in the chest in the same place knocking me down on the ground again.

For the second time, I got up. I was mad. I got a big stick and stood in front of the goat. When it came after me, I backed off until the chain was tight, and the goat couldn't reach me. Then I hit it hard right between the eyes and then right on the top of the head between the rolled up horns. The goat ran in the opposite direction toward the fence and tried to clear the fence, but when it jumped, its chain was too short. The goat spun around, so its hind legs were on the ground, but its front legs and the front of its body were suspended in the air.

I ran back to Dad and said, "Dad your Billy Goat's hanging in the air!"

Dad untangled the chain from the fence, led the goat to the pickup, and loaded it. When we pulled up to the Busy Bee to deliver the goat, the parking lot and the store had filled up with customers. Mr. Goodson's advertisement had drawn a large crowd. As we parked, all the bullies and big men in Oakdale gathered around the truck to take a look at the "big" goat. They bet on who might be tough enough to wrestle the goat touching its forehead to the ground for one second. The person who could, would win a case of Coca-Cola. A big sweaty guy in overalls tried several times but just as he got the goat's forehead on the ground, the goat twisted out of his grasp and managed to stand back up again. Lots of guys who hung out around there tried, but none got the goat down to the ground so that its forehead touched long enough for Mr. Goodson to count even one second.

There were several drawings for prizes. I had my heart set on winning a new bicycle. I entered the drawing for the Galaxy 500 bicycle with the big knobby tires and the headlight built right into the frame. Mr. Griggs, the man in charge of the drawing, gave me a whole bunch of tickets to drop into the box. I just printed BRAD on each ticket in big letters. I think he wanted me to win. He was a good friend of Dad, and he knew I needed a new bike since my old bike had a broken pedal and dents from being wrecked a few times. Well sure enough, I won the Galaxy 500. Now I could outrun Tophat and Rooster in the afternoon races down Hill Street to my house.

After the grand opening of Busy Bee was over, Mr. Goodson called Dad. "Come get this goat. He's mean and keeps butting me."

"How much do you want for him?" my dad asked.

"Oh, you can have him. I just want him out of the way." Mr. Goodson replied.

We kept the goat only a few days before we sold it for fifty dollars, but I still had my new bike which almost made it worth getting butted around.

6.
Uncle Sycamore

My favorite relative, Uncle Sycamore, came by one evening after school to see my new bike and to help Dad around the farm. Silvey was his real name, but everyone called him Sycamore. He spent a great deal of time hunting and fishing. He was small, neat, person and just a plain, country farmer. Dad said Sycamore was "quick like a squirrel."

Sycamore wore a camouflage shirt and overalls. He had black hair but some of the hairs were white, and he wore the kind of hat railroad workers wore—navy with white stripes. This kind guy became everyone's favorite uncle, brother, or friend wherever he went. He never married, but became the glue that held the family together. Whatever you needed, Uncle Sycamore worked hard to make it happen.

Because of injuries he had sustained in World War II, Sycamore couldn't control his right hand from shaking, and he walked with a limp. Aunt Lilly called Sycamore "shell shocked." Daddy said he served our country well. I loved spending time with him.

One Saturday morning, Uncle Sycamore came by early and said to me, " Come on Bradley Boy, let's go drown some worms." We grabbed our fishing poles and headed toward the creek, where it widened down under the railroad bridge about a mile from the house. We spent all day and caught two bass and one crappie.

In the late afternoon, we went over to his small, white framed house. Even though the house had only two rooms, they were the neatest and most orderly rooms I had ever seen. In spite of Sycamore's shaking hand, he cleaned the fish and managed to fix fried fish, hush puppies, and french fries for our supper.

After we ate, he showed me a framed picture of himself dressed in his army uniform. He took a small gold foil box from his top bureau drawer and held it down for me to see the contents as he carefully opened it. The box was filled with army medals—awards he had received for his service during World War II. He showed me one interesting heart-shaped medal which hung from a purple ribbon. It was purple in the center and had gold trim with a raised gold silhouette in the center.

"Sycamore, what's this one?"

"Oh. That one's called a Purple Heart. I received it when I got wounded," he replied. When I questioned him about getting wounded he didn't want to talk about it.

He only said, "Brad, that was a long time ago and a lot of bad things happened. I know I limp and have a shaky hand, but really, I'm lucky to have survived the war." Then he said, "You can have that one." He referred to the Purple Heart medal.

"Oh, Sycamore, I can't take that."

"Yes, you can and I insist." With his hand shaking, he put the Purple Heart medal into my hand.

I put the treasure in my pocket to later put it in a small keepsake box I kept on my bureau, when I got home. "Hey Sycamore, tell me how you got your nickname." I had heard this story many times but I liked the way he told how his name, Silvey, became Sycamore.

Sycamore grinned at me, pulled up a chair to the kitchen table where I sat, and begin his yarn. "Well as a boy, my dad and I went out squirrel hunting. We found a squirrel nesting in a dead, hollow sycamore tree. We decided if we set fire to the tree, the squirrel would come out then we could shoot it and have squirrel stew for supper.

We had a plan. So we started a fire in a hole at the base of the tree, but the smoke came out toward us. I put my hat over the hole, so the smoke would go up the tree and drive the squirrel out. While we were looking at my hat and the fire in the smoke-filled hole, the squirrel escaped out on a limb and got away. The tree burned up, and my hat smelled like smoke. After that everyone ribbed me and have called me Sycamore ever since." As he told the story, his right injured hand began to shake even more, and a bright excitement came into his eyes. He let out one of his hardy laughs similar my Dad's laugh.

Sycamore definitely became my childhood hero and best friend. As a very small child, when Sycamore came to my house I flew to hug him around the knees. He lifted me to his shoulders and took me for a walk down the rows between the tall summer corn. I remember how the sun shown high, and the day was warm as the June bugs made their thin shrill sound. Sycamore carried me so high in the air, I could touch the tops of the corn tassels as we walked down between the rows making a trail of corn-tassel dust fall behind us on the red Georgia clay. I held onto Uncle Sycamore's forehead with my other hand and felt high as the top of the world. Back then when I was small I didn't notice his limp when he walked or his shaking hand when he held me on his shoulders.

After I started school, Sycamore gave me all his pocket change each time I saw him. This is where I got my change I spent on candy at the Pac-a-sac after school. He always came around to help gather corn or take me fishing.

The night after I had gone fishing with Sycamore, I placed the Purple Heart in my treasure box in my top bureau drawer with my other keepsakes. Dad came into my room, and I showed him what Sycamore had given me. He patted me on the shoulder and gave me a big smile to show his acknowledgement of the gift and his approval on how I was going to value it as a keepsake.

Then he said, " Son, tomorrow is hog killing day. Do you want to help?" My eyes got big. "You mean we're going to kill the ol' sow?"

"We've had to wait for cold weather. Today we had our first frost, so it's time. We're getting started early, at six. I'll call you then."

I went to bed early. The next thing I knew, Dad leaned over my bed. "It's six o'clock. Time to get up. Shake a leg. Let's look alive."

On this very cold winter day, Sycamore came over and some guys from church came to help. I became Daddy's shadow again, asking questions. We pulled the huge sow out of the barn and brought out the big pot. I asked, "What's the pot for?" Dad patiently replied, "We boil water really hot to blister the hairs off the hog as we pour buckets of scalding water over its skin." I helped bring the logs to build the fire under the pot. I also helped bring buckets of water from the kitchen to fill the pot.

As Dad got the 22 rifle and loaded it, I pleaded excitedly, "Let me, I want to shoot it."

Dad agreed and showed me how to hold the gun. "Aim between the sow's eyes. When the bullet goes into the brain, the hog dies."

All of the men who were there to help, stood behind Dad and me. I pulled the trigger and the hog fell, twitching on the ground, screaming a high pitched whine.

"Nope. Sow's not dead. Shoot again," Dad said.

I pulled the trigger and blood went everywhere. I hit too high and missed the brain. I felt like I couldn't breathe. When I did take a breath, I could see white steam puffing out in the icy cold air. On the third shot, the hog quit screaming and thrashing around. Pools of blood splattered on the ground all around. I gave Dad the gun and walked off. I felt kinda sick. I stood back and watched.

"We have to bleed the hog out," Dad said in my general direction for my sake. "Or the meat won't be any good." He took a knife and cut the hog right at the middle of the neck and blood came out in gushes.

Dad then brought the horse around to drag the sow up to the biggest oak tree, further back behind the barn. The hog's hind legs were bound together with a rope then it went as a hitch to the saddle horn. When the horse dragged the hog over to the tree, the men hoisted it up to a heavy thick logging chain that had hung from that tree for as long as I could remember. When the hog hung high in the air, attached to the chain, the men cut its belly. I thought it had been bad to see a chicken get cut, but a whole lot of guts came rolling out.

The colored folks in the community came to get the insides of the hog to make chitlins. They washed out the insides while they were at our house and put everything in a big tub. Dad said they didn't owe him anything. They left happy, thanking Dad.

The men spent all day cutting up the meat into pork chops, pork roasts, and sausage. Momma and Aunt Lilly prepared the meat as the men brought it into the kitchen. The women folk put some of the meat in the big freezer, and the rest, they canned in jars for our meals. I heard Dad say we got enough meat from one hog to last all through the year. I thought about the sausage Mom fried in her big, black iron skillet when we had hot biscuits and sausage for breakfast.

Since I had killed the hog, my Dad treated me more like a buddy, like I had become more grown-up than my short eight years. As Christmas time neared, my parents asked what I wanted. I told them a BB gun. Dad smiled to himself but Mom openly protested saying, "Brad, you're not old enough or responsible enough to have a BB gun." Dad calmly looked at us both and said, "Now Lila, who killed our hog this year?" She only shrugged and walked way, not happy about it, but she could not protest.

When Christmas morning came, my BB gun lay in a long box underneath the tree. I immediately begin to shoot the gun in the backyard and took it everywhere with me. At the time we did not know this new BB gun would save my life when spring came.

When the redbud trees started to bloom and the spring rains came non-stop for three days our whole backyard flooded all the way from the creek bank up to the back steps. Two feet of water stood surrounding the big granite rock in the middle of the backyard. Dad said to be careful of snakes.

That night I had a dream that saved my life. I dreamed two big water moccasins were curled up on the creek bank in the place where I jump over to get to the barn. The next day when I came home from school, I found the water had receded somewhat. The swollen creek barely spilled out of its banks, and the backyard had turned to brownish red mud. I headed for the barn to see Thunder. Just as I started to jump the creek, I remembered the dream. I stopped short. Right there in front of me on the ground, across the creek, not six feet away, were two water moccasins curled up together just as I had seen in my dream.

As I turned to run back toward the house, I glanced back over my shoulder. I got a glimpse of the two snakes, uncurling, and slowly moving in my direction. Their heads were pointed toward me and their forked tongues were shooting in and out. If not for the dream, I would have jumped right onto the top of those deadly snakes.

I ran into my room and got my BB gun. Back outside, I shot the two snakes again and again. One slithered away wounded, but I kept shooting the other one until I killed it and it just floated there in the creek.

When Dad got home, I brought him over to see the water moccasin, and said, "Look Daddy. I killed it."

"Good boy," Dad said as he stared at the dead water moccasin. I could see his shock at how dangerous the situation could have been if I had missed. As he looked at me, I could see his pride in what I had done. The next day he bought me a pellet gun.

7.
Train/Car Crash

On Saturday, we had a leisurely day that turned into turmoil. Dad and I took Mom into Oakdale to see Dr. Pennell who wrote her a prescription to increase her insulin. He told Mom to give herself one insulin shot each morning. She could do this because of her nursing background. He also told her to stay away from all sugar and sweets.

After we left the doctor's office, we went to the Daniel's Pharmacy and got the prescription filled. The three of us went to the soda fountain to have a cherry coke. Mom said it would be okay for her to have a soda, this one time. I had a sundae, and we listened to Big Band music on the juke box. The sounds of the horns filled the pharmacy while we sat there enjoying being together. I loved being with both my parents.

After we left the pharmacy, we strolled main street. Dad laughed at the big sign on Matt Murdock's gas station, "Don't Fuss - Phone Us." We greeted Rex at the Pac-A-Sac Groceries when he went in the back to see Jed Saxton, the meat cutter. Jed said he would have a big box of scraps and bones for Dad's dog that night when he closed.

Dad spent a lot of time collecting and storing things for the family, for the animals, and for the livestock. The school gave us leftover food to slop the hogs. Dad got boxes of broken candy from a friend who worked at a candy factory. He stored this extra candy in a shed which backed up to the barn. He brought the candy out on special occasions like birthdays and holidays.

We were walking toward the taxi stand when I heard Dad say, "How ironic that Dr. Pennell, one of the town's richest and most educated men, who spends all his life fixing up other people's bodies and ailments, has a son with an ailment he can't cure, retardation."

I saw Dad meant Mayor Mortimer. I hadn't known Mortimer's dad was Dr. Pennell. I never thought about Mortimer being retarded. I just thought him dumb, dumber than a sack of hammers, dumber than a bucket full of rocks. But the one thing Mortimer knew—his animals. My guess he might be on the same level as them. Often I saw Mortimer shuffling down the street with a brood of chickens, or a couple of dogs, or a fat pig following him. He would trade an animal for anything shiny, sometimes a coin or even a bottle cap. Some of the shopkeepers complained about the feathers and mess, but mostly the men tolerated him on account of getting a good hunting dog for six bottle caps.

We walked up to Mayor Mortimer and Dad said, "Hey old buddy. How you doing?"

Mortimer had his usual look being he was dressed in a white long-sleeved shirt, checked pants with red suspenders, and shiny black boots. His mouth hung open like always until he saw us. He came over and shook our hands. We knew he wanted to make a trade, and he looked as serious as if this could be a life and death situation

He said, "Got a g'd knife here. I like to give it for a g'd dog. You got a g'd dog fur me?"

"We have a good dog, but I want to keep it, and I don't believe I need a knife today," Dad replied.

Hanging out there under the oaks on a bench telling yarns and swapping lies were a few of the locals who came to town to trade. One man had a pocket watch, and another had a bird dog and one had a Bluetick hounddog. Two old farmers sat nearby listening.

Instead of saying, "What do you want?" one of the farmers asked, "What do you allow?"

Dad just laughed at all of them but I knew he liked to trade as well as the next one. All of the animals he brought home to entertain me for a short time came from a trade. I kept them until he traded them for something else.

I heard Dad say the word, "troublemaker" as we left. I looked back behind us to a group of teenagers hanging out on the sidewalk. The oldest Blackmon boy, the one who had cut my hair with his switchblade stood in the midst of the group. I wondered if Dad knew these guys harassed us after school. If I had told Dad about the Blackmon boy cutting my hair, he would have come into town and had a talk with him. Then us little kids would have really gotten harassed for being a tattletales.

Dad took us down the alley beside the taxi stand. Parked there sat a tall, open vehicle with three wheels. It had only a single seat. "Bradley Boy, you see this little three wheeled scooter?" I didn't say anything as I really took in this strange sight. "This is what Mortimer drives around town. Dr. Pennell got a license for him to drive just in Oakdale and not beyond the city limits. There are no provisions for a three wheel scooter, but as the son of our prominent doctor, this exception became permanent for Mortimer."

As we walked to our car, I looked back at the tiny vehicle and back down the street to Mortimer who still tried to trade a knife for a dog. I thought to myself about this man and his car and how strange they were, but I thought they made a good match.

After we left town, we rode in our '55 Chevy to the country. Dad had said to Mom, "Hun, you need to get out of the house for a while and have a nice little drive in the country and some fresh air." I looked out the open window at the countyside which appeared to be flying by and at the cows and horses out in the pastures. The wind blew in my face and on the radio, Elvis sang, *Love Me Tender.* When we came back to Oakdale, we stopped by the Hess station. Dad read the big sign from the car lot next door, "Call Us—We will not Betray your Trust."

I felt happy there in the back seat of the '55 Chevy. I loved this kind of day. Mom and Dad were talking and even Mom laughed a lot. I wished these times could last forever.

After our ride in the country, we headed down Hill Street toward home. When we crossed the plank bridge, we saw my sister's car parked in the front yard. We had locked the front door, so I went running to the back yard to find her. Kay sat on the big granite rock, huddled over. As I got near her, I could hear her crying, sobbing. I slowed down unsure of how to react. I just stood there a few feet from her. She saw me but did not stop crying. In a moment, Mom came through the house and out the back door.

I heard the screen door bang and Mom exclaim, "What in the world?" She ran to Kay. I heard Kay crying out, "George left me. The money's gone."

Dad came up behind them now. He put both his hands on top of his head and exclaimed, "Kay, how did he get your money?"

"Because I'm dumb," she sobbed. Dad hugged her. "We had a joint checking account, and he cleaned it out and left."

As they walked toward the house, Dad put his arm around Kay. I went to the pasture to check on the horses. I came back in a few minutes and sat on the back steps, listening to see if I could understand what happened to Kay. She had quit sobbing.

I heard Mom say in a distressed way, "How much more can this family stand? Why is all this happening to us? We are a God fearing family. We go to church, work hard, and try to live right. What did Kay ever do to deserve all that has happened to her?"

They remained quiet for a moment then Mom complained, "This shouldn't have happened, Frank. It's been nine years." I knew she referred to the train-car wreck Kay had been in when she was sixteen. I did not understand about the money George got out of their account and how Dad and Mom knew about her money. I heard Dad quoted the Bible—something about, *"God will not put on you more than you can stand."* Kay said she needed to take a nap and Mom said that would be a good idea.

I went out to the swing and did a lot of thinking while I tried to see how high I could go and if I could touch a branch of a tree high above me with my toe by stretching my leg as far out as I could and by pointing my toes. I knew there were things I had asked about in the past and had never gotten all the answers.

While Mom cooked supper and Kay took a nap, I stayed in the backyard close to the house. I smelled something really delicious cooking. Finally, Dad called me in to eat. Mom put everything on the table, and Kay got up from her nap and came to the table. When we were seated, Dad said a blessing.

Kay started to talk about her problem, but Dad said, "Let's have a peaceful meal." When Mom served the ice tea, I noticed her hands were shaking. We ate our supper in silence. Well, almost. Kay sniffled every now and then while we ate whipped potatoes, meat loaf, fried green tomatoes, pinto beans, and corn bread. Finally Mom said, "We have blackberry bread with whipped cream."

I said I would have some. Kay said she would have dessert, too. Dad said, I'll be at the barn feeding the animals."

Before he got up, I asked, "Will someone please tell me what's going on? I'm old enough to know what's wrong with Kay."

Mom and Dad and Kay exchanged glances before all three of them looked at me.

"He's right," Dad said as he pushed back his chair. "Kay, you go ahead and tell him what happened to you."

Mom said she would do the dishes later, then she served the dessert and left the kitchen. As I took a mouthful of whipped cream, I heard the front screen door close. The porch swing started to creak and the chain on the swing clinked, so I knew Mom had taken a retreat to her favorite spot.

Kay started her story. "When I was sixteen, Garner, a friend from church came by to ask me to go for a ride as he carried his brothers to church. Mom had not gotten home from work, but I thought a short ride with him to church would be okay. I could still get home in time to fix supper for Mom and Dad. So I got into Garner's forty-nine Ford. When we went down Oakdale Road toward the church, I noticed he didn't stop at the crossing. We were talking, and he drove fast. We picked up Garner's two little brothers and dropped them off at church, and drove quickly back toward Oakdale, so he could drop me off by our house."

"I sat facing Garner, and as we neared the train crossing, I looked up to see the sun glaring right off the Silver Comet streamliner passenger train as it neared the crossing."

"I screamed, 'Oh! Garner the train!' "

"He slammed the brakes and cut his wheel to the left. I crashed into the windshield and bounced back into the car as the train collided with the car on my side. This knocked me unconscious and I woke up as the train carried the car backward down the tracks, ripping and twisting it."

"The passenger side of the car tore open by the impact, and was caught under the edge of the speeding train. The remains of the car were dragged 300 yards down the track toward our house. Garner was thrown out of the car on the driver's side, and I was trapped by twisted metal on the passenger side. I hung half in and half out of the car as my right leg and right side were out of the car, but somehow as I regained consciousness, I managed to hold onto the center divider between the front and back seats as the train dragged the car. ”

Kay stopped talking and put her hand over her face and then took a napkin and wiped her eyes. I had stopped eating and stared at her. I had felt my heartbeat pounding in my chest as she told about what happened. “Sister, I knew you were in a train-car wreck but I didn’t know how bad it was. I’m glad you lived.” I patted her arm hoping she wouldn’t cry anymore.

“Mr. Elderberg, our neighbor, had been walking down the tracks toward his house after just getting off work. I sobbed hysterically and screamed, ‘Please get me out of here.’ He looked at me helplessly. I screamed for my life. Screaming is all that kept me alive.”

“Much of my injuries were sustained on impact, but the car, caught under the edge of the train, which dragged it backward slashed my body. The shredded metal of the car shook and rocked as it went backward down the tracks.

“The engine of this passenger train did not stop until it got to the Church Road Bridge, a half-mile passed our house.

“I remember the sound of the collision and the sharp noises that followed. Even in the moments of unconsciousness, I could still hear the sounds. When the train dragged the car passed our house, the screeching sound scraped like a thousand fingernails on ten thousand blackboards. There was a slowing down and breaking sound and sharp noises, like click, click, click.

“When the train came to a stop, people were running toward me. Mr. Elderberg had caught up to the wreck. I screamed, ‘Momma! Momma!’ My left side was trapped in the car, and I hung partly out of the car like a rag doll. I went in and out of consciousness. Mr. Elderberg kept talking to me.

“In a few minutes, firemen were trying to free me and get me on a stretcher and into an ambulance which had just arrived. As they put me into the ambulance, I saw the silver train snaked out behind me and smelled the diesel fuel. The cold wind November wind blew and the smell of my blood came from the mangled car. I remember wondering if I were going to die.

"As the firemen put me into the ambulance, I saw the remains of the twisted car. It looked like a crushed ball of metal some angry giant had wadded with his fist. The roof of the 49 Ford was pushed up into a canopy over the mangled mess, and the only way I recognized it as a car is that I could see one of the wheels underneath the tangle.

"Garner came running down the track crying and screaming, 'I didn't mean to kill her! I didn't mean to kill her!'"

As Kay told her story, I finished my dessert and she continued to wipe at the tears still rolling down her cheeks. I patted her arm again and said, "Sister, how long did it take you to get over the cuts?"

"The fireman put a tourniquet on my leg to slow down the bleeding to keep me from bleeding to death. This saved my life. I had a serious cut on the tendon in my foot and blood was everywhere.

"I heard the ambulance driver say, 'We've got to give her blood, fast.' They took me to Crawford Long Hospital. Garner became too distraught to go in the ambulance to the hospital. Later a doctor admitted him to Crawford Long.

"It was a hard time for Dad and Mom. They were very strong during all this. It was terrible for them that I was not expected to live." I felt badly for Kay as she continued her story.

"When my parents wasn't at my bedside, they were in the hospital chapel down on their knees. They trusted the Lord to bring me through all this terrible time and He did.

Kay continued, "It's been almost nine years, and I've had reconstructive surgery four times. I know of two more surgeries the doctors say

I will need."

Kay said, "I stayed in a wheelchair about a year. The doctors said I would never walk. But after all the surgeries, the right side of my body healed. It took me another year, trying, but as you know I can walk well—even without a limp."

I studied Kay's eye and face. I had never looked at her up that close. She wore a lot of makeup. I noticed her right eye had faint scarring around it and there were scars on her cheek, chin, and neck. It seemed to me Kay had been through hard times. I did not understand all that happened or why God let it happened.

Mom came in from the front porch and said, "I'll never forgive Garner for what happened. I hate him. If it hadn't been for him Kay would never have had all this pain and heartache."

Kay said, "I can't blame Garner. It's just something that happened. I'm just thankful to God I survived."

From what I heard, I pieced together the events after the train accident. Mom took care of Kay. About a year later when Kay could walk perfectly, Mom went back to her job, as a nurse at Piedmont Hospital. Shortly after then, she got pregnant with me. Because of her bad health and being pregnant, she stayed in the hospital almost as much as she worked there.

When it seemed Kay would soon be finished with her surgeries Dad decided it was time for a settlement with the railroad. In a settlement all the hospital bills were paid, and Kay received enough money to pay for a two year education at the Massey Business College. She put the rest of the money in the bank for the last corrective surgery on her heel and for the last plastic surgery on her face.

At Massey Business College, Kay met George Lee and they dated for several years. After they both graduated, they got married. They rented a house from Dad, the one George accidentally set on fire. After the fire, Kay took some of her savings and put a down payment on a two story house with a full basement in a nice neighborhood, but then George walked away with the rest of her savings.

After Kay told her story to me, I felt really sorry for her. Mom and Dad sat down at the kitchen table with her. “Dad, what am I going to do?” she asked. “I’ve just bought this house. I can’t make enough money to keep up the payments by myself. I don’t want to lose it. And what about the last plastic surgery on my face?”

Dad hugged Kay and said, “We’ll think of something. We always do. In the meantime you can stay with us. We’ll get through this. You’ll have your surgeries, somehow, and we’ll think of something to do about the house.”

In the end, Kay decided to stay with Mom and Dad for six weeks and commute to her job in downtown Atlanta where she worked for the state government.

Kay had been staying with us for two weeks and started feeling much better when I came in the house one Sunday afternoon right in the middle of a big discussion. When Kay and Mom were together, they always got into an argument about church.

“You were too strict on me,” Kay said to Mom. You wouldn’t even let me go to the picture show or a ball game. And heaven fall down if I thought about going to a dance,” she said. “And my hair! Remember you wouldn’t let me get my hair cut? My hair got way down my back. At thirteen I wanted it cut. Every morning before school I had a big tangled mess. Remember how I begged and begged until you finally took me to get it trimmed.”

“Well, young girls should have long hair,” Mom protested.

The conversation heated up and Kay said, “I always told you, when I got old enough, I would not ever go to church again, and I would do just what I pleased. Well, I admit I do attend church. But I’ll never go back to your and Dad's church. I grew up afraid I would do something wrong, and God would strike me down dead. You even told me once that if I wore lipstick, I'd go to hell."

"I did not," Mom said in a small, quiet voice.

"That's what you told me. Mom, that's crazy. God has got more important things to do than keep up with who's wearing lipstick!" At this, the two of them laughed.

"Anyway, when I got to school, I put it on."

Kay laughed at this. Mom gave her a hard look. Kay just would not leave it alone, "I just wore light pink. I figured God wouldn't notice if it weren't too dark." I thought Kay was going to fall out of the chair she was laughing so hard, teasing Mom. Mom started to get mad, so Kay quit teasing her.

"Seriously, Mom," she said. "God is love. God is not out to get me, and that's what our church taught. You brought me up to believe if I wasn't perfect, He would destroy me or do something to me. I don't like that way of thinking. Many times, when I went into the church on Sunday I feared God so much, I would go back out and throw up in the bushes outside, in the church yard."

I went into the backyard to the swing. I swung as high as I could, thinking the whole time about all that Kay had said. I liked the idea that God is love and He was not just out to get me. But why did he let the train wreck happen to Kay? I couldn't understand it.

8.
Blotter Acid

For the six weeks Kay stayed with us, most of the family's attention turned to her. She and Mom continued to argue about church and religion. I stayed out of the arguments, but still felt confused.

I spent time in the backyard with Rooster and Tophat. We were innocent kids who started out doing innocent things—things that all boys had done or wanted to do. But there came a slow unraveling we were not even aware of and our parents would not know about for a long time.

Rooster Roberts and Tophat Taylor came over more and more, so we decided to build a hut in the middle of the backyard, just past the big granite rock. We got discarded pallets from the dumpster at a nearby factory for the sides of the hut, and old shingles from the school when they replaced the roof. Dad framed the hut for us and put in four windows. He showed us how to put up the siding and the roof, and we guys did the rest of the labor. We put in two bunk beds, so we could sleep four guys out there. We put in a wood burning pot-bellied stove to use in the wintertime.

The first Friday night after we finished the hut, Mom and Dad said we could spend the night there. About dusk, Rooster said, "Let's go into Oakdale. I've heard the older guys drag race. I want to see what drag racing is all about."

After I asked permission from Mom and Dad to go into Oakdale, we were on our bikes and up the street in a few minutes. When we got there, we stayed back out of the way of the tough looking guys. They were parked under the big oak trees in their fast cars with the big motors. I felt kinda excited watching. I did not know what to expect. These tough guys were wearing levies, tee-shirts and had slicked-back, greased hair. We watched as these big cars with powerful motors burned rubber in front of Pack-a-Sack.

Sure enough, I heard them say drag racing, but I didn't understand what they meant until we watched two cars race toward the river, a few miles away, and then race back toward us. We waited and watched them come barreling into town. Watching this action with the noise and speed was spellbinding to me. I loved the sound of the motors and I loved the speed. I could not wait to see two more cars race. Rooster, Tophat, and I had each just had our ninth birthdays within a couple of months of each other. We were at the end of our third grade, so we had never been out on our own or had seen anything like this.

I saw Mike Blackmon, the big kid who had held me down and cut my hair with his switchblade last year after school started in August. He had a scar on the bridge of his nose where I had hit him with the quart beer bottle. His right eye lid looked kinda turned inside out. I ducked behind the crowd before he could see me.

Jeff Kilpatrick, one of the local teenagers, stood between the hot rods outside the Pack-a-Sack with a group of older boys. He had done some work for Dad and had been by the house several times to pick up his paychecks. "Hey Brad." Jeff said. "What are you doing up here."

"We came to watch the drag racing." I didn't know if he would rat on me to Dad. He shrugged his shoulders. He had a few beers in a cooler sitting behind him on the ground. He then urged me, "Come on, Brad, we'll drink some Papst Blue Ribbon."

I didn't like Jeff. He meant to be a smart ass, and I really didn't want any of that stuff. "No," I said as I shook my head.

He balled up his fist and put it right in my face. "Have a drink or have a busted mouth. You're one of the guys. You think you're too good? Then you're a sissy and a whimp. You want a broken tooth?" I couldn't believe he would treat me this way. I couldn't tell Dad or he would know I had watched the drag racing. After a few minutes, I remembered Dad had laid Jeff off as he had proven to be a lazy worker. Maybe he threatened me because he was still mad that Dad let him go from the job.

Rooster and Tophat drank about half of the one he gave them, and then they said, "Let's go." They ran but Jeff grabbed me. I faced my choice—either drink or get beaten up. I figured it couldn't hurt to just go ahead and drink the beer. It tasted bitter and nasty, but I drank it. I could stand it better when he put a little salt in it. I drank half the beer, and when Jeff turned his back, I ran away from him.

I found Rooster and Tophat waiting for me nearby. "Sorry, man. We didn't mean to leave you. We thought you were right behind us when we left," said Rooster.

The next Friday night, the three of us went into Oakdale again to watch the drag racing, and found ourselves in the same situation as before. We began to learn to drink, so we didn't get beaten up. After a few weeks, we could stand the taste a little better. After a few more weeks, we even grew to like beer as it quenched our thirst on the warm spring nights. We liked being treated as "one of the guys" and being a part of those who watched the drag racing. We thought we were being cool.

One Friday night after Rooster and I watched the drag racing, we rode our bikes down Hill Street and got almost home when we decided to sit down in the middle of the street and drink the beers Jeff Kilpatrick had given us. We put our bikes in the ditch and sat down just beyond the crest of the hill up the street from my house, so my parents couldn't see us. We could still see the lights and hear when a car came. There were only four driveways on our end of the street and it seemed unlikely any cars would be down this way. We drank our beer and threw the cans in the ditch next to our bikes and lay down. When the nine o'clock train roared by, we watched the headlights shine down from the bluff above my house. I said, "Hey, the train's headlight looks like a giant's flashlight."

The train sounded so loud, we didn't hear the car coming until I felt the vibrations on my backside at the same moment Rooster screamed, "**CAR**!"

We each rolled to the opposite sides of the road—Rooster to the right side and me to the left side. Dad's car passed just where we had been laying, seconds before.

Dad stopped the car when he saw our bikes in the ditch and got out with his hands on his head, "Well my swanee! What in the Sam Hill are you two doing laying in the road?! Bradley, I went up to Oakdale looking for you."

I did not say anything. Rooster took off home. "You come on to the house," Dad demanded. He didn't see the beer cans we had thrown into the ditch five minutes earlier. I got on my bike and followed his car down Hill Street across the plank bridge and into the yard. I went straight to bed as I didn't want Dad to smell beer on my breath. I heard him telling Mom what happened. I felt terrible, and the next day I felt even worse as I experienced my first hangover. Dad never had any idea Rooster and I had been drinking beer sitting in the middle of the street at night when he came by in the car.

My life gradually took a turn. It began so gradual that no one noticed, not even me until I let go of control. It all started with one phone call. It's funny when you look back and see how one little phone call can change your whole life.

My Daddy's cousin, Aaron Berkshire, phoned Dad and said he and his wife, Mary, and their son, Kelly, were moving to Oakdale. I had never met any of this part of my Dad's family. Aaron got a job at the local electric company and Dad found a house for them to buy on Hill Street near us. When they moved into a house, we went to meet them. Kelly was three years older than me and seemed pretty nice. He told me everyone just called him Kell.

After I got to know Kell, we met after school and walked up to Oakdale before going home. By this time, we were in the last two months of school. I knew I had fallen so far behind, so I looked forward each day to meeting Kell outside after school. School bored me. Being with him and doing what he did, I hoped to become a tough guy.

When Kell and I went up to Pàc-a-sac to buy bubble gum, he acted like we were buddies until we got to the store then he began shoving me around and calling me names in front of the tough guys there. The others followed Kell's pattern, and I became their subject for abuse. I guess they shoved me for their amusement.

"Hey, Pànsy, Whimp." Kell shoved me into one of the bullies who shoved me back to Kell. I left there with a bloody nose and bruises on my arms and shoulders, but mostly I had a bruised ego.

I avoided Kell for a while. Then I figured out I needed to be tough to be accepted, so I would not be beaten up. Whenever I hung around Kell and the other guys, I drank a beer, so I would seem tough and like I belonged to their kind.

The next time Kell came over, he brought marijuana into the hut where Tophat, Rooster, and I were hanging out. He showed us how to smoke a "weed." He also had a bottle of wine. I ran into the house and got paper cups, filled them, and we began to sip the wine. Pretty soon we were giggling and feeling pretty good. I guess Dad heard us giggling and making a lot of noise and out of curiosity decided to check on us. When he opened the door and stepped into the hut, he exclaimed, "Well, heck fire! What is going on in here!?"

He saw the almost empty wine bottle. "Where in the Sam Hill did you boys get wine?"

I told him that Rooster, who had already left, had brought it.

Dad said, "I'm not going to have this, Bradley Boy. Drinking is no good. Before you know it, you will have a habit. People think it's the thing to do when there's a group or a party. You can be influenced by other people to drink, but it can ruin your life. Drinking can become so addictive it will become your God. This is one thing you boys don't want to become a habit. Promise me you won't ever bring any more wine into this hut."

We all said, "Yes sir," as he gave each of us a stern look. He then took the bottle and poured the contents on the ground outside the hut and went back into the house carrying the empty bottle.

Dad didn't notice the smoke or the smell of marijuana. I guess he didn't know what marijuana smelled like. We had a little fire going in the wood burning stove that probably masked the marijuana smell.

A couple of the older guys gathered after school behind the stores in Oakdale and smoked pot. They said it made you feel so good when you got high, so I smoked several times. I bought a "nick" from Kell. A nick meaning a nickel's worth. Then I found out I could get a quarter of a bag, for five dollars—eleven to twelve joints of marijuana cigarettes. After I bought my drugs, I went out back to the hut and smoked. The first time I got really stoned alone, I walked over to my neighbor's house and sat on the porch swing with the Renee and Teresa Walker.

They said, "What's wrong with you, Brad? You're acting weird." Instead of answering, I threw up in the bushes, left, and went back to the hut.

Kell told me I could buy five dollars worth of drugs a week from him with the money I earned from mowing lawns in the summer around our neighborhood. Sometimes I got the money from doing odd jobs for

Dad as he gave me a dollar for helping him work around the yard or for taking care of the animals in the afternoon. My parents were unaware of the drug culture. To them, a pot was what you used to cook a meal. A weed was what they pulled out of their garden. And drugs were what they bought from the pharmacy when the doctor wrote a prescription. Then one night on the national news, a broadcast reported on hippies doing drugs. "Son have you ever heard of your friends doing drugs? This report says drugs are being sold in the suburbs."

"That must be happening somewhere else in the world." I had never lied to my Dad before and I felt badly about lying to him. Kell told me everybody smoked pot. "It don't hurt anything or anybody. It makes you feel good. Just do it anyway and don't tell your Dad." For some reason I did what Kell wanted me to do. I let him influence me and I influenced Rooster and Tophat. Anyway I liked the way pot made me feel.

Then Kell sold me LSD in the form of blotter acid. This piece of paper looked like a stamp. He told me to put it in my mouth and chew it. I did and then I really began to feel strange and see strange things. The next day, I took a stamp over to Rooster's and showed it to him.

He said, "What's that?" referring to the stamp. I said, "It's LSD."

"I thought LSD had something to do with a needle and syringe," he replied.

"You trip for nine or ten hours and then you come down," I said quoting what Kell had told me. We each chewed a half. I had planned on walking around for an hour or two, but after we walked around for thirty minutes, Rooster headed home.

"I don't think you should trip around your parents," I said.

But he went home anyway to eat supper. I decided I had better go and see what would happen to him. When we got to his house, he sat down at the supper table with his parents. I tried to tell him not to eat by getting his attention and shaking my head. I had just remembered Kell told me not to eat when I took LSD. But Rooster helped himself to the boiled cabbage and cornbread and began packing it in. "Brad, that's some mighty fine cabbage your Dad gave us from his garden for supper tonight, son," his dad said to me not noticing I was trippin.' Kell had told me LSD contained strychnine which has a poison and would blow up your stomach, making it swell.

Now as I sat there with the family, I didn't want to eat. I stared at the floor tiles as they looked like they were rising up off the floor. Pretty soon Rooster's stomach swelled up like a watermelon. I kept trying to tell Rooster not to eat.

All of a sudden he sat back from the table and said, "I think I'll go to my room." I followed. When we got to his room, Rooster turned around and exclaimed, "Berkshire! Berkshire! What's going on?" He started taking off his belt and loosening his jeans. "I tried to tell you not to eat. LSD makes you swell," I said. I looked around Rooster's room. The walls were starting to melt. Just then Rooster's mom came in. "What's going on?"

She looked at Rooster who still had his shirt pulled up looking at his stomach. I knew I hallucinated, but his stomach really looked like a balloon just like when a balloon gets so big it starts to look lighter in color. Rooster's stomach had turned big and white! "Oh, he ate too much cabbage," I said.

I glanced up at her, and saw her forehead melting over her chin. She laughed and left the room. The walls were curling and sagging. The floor waved and rose up.

"Damn, Berkshire. What kind of stuff is this anyway?" Rooster said.

"You'll be all right in nine or ten hours," I replied.

Rooster's mom called from the kitchen, "What's wrong with

y'all?"

"Rooster's got a stomach ache," I called back. "He just ate too much cabbage."

She did not dream her kid did drugs, much less LSD.

"Kell told me you'll peak in five hours." I said. "You gotta maintain. Be cool," I said. I headed for the back door. "Berkshire. Don't leave. Don't leave." I passed Rooster's dad. He said something like, "Tell your Daddy that Rooster sure did like the cabbage."

It scared me trippin' at night walking home along. The wind blew the trees and bushes. I thought spiders were coming out to get me. The leaves rattled like the paper skeletons on Halloween. I headed straight to my room without eating supper. I told Mom I felt sick and went to bed.

All night long—every two hours, the train roared by like a monster. The noise vibrated my bones flat into the sheets. The hot breath of each monster breathed fire on my eyelids and forehead. When the sun came up, it seared my closed eyes. When I refused to go to school, Mom said, "Bradley, you don't need to miss school. You need to keep up with the reading. You're already behind."

"I've got a headache and I'm sick at my stomach." I turned over and pulled the cover over my head, so Mom left me "home sick." I laid in bed until two, getting up just before she came home. Even though I threw up, I still took more blotter acid. As long as I took this, I felt good. I didn't worry about school.

About this same time, things were changing around our land. The Georgia Department of Transportation cut Interstate 285, laying the interstate out in a circle around Atlanta. The west side of the perimeter cut through a section of our back pasture and took a slice off the back thirty acres of my Dad's land. Part of Pine Street where my Mom's parents had lived for several generation would be totally eliminated. From our house each afternoon, I could hear the bulldozers getting closer.

As I ate breakfast one morning, I glanced out the bay-window in the kitchen and saw a big yellow bulldozer far in the distance over on Pine Street. "Mom they're here!" I yelled.

Mom leaned over me and peered out the window. We both hurried to the back of our land as far as we dared go. The bulldozers were in the yard of my grandparent's old abandoned house. Mom folded her arms tightly around herself. As I watched her, I knew tears were close.

"Lilly and I grew up there," she said almost to herself. "A lot of living went on in that house. Mother and Daddy raised seven boys and us twin girls there."

I barely remembered having my second birthday party there in the old home-place. The house had been empty since Granddaddy O'Neal died and Grandmother O'Neal went into a nursing home when I was four. I don't have any recollection of Grandmother O'Neal except when she rolled up a newspaper tied tightly with rubber bands and hit me up the side of the head with it.

"Children should be seen and not heard," she had shouted, chasing me. "OW!" I'd grab my head and stood off looking at her not knowing what I had done to provoke her. I never had anything else to do with her after she hit me with the roll up newspaper.

We watched as a bulldozer pushed the walls in, breaking up the house and exposing the empty rooms. When the house crumbled, the roof fell in on top of the rubble. A bulldozer scooped up all the debris into a pile while tears streamed down Mom's face. Finally she went back home with her head down. She let me stay out of school to watch the rest of the work. I went home for lunch then went back and watched again, all afternoon.

When Dad came in from work in the evening, he came back to the clearing, and we watched the pile of debris burn. He said, "It's like watching the past go up in flames." A little later when the fire had consumed almost all the debris, he added, "Time waits for no man, it just keeps on going."

When everything had finished burning, the digger put the left-over debris into a dump truck to be hauled away. Then the bulldozers scraped the area until all traces of the house were gone and left only a smooth dirt surface. Dad and I walked slowly home in silence.

The next morning before the bulldozers started plowing into our pasture, Dad and I rounded up our two cows and four horses, and moved them to a pasture nearer the house. I ran shouting and herding the livestock. I saw the men on the equipment slow down and smile at me running, and waving at the livestock, sweating the whole time. When we had all the animals in place, we reset the barbed-wire fence out of the way of the bulldozers.

Every afternoon after that, I sat on the railroad bridge and watched from a distance as trees were pushed over and the grading continued for the interstate. Month after month, we heard the distant sounds of the bulldozers as they cut into hills and graded the land flat for the paving to begin. This interstate not only took our old family home-place and a chunk of our land but the beautiful woods surrounding our land. This did not necessarily narrow my world. I could still walk the railroad and go under the I-285 overpass to the surrounding neighborhoods.

There were other changes going on that I didn't like. Both Mom and Dad were away from home more. Mom took her insulin shot every day and felt better, so she went to her nursing job every day and didn't get home until about five-thirty. I came home to an empty house every day. Daddy had a great job at Southern Railway as a teletype operator, but one day he came home and said he had to take an early retirement. A microwave company had bought out the division of his company and did away with his job.

Southern Railway offered those who would lose their job an early retirement. Dad knew he had to take the retirement package and be glad of the offer. But his retirement income did not amount to nearly as much as he usually brought home.

Daddy could not afford to continue his sideline business of building rental houses, so he hired a few men and went full force into cleaning new apartment buildings. He and his crew cleaned stairwells, and laundry rooms and made needed repairs and did maintenance work.

As a small boy I had spent a lot of time with Dad. He had shown me how to work. The component of his work ethic meant you produced and you produced well. I worked right beside him when he did yard work, tended to the animals, or made repairs around the house. He taught me not be afraid of work, and he gave me jobs to do around the house every afternoon before he got home from work. He gave me a dollar or so every now and then for the work I did. Dad promised when I got older, I could work with him as one of his crew members.

With the money Dad made from the sale of our back pastures to the Georgia Department of Transportation for the new interstate, he had the money for Kay's last two surgeries.

In the meantime, Kay rented out her new two story house to a nice family, the Hershel Johnsons, with the stipulation she live in the basement. She stayed with us after the surgeries, but soon went back to work then she moved into the basement of her house to live.

Our house stayed mostly empty except for early morning when we got up to eat breakfast and to get ready to leave for school and work, and when suppertime came. After Kay moved out, I stayed there by myself when Mom worked at her nursing job. Dad didn't get in until seven many nights. I rambled—on the loose. At that time I could get away with a lot. If people didn't know what I did, they didn't know.

Rooster, Tophat and I created our own adventures. We roamed the woods, going over several hills and valleys and found another railroad track and a fishing hole called Nickajack Creek.

School let out for the summer, so I took Rooster down to the swimming hole to scoop around for minnows. When we couldn't catch any minnows, we'd go back home and get a loaf of bread for bait. If we didn't have fishing hooks, we used safety pins. As we walked the tracks home, passenger trains passed us. We'd stepped off the tracks while the trains passed us like jets, and then we'd step back on the tracks and head home. I loved the speed and sound of the trains.

I guess I got my love of trains from my Dad. He loved the power and the idea of a train. When we were out in the yard, he'd say, "man, that engine's pulling hard." I'd say, "How do you know that?" "Listen to that diesel straining. That's two or three miles of steel it's pulling. It's even got a helper engine about midway."

On the weekends, a favorite pastime on the Southern Railway tracks became riding the cars, seeing how long we could stay on as the train built up speed before we'd jump off.

Once Tophat and I were hiding in the bushes when the train came in, slowed down, and prepared to switch tracks. Then a train came by going in the opposite direction. We jumped on the side ladder of the train and climbed into an open box car, as the train slowly picked up speed. The engine made a big jolt, and then came a surge in speed. When the train got to what felt like five to ten miles per hour, I jumped off.

Tophat, being more of a daredevil than I, kept on riding. He turned and looked back at me standing on the side of the tracks. I saw his head poke out of the door then he looked toward me. I thought his bright red hair, and the way he wore it out front off his forehead like he did, flapping in the wind, looked like a flag waving.

I screamed as loudly as I could after him, "You better jump now or you'll end up in Alabama!"

Another jolt and surge of speed put the train up to about twenty to twenty-five miles an hour. Tophat decided to jump right when the train got to a curve.

After Tophat jumped, he rolled right into a tangle of bushes. I ran to see if he was hurt. I found him just laying there, his face white. I pulled on his shoulders and brought him upright. I heard a rush of his breath and saw him suckin' in air through his open mouth. He had gotten the wind knocked out of him. He struggled to get up, took a few more forced breaths and started to take a step, then howled out. He had sprained his ankle, so I helped him as he hobbled home.

In a few weeks, we were back on the tracks riding another train. All summer long, we continued to ride the rail. We began to have a clear understanding of what rocks, gravel, and briars felt like. However, we didn't get seriously hurt and each time we jumped, we lived to ride another train. We got through the summer without any mishap and then school started back.

I started the fourth grade and did just as poorly as Mom and I expected. My teacher, Mrs. Betts, soon found out what a challenge she had in helping me read. Mrs. Betts and the class moved on in the assignments and left me not understanding even the first assignment in the book. I had a hard time sitting in class all day not knowing how to do the work and not being able to do anything when instructed. I became restless after running loose over the countryside all summer. So Mrs. Betts had to get after me to sit still many times every day. I became such a challenge. I know she didn't like me.

When Mrs. Betts asked the class what we all would like to do when we grew up, the little boy in front of me said he would like to be a truck driver. That sounded like it would be fun to me, so I raised my hand, and she called on me.

I said, "I would like to be a truck driver when I grow up."

Mrs. Betts looked at me real hard and said angrily, "People like you will be a ditch digger all of your life."

The whole class laughed at me. I felt my cheeks growing red, and I just stood there studying my shoelaces. I felt humiliated, and from that moment on, I hated school. I wanted out as soon as I could get out. The year turned into one long miserable time for me. All week when I went to school, I looked forward to spending the time after school and the weekends with Rooster and Tophat.

The three of us roamed the neighborhood doing what most boys our age were doing, seeking adventure. We rode our bikes for miles just to see what we could discover. We went over to the Kentwood neighborhood and met some tough boys in a gang, Billy and Johnny Hatchett. We realized they were bad news and headed back to Oakdale.

More and more my real hero became Kell because he supplied us with marijuana and beer. I hung out with him, so I could learn to be tough and, of course, have access to drugs. He pushed me around in front of the older guys on Friday night, so I learned to stay clear of him when Tophat and Rooster were not with us.

Kell, Tophat, Rooster and I went into Oakdale drag racing every Friday night and came back to the hut and got high. We asked beforehand to spend the night in the hut. So if we came home stoned, we didn't have to face my parents. So in the fall and on warm winter nights we slept in the hut and many of those nights we were stoned. We fell asleep with the transistor radio blaring out rock and roll music. When I got high, I didn't have to think about being a poor student or how much I worried Mom and Dad and the teachers about my low reading ability.

I still went to church with Mom and Dad on Sunday morning, but I got high on Sunday afternoon, so I didn't have to worry about what the preacher had shouted that Sunday morning—about being a sinner and going to hell. I felt pretty sure by now I had become a sinner with all this drinking and smoking pot, and now I lied to my parents all the time about what we were doing and where we had been. Being dishonest worried me and gave me a new feeling of guilt.

One Friday after school, I rode my bike home from school and saw that the city workers were paving a sidewalk. They had the concrete smooth and a section looked dry. I rode my new Galaxy 500 bike toward the sidewalk and a city worker called out, "Don't go there! It's not dry!" I plowed my new bike—the one I won last year—the one with the knobby tires— right down the middle of the sidewalk. My Sunday School teacher, Mrs. Couch, stood in the parking lot of a nearby store and stared at me doing this. Mrs. Couch called out a warning to me, "Bradley Berkshire, you'll go to hell for that. I'll tell your Daddy on you."

I felt a little high that afternoon and just laughed to myself. Later at dusk dark, I went back and wrote my name beside the knobby tire tracks. I felt rebellious. I also didn't like hearing grown-ups threaten me with hell. If I went to hell, it would not be because of riding my bike in the wrong place.

I went into the house one Sunday afternoon and heard a rigmarole going on about Mom's new "red-bird vase" Dad had given her for her birthday. This cornucopia-shaped flower vase had a hand painted, red bird on each side. What was so unusual about it, Aunt Lilly said, was that it attached to the wall. The vase being so unique and so beautiful caused Aunt Lilly to say she just loved it and just had to have one like it.

She kept going on and on about the gift until Dad just went back to the store and bought one like it for her. Lilly said when he came back into the kitchen with the package, "Well, after all, it's my birthday too." When she unwrapped her new red-bird vase, she was so excited. She kept laughing as she hugged Dad and gave Mom a "well-I've-got-one-too," look. The day seemed to be about Aunt Lilly getting the same gift as Mom had gotten—not about Aunt Lilly's birthday with her family. I would have enjoyed the time with Mom without Aunt Lilly who always seemed to be butting into our family matters. I couldn't understand why she came as she had her own party to go to later in the day.

I took all this in and stayed for Mom' s birthday dinner. I had bought her a string of beads with the money I had earned helping Dad. When I could, I slipped out the back door unseen. No one would miss me and no one would come out into the hut where I would be getting high, stoned on marijuana. No one would know. No one from the house ever came outside looking for me. My hut became my refuge.

My world opened up. I ventured out, not so protected as I had been there at the end of Hill Street with my Mom and Dad. They were gone more and more from home. I crossed the bridge in my yard and went beyond what I had known. My childhood, like the dirt in the pasture, had been pushed away by my new experiences—and more were to come.

Part II — Don't Cross That Bridge

9.
Hippie Festival

At ten years old, I started the fifth grade, but I was too young for the experience coming—one that would really shake me up.

I had started eating hardily and had grown to five foot eight inches tall and weighed a hundred-and-fifty pounds. When I was younger and much smaller, Mom had always tried to make me eat. Now she delighted in how healthy and strong I had become.

My fifth grade teacher, Mrs. Bennett, ignored my other problems of falling asleep and of sometimes being high. She helped me with reading more than any teacher. Somehow she helped me realize the accomplishment of learning. I could only read a few second grade words, but she built on these words—teaching me compound words. She taught me to sound out syllables using phonics. Then I started learning consonant blends. "Brad, think of the BL sound—the B and L sounds blend together. Try reading these flashcards."

I read, "BLACK, BLOCK, BLUE, BLIND," then paused and looked at her for approval.

"Brad, that's exactly right." She smiled at me and said, "You are doing very well."

I immediately felt lifted up and happy. I could learn. I went home so hopeful and my whole day seemed happier. The next week, when Mrs. Bennett helped me after school, I learned a few third grade words then she helped me in language arts. For a short time, I became interested in school and became hopeful that I could learn to read well enough to catch up to the fifth grade level, the level of my classmates.

Mrs. Bennett planted a seed, but that seed did not get a chance to sprout and grow for a very long time because of what happened one Saturday in late September. I had my first true drug culture shock.

On one of those beautiful, early autumn days in the South, Kell and I hitch hiked into Atlanta to Piedmont Park. Kell, who had turned thirteen, dressed in plaid bell bottom pants, a buttoned up shirt—open at the neck—a hippie headband and boots. He had grown tall and skinny and had a bad case of acne—which altogether made a disagreeable-looking kid. But he could turn on the charm especially to girls. He brought a couple of girls, a few years older than him, along with us to the festival. They were dressed in long, flowing, bright dresses, had long straight hair and wore flowered headbands. I talked to them. They seemed nice in spite of the weird way they were dressed.

We thumbed on the side of the road and walked toward Atlanta to get to the festival. Finally someone driving a U-Haul truck gave us a ride. He put us in the back of the truck and pulled the door closed. This closed off the light, and it got hot fast, but the driver soon pulled over and let us out at Piedmont Park where a hippie festival spread over several acres of rolling park—a spectacle like nothing I had ever seen.

I turned around amazed at the amount of people everywhere—hundreds, maybe a thousand. I stood and looked and turned slowly in a circle. There were people over the green hillsides, under the large oak trees, and around the lake. Everyone dressed strangely to me in colorful, loose clothing. Both men and women wore their hair very long and had on headbands. The music blared loud and continual.

Some people were sprawled out on the lawn and appeared as though they were half asleep, even though, they were talking to those around them who also appeared to be half asleep. Hippies were acting like they were there but not really there. Everyone smoked until a smoky film hovered over the entire park. A black guy sitting on the ground near us talked to himself. He slumped over, his head bobbing before he started slobbering. "Kell, what's wrong with him?" I pointed to the man.

Kell replied, "He's doing junk." I didn't understand what he meant. I heard strange words. A guy with long hair down his back walked by me, looked me in the eye, and mumbled, "Reefer?" When I didn't answer, he staggered on by with a glazed look in his eyes. Some walked around with leather pouches strapped to their sides and went through the crowd asking if anyone wanted to buy what they had to sell. They simply looked at you and asked, "pounds, reefer, triple A, heroin, smack, O-Zs, Mexican MDA, THC?"

Kell and I walked around looking at the sight of all these crazy people. A policeman stood nearby, also watching. Kell passed me a joint. I glanced over at the policeman. I didn't take the joint from Kell. I felt afraid I might be arrested. Then I realized there were too many involved in this illegal activity for him to do anything, but it seemed he still watched me, yet he did nothing.

When I didn't take the joint from Kell, he walked off and left me standing there in this weird crowd. After a few minutes, I quit searching for him and just watched these insane people.

All around, I saw banners with slogans, "If It Feels Good, Do It." "Peace-Love." "Keep on Truckin." One guy with very long hair approached me. When he got right beside me he asked, "Orange sunshine, purple microdot?"

What kind of language are these people speaking? I wondered to myself. Are they from another planet? Then I began to see milk jugs and fruit jars filled with liquid. I asked a hippie who stood close by watching, "What are they drinking?"

He replied as if he were in a drunken stupor, "electric tea." It's Kool-Aid with two hundred hits of THC, enough for two hundred people."

I looked quickly back to the eight or ten people who sat in the circle passing the jug around. Everybody took a sip then waited for a minute before passing the jug to the next person. With only a little liquid left in the bottom of the jug, the next man took a sip. In a few minutes he fell back, flat on the ground and began to twitch. He jerked and his eyes rolled back in his head. He arched his back. He began to throw up. Then he began to jerk in convulsions.

I felt shocked. I had never seen anyone have a convulsion. I didn't think anyone my age should be seeing this. Some people began to run away from this guy like what happened to him could be their fault. I stood in a crowd of curious on-lookers that formed around the guy on the ground. Several policeman came over and told us to step back and clear a space. One called a near-by ambulance attendance over to help the man. As the ambulance came over, I heard one of the ambulance attendance say, "The liquid in the bottom of the jar hadn't been stirred—too concentrated—the THC wasn't dissolved fully. He got a big dose of the raw drugs. We have an overdose here."

With all the commotion and the ambulance leaving with the siren turned up full blast, Kell came back to find me and to see what had happened. "The ambulance attendance said a man overdosed. You shouldn't have left me here. I'm not used to this crowd. I'm just ten years old and shouldn't have seen that." I felt pretty shook up. Kell gave me a slap on the back and said, "Grow up. Sissy."

I tried to keep Kell in sight as he walked the park. I heard the love and peace slogan from the hippies. Maybe that would not be so bad,

I thought, to exist in peace and not have to fight. You might have peace and love while doing drugs but then have convulsions right then and there. The hippie overdosed because of what he drank, and he drank it of his own free will! That seemed crazy to me. Also the hippie slogan, "If It Feels Good, Do It" scared me.

As we walked and hitched home, I felt stunned and confused. I worried about what I had seen. I had a good look at the hippie generation and when I compared them to the way my friends and I lived, I felt repulsed. I didn't care for hippies. But then, I really didn't care for the rednecks, the bigger guys in Oakdale who picked on me and shoved me around. I thought of them as stupid and ignorant. These rednecks with their hot rods, drinking beer, and wanting to fight and act ignorant were always trying to prove how tough they were. It didn't seem like much to me anymore, but I knew one day I might fall into the category of redneck. I knew I might be forced to be one to survive. I didn't want to be a hippy, and I didn't want to be a redneck either. I really didn't fit into either category or fit in with everybody else I knew.

I didn't tell my family about the man having convulsions or about his overdose or about the festival. But being confused about what I saw and what I felt did not reform me. I did just the opposite. I started doing drugs more and more. I soon forgot the reading my fifth grade teacher, Mrs. Bennett, helped me with at the first of the year. It felt like my education went down the drain. Many times, I fell asleep at school because of being on drugs. I attended only enough to keep the truant officers away. Mrs. Bennett never gave up on me, she just could not get me to cooperate when I did come to school.

Toward the end of the year, Mrs. Bennett convinced me to stay after school again, so she could help me with reading like she had done at the first of the year. She showed me the third grade level flash cards of phonics. We took up where I left off last September. I learned a few of the new words.

She stayed late to help me, but I couldn't function—as I had taken drugs that morning before school. When she got up to get a few more cards, I went to sleep, sitting there in the classroom. When she sat back down at the desk beside me, I gave a start and woke up.

"Oh!" I said as she frowned at me. "I'm sorry, I fell asleep," I apologized. I embarrassed myself when I could not read the next five flash cards. I saw tears in her eyes and realized just how much she wanted to help me.

"Oh Brad. You could do this. I know you are capable of learning. I wish I could help you learn to read, and I wish I could help you get off drugs. Do your parents know you are stoned every day at school?"

I pretended I didn't hear that last question. I told her again, "I'm sorry I can't stay awake. Thank you for trying to help me. I just can't remember those words." I left abruptly because I felt like crying when I saw her pretty, caring face and saw the tears I caused her. Everyone knew I couldn't do the work. It was ridiculous to even try. I had the feeling of inadequacy and really didn't want to be in school anymore.

The next day the kids were taken into the gym where we sat on the floor to watch a film called "Reefer Madness." Mrs. Bennett said this would help educate students against taking drugs. Mrs. Bennett stood with two other teachers behind the projector and they kept glancing my way while the projector ran. I knew Mrs. Bennett had been instrumental in getting this film shown to all the fifth graders, especially with me in mind. Maybe she thought she could help in some way, but I should have seen this film back in the third grade. A movie could not help me now.

In the film, someone smokes half a jade and then runs and jumps out of a window. Another kid in the film smoked a joint then wrecked a car. Well, I had smoked pot, and it had made me laugh then I had become quite tranquil. I didn't jump out a window. Rooster and Tophat sat next to me, and we began to giggle during the film. "Hey," I said. "We better be careful the next time we smoke not to wreck a car."

"That would be hard to do," Rooster replied. "Since we're ten years old and don't even drive." The three of us fell back on the gym floor laughing.

This film came off as a lie. I decided society believed wrong about marijuana then they may be wrong about other drugs. In my small mind, in this free country, I could do what I wanted to do. I would be an individual even if I shocked people. I would not be afraid to try hashish. After that I became complacent. I saw I could get stoned and do nothing real easy. I felt content to sit and watch television for hours and even days. As the school year went by, I felt lost as I smoked pot, jade, and reefer and spent a lot of time in a stupor.

In the hut, I told Kell, "Twist one up." We were rolling them up in zig zag papers. Kell said, "Wait until you see the strip."

I said, "What's a strip?" He took me to an area on Peachtree Street in Atlanta—nine to ten blocks around Tenth and Fourteenth Street where you could buy anything twenty-four hours a day for two dollars a hit. There were the head shops where you could buy drug paraphernalia. I pointed to a strange piece of glass and said, "Kell, what is that?" "That's a water pipe."

"What's that?" I enquired about another object.

"This is a rolling machine," Kell explained. This just doesn't make sense to me because I knew all these drugs and all these paraphernalia were illegal.

As Kell and I walked down the busy street, I listened to the sounds of the many cars starting and stopping in traffic like background music and all the people walking and talking around me set the tempo of this music. I felt like each step we took added to the sound. I looked up to the traffic lights changing and heard policemen blowing whistles. It felt good to be there. I felt independent. I looked around at all the white dogwood trees in full bloom and all growing the same height lining the edge of the sidewalk all the way to a plaza where a fountain sprayed and where bushes flowered and cut flower grew. I liked Peachtree Street.

I realized if you belonged to the hippie crowd, no one came up to you and beat on you, and I didn't have to go up and beat on anybody else, so I thought being a hippie would be a great new life-style. When I wasn't doing drugs, I ate. I really packed in the food and really grew taller.

By the end of the fifth grade—after I had my eleven birthday, I began to dress like the hippies and let my hair grow down past my collar. I got an army shirt, cut out the sleeves, and painted peace signs on it. I wrote the word love in big letters across the back. I wore bell-bottom jeans and dingo boots. On one of my jackets I wrote the hippie slogan, "If It Feels Good, Do It" just like I had seen at hippie festival.

I tried to become a complacent hippie, but in this rough school the same unwritten ordinance applied like the one around Oakdale—be a tough guy or you don't make it. All the tough guys carried a Barlow or a banana knife and everyone had a chain like one you could use to chain your dog. I carried a chain either in my pocket or on my belt loops. No one had ever gotten hurt with a chain or a knife. I stayed as far away from these bullies as I could, but it gave me a sense of security to carry the knives and a chain.

Tophat, Rooster, Kell, and I continued to be hooked on the path of drugs. When we were in the hut doing drugs, we listened to the popular hippie music of the day like *"Stairway to Heaven"* and heard lyrics speaking directly to us urging us to change the path we were going down.

In the backyard, the summer night heard the bullfrogs croaking beside the babbling creek, the shrill seesaw sounding of the tree frogs, the music of "*Amazing Grace*" drifting through the screen door from the piano in the living room where Mom played and sang, and my music blasting from the transistor radio through the open window of the hut where I laid on the cot, stoned, hearing nothing.

Influence. I went for that. I blamed it on Kell, but I became what child psychologists call a blank slate waiting to be written upon. Some would say peer pressure might have been the cause of influence or the lack of it. Though my parents tried, I went beyond their control by age eleven.

I became illiterate by default, being absent, being in trouble, and being a discipline problem all contributed to my not getting an education. I was socially promoted again at the end of the year.

10.
Molotov Cocktail

My sixth grade teacher, Mrs. Starky, and I were such bitter enemies we ended up in court. The first day I saw her I didn't like her because of how she treated the students. She appeared to me to be about retirement age. I complained about her to Kay who said, "Mrs. Starky has to be old. She taught me in the sixth grade, seventeen years ago. I can't believe she hasn't retired."

Mrs. Starky had silver-blue hair and wore glasses that pointed up in the corners. Her large eyes appeared even larger because of the thickness of her glasses. Her back had a curve in the shoulders, and she slumped when she sat down. "You boys and girls will have to listen to me this year. I don't tolerate any misbehavior or any late assignments. If you try me, I'll have to show you what being tough means."

The first week, she picked out the "bad boys" and lined all their desks down the left wall by the windows. Of course, I became a part of her line-up. If any one of us caused a problem, we were all punished with a lick across the hand with a yardstick. Mrs. Starky called it the "pepper stick." She asked each of us to open our right hand, so she could strike it. If we didn't, she took us out into the hallway and struck our hand out there.

By the time I got to her class, I had given up on learning. I could only read a few second and third grade words. I couldn't keep up with what went on in the classroom. So, I figured if I slept instead of harassing her or anybody else, everything should be okay. But my assumption proved wrong. I had my head down dozing when Mrs. Starky came by me and whacked me two or three times about the shoulders and head with the pepper stick for an offense someone else did while I had been asleep. I raised my head and just sat there trying to maintain control. I sat there stunned, hurt, and angry. She said, "Bradley Berkshire, if you could stay awake you might learn something for a change."

This caused the whole class to laugh. I left the room, went home, and told my mom what had happened when she asked why I came home so early. She went up to the school to find out why Mrs. Starky had hit me. Mrs. Starky only told her I had been sleeping.

I refused to go back to school for several days. What a mistake. The truant officer came by my house and said if I did not come back to school, he could put me where I would have to attend school.

Well it all happened again exactly the same. I fell asleep again. Mrs. Starky began hitting every one of the bad boys, and she hit me about the shoulders and head. I raised my head and just sat there gritting my teeth and clinching my fists. I felt just as I had the week before, angry and hurt but trying to maintain control, but this time, I could not believe she had gotten away with the same thing.

"What are you going to do? Go home and tell your mother?" she said. Everyone in the room laughed. I just got up and walked out. She had humiliated me again. So I went to the school office. Everyone in there turned to look at me expecting trouble. I told the head secretary, I needed to talk to Mr. Hastings, the fill-in principal. He heard me, came out of his office, and asked me to come in and tell him what was on my mind.

"Mrs. Starky disciplines all the students she has lined up against the outside wall every time one gets into trouble. She hits the other students who have not done anything by punishing all when only one should have been punished for what he or she had done. She also has a board with holes in it and when it comes across your backside, your flesh can go up into the holes. Once she gave me fifteen "licks" from this board for sleeping in class."

Mr. Hastings had neglected to close the door. I wondered if he had done this on purpose. All the instructors, aides and secretaries heard what I told the fill-in principal. He told me to pay attention and not sleep in class. My telling the principal had done no good whatsoever.

I went home in a stew. Timmy Mitchell, a good student and a good friend, went home with me. He hated Mrs. Starky for treating students like she did. Well, after I had been humiliated the second time, I stayed out of school again. Timmy stayed out with me. We stewed for a few days. I had once heard of an older student making a Molotov cocktail and leaving it on the baseball field when he had a difference with the coach. No one had known who had made the Molotov cocktail which caught the field on fire. He had gotten away with throwing it. Remembering this gave me the idea of how to get back at Mrs. Starky, the principal and the students who had laughed at me.

"Timmy, we're going to make a Molotov cocktail and burn down the damn school," I vowed. Timmy, a small, neat, nice little fair-haired boy, seemed to feel safer with me than he did alone. I guess he knew there were so many bullies around he felt I would protect him.

The same week Mrs. Starky had hit me twice, Timmy spent Friday night with me. At eleven o'clock, we put on our jackets and caps and snuck out the back door and up to the school. I carried a Dr. Pepper bottle filled with gasoline and a rag saturated with gasoline.

"Let's don't do this," Timmy whimpered. I saw his hands shaking as he took the match box out of his pocket.

I said, "You're going to strike the match and light the rag in the bottle, and I'm going to throw it.

Timmy said, "I don't want to do this but you're my buddy and I don't like the way Mrs. Starky treats people. This will show them all."

On this cold, windy Friday night we walked up to the double, back doors of the school. Like I planned, Timmy lit the rag in the bottle. As I threw it, a three foot flame shot past my knees. The bottle hit the door, and we ran. I glanced back to see black smoke rolling into the air. Timmy and I ran as hard as we could and got back to my bedroom where we turned out the light and pretended we had already gone to sleep.

We laid quietly in bed listening to the night sounds, waiting to hear fire truck sirens, but nothing happened. The next morning, early, we sneaked back up behind the school to see if there had been a fire. Much to my chagrin, and maybe secretly to my relief, either someone had put out the fire or it had just gone out by itself. Maybe the wind had blown it out. We never knew. The paint on the double doors had burned about two feet up from the bottom. We had a tense weekend worrying.

On Monday Timmy went back to school but I stayed away for a week. I left the house every morning as if I were going there, but I never entered the building. Instead I hid out in the woods. After a few hours, I got a kick from being out behind the baseball field where no one could see me. I climbed a tree, light up a Tampa Nugget cigar, and watched the kids on the playground. I felt like Mr. Big Man who had gotten away with what we had done. At one point, I wished I were on the playground as I missed playing with the kids. At the same time, I wanted them to be impressed by knowing I was brave enough to stay out of school. I felt like Mr. Big Man, at least for the short time.

One morning while I sat up in the tree, suddenly I heard a noise to my right. I turned around and there in the briars and vines stood the fill-in principal, Mr. Hastings. He stood there with his horn-rimed glasses, flat top haircut, suit and all, and surprised me so much my cigar fell right out of my mouth, out of the tree, and to the ground. "Brad, get down from there. I want to talk to you."

I skinned out of the tree and took off running as hard and as fast as I could. After a few minutes I found myself in unfamiliar territory in somebody's backyard, but I didn't slow down. As I glanced back toward the school to see if anyone came after me, I ran off a twelve foot cliff with a creek at the bottom. When I hit the ground, I hit my head and hurt my neck. I almost passed out because of the pain. I felt nauseous. After a long time, I finally crawled up the bank on the other side and got to my feet. I'm some Mr. Big Man all right—cigar, leather jacket, Barlow knife, and a chain on my belt loop. I stood there crying like a kid.

The next Monday morning, I decided I had stayed out long enough. The time had come for me to face Mr. Hastings. I still didn't know if anyone knew what Timmy and I had done. Timmy had sworn he had not told anyone. So Monday morning I walked in as though nothing had happened, ready for anything but what did happened. I felt anxious and wondered if the principal would call me in his office for being out all week. I expected trouble. Right then, an older boy walked up to me, pulled out his knife, popped the switch blade, and put the blade against my belly. This shook me up, but I remained calm in appearance and said, "Where did you get that?"

He replied, "Mr. Brad Berkshire, you think you're so tough don't you. That unnerved me. Did he know about the Molotov cocktail? Did he know about Mr. Hastings seeing me in the woods and about me running? I thought, he's only messing with me. I felt anxious, but walked right by the principal's office and went to class with a confident air.

About one o'clock, Mr. Hastings appeared at the classroom door and said, "Brad, I'd like to see you in the office." When I got to the principal's office, I saw Timmy Mitchell sitting there crying. I knew the jig had come to a close. Mr. Hastings really sat me back when he introduced me to the FBI agents who were already there in the office.

I didn't confess. I didn't own up to anything. One FBI man said, "We know you did it. Your fingerprints are on the bottle." I knew they were trying to trick me because I had put on work gloves, so I wouldn't burn my hands when I threw the bottle.

The FBI men took me from school down to their office in Atlanta and called both my parents who came immediately. Mom and Dad both knew about the trouble I had with Mrs. Starky the first time but had no idea she had struck me again. My parents were shocked I had thrown the Molotov cocktail. The FBI booked me, and a court date was set. Dad remained rather quiet on the way home. He tried to be understanding. I know he prayed for me and about the situation. Mom announced immediately, even as we rode home, "Bradley Elijah Berkshire, I'm literally horrified you would break the law. What will our family think? No one in this family has ever done such a thing." I knew she thought about Aunt Lilly's opinion and of how judgmental she had become about my behavior.

Mrs. Starky's way of conducting her class changed right away. She stopped hitting all the bad boys. Only the one in trouble got punished. She allowed me to sleep in class. She barely spoke to me or glanced my way. One day I thought about the paddle with the holes. I didn't see it when I searched around the room. After school, I waited down the hall out of sight and when she went to the copy room, I slipped into her room and found it in the waste paper can behind her desk. I took the paddle. She wasn't going to do away with the evidence.

Two months later my Mom, Dad, Mr. Hastings and the FBI officers were in the Fulton County courtroom when my case came up before Judge Abraham Rourke. Judge Rourke was a tall, thin, middle-age man with graying hair who peered down at me with his dark eyes over his half glasses. He called me down to sit in the chair beside his high podium. "You did this didn't you?" He studied me intensely over the half glasses. I watched the heavy, thick black eyebrows that caused him to look so intimidating.

"Yes sir," I replied.

"Why?" he asked me.

I told him about Mrs. Starky, about not being able to read, about falling asleep in class, and about her hitting me for something someone else had done. I told him about her paddle with the holes. In fact, I showed him the paddle I had brought to court. I talked directly to the judge who continued to study me with his piercing dark eyes. I forgot about everyone else in the courtroom and just told my story. I felt pride in representing myself well and some relief in the fact someone listened to me, finally.

When I held up the paddle to show the judge, I noticed Mrs. Starky sitting on the back row of the courtroom very close to the back door. I knew she had left school to be there, probably she had been ordered to be there. Her eyes threw daggers at me.

After listening to my story the judge made a decision. "Well, this is your first offense. I order you to sand and paint the doors, and pay for both the sandpaper and the paint," he said.

Dad told me, on the way home, he thought the judge gave me a fair penalty for the offense.

Everyday the following week, Dad gave me work to do and paid me, so I could pay for the sandpaper and paint. I spent the next Saturday refinishing the school doors in the same green enamel paint.

Even though I had been before the judge and many students knew I had been in trouble, I had more confidence in myself just because I had represented myself and had spoken up. Even for a few minutes, I had everyone's attention when I told about my problem of not being able to read and with falling asleep in class. I had not mention doing drugs.

What I had done changed nothing between Kell and me. The first day after the court hearing, he came off just as cocky, and strutted around like Clint Eastwood in one of the rip-roaring westerns. Ever since

I had met Mr. Strutting Eastwood he had always shoved me around and slapped me and called me names. Right off, he slapped me hard on the right side of the head then he slapped me on the left side of the head and called me "Candy Ass" for being caught by the FBI.

Later that same afternoon at my house, I noticed Kell and I were the same height. I knew I didn't have to put up with his abuse. I decided I'd had enough. I doubled up my right fist, swung around in a half-circle, windmill fashion, starting with my back to him, and hit him right where the breast bones came together. My fist on his chest made a "whoosh" sound. Kell blinked and just looked at me with a tight-lipped grin. He strutted off around the corner of the house while I waited to see what would happen next.

"Oh, Lord, he's going to get a stick and come back and kill me," I said to myself. I waited for a while longer then walked around the corner of the house. I saw him bent double in pain, on the ground. I stayed friends of a sort with Kell. I needed him for the drugs. But he never beat up on me again.

After the incident with Kell, I learned I could take care of myself. My size would keep me out of trouble but would also become a source of trouble. Many times guys wanted to fight me to see if they could beat me. At school, there was always a threat of a fight. It became a challenge around school to find someone who can "whip Brad." I hated when the teacher sent us to the rest room. I knew the bullies hanging out there would pick on me, and I would have to fight, or they would pick on someone small, knowing I would come to their defense. The teacher usually had to come into the rest room to separate the boys and stop the fighting.

I walked around the corner of the lower hallway and right into a fight. There stood Matt, a leader of he bullies, beating up on my little friend, Timmy. Little blond-headed Timmy, smaller than everyone else, had blood running from his nose and mouth as he had gotten pounded on by a big coward. As I approached, I could see Timmy getting the stew beat out of him. I tapped Matt on the shoulder. I had learned from punching Kell how to come off confident like Clint Eastwood, like go ahead, Punk, make my day. I said, "You want to fight someone? Well here I am. Fight with someone more your size."

"No, Brad. I don't want to fight you."

I picked Timmy up, straightened his shirt, and told him, "You're okay, but you need to go to the school clinic to get cleaned up," I said referring to the blood on his face.

As I turned loose of Timmy, I came from the left with a haymaker and knocked Matt into the locker. "When you want to fight again, look me up. Leave my little friend alone." I walked away leaving Matt laying against the locker with his lip bleeding.

It made me so mad when, for no reason, Matt beat up on little Timmy. He had never hurt anyone. Timmy tried to be a good kid. He did everything right and never got into trouble. Timmy did his homework, cleaned his room, and obeyed his parents and his teachers. He knew if he didn't, his mom would give him a swift and through whipping. Everybody liked this easygoing kid, and he didn't deserve to be beaten up by a bully.

I soon got a chance to look out after a kid of another color. When we heard that a black child had been admitted to school, everyone talked, saying "A nigger is coming to school." I expected a monster because of the way everyone acted. When the day arrived for him to attend, we all looked out the window. I saw a black lady come up the front steps of the school with a little, bitty black boy. I recognized his mom as one of the black ladies in the community my Dad and Mom had given hog meat and chitlins to when we killed the hog a few years back.

I said to the kids who were looking out the window, "What's the big deal? He's just a little kid."

Everyone knew Willie, the black kid, but no one talked to him. When I passed him in the hallway, I spoke to him and smiled and said, "How you doing, Willie?" He didn't answer. He just kept looking down at the hallway floor in front of him as he walked on to class.

After a couple of months of speaking to him, Willie began to make eye contact when we passed each other. A couple of months later he returned my smile. By the end of the year, he said, "Hey, Brad," when I saw him.

When I walked out of my classrooms each day, I could see all the way down to each end of the hallway when the bell rang and the hall filled up. Willie kinda stood out being the only black child, so I found him easily. I never heard of anyone causing him any harm.

As the school year progressed, I began to look out for more and more kids who were being pushed around. Many times I tangled with their adversaries. I gained a new respect. I got into fights less and less. When I came around, no bullying or fights happened.

Each day when the bell rang, and I walked into the crowded hallway on the way to my next class, a path would clear in front of me as I walked. One day I noticed kids going into classrooms they did not belong in, until I walked on down the hallway. They went into classrooms of another grade level than their class. They were trying to avoid me. I realized they were afraid of me. It seemed my tough demeanor preceded me.

A few months into the school year, Mom stayed home from work, sick, just about every day. One day, I asked her if I could drive her car, a 57 Chevy, around the yard. She just nodded and gave me her keys. "Just be careful." That afternoon, when Dad came home, I backed the car and drove around the front yard to show him I could. He just smiled at me because he had probably driven a tractor or a truck or even a car at twelve years old too, but back then there were pastures and country roads and wide open spaces.

The next morning after Dad left for work, Mom stayed in bed, sick. I got up early and wanted to drive before school, so I drove the car around the yard and practiced backing. I would be twelve in a few months, so I kept thinking to myself, in about four more years, when I turned sixteen, I would be ready to get my driver's license.

There I sat in the car with it facing toward Hill Street. My heart began to pound with excitement. Should I do it? I knew I could drive without wrecking Mom's car. I glanced toward the house. I knew Mom still slept. I looked up Hill Street and thought about the school only one mile away. I let off on the brakes and slowly pressed the accelerator, crossed the plank bridge, and went up Hill Street in a couple of minutes. As I drove up Hill Street I felt very excited. I did not pass a single car. Then I eased into the parking lot next to the lower baseball field. I looked around before I got out to make sure no one came around. I got out quickly and went inside the school. I told no one.

That afternoon, I waited until the lower parking lot cleared, got quickly into the car and went home, again passing no one. When I went into the house, Mom still wore her housecoat and lay on the sofa watching television. She had not even missed the car. I said, "I drove the car to school." I stood there watching for her reaction.

She just smiled at me and said, "Oh Brad. You're growing up way too fast." After that, any day she stayed home, I just drove. I didn't ask or tell her. She figured it out when she looked out the window and noticed her car was not in the yard. After a while, a few of my friends knew I drove, but we mostly kept it quiet. Anyone who might see me driving would never guess me to be just twelve years old and in the fifth grade.

Dad didn't know I drove to school. I left for school after he left for work and got home, of course, before he come home from work. One day about six months after I started driving to school, I got home from school and could not wake Mom. I shook her. She moaned and had become very pale. I could not get Dad on the phone. So I picked Mom up, placed her on the back seat, put a pillow under her head, took a deep breath, and headed for the Atlanta skyline.

I knew I needed to take her to Piedmont Hospital where she worked. I had visited Mom there the last time they admitted her to the hospital, but at three-thirty, the afternoon traffic picked up and became heavy. Driving on the interstate made me very anxious. How would I find the exit ramp to the hospital? I knew what the hospital looked like, and I could see it on the distant horizon. I keep going in the direction of the hospital. I got closer and closer. I could make out the **H** sign for Hospital. I knew that Piedmont started with a **P** and had many letters. Soon I found the exit.

I kept checking on Mom in the back seat. Her face looked as pale as the pillow she lay on and sometimes she moaned, but she never spoke or opened her eyes. When I glanced back at her again, I saw a little moisture coming from her mouth and seeping toward the pillow. She had started to drool. I knew then she had a serious problem.

When I turned into the entrance of Piedmont Hospital, I found the emergency sign by looking for a long word starting with **E** on a large sign in bright red with a red arrow. I found the parked ambulances and pulled up to the emergency room door beside them. I got out and started getting Mom out of the back seat. An orderly noticed me and came with a gurney. I told the orderly my Mom had a diabetic problem and to call Dr. Pennell.

Dad came rushing into the hospital after I called him from a pay phone in the lobby. After the doctor reassured him of Mom's recovery, he came over and sat down by me. "Son, I'm proud of you. You saved your mother's life. The doctor said Lila had gone into diabetic shock because she had taken too much insulin in her shot. It had just taken her out. If she had not gotten the help she needed—when she did—she would have died in a few hours." He patted me on the shoulders with his broad hands as he talked. He had tears in his eyes. The doctors and nurses treated me like a hero and told me I had saved my mother's life. No one ever thought about a twelve year old kid driving without a license or, of course, driving in downtown Atlanta traffic.

While Mom stayed in the hospital I found out more about the inoperable tumor growing on her pancreas. She first became aware of the tumor when she was pregnant with me. I felt guilty about this. I felt responsible, somehow, for the problem. The tumor could not be removed because of her pregnancy. Now the tumor had grown larger and had become inoperable. "Son, my having that tumor is not your fault. I had it way before my pregnancy with you," she reassured me.

When Mom went home, I found every excuse to stay with her, so I could make sure she did not overdose on the insulin again. She wanted me to stay out of school every day for several weeks to care for her. It made me happy to miss school.

While I stayed home with Mom and saw that she got better, I noticed she went to the backyard at least once a day. Since Dad and I did everything with the animals, I could not understand what she needed from the backyard, so I watched her. I saw her take the key from Daddy's top bureau in the bedroom and go to the shed out back behind the barn. When she saw me watching her come from the shed with a handful of candy, she put her finger to her lips and motioned for me not to tell.

It hit me then. This was the broken candy Dad got from a man who worked at a candy factory, and he kept it locked in the shed to give to us kids on special occasions. For a split second, I thought Mom had gotten the candy for a snack after supper as a surprise. But then I realized she consumed this candy as a "fix" for her diabetes. I stood there, stunned, as she went into the bedroom with the candy.

I began to watch and came to the full realization that she ate a pack of candy or several candy bars every day. As a nurse, she should have known this to be harmful to her diabetes, but, I guess, she couldn't help herself. I thought she might have been doing this for quite a while as Dad had been storing the extra candy for a year. I realized Mom ate candy like I popped blotter acid. I could understand sugar gave her a pickup when she hit a low just like my drugs gave me a pickup and wiped out all of my worries.

The fact that she had become as addicted to sugar as I had become addicted to marijuana and acid hit me full force. Both of our habits had the potential to destroy each of us.

11.
Kid Junkie

The summer after I turned twelve, I graduated, not from school, but to hard drugs. I meet up with the big boys, the big drugs, the big times, and death.

I had been helping Dad for about a year on Saturdays with his cleaning and construction crew. Dad said I could handle the hard work, and I did. I thought I did as good a job as any of his workers. I told Dad I saved the money, but it went to buy marijuana from Kell. When I bought extra drugs to sell, I felt empowered, like "I'm the man."

I loved drugs. I loved marijuana. A couple of us guys started making regular trips to the strip to buy LSD. Sometimes the drug came in stamp form, other times it looked like saccharine tablets. I started bringing drugs back to my friends.

It happens this way. One person gets high, gets turned on, starts doing drugs, starts using. It's not so bad. It's funny. You laugh. You have a good time. Then you come down. The drugs are available: black RJS's which were highly addictive amphetamines, detoxins, LA turnarounds, Christmas trees, THC. A small powerful amount of cocaine you called a matchhead because if you got it when they first made it, you could get a buzz on just a matchhead amount snorting up your nose. Some of these were pharmaceutical drugs. Some were illegal drugs made on the open market.

On one trip to the Peachtree strip, I saw a yellow-looking man on the street. Someone said he had hepatitis. I saw people who looked like they were dying. I said to myself, "Where do all these drugs come from?" I couldn't understand how all this illegal activity could be allowed out in broad daylight.

I started hanging around with the older crowd which turned out to be a major mistake. These older guys really had an influence on me. They became my peers, and I wanted to do what they were doing. I started thinking about what other people thought about me. I wanted to do what they did so I would be accepted. I grew tall and wanted people to think I belonged to their crowd. As I sold drugs, many people called my house wanting what I had picked up on the strip each weekend. I had so many friends my parents put in a separate phone line for me. But, of course, they had no idea why I had so many calls or what I was doing.

My mother started getting suspicious of these people coming to the house then leaving. I think she might have been jealous of the amount of time I spent with them instead of spending time with her. One day she gave me a hurt look and said, "These people who you think are your friends, are not really your friends." She must have had some insight into the future events to come.

"Momma, you don't know what you're talking about. These are my buddies, my pals to the end. Friends forever."

"Brad, why are they coming by here? What do they want? They're not staying long enough to be friends with you. What do you have in common? Why do you always go out and don't invite them into the house to meet your parents?" I knew then I had to move my business elsewhere or I would be found out.

When six of my older friends who were seventeen to twenty years old, rented an apartment in Marietta, the next town northwest of

Oakdale, I went there to stay with them on the weekends. Kell got a job working at Morris' Cafeteria and I led Dad to believe I had gotten a job there also. Dad let me go with Kell, trusting him to look after me. Since Kell counted as family and since he happened to be three years older than me meant, in Dad's eyes, he could be trusted to watch after me.

These other guys who were five or six years older than me soon accepted me and thought me equal to them in size and age. At twelve years old, I had grown as tall as them, and I recently had put on a lot of weight. I could easily have been mistaken for eighteen. I felt equal to them. My ego pumped up. I felt like, "I can do anything."

I still worked with Dad during the week and he thought I wanted to work with Kell on the weekend to earn extra money for myself. But instead of working, I just hung out at the apartment doing drugs, eating, sleeping, or being complacent. Kell brought in food for the two of us each night when he came home from the cafeteria.

I liked the idea of the freedom of it all, but the first day when I walked in, the smell repulsed me. The worn carpet smelled old and dusty as though it had never been vacuumed. A look in the bathroom sickened me. It looked as though the toilet had never been cleaned, and vomit had dried on the floor. The kitchen smelled of weeks of garbage piled up, and dirty dishes piled a mountain high in the sink.

Fat Jack, Rock Mantell, Danny, Don Pace, Larry Coots and now Kell and I lived here in this apartment where I had my first experience of seeing someone using intravenous drugs. They were injecting heroin, and I remember hearing all the propaganda about drugs which I didn't think could be true. These guys weren't hurting anyone. They wanted to get high, so they did. I watched, but I wasn't crazy about the idea of a needle. As I watched them shoot up their heroin, I learned lots of new names: smack, horse, junk, white China, Mexican brown. I watched these guys take heroin and sit there and nod off, falling into a stupor. They said,

"Man, this is good stuff."

They just sat there in the apartment listening to the Woodstock album and shooting up day after day. I either got high or I remained complacent, just sitting, sleeping, or laying around for hours each day. I also watched them to see what they did and to see the results of what they did.

I careened into the drug scene like a rocket on a delightful path to destruction. We went into Atlanta each weekend to get the drugs. The others got heroin. I got marijuana. A bag cost seven dollars each or fifteen bags for sixty-five dollars.

Finally one day I said, "Well, heroin didn't kill any of you guys, and you seem to be enjoying yourselves. I'll try it." So I came up with my money and they gave me a half bag of Mexican brown heroin. But I didn't know how to operate the syringe. They were more than willing to help me. Fat Jack took the heroin and injected it intravenously into my arm. I got a rush from my stomach up, a warm feeling. I felt really good, like a feeling of being submerged in a tub of warm water. I nodded. I went into a semiconscious state, almost like being asleep, but I could hear everything that went on around me in the room.

As I did heroin, I found why it could be so dangerous. The closer you take it up to death the better it gets. You try and take it right on up to the point where you're about to overdose. If you start to throw up, your body is rejecting it. But this is where you want to be, right on the edge, just about to overdose, but not going over the line. This's why so many people have died taking heroin.

I began to feel guilty. I thought, I need to get up from here and go home. I shouldn't be doing this.

Hours later as I started coming down, I wanted more drugs. All of a sudden I realized I had a need for the drug—one I couldn't overcome, so I stayed at the apartment and didn't go home on Sunday night. I called my parents and told them the cafeteria manager needed me to work during the week for a couple of weeks.

After a week of doing heroin, I developed a desperate need. After a month I had a bad addiction. My guilt became overwhelming. Here I lay—almost passed out, twelve years old, with a heroin addiction. I'm an illiterate, living away from my parents, lying to them, and being influenced by these older guys.

The guilt of it all lay on me heavily one night after Fat Jack shot me up. All the junkies were asleep or passed out. I slipped into the living room. I thought and thought about what my parents had said. What if Jesus came back now? I would be burned up. As a twelve year old child, I should be enjoying my youth and having some of the best times of my life, but here I am addicted to heroin. When I came down, I wanted to shoot heroin again. Don Pace said, "Big Guy, I'll be glad to get you off." I still didn't know how to use the "rig" to inject the heroin into my veins, so he showed me how.

"Kell, I'm just going to give him half a bag," he said.

Kell replied, "He can take it."

Don Pace became our real leader in crime. He was a cold hearted individual with the coldest blue eyes who wore his long hair over to one side. He wore bell-bottom jeans and a jeans shirt and a look of toughness. He told stories of being in the reformatory and how he could fight and handle it all. He bragged about fighting, and showed me, playacting in a mock fight, how to fight using his elbow to bust out the opponent's teeth. I got up and followed his lead, pretending to fight him, using my elbow, pretending to knock him in the mouth.

As time went by, I learned he could be cruel and calculating, but I admired him. He, for a time, became my role model. He qualified as a "plastic hippie" meaning he fit in well with both the rednecks and the hippies.

When Don injected me with heroin, I had the impression that he hoped I would fall into unconsciousness, so he could beat me in the face and say, "Big Guy, wake up. Big Guy wake up," because he enjoyed hitting people in the face.

The police had been watching us as we came in and out of the apartment. They knew we were dealing in heroin and were ready for us. We were always aware of our surroundings and on the look-out for them. One Friday about mid-summer when my parents were at work, the guys came by my house to get me. They drove a yellow Corvaire van with a big white star on the side. We were headed for Atlanta to make our weekly run and build our stock of drugs. After we bought our weekly supply, we started toward Marietta and the apartment. As we passed back through Oakdale, we could not wait for a fix, so we stopped on a dirt road to shoot up and get our "fix."

Don Pace injected me while I stood outside the van. It had to be some of the strongest heroin we had ever had. It almost sent me out. My eyes turned up toward the sky and he slapped me in the face bringing me back to consciousness. As I glanced upward, I saw a helicopter hovering above us. The police had followed our van from Atlanta to this dirt road in Oakdale.

There were woods all around the dirt road, so the helicopter didn't have a place to land. It came down closer and closer until I could see the badge on the pilot's shirt. The wind from the helicopter blades whirled the oak tree leaves and blew dirt into our eyes, hair, and clothes. The pilot had a megaphone and demanded we lay down and put our hands out in front of us. We looked around and saw no way for the helicopter to land as the trees were too close to the dirt road. We saw no police car coming.

We all jumped into the van and Fat Jack got in the driver's seat. Don had to help me into the van. He kept slapping me as I passed out. "Don, I'm okay. Stop hitting me, man." All this time, I kept watching the helicopter. Don just knew he had saved my life. But at the same time, he brutalized the hell out of me. Fat Jack floored it.

We had a real nice name for cops back then, "Pigs." I didn't know how the name came about. I guess we were supposed to hate pigs and cops, so we called cops, pigs. We were involved in criminal activity here, and I'm thinking they have a right to be after us.

We drove; and we drove; and we drove. We drove around for a couple of hours. Either the helicopter ran out of fuel, or we were over into another county where they did not have jurisdiction.

We continued to drive long after we lost sight of the helicopter then we went to Don's friend's house and borrowed his Rambler. This cool hippie car had a Grateful Dead sticker on the dashboard. From here, we drove on into Marietta with our weeks supply of heroin.

We began to deal more and more in a lot of drugs. We took drugs ourselves and then we sold drugs for profit. Our supplier, Poppie, got angry about our selling for the profit he usually got for himself. He could not keep up with our demands. We paid him in advance for drugs he promised to deliver when his supply came through.

When we got to the apartment, everybody went ahead and got off. All were at peace with the world, for at least seven hours. Larry Coots, a tall, skinny kid with red pimples all over his face woke up first the next day. He got excited after a run because he had set up a large client list in his community. He went over to the kitchen table and started figuring on all the money he could make from what he had bought. He then figured how much drugs he would buy next time, and how much profit he could make when he sold the next batch.

Larry still sat at the table figuring, when a knock at the door awakened me. I got up and opened it not knowing what to expect. Poppie, our supplier, stood there. I knew him, but I didn't know what to say. He looked like a dried up old man with a thin, sickly, weak-looking body.

His gray hair looked thin and unwashed, his face unshaven. He looked as though he had never taken a shower or changed clothes. He had on the same old jeans, and faded, plaid shirt, and flip flops that he had worn the few times I had seen him. He handed me several bags of drugs and said in a threatening voice, "This is your last order. Don't bother me again."

I walked into the kitchen and put the bags on the table and told Larry, "Poppie delivered the other drugs. He said not to order again." Larry looked surprised at what I said. As the other guys awakened, they immediately opened the bags, each getting what they had paid for.

If you were any kind of a junkie, you could do a whole bag, but with a whole bag we skirted death mighty close. Every time we shot up, somebody passed out and hit the floor. "This is going to kill you," became as common a saying as one would walk to the window, look out, and say, "Looks like rain today."

Don in his coldhearted way with his glaring, deep blue, eyes flipped the syringe to get the air bubbles out and aimed the needle at Fat Jack. "This is going to kill you, Jack."

"I can take it," he said in a dreamy way, already feeling the drug enter his bloodstream. We called Jack the "greasy headed ape" because of his appearance. He was fat, had a full beard, and long hair parted right in the middle. When Don shot him up, he fell out of the chair and hit the floor unconscious. I couldn't believe the next twenty-four hours. Poppie had given us "bad stuff" which made everybody sick. Everybody threw up everywhere, then passed out. Larry lay on the floor groaning all night. We all survived, but I took a week off and stayed home recovering. Mom thought I had the flu or a virus.

Two weeks later I walked in on the same scene. "Jack, this might kill you, man," Don said in the same tone he would have said, "It certainly is a beautiful day."

Don had a nonchalant attitude about the drugs. I said to myself,

"This is my role model!" I began to see the craziness of my situation, and knew I had gotten myself into deep trouble. Fat Jack continued to be shot up, but it didn't kill him.

Then they began to play games with me. Instead of giving me my normal dose of a half bag a day, they began giving it to me in hits three times a day—a whole bag.

That night the guys brought in Kabanol and THC. Don fixed me up with a shot of both, mixed. I had to walk outside immediately. I thought, this is it—I'm a goner. An overdose. Instead of having a good feeling, I turned completely numb. My arms and legs felt like rubber, and I couldn't feel anything. I glanced back when I heard laughing. Fat Jack and Don Pace were standing in the door laughing at me, "Hey, Big Man. You all right?"

I saw them standing there in the doorway of the rundown two story red, brick apartment building. The light glowing from the doorway around them lay on the concrete walkway. I sat down on the sidewalk. I didn't trust my legs to carry me back inside. I don't remember getting up or going back inside, but around noon the next day, I regain consciousness and found myself on the floor just inside the apartment door. I had no idea how I'd gotten there, unless they'd dragged me back inside. The next time I saw Don Pace, when he and I were both conscious, he said, "That THC and Kabanol really put you out." He started laughing at me, again.

I decided I had to learn how to run up myself or continue to risk what these guys would do to me. I couldn't get the hang of it the first time I tried, so I let Don Pace get me off one more time. He shot me up with Delata, an opium drugs. I sat in a chair, and he put the needle in my arm. With the needle still in my arm, the drugs hit me in my stomach and started a sensation coming up. I had never had a feeling like this. I called it the "death rush." I jumped up before all the drug went into my arm.

The syringe came out of his hand and flipped across the room. He said, "What are you doing?"

Blood dripped down my arm and on the floor. I started walking immediately because I thought, this is it—I'm dying. From far away, I heard all of them laughing. I looked back into the living room as I went through the door. They were laughing so hard they were slapping their knees and bending over double laughing and pointing toward me.

I thought, I'm dying. I'm dying. The rush came on up to my chest, then up to my neck and into my head. Then it mellowed out into the most beautiful heroin type high I had ever imagined. After I woke up the next day, I spent time learning about the syringes and needles. I practiced injecting water into my veins.

I had an obvious source for syringes—Mom. She sent me to the drug store about twice a month to pick up a dozen syringes for her insulin shots she took every day. The druggist always had them ready and in a bag. After I left the drugstore, I took a few syringes for my drug habit. Mom never counted to make sure there were a dozen. I don't think she knew the druggist sent a dozen. She never missed what I took.

We listened to the radio as we walked up and down the strip seeing drugs flowing openly. We heard one song which had an acronym LSD. "*Lucy in the Sky with Diamonds.*" If you took away the drugs, the music didn't seem as important. With the drugs, the music lyrics played out the culture, the time, and my life, it seemed.

Getting drugs got to be very dirty business. The police cracked down. I think some of the cops were straight out of the penitentiary themselves. A couple of cops pulled Don and me over when we were leaving the Krystal after we had gotten hamburgers for everyone at the apartment. They demanded drugs or money. When they didn't find drugs nor any money on us, they put us into the patrol car. We thought they were taking us to jail. Instead they took us to a wooded area and began to beat the hell out of us. Don came back at them a couple of times with his elbow, but he proved no match for both of them.

They slammed me up against the patrol car. Don who lay on the ground after they had beaten him, raised up and shouted, "He's a minor."

They paid no attention to him and began beating me. One of them searched me and growled, "Where's your license?"

"Sir, I'm not old enough to have a driver's license. I'm only twelve years old." They left.

We were bloody and beaten but had no broken bones. We walked to a service station and called Fat Jack, who owned the yellow Corvaire van, to come and get us.

Larry Coots continued to be greedy. He kept hounding Poppie for more and more drugs as he didn't have enough to continue selling in his community during the week and shooting up with us at the apartment on the weekends. Larry really rolled in cash and kept demanding drugs from Poppie who gave him one more run and warned him again, "This is the last batch. Don't ask for more."

The next Friday night when Fat Jack couldn't pick me up at home, I caught the bus to the apartments. When I walked up to the apartment building, I could see the guys standing outside the door. They were quiet and pale and nobody said anything to me. I started to go inside.

"Larry's laying in there, dead," Don Pace said in a choked voice. I looked at each of their faces quickly, then pushed the door open. Larry Coots lay sprawled in the middle of the living room floor. I turned around and glanced back at Don Pace. He didn't make eye contact. None of them made eye contact with me. When I began to grasp what had happened, I felt the air had been sucked out of my body. I had to make a strong effort to breathe. I sat down on the curb.

Just then the coroner's ambulance turned into the apartment

driveway. People began gathering around. I saw a police car pull into the other side of the driveway.

I left. I didn't want to see Larry's body again. I knew I couldn't stay there any longer. I walked back to the bus stop and caught the bus home. I felt stricken. Shock now numbed me as much as some of the drugs had.

When I got home, I called Kell at the cafeteria where he'd been all day, working. Fat Jack had called him so he didn't go back to the apartment as he might be implicated. Jack told him all those guys at the apartment—Jack, Don, Rock, and Danny had been arrested when Larry's body had been picked up. They had gotten rid of all the drugs, but all of them were in some stages of being high. Nothing at the apartment showed I had ever been there, and I knew no one would rat on me.

We figured Poppie had gotten rid of the so-called "Larry problem." Poppie had sold Larry uncut heroin without warning him about it being uncut. Larry had bought it on Friday afternoon and tried it himself at the apartment before he went to sell it back home. He overdosed, dying right there in the living room when it hit his bloodstream.

Thank goodness he hadn't shared his store with us, but kept it to sell when he got back home. We couldn't believe Poppie could be so malicious as to cause a death, knowingly. Later we learned Poppie had sold uncut drugs before, just to get rid of a bothersome dealer. We found out an acquaintances of ours had overdosed on seemingly a small amount of pure uncut he had also gotten from Poppie.

Back home, I talked with my dad about drugs in general and about a friend, Larry, dying of an overdose. I didn't tell him about the apartment or how I knew Larry, but I did say some of my friends were using drugs. He questioned me about drugs in general.

"You mean this speed takes you up and makes you feel real good and gives you a lot of energy?"

"Yes," I replied.

"And then it lets you down and you have to take more?"

"Yes."

"What good is taking drugs, if you later crash then have to take more to feel better, then crash again?" He thought a little while and said, "I would just rather go along like I am."

He put his hands on my shoulders and looked into my eyes. My Dad had a lot of wisdom and I admired him as one of the best people I knew. "Drugs can ruin your life. Son, are you on drugs?"

I hesitated and glanced at the floor then back up to him. Our faces were close together. I didn't know what to say. I had so much respect for my Dad and didn't want to hurt him.

"No, Dad. I'm not on drugs." I felt to ashamed to tell him the truth. I felt guilty lying to him, but I said this with a hope I could come off drugs, so he would never find out. In a way, I felt relieved I hadn't told him. But I had lied to him. My whole life felt like a lie. My chest felt funny and my stomach felt like it had a big rock right in the middle. I'm not sure he believed me. Dad let go of my shoulders and said, "Drugs will ruin a person's life. Your friends need to let go of this."

I nodded. I wanted to quit, but I didn't know if I could.

Afterward, I went into the living room and got the Bible off the mantle. I took it to my room and stared at the pages, trying to read some of the words. After studying the words for a while, I discovered I could read a few of the words where Dad had highlighted the scripture in red. I picked it up amazingly quick. It could be I had heard Dad or the preacher quote these certain scriptures enough I had memorized them. But I thought I read them.

All this time up until now I'd been thinking, "I'm stupid, I'm dumb, but wait a minute, I'm learning to read almost on my own." I couldn't understand it. Was I smart? Was I dumb?

Over and over in my mind I kept thinking: "I'm addicted. I'm lying to my parents. I'm illiterate. I can't succeed in school. But I could read the Bible words. I love drugs. But drugs will ruin my life."

I could hardly bear what went through my mind. The only pleasure I had, the drugs, were going to ruin my life, Dad had said. I believed him and wanted to quit but knew I couldn't. Mom and Dad had said many times, "Jesus is coming back, and you need to live your life in a way so as to prepare for His return. You need to understand you're going to be with Jesus for eternity." Now I could hear those words echoing in my mind.

I read some more verses from the Bible. In Proverbs I sounded out the words and read, *The way of the trans-gress-or is hard.* I thought this sounded true, and I believed the Bible. I thought, time will play out and you will see what you can get away with. But it seemed, time had caught up with me.

I had a plan. I told my parents I had to work all week at the cafeteria, so I went back to the apartment one more time, for a week. What I really did though, that week in the summer of my twelfth year, I quit. I went cold turkey.

I lay on my sweat-soaked bed at the apartment. I shook. I sweated. I threw up. Pain wracked my body. I lay there in a stupor, too weak to get up. I fell asleep listening to the sounds through the dull haze forming around me in my room. The outside sounds were of children at a pool in the next group of apartments over from ours.

I thought, I should be out there swimming and having fun not lying in bed, missing my childhood. I don't want to be an addict. I thought this over and over. I fell asleep then woke up in agony, sick of the apartment, and the life style, and sick of what the heroin had done to me. Heroin made me lose all my will power and all my freedom. Heroin had been all I had thought about for months.

What is life all about? I thought about these guys who had been arrested. I thought about all of us being involved in this criminal activity. I thought about Larry Coots' death.

When the guys got out on probation and returned to the apartment, they began to go back to their old habits. Don Pace and Kell came into the bedroom to check on me. Mostly the others stayed away from me. Don said, "I just can't understand why you want to do this to yourself. I can shoot you up and you will mellow out and feel great."

I shook my head from side to side on the pillow and turned away from him. Suddenly I felt sick and threw up in a pan I had on the bed beside me. They left and did not come back. I kept repeating a Bible verse I had heard Dad repeat many times back at home. "*I can do all things through Jesus Christ who strengthens me.*"

As I lay there, I thought about my lack of education. I thought about all the education I had missed. I wondered if it were too late to ever go back to school. I read on the second or third grade level, but would be in the seventh grade when school started back.

After three days of laying in a stupor, sweating, throwing up, and being in the worst pain I had ever had, I managed to get up then collapsed in a big overstuffed chair in the dingy living room. I turned on cartoons and watched them for hours. Finally, I stumbled into the kitchen and got a soda from the refrigerator. I felt so weak. Kell brought food for me from the cafeteria when he came in at night. He realized what bad shape I had gotten in, and he feared my parents would find out and blame him because they had trusted him to take care of me. I stayed four more days in the apartment sleeping and eating what Kell brought from the cafeteria.

On Sunday night when Kell got off work, he got Fat Jack to carry us home. I lay in the back seat, very sick, with my head back and my eyes closed. "Brad are you going to be alright. Do you think your parents will know you've been sick?" Kell's concern centered on himself not on me. He didn't want to be blamed.

"Mom will know something's wrong with me. I'll tell her I had a stomach virus or something again. Telling her that should give me a few more days to recover. I didn't know if I could live through this withdrawal. I vowed to myself, "I'm never going back to the apartment and I'm never going to do heroin again." I can't stand being on heroin and I'm certainly not ever going through withdrawal again. In the years to come, I did keep part of my vow.

As we drove toward home, I closed my eyes and thought about what Dad had always said, "You can't play with fire and not get burned. Just like a moth drawn to the flame, you can see the glow and feel the heat, but one day it will get you." I hoped I had learned my lesson.

12.
Trippin' in Strawberry Fields

I finished out my summer at home recovering from coming off heroine on my own. I never let my parent know why I had been sick when I got home from the Marietta apartments. I planned to go back to school in the fall.

Uncle Sycamore came over to go fishing with me about a week later on a Saturday. I knew Dad might have told him about Larry Coots dying of an overdose and about my concern for my friends who did drugs. If Sycamore knew, he never mentioned it to me. Neither of them knew I had done drugs, how bad it had gotten, or about me coming off heroin.

As Uncle Sycamore and I loaded minnows and rod and reels into his pickup, he looked up at me, smiled and said, "Let's go drown some worms."

I grinned and got my rod and reel out of the barn.

"I always wanted to be a big man," he said. "If you're this big now at twelve, I know you will get even taller before you are a grown-up."

As a kid, I had thought of Uncle Sycamore as being very tall when I rode on his shoulders, but now, I had grown at least three inches taller than him. I stood six feet and weighed two hundred pounds.

For a few minutes I got quiet. I realized I might be taller in statue, but I really didn't see the prospect of ever being as great a man as

Sycamore, at least not the way I had been going. I might have had bigger feet, but I realized I could never fill his shoes.

After I got home, I caught up on what had been going on with my family. Kay came over with her new husband, Sam Ellis, whom she had met last year when she went into the hospital to have the last plastic surgery. This last surgery fixed her eye and the scars on her face and neck had been erased. Dad helped finance this last surgery with money from the sale of his pasture land to the State Department of Transportation to build I-285.

Kay's life finally had began to turn around. Sam worked there at the hospital as a male nurse. That's how they met. After dating for six months, Sam had asked her to marry him. They now lived in the basement of Kay's house, the one she had bought before her first husband had stolen all her settlement money. Seeing her now, three months pregnant made us all happy.

I tried as hard as I could to leave the drugs behind and to find some old friends and get my mind off my summer experience and off the fact I would start to school next week. I called Tophat Taylor, but his phone had been disconnected. When I didn't see Tophat in Oakdale, I asked around. A kid told me to call his grandparent's house. He answered the phone. "Hey, you want to come over and hang out in the hut," I asked.

"A lot of things have happened to me this summer," Tophat said. "My parents have divorced. Mom and me live here now." He hesitated. "Brad. Uh—I've decided to go straight. I'm not doing drugs any more. Anyway. I've got a job at the Tastee Freeze after school. I give Mom the money I make. She needs it to help provide a living for us. I'm going to a different school than you. I'm going to start Lindley Middle School next week, so I won't be hanging out with you and Kell." After a few minutes of small talk, I hung up.

Even with Tophat's dad out of his life, his having to move, and having to get a job, I saw him as my hero. I envied him for coming off drugs. I wanted to be clean. I wanted to be clear of this drug obsession. I felt sad to not be seeing much of Tophat, but I felt so happy for him and wished somehow I could be like him in coming off drugs.

I lay in the hut listening to my transistor radio. On the radio, the Beatles sang *Strawberry Fields.* Rooster and Kell came into the hut. Kell had marijuana and gave me some. I put it under the pillow on my cot and planned on throwing it away later. The drug culture had spread all around Oakdale. But Kell told me after Larry Coots died of the overdose, he had decided not to go back to the Marietta apartment either. "I'm finished with those guys. Things got a little too out of control there for me," he said as he took a draw.

The morning I started seventh grade at Lincoln Middle School, I had a knot of fear about being found out that I couldn't read, so I went out to the hut and smoked the marijuana I had left underneath the pillow on the cot. So when I went into the school, I had already gotten high. I met Mrs. Kontz, my teacher, a beautiful blond lady—a knock out. The first week I actually thought about trying to learn, but everything fell into place—the same as before. I still read on the second or third grade level. It didn't take her long to figure this out. It felt so humiliating I couldn't take it. But she did everything she could to help me.

Even with all I had been through, everyday when I got to school, I would already be stoned on marijuana. Kell kept me supplied. I made an excuse to myself when I told Kell, "I'll just take it to help me detox after coming off the heroin. By lunch time, I wanted to leave. I didn't want to be in school. One afternoon, Mrs. Kontz saw me in the hallway and said, "Brad, come here. Get in this room."

She took me into her class and sent a note to my next class. She kept me with her for two or three class periods until time to go home. She even escorted me out to the bus after the last bell rang. If I had been caught being high on drugs, I would have been expelled. She did this almost every day. I think her motive was to keep me from being expelled and somehow help me stop doing drugs. I think she thought she might have a chance to teach me. Somehow she picked up on my desire to learn even though my actions were in direct conflict with what I wanted to accomplish for myself.

When Mrs. Kontz wasn't there to put me on the bus, I met Kell after school like I did last year. "Hey, Brad. Let's go see this man I know. He'll sell us drugs and let us stay at his place for a while," Kell said. I figured in my mind a little marijuana could be a way to wean myself off the hard stuff. I would pamper myself and go along with Kell. I had nothing else to do.

So, Kell, Rooster, and I went to the Cumberland community on Jones Road. We walked the track about a mile down from my house, turned left, and walked another mile north. The three of us told our parents we were each staying over at the other one's house. When we walked up to a low, unpainted shack of a house sitting back in some trees off Jones Road, the chickens scattered in the dirt yard.

I saw an old black man in the front yard who looked like a dried up old scarecrow. He turned to look at us. When we got closer I saw he looked about one-hundred-years-old as his face had withered up like a peach drying in the sun. He had a full head of white kinky hair and a white mustache and beard. He sat in a worn-out lawn chair under a big tree. A cane lay against the chair and he had a fly swatter in one hand. Beside him on a small table were a couple of cups and a pint of whiskey. His shack behind him had two uneven windows covered completely inside with dark curtains. When he saw us, he waved and motioned to us like he had been expecting us. Kell knew of him but had never met him. "Brad, this is Uncle Vern," he said.

"Uncle what?" I questioned.

"Vern. V-E-R-N." Uncle Vern spoke with a voice sounding like gravel tumbling out of a glass. "You longhaired white boys are up to no good? Well, so am I! Come here and have a cup of oil with me," he chuckled.

The oil he referred to turned out to be whisky, Wild Turkey—one hundred one percent proof. We watched him pour this whiskey into three unmatched, broken coffee cups. We each took a cup. Uncle Vern downed his immediately. Kell, Rooster, and I took a cup and sipped more slowly. I wondered why Uncle Vern seemed so friendly and why he would give strangers his liquor.

Vern said, " Boy, that oil will wake you up."

It burned as it went down—strong, and bitter, but I drank it anyway. I didn't want to seem rude to refuse it. Also I felt a little curious. As I drank the last of it, I felt a buzz. I looked up at the trees which began to sway, but the wind wasn't blowing.

Before we left, we had met the whole family: Vampire and Bug were Vern's sons and Leing, Vampire's wife.

"If you boys want drugs," Vern said, "You can get anything you want from Vampire. He's named Vampire because when he's high, he thinks he can really go outside and "fly." And he loves to wear black. Everything he wears is black." Vern laughed at his last remark.

I looked at Vampire. He had very dark skin, and probably if you saw him in a dark alley at night, only his teeth and the whites of his eyes would be visible.

Vampire's old lady, Leing, had an expression like she had just put her finger in an electrical outlet and been shocked. She walked around in a daze with her eyes popping out of her head.

"This here's Bug, my other son," said Vern. I thought, how could Vampire who had very dark skin possibly be Bug's brother as he had very light skin. "Bug can stay high two or three days on one joint."

Vern laughed at him and reached out to playfully hit him on the shoulder. I watched Bug for a few minutes and decided he might have been kinda half-retarded.

Vern seemed like an innocent, friendly old man just sitting in his yard waving at anyone who walked by and sat swatting at an occasional fly. He sipped on his "oil" and offered it to anyone coming into the yard. But things seemed just a little too casual for all the illegal drugs going on here.

On our next visit, we went inside Vern's shack. From behind the closed curtains, we watched the police drive by and glance at Uncle Vern's shack. They then cruised the empty church parking lot of the Cumberland Church directly across the street. We stayed quiet until they left.

Vern said, "I think the cops are afraid of this place." He gave us a knowing look I did not understand and then he chuckled to himself. I let the curtain close, and we had some more oil before I snorted some meth crystals he gave us.

Vern's neighbor, Junebug, a skinny old woman who had hair sticking up like a rooster's comb, walked into the yard. She wore an old crumpled cotton dress with a big apron. I think she kept her drugs in her apron pockets because when anyone went toward her, she immediately put her hands in her pockets. She walked around wringing her hands, talking to herself in a high-pitched voice.

When the weekend came, we boys, again, each told our parents we were spending the night at the other one's house or were sleeping in the hut in the backyard. My parents never checked to see if we were in the hut or not. So we walked over to Uncle Vern's, bought our drugs, and sat on the cement driveway of the Cumberland Church which sat up on a hill across the street from Vern's house. We got high behind the tall shrubs lining the driveway, yet we were close enough to Vern's house so if the cops came, we could run and get inside his shack before they spotted us.

Kell, Rooster, and I got really high. We didn't just smoke a joint or two, then stop. We smoked all we had purchased.

The next weekend we chose to sit in the driveway of the church again but stayed all night. Junebug sat up in the parking lot not too far from us, trippin' out and singing "I'll Fly Away, Oh Glory, I'll Fly Away." Her sharp, grating voice distracted us, and we moved away from her so we can trip in peace. I'm sure she literally felt like she could fly away.

The next week we earned money after school and looked forward to Friday night. This time Uncle Vern sold us blotter acid. A few minutes after we chewed one stamp of the blotter acid everything we saw began to move and had little swirls twirling around it. I looked up into the clouds and saw letters and messages in the sky.

The older blacks in the community didn't like having white boys hanging around. Junebug actually told us, "You longhaired, white boys have no business in this neighborhood. You need to leave and not come back or you'll be asking for more trouble than you can handle." I figured we were intruding on her turf and white boys in a black neighborhood might call attention to any illegal activity going on there. One Saturday afternoon, we were coming out of Cumberland, and a cop car turned into the community. The patrol car slowed down and pulled over to us. The patrolman, Detective Reed, rolled down the window and demanded, "Hey, what are you boys doing over here?"

I shrugged my shoulders and said, "We're just walking."

"You need to stay out of this place. It's dangerous over here." He left, and we went home.

We boys were either in the hut in my backyard, on the tracks, or in the Cumberland community. When I really wanted a refuge to get high, I went to my secret places: Dead Horse Road and Split Rock Creek. These places were where Dad and I first made a father-son bond. They were now my places of silence where I went reflect and feel remorse. Yet despite these places being a hideaway I went there when I wanted to get high. These were places where no one could find me.

A couple of weeks after we met Vern and started buying drugs from Vampire, we were running out of drugs and money. Vern said to us, "You boys want to earn some extra cash?" We were eager to hear what he had to say. "There's a flea market in Sand Town needing wagons wheels like the ones on the wagons the Clydesdale horses pull. People buy these wheels and put them in their yard for decoration. This Sand Town Flea Market will give seventy five dollars for wagon wheels like those. They are all sold out and need more. I know where some are if you're willing to help us."

I knew what Uncle Vern asked, but the way he described things seemed like we were doing everyone a favor including ourselves. My parents had raised me to be honest, and I had been to church and knew one of the commandments stated, "Thou shall not steal." As a child I knew better than to steal. For one thing my Dad would have whipped me with a belt if he ever found out I had stolen anything, so I had never been tempted to steal. Vern interrupted my thoughts, "I can't give you the whole seventy five dollars, but I will give you a finder's fee. Are you in?" I gave Kell a questioning glance. We were wanting some drugs pretty badly. We nodded and I said with my heart starting to pound harder, "Tell us what you want us to do."

"Be back here tonight at nine, and I'll tell you what to do. Bring some dark clothes to wear."

We left not knowing what to expect, but we did as he said. At nine o'clock, Vampire waited for us with a flashlight. We walked a mile from Cumberland to the Clydesdale Horse Farm where we hid in the bushes. A fine white Victorian two story house sat on the hill with sprawling green pastures around it as far as we could see in the dark. All the lights were out. High white fences surrounded the pastures where the barns were the tallest and biggest I had ever seen.

While we stayed quiet, just waiting, the security car came around to check the place. I could hear my heart thumping in my chest. I didn't dare breathe. I crouched low and waited for the security car to leave. We listened to the roar of the car getting quieter and quieter as it went away from us going on down the road. I understood better why Vampire wore black all the time. After the security car left, we waited half an hour more. The only sounds were a million night crickets chirping so loudly together in one ominous sound vibrating your ear drums like a high-pitched *see-saw sound, see-saw sound*, back and forth.

When Vampire gave the signal, the four of us ran quickly and quietly across to the fence, and went under it one by one. The main horse barn stretched out closer to the house. We ran to the low, side-barn where the wagons were kept. We went into a smaller wagon barn, but I could hear a horse in one end of the wagon barn. He snorted and kicked the stall when he heard us coming into this low dark barn.

Once inside, Vampire turned on the flashlight. I glanced toward the huge Clydesdale horse which loomed over us. His nostrils flared and he attempted to rear-up uneasily a few feet several times because of us being there. The wagons were huge and the wheels were too large for one person to handle. After Vampire got two wheels off, it took Kell and me to roll one wheel, and he and Rooster got the other one. Then we rolled them slowly to the fence. We each lay one flat on its side and pushed and pushed until we got both under the fence.

Then we rolled them slowly the mile back to Vern's. We got back to Uncle Vern's at one in the morning and rolled the wheels into his shack. He said, "Vampire will load them into his van and have them to the flea market in Sand Town by five in the morning, probably before the wheels are missed." We walked in the dark back to my backyard and slept in the hut. We rolled the dark clothing and stored them under the cots. The next afternoon after school, we met and walked over to Vern's. "Here's ten dollar each." He gave us the money and immediately Vampire brought out more drugs than we had ever had at one time. We bought enough blotter acid and marijuana to last us for weeks. We stuffed our pockets and walked back to my house and stashed the extra drugs under the mattresses in my hut.

We waited a month and made another run to the horse farm. I kept thinking about the huge horse on the other end of the wagon barn. So I put a couple of apples in my pocket just in case. Everything played out exactly the same as before, except frost sparkled over the countryside and there were no cricket sounds. We hid in the same bushes outside the farm. We waited for the ten o'clock security car to go by and then disappear down the road, leaving only silence. We waited another half hour and made our move. We went under the fence as before. But as we turned on the flashlight to find the wheels, we saw the Clydesdale in the stall beside the wagons. He had been moved much closer than he had been before.

He gave a start, jerked his neck back, kicked the side of his stall, and neighed. His large eyes glared down at us like a monster's eyes. He shuffled, restlessly in the stall. Vampire did not cut the light out, but lay it on the floor of the barn shining it toward the wheels. As Vampire, Kell, and Rooster, tugged at the wheels, I took an apple out of my pocket. I knew I had to distract this huge animal before he made any more noise and awoke the owners up in the house. I eased over to him slowly with my hand out and the apple balanced on my hand. I thought, this horse could bite my arm off, or my hand, or a couple of fingers. "Easy boy," I said.

I glanced over my shoulder at the others who were working fast. They almost had the second wheel off the wagon. The stall and huge horse were in the shadows as the only light came from the flashlight which pointed toward the wagon. As I neared him, he jerked his head back. I made out in the shadows the gray hair which showed his age. He had probably been put out here away from the others for some reason. Maybe he had become a "watch dog," of sorts, for us. When I put my hand under his nose, he suddenly just nipped the apple up and after one or two chomps he swallowed it. I dared rub his soft nose above the nostrils. "Easy old boy." I had to reach way up to his head far above mine.

After a few minutes, someone whispered, "Let's go." I took one quick look back at the Clydesdale who smacked his lips like he wanted another apple, so I quickly gave him another thinking it would keep him quiet while we got out of there. It worked. No more kicking or snorting. In a few minutes we were under the fence and on our way back. As before, we each made ten dollars, bought drugs and kept our store in the hut. We had to ration ourselves on these drugs as we decided to wait a longer time and go on a very cold night.

After two months we made our next move. We made only one change in our routine. We went at three in the morning on the weekend. As we entered the barn, the Clydesdale moved and I said, "Easy boy." When Vampire lay the flashlight on the floor of the barn and turned the light on, we all looked toward the horse. His breathe came in white puff out his nostrils as this winter night had turned very cold. The Clydesdale made more noise this time because he remembered me and knew the apples were coming. I kept him busy giving him several apples and petting him as the others worked fast. We didn't get the wheels back to Uncle Vern's shack until five o'clock in the morning. Vern had the van hidden behind the shack. We loaded them and Vampire sped off to the flea market.

The next day after our third run, Detective Reed came out to the school gym and arrested me. The patrolman put me in the car and Reed said, "I want to ride in the back seat with Brad." He slapped me on the leg and said, "We've finally got you. We've finally got you, and right before I retire." He grinned in a triumphant way.

He tried to trick me—to trip me up, but I had some streetwise. I knew he didn't have any evidence I could be involved with Vampire's ring other than he had seen me walking on Jones Road, coming out of Cumberland. He just guessed I was involved, and tried to scare me into a confession.

"Detective Reed, you haven't got me," I said. I haven't done anything. I am completely innocent of whatever you think I did." I stared at him, looking him in the eye.

"Brad, I know you and your friends were involved. Why don't you tell me all about it?"

"I don't know what you're talking about. I'm just a thirteen year old kid going to school every day." He never told me what he knew, and I didn't fall for his trying to bait me into a confession. He never gave the reasons he had come to school and arrested me.

He pushed the door open and let me out of the patrol car, disgusted he couldn't make me confess. "I will be watching you. I'll get you sooner or later." He slammed the door angrily.

I had to know what had happened and why Detective Reed had picked me up. He had to know about the theft ring. At dusk dark, I went alone to the Cumberland Church and hid in the bushes beside the parking lot behind the church. I had a flashlight with me. When all traffic quit coming in and out of the community and when all the lights in the houses were out, I turned on my flashlight and ran to the door of Vern's shack.

I rapped three times, and Vern jerked the door open as if he had been waiting for someone. By the dim light inside, I could tell the whites of his eyes were bloodshot. He looked tense as his fists were balled up and his neck jerked as he said, "Vampire got caught in Sand Town at the flea market when the owner paid him for the wheels still in his van. The cops had been staked out here in this community but could never catch you guys, but the cops in Sand Town kept up a patrol going by the flea market early every morning. They just got lucky coming by at the right time."

"Vampire and the guy who paid him were both arrested. They each insisted they were the only two involved. Vampire won't rat on you white boys." He rubbed his white bearded jaw and had a distant look in his eyes. "In fact, no one would believe you three white boys would even be over here in this neighborhood let alone be involved in stealing," Uncle Vern said emphatically.

I knew someone who would believe we were involved. Detective Reed would believe it if Vampire chose to tell. I hoped with Reed retiring soon, the case would never come under his questioning again.

"You better get out of here," Vern warned. "The detectives have been here trying to make me talk. They know Vampire couldn't carry those big wheels out by himself. You and those other white boys better not be seen here again."

I left, running and hiding all the way back home. When I got back, I slept in the hut. We didn't dare go back to see Uncle Vern. It would not do to be seen in the Cumberland community again. For us three guys, the Cumberland days were history.

My stealing and being part of a theft ring had come to an end and I felt glad about it. I didn't mind working for my money. I hoped I would never steal again.

13.
Kingpin

The drug culture moved steadily into the suburbs and the schools. Drugs were moving into Oakdale. I had sold drugs. The guy down the street sold drugs. The next neighborhood, Kentwood, had drug gangs. You could do okay, but your profit went out the window with such easy availability. I still felt remorse for being involved with all of this illegal activity and for not getting the education I wanted. But I lived to take drugs. They ruled my life. Turning back felt beyond my control. The current pushed this lost child along like a pebble in the stream. Kell made it so easy for me to get drugs. Rooster went along with taking drugs. Together we had some literally "high" times.

We found a new supplier—a kid at the skating rink. We got Mom or Dad to drop us off at the skating rink and after they drove off we could go to a small house a block behind the skating rink and get marijuana, no questions asked. We got our drugs, got high, went back to the skating rink, and skated for a couple of hours. When our parents picked us up later that night, we were outside waiting for them. By then we had come down somewhat, and they never suspected we had been high.

Then we met the ultimate drug contact—a drug dealer. On a Friday night in the early spring, Tophat, Rooster, and I had gone to the Atlanta Fox Theater on Peachtree Street to see Black Sabbath in concert.

Tophat had asked off work at the Tastee Freeze for this special occasion. He stayed over at my house for the weekend. He had been off drugs for a long time and when he took some acid before we left for the concert, it really affected him. He chewed a blotter acid, "Hey, Man. I forgot what this felt like. I feel like I'm floating. My arms feel like rubber." We just laughed at him.

We were really enjoying the concert, but Tophat started having hallucinations. "What's that light?! The music is getting me!!" We had to leave the concert early as Tophat freaked way out. As we started hitching home, walking along the interstate toward Oakdale, an expensive, top-of-the-line black Mercedes Benz pulled over on the shoulder of the road in front of us. A dark-skin, slick-haired dude with a mustache motioned for us to get in. He looked the part of a drug lord—kingpin, and had a real playgirl type girlfriend with a fine looking, sexy body and blond hair.

"What's happening?" I said as we got in.

"Yeah, what's up? Rooster asked,

Tophat didn't say anything as he got into the car.

The driver introduced himself as Marcos. "This is my girlfriend, Candy," he said. She leaned over the front seat and shook hands with each of us. I think she did it just to tease us as she had on a low cut blouse that partly exposed the biggest bosoms I had ever seen. When she shook hands with us, her cleavage jiggled. Tophat's eyes bulged out, staring at her jiggling bosoms because in his mind he thought them to be part of his hallucinations. When she smiled, I noticed her lips were as red as the bows on Mom's Christmas packages. In a few minutes we got to the point, "Got anything for the head, Man?" I asked.

"I've got the finest Berkeley acid, made in California," Marcos replied.

"If your acid is so good, let us try it," I said. "How much?"

"This one's free." Miss Candy passed us the drugs over the seat, smiling at us again.

We each rolled up a joint and lit it. This could be the best I'd ever had. After we were stoned, he started telling us what he wanted from us. He showed us a leather pouch filled with drugs—ecstasy, cocaine, Colombian marijuana. Some of the finest to be had.

I thought, it would be good to have a connection to grade A, prime drugs. Some people had tried to rip us off by selling us fake drugs, even rat poison, just to get our money. I remembered the uncut Larry Coots had gotten that had killed him. Getting top quality would be worth paying a little more.

Marcos pointed to me, "I want you to distribute for me. If somebody wants something I don't have, I can have it to you in one hour. I have the machine," he said, meaning he had a lab and a chemist to make it for him. "I want someone to get it into the high schools for me. I want a juvenile. If a kid gets caught, they won't send a kid to jail as quickly as they would an adult. If you ever get locked up, I'll make your bond in one hour."

I took it all in. I felt pride he had chosen me to distribute, but at the same time it bothered me I would be the one to help hook kids on drugs. I listened.

"If you ever narc on me or try to rip me off, I will kill you. I will eliminate you. I have a 45 tommy gun in the trunk. You want me to stop the car and show it to you?"

A fear crept into my chest as I thought about the gun, "No I didn't want to see it," I replied.

"I will call you Sunday afternoon at five. I'll let the phone ring five times. If you pick up the phone, we're in business, forever, and there is no way out. If you don't pick up the phone by the fifth ring, you'll never hear from me, again."

I gave Marcos my phone number, and he let us out of his Mercedes at the Fox Theater on Peachtree Street back where the concert had been. We started walking and in a few minutes we were really stoned on this green Berkeley acid.

Tophat looked at the full moon and said, "There's a bullfrog up there on the moon!"

Rooster looked up and said in amazement, "I see it too—there's a bull frog on the moon!"

"You two are crazy. You're hallucinating. There's no bullfrog on the moon. That's impossible." We argued for a mile or two. By this time we realized we had been walking in the opposite direction—away from home.

This Berkeley acid proved to be good stuff. We were trippin' out of our heads. The moon began to swirl, then melt. We could smell colors and see sound.

In the wee hours of the morning, we finally got a ride to Oakdale after a guy on the interstate gave us a ride. We were so stoned, all I could murmured was, "Oakdale."

He kept asking, "What's wrong with you guys? Now you are sure this is where you want to go?" As he let us out, I looked at the "Welcome to Oakdale" sign and saw it melting.

I said, "This is Oakdale?" He pulled away and we walked the rest of the way to my house and to the hut.

On Sunday afternoon a few minutes before five o'clock, we waited for the call from Marcos. Tophat, Rooster and I sat in my room close to the phone, staring at it. Rooster said, "I think you should sell for him. You can make enough money to have a big car like his in a few years. I'll bet his car cost sixty thousand bucks. We'll help you sell."

"Rooster, I'm thirteen years old. Even if I had sixty thousand dollars, who is going to sell a Mercedes Benz to a thirteen year old kid!? Anyway I don't have a driver's license."

The three of us continued to stare at the phone. Tophat leaned forward and whispered, "If you get in with Marcos, you can't get out. He'll kill you. He might kill us too!"

Exactly at five o'clock, the phone rang, and Tophat jumped back like he had already been shot. The phone sounded louder than usual. We sat tense as it rang four more times. Rooster said, "Go ahead. Answer it. It might be him."

Tophat and I glanced at Rooster then continued to stare at the ringing phone.

"I really want the money and the power of being the big man with the drug connections," I said. "But I feel guilty about being on drugs, and I didn't want to contribute to wrecking other people's lives like I've wrecked mine. And Marcos had told me once you're in, there's no way out." I thought about the gun he had in the trunk. I had already seen someone die because of drugs—Larry Coots, back at the Marietta apartment. Tophat and Rooster were looking at me. I just sat there and let the phone ring again. Then it stopped ringing after the fifth ring.

I didn't answer it. We never heard from Marcos again.

With all my weakness toward addiction and in spite of my youth, I managed to make the right decision. I guess you can say I had the ultimate connection, and I let it slip through my hands. I knew I had to do the right thing. I felt more power after that than if I had agreed to become the "Big Man" selling drugs. This one time in my young life, I showed some strength.

14.
Incident in Middle School

In my thirteenth year, I started the eighth grade at Lincoln Middle School. The year started out as expected, like all the previous years. I started out behind, of course. I baffled each of my new teachers by my lack of reading ability, or when I didn't perform in class and when I didn't turn in homework, they may have thought I was being unruly or belligerent.

A few months after school started, a tragedy happened—one that stayed with me the rest of my life: When the afternoon bell rang, kids piled into the hallway. Most got on the buses to go home. I waited for my friend, Timmy Mitchell, who rode the same bus from school to Oakdale as I did. We rode together every day. Timmy knew about my problems but did not condemn me. He said he would never do drugs and he wished I could quit. He had been a friend for a couple of years and saw what a turmoil I stayed in because of my addiction.

When the bus reached Oakdale, all the kids who lived there got off the bus. Some of the high school students were there waiting for a brother or sister. Also some of the older guys who hung out in Oakdale were there waiting for their friends to get off the bus. Hiram Smith, one of these older guys, sat in his '66 Chevy in front of Pac-A-Sac Groceries waiting to pick up his brother. Hiram Smith seemed like a regular kid. He wasn't a bully, just a kid picking up his brother. I started talking to some kids near the bus-stop. Timmy went over to Hiram's car, and jumped up on the hood. He sat there perched on the hood, goofing off, laughing and clowning around with Hiram and a couple of other guys.

I glanced over toward Timmy. It seemed I had a habit of looking after him. Hiram began to ease his car forward slowly, going probably only 5 m.p.h. Timmy held his books in one arm and sat, perched on the hood. Suddenly Hiram tapped the brakes, and Timmy lurched forward off the car. The next thing I knew, Timmy fell on the asphalt, face down, and I started running. I knew his forehead had hit the curb. By the time I got to him, he lay sprawled out. Blood came from his ears, nose, and mouth. Several kids gathered around him, stunned. Some girls began to scream. One girl ran into the Pac-A-Sac store to find an adult and to ask for help.

"Don't touch him. Don't move him," I said dreading what I would find when I knelt down. I put my finger on the side of his neck. No pulse. I know I turned pale. I felt all the blood drain down from my face. I stood up, and the crowd of students looked at me. I could not speak. I just shook my head as Jed, the manager of the Pac-A-Sac, and several customers rushed out of the store toward us.

I stepped back. By this time, blood pooled all over the asphalt around Timmy's head. The adults made the crowd clear back. We all stood in a circle, back from Timmy, and I heard someone say in a low voice. "Dead." In just minutes, the fire truck and an ambulance arrived. Then the police were on the scene and questioned everyone. Hiram Smith, the driver of the Chevy, went berserk crying and moaning, "I didn't do anything. I barely moved my car. I didn't tell him to sit on the hood. I didn't know he would fall off. Why did he die?"

The other students, when questioned, confirmed Hiram had been barely moving. Everyone said Hiram should not be blamed. There were a lot of kids crying.

I had been quiet, standing there all this time—my insides shaking. The ambulance crew checked Timmy. They looked shocked and whispered and nodded amongst themselves. They placed Timmy on a gurney they had just taken from the ambulance and then loaded him into the ambulance. They turned on the siren and blue light and took off.

When the ambulance left with Timmy, I felt a knot in my chest. My neck felt like a wet cloth twisting. I remembered how Timmy—my little buddy—the one I saved from being beaten up when we were in elementary school, had always been there for me. When I went through my situation with Mrs. Starky, he had even helped me make the Molotov cocktail though he had been against it all the time.

I wondered if Timmy's dying could be a punishment for lighting the Molotov cocktail when I threw it at the school? I didn't think so. The fire had only scorched the door and no real harm had come to anyone. As far as I knew lighting the Molotov cocktail might possibly be the only rebellious thing Timmy had ever done, and I had been the cause of that.

I couldn't understand why Timmy died. I thought of his Mom who had been so strict on him. He had always been such a good kid. He had never gotten into any trouble with his parents or teachers.

I walked slowly down Hill Street toward home. When I walked into the kitchen Mom glanced up at me. "Bradley!" She exclaimed, "What in the world happened? You're as white as a sheet—you're trembling." I sat down at the kitchen table. I noticed my hands were shaking.

"Timmy's dead." Mom sat down beside me and held on to me while I told her. I heard Dad's truck in the driveway a few minutes later. He ran into the house, came into the kitchen, and put his hand on my shoulder glancing up at Mom at the same time. He already knew. On the way home from work, he had stopped in Oakdale and someone had told him. When I told him about what happened, tears ran down my face. "Dad, why did this happen?" I sobbed, putting my head and arms forward on the kitchen table.

Dad had knelt down beside me patting my shoulder. "Only God knows. It's not for us to understand," he said sadly. I went to my room and lay on the bed, still stunned.

When Mom had supper on the table, we sat down to eat. Dad prayed for Timmy, for his family and friends, and for me. I didn't eat much. Then I went to my room and lay on the bed, again, seeing the accident over and over in my mind. I didn't sleep much that night.

The next day at school, we had a special assembly. By this time, everyone knew about the tragedy. There were speeches and prayers and counseling in each classroom. One of the counselors came up to me in the hallway, "Brad, I know you and Timmy hung out together. I know this is hard for you. Do you want to come in my office and talk?" The counselor looked genuinely concerned. I just shook my head and walked slowly away with my head down. I didn't think I could talk about it at school. I kept to myself.

On Sunday, the faculty and staff of Lincoln Middle School held a memorial service in the school auditorium. I went, but stayed back from the crowd and didn't talk to anyone. A few students hugged me or patted me on the shoulder. Several other teachers wanted to talk to me, but I shook my head and looked down as I walked away. I left when some of the girls started crying.

For all the years after Timmy's death, I still felt shocked when I thought about what happened and have always wondered why he died in such a freak accident. There wasn't even an accident—it was like a no-accident. He had just slipped off the car. I never got over it.

About a month after Timmy's death, the football coach called me into his office. I had no idea what he wanted. Coach Morton acted strict, stern, and tough. As I faced him, I noticed his flattop haircut and his very straight upper row of teeth. He had a tight, toothy smile and tried to come across as friendly but I knew all the time he sized me up when he said,

"Brad, have you ever considered playing sports?"

I had a desire to play sports, so I listened to what he had to say. "Well Boy, you're pretty big, and I can probably use you as a lineman. You'll have to cut your hair. You can't play with your hair long, Boy."

He always called the players, "Boy" when he talked or yelled at them on the field, but I still didn't like it. I had long hair touching my collar, and I wasn't willing to have it cut. I just gave him a hard look and walked off. I fooled him. I wasn't going to cut my hair to be a jock. Who wants to play damn sports anyway? That's for a bunch of ra-rahs.

I felt like I looked good, and I got a good reaction from the girls. At six foot two, I kept my weight just under two hundred. I kept trim and muscular. When I worked out, I could press one-eighty. With one arm over my head, I could press one-fifty.

In study hall at the library during fifth period, I started talking to Marianne, a girl in the eleventh grade. Every day she saved a place for me at one of the tables back in the corner away from the librarian's front desk. I looked forward each day to seeing her friendly face. We started out whispering, then talking and laughing and joking. The librarian kept coming around the corner warning us, "Quieten down or I'll have to ask you to leave."

That just made us laugh more. I didn't know what to make of Marianne when she kept touching me. Was she being friendly or coming on to me? She ran her finger across my knee and touched my shoulder then she leaned close to whisper. "Brad, I would like to get to know you better."

Then she asked me to cut class and go to Belmont Hills Shopping Center with her. She had just gotten her driver's license and drove her mother's car. We had it planned. One morning, I just didn't get on the school bus when it stopped in Oakdale, but met Marianne. When we shopped, she wanted to buy a shirt for me. She held many shirts up to my chest to see if they were the right size and how certain colors looked with my blue eyes and blond hair.

Finally she bought a blue knit shirt and then we went back to her house. Her mom would not be home from work for a couple of hours. We sat in the kitchen, had a cola and a sandwich, and talked for a long time. I told her about Timmy and what a good friend he had been. She told me she knew about his death, but had not known him. She listened and acted like she understood how his dying had affected me. She said she felt genuinely sorry for what happened to him.

She said, "Oh, Brad. That is so bad." She hugged me and kissed me on the mouth. Then she hugged me again. We stood up embracing. She quickly put the dishes away and began to show me through her house.

Then we went into her bedroom. This girl's bedroom had the color pink everywhere. Her curtains and bedspread and the walls of her bedroom were pink. There were stuffed animals on the bed. I felt a little out of place as I glanced around at her clothes in the open closet and on the floor.

She asked me to try on the new knit shirt. I stripped off my shirt and put the new one on quickly. It fit snugly. She hugged me. Then she reached up and cupped her hand against the long hair at my neck pulling me to her, kissing me on the mouth. It felt so good to have somebody hug me and love on me. We were laying on her bed before I knew it. Then my heart started pounding as she started unbuttoning her blouse. I couldn't believe this. This surprised me. I knew she had been coming on to me, but I wasn't expecting this. I thought, I'm too young for this. I remembered being at Piedmont Park at ten years old and having the same thoughts, that of being too young for a situation when I saw a man take an overdose. But, like the park situation, this new experience overtook me and I saw it through.

I came away educated in the ways of sex and of a naked woman.

I had imagined what I had just experienced as other young boys my age had. After Marianne brought me back to Oakdale, I walked home. I relived the experience over and over in my mind for several days and nights. She had shown me what she wanted and I happily obliged her. This young man's fantasies had come true that day.

The thing though—I really didn't like Marianne that much. I didn't find her cute or attractive as I did my other casual girlfriends. She listened to me talk about Timmy's death. She had a way of consoling me. But Marianne, who was three years older than me, had come after me. Even though I felt guilty about what went on and even though I did not particularly like her, when she asked, I went back to her house several times that year.

In my sadness over Timmy, I reached out to Marianne more than I did the drugs. I needed one or the other to get my mind off the things that I had no power over. For this short time, I allowed her to console me.

15.
Devastation

In school, I continued to do drugs and still didn't do well in class, but with my great body and some experience, lovemaking became my new diversion. I always had a new girlfriend. When I did drugs before going to school, my girlfriends, each, tried to keep me from getting caught and suspended. When I fell asleep in class, my girlfriend woke me before the teacher discovered me sleeping. Each girlfriend wanted to rescue me from drugs. None of them did drugs themselves, and each tried to persuade me to stop.

While many of the girls wanted to help me, the bullies wanted to see if they could whip me. When any of these tough guy wanna-to-bes picked on a little kid, I remembered Timmy and went to their rescue. I tried, but it seemed I couldn't avoid a fight with Matt still around. He had pushed Timmy around in elementary school, and I had come to his rescue. He provoked me again when we got into a confrontation in the bathroom when he said, "Hey Brad, you don't have anybody to protect today?" I had wanted to be left alone, but when he shoved me and said what he did, I went berserk. I thought he referred to Timmy. I knocked him down on the first punch and grabbed a handful of his hair and just kept punching him in the face. Some kids heard the commotion and ran to the principal's office. Coach Morton came in no time and restrained me. I tried to control my anger but still wanted to hit Matt. The coach suspended me for a week. I left red-faced but relieved. The coach had not realized I had been high. I had rather be suspended for fighting than for being on drugs.

The first day after I came back at school, I walked into study hall with my latest girlfriend, Sandy. Coach Morton whom I think followed me down the hall watching for an excuse to expel me said, “Get rid of the chewing gum.”

I came back at him, acting cocky. He put me down in front of Sandy. He called me out into the hallway and grabbed me. I stumbled. “You don’t put your hands on me, Buddy,” I said as he snatched me away from Sandy.

“You’re high. You’re doing drugs,” he said.

“I’ll whip your ass,” I threatened.

“We’ll see about that.” He took me to the principal’s office.

I went in and sat down in front of the principal, Mr. Hopper, an unnaturally skinny guy who looked like he came from outer space. He had pointed ears, a sharp nose, and bug-eyes. He carried a paddle with him everywhere he went. This paddle looked like Mrs. Starky’s—with holes drilled in it. He would go into an area where students were not supposed to be and threaten in a whining voice, “All right ya’ll, get up right now or I’ll start paddling.”

In his office, he listened to Coach Morton and then said to me, “You know, you’ve been nothing but trouble since you’ve been here. You’re always fighting. You beat a boy senseless last week. You can’t even read. Can’t write. You can’t do anything but cause trouble. Tell me right now you’re not high on something,” Mr. Hopper said.

I gave him a blank look and shrugged. I felt hopeless to deny the obvious. I had gotten by this long without being caught. Coach Morton said, “He comes in just trying to act big in front of his friends.”

I jumped up and threatened, “I’ll whip your ass in here just as quick as I'll whip it out there." Coach Morgan stepped back. I think he realized I meant it.

"Either he's going or I'm going," Coach Morton said to the principal.

So guess who goes? The principal expelled me for the rest of the year, the last six months of the eighth grade for drug use at school and for threatening to attack Coach Morton. He could have given me less time, but expelling me for six months got me out of his hair. Now I had to tell my parents about being expelled and about my problems.

My parents knew I hated school. They were aware I couldn't read and couldn't be a good student because of not reading. Each year, after I got a promotion to the next grade, I guess they thought things had gotten better for me toward the end the year. My parents just hadn't caught on to the fact the school system didn't know what to do with me. For one thing, I stood a head taller than anyone else my age in class. If I had been detained each year, I would have been over six feet tall and still in the third grade.

Mom and Dad knew I played hooky. The school called whenever I stayed out a few days. My parents had talked with me, asking me to please not stay out. They had told me how important my education was, but they weren't paying close attention. Dad worked long hours, and Mom worked at her nursing job or stayed home too sick to catch me playing hookey. I don't think they kept tally of how many days the school called.

Each time I stayed outside in the hut or away from the house wandering around, my parents thought, I was only doing what most young boys do. They had no reason to suspect me of any wrong doing or think I could be in any serious trouble. A few times when I got high and came into the house to eat, I just kept quiet and went to my room later to play the radio, watch TV, or sleep.

Now by being expelled for drug use at school, I guess my time to "fess up" had come. I waited until we were finishing supper and said, "I can't go back to school. The principal expelled me today."

"Well, Bradley, what in the world?" Mom exclaimed.

I studied her face, dreading what I had to say next.

"I'll just go talk to them and see about that," she said.

"Mom, I've been expelled for six months. I can't go back this school year."

Mom's mouth dropped open and her eyes were big as she stared at me. Dad lowered his head and studied the last bites of his food on his plate like the answers were written there somewhere. He took a deep breath and let out a sigh.

They both sat still as I explained. "I've been in trouble for a long time. Dad, you remember, last year, when I told you about Larry Coots dying of an overdose of drugs? You remember when we talked about drugs?

"Son, you told me you weren't on drugs."

"Well I lied. I just didn't want to hurt you. I didn't want to tell you about my addiction. I thought I could come off drugs and you would never have to know. I did come off heroin by myself."

When I said heroin, Mom went pale. "Bradley, we had a patient at the hospital last week who died of a heroin overdose. Those are dangerous drugs." Her mouth tightened into a thin line and her eyes got moist.

"Mom, I'm off heroin."

She looked at me as though I were a stranger whom she couldn't believe. "Bradley, coming off heroin is horrible."

Dad had been listening. "Son, how can we help you?" he asked.

"Dad I've tried to quit. But I feel so good when I'm on drugs. I don't know how I can try any harder." I didn't have a chance to say anything else. Aunt Lilly opened the kitchen door and came in without knocking, interrupting our conversation. She saw the expression on my Mom's face.

"What's going on? Am I interrupting something?" We were all quiet. Mom pushed her chair back from the table and went to the bedroom. Aunt Lilly followed whether Mom wanted her to or not.

Dad and I were quiet as we continued to sit at the table. We could hear Mom crying and talking quietly. Then we heard Aunt Lilly say in a strong voice, "Lila, I told you that boy of yours ran wild and you didn't believe me. I knew he would be in trouble one day having that long hair and all."

In a few minutes, Lilly came through the kitchen headed toward the back door. "You should be ashamed of yourself. No one in this family has ever acted like you're doing. We were all raised Christian. Your father and mother do *not* deserve to have all this trouble. They are good people and have raised you to do better than this." She snorted as she left pulling the back door closed with a strong thud.

After Mom lay down for a while, Dad called us back into the kitchen. We sat at the table.

Mom said, "Son, I had no idea you were in trouble. I wish you had confided in me. I know you can stop taking drugs if you just try."

"If I knew how to stop I would," I told Mom.

"Son, what did we do wrong that caused you to act like this?" She asked in an anguished voice.

I looked down at the table and studied the small, geometric lines in the yellow formica. I shook my head.

Dad kept hitting the how-can-we-help-you angle. "Son, tell us what to do for you. How can we help you?" But I didn't know what to tell him. I kept saying, "I don't know how you can help me. I guess it is up to me."

I went to bed, but didn't sleep. I had a lot to think about. I felt badly for my parents, but I felt relieved to be out of school. I didn't know what I would do with myself with all my days totally free. Also, how could I do drugs now? I would be home all the time with Mom and Dad. I knew I had quit. I had promised them and now I had to promise myself that I would try to stop doing drugs.

The next day after I had been up to Oakdale, I walked down Hill Street toward home and passed the next door neighbor's house. I saw Mrs. Walker sweeping her front porch and started to speak. When she saw me, she looked scared, went into the house quickly, slammed the door, and I heard it lock behind her. I knew Aunt Lilly had told her and everybody else about my being on drugs and about me being expelled. It hurt my feelings knowing Mrs. Walker was afraid of me. I had been to her house to see her and the girls, Teresa, and Renee all my growing-up years. I figured all the church ladies and my former Sunday School teacher, Mrs. Couch, knew about my downfall. I don't know how I expected anybody to treat me any differently than Mrs. Walker had. I dressed like a hippie—in jeans, a jeans jacket with the arms cut out with symbols drawn all over it, dingo boots, and unkept hair touching my shoulders. And most of the times when she saw me, I had been doing some kind of drugs.

After I worked with Dad's crew for four months, I told Dad I had been saving all I made to buy a motorcycle. "Brad if you want a motorcycle, I will pay half. I'm proud of you for being off drugs and coming to work with me. You work as hard as any man I have. I knew he felt relieved when I stayed with him every workday, so he could keep an eye on me.

I completed the picture of a true hippie when I got my motorcycle. I stayed in contact with my friends. Rooster and one of the classmates, Jimmy Henderson, came over to see my Harley. "Man, I've got to have a motorcycle. He rode it around the backyard a few times then up Hill Street. Soon Rooster's Dad bought a Honda for him. We rode around the yard and through the pasture and the woods nearby. We were having a blast.

One Friday when I didn't go to work with Dad and Mom had gone to work, I hung around, still expelled, with nothing to do. So I went for a ride on my motorcycle with Jimmy who played hooky. Even though I didn't have an extra helmet, I let him ride on the back of the motorcycle. We were on our way back from buying beer from Jeff Kilpatrick who had been our source from the first time I had bought from him, at nine years old. Jimmy and I were both a little high on marijuana we had done earlier. It had been four months since I had been expelled or since I had done drugs. We had also drank a few beers at Jeff's house.

As Jimmy and I went down Atlanta Road, I noticed a protective custody car parked at an intersection. The cop stood outside his car. I did a wheelstand across the road right at the intersection in front of the patrol car.

The cop hollered at me, "Hey where's his helmet?" He started walking toward me.

He pointed to Jimmy. I circled the intersection. He motioned for me to come over to him.

"I'm not going with you," I called out. "You're not going to get me, you pig."

He got into the patrol car and turned on the blue lights.

He hollered back, "You longhaired hippie. I'm going to show your ass."

I told Jimmy, "I'm going to run, Son. What do you want to do?"

He only had time to say, "Go, Man go."

We cut out and went in the opposite direction past the patrol car, knowing he would lose time turning around. I headed toward a little gravel road on the other side of I-285 called "Reefer Road" where we had gone several times to smoke pot and get high. “Go, Brad, go,” Jimmy screamed. He held on to me for dear life.

When I crossed the I-285 underpass at the end of the bridge and turned down the gravel road, I glanced down at my speedometer. We were doing ninety. We almost hit a bank. Jimmy began to scream, “Slow down; slow down!” You’re going to kill us!”

Somehow I held the motorcycle in the road. It jumped and vibrated, and took a beating on the gravel. I quickly glanced back—the detective car crossed sideways and bounced off the bank. They were having a rough time too. We had gone into the road too fast. I went down a hill and into the woods. The detective drew his gun and fired two times. *Pow, pow.*

“Oh, God. Oh, God!” Jimmy screamed pressing his face into my back. I thought the cop had shot Jimmy. I put on the brakes, and lay the motorcycle down sideways before it came to a full stop.

I thought, if he’s hit he’ll have to go to the hospital. I can’t let my friend die.

Jimmy hit the ground when I laid the motorcycle down. He turned a flip, got up, and ran for the woods. I glanced around and saw the detective had jumped out of the nearby patrol car and ran toward me as I tried to get up. He pointed the gun at me and pulled the hammer back.

“Just go ahead, run!” he shouted.

I knew if I did, he would shoot me. I stayed still.

He made me push the motorcycle back up the hill to a point where I became so exhausted I couldn’t push it anymore.

He said, “I’m going to let you crank it up and walk it. If you take off, I’m going to blow your damn brains out.”

The other detective drove the car out as the detective with the gun walked beside me with his gun pointed at my head. When we were back up to the street, I took off my blue metallic helmet with the American flag on it. He took it from me, held it for a moment, then threw it at me, hitting me full in the chest. I double over from the impact. It hurt.

"Don't treat him like that," said the detective in the patrol car as he pulled up alongside us.

"He just ran us down a damn pig trail. He could have killed us all," the other cop said.

"Where are you taking me?" I asked.

"I'm taking you and putting you in a damn cage with the rest of the damn animals where you belong."

In the end they charged me with riding a motorcycle without a license, riding someone on the back of the motorcycle without a helmet, driving too fast, eluding a police officer, resisting arrest, and reckless endangerment. They also found two joints on me.

My parents were called. Dad got me out on bond with the provisions I had to stay home and not leave my parent's custody until the hearing. Dad looked so hurt. "Son, I thought you had changed. I thought you had given up drugs. See how you act when you are on them." I nodded, but did not reply and followed him to the car. "Mom stayed home. She's too upset to come."

I continued to go to work with Dad each day. In the afternoons and on weekends, I could have guys over, but could not leave the yard. I rode my motorcycle only with Dad around. I had not one chance to smoke pot.

Two miserable months later on the day of the hearing, I faced Judge Rourke. I represented myself and said, "Your honor, this is just not me. I hate violence and trouble. I hate buying drugs and being involved with the kind of people who sell them. I can't understand why I get so wild when I'm on them. I feel like a victim of circumstance. I act so differently when I'm taking drugs. I've tried to stop. I stop for a while. But then I take drugs when things are going badly for me. I promise I'm going to do better."

He studied me as I spoke. I felt his focus on my every move as I walked around speaking with animation, probably out of nervousness. I kept glancing back at him, aware of those heavy eyebrows, half glasses, and those small black eyes following me. I'm not sure the Judge even blinked. He never moved until I finished.

When I glanced around at my parents sitting in the court room I felt so sorry to be standing in front of the Judge. Mom had dressed like she did for church on Sunday, in a nice dress with makeup and jewelry. Dad had on his best suit. They both looked really nice, but so ashamed. I looked around the courtroom. My parents seemed out of place. They didn't look like they should have even known anyone in trouble much less have a son who could not stay out of trouble.

My poor dad had tried to do something with me. He had been patient and had taken me as a trainee at his job, just to keep me out of trouble. I know he prayed about me and for me. I guess he felt like a coach standing sadly on the sidelines watching his star player in one fumble after another and with each fumble I managed to pain him to the core.

Judge Rourke spoke when I finished. "Son, I am fining you three hundred dollars. You are to work and pay the fine yourself—not your parents. I am placing you in your parent's custody for three more months. You are not to leave the yard unless your Dad is with you. Your Dad is to lock your motorcycle away for six months and you are not to ride it until you can show you are responsible.

"You have placed yourself and your friend, Jimmy Henderson, in danger. You have put your community in danger while you were on drugs and when you were speeding on the motorcycle. The patrolmen were doing their job, but they are there to protect our community from criminals.

"When I have a young man from a good family to do what you

did, it embarrasses not only the family but the community. You should be ashamed. You make me ashamed. I am embarrassed for your parents. You were raised better than to do this. I want to see you here again in three months with your father, and I want to be told you have been clean. I want this to be the last time I see you. I do not want to ever see you again, for any violation. Do we have an understanding on this?"

I had been sitting with my head down, truly embarrassed, while he spoke then passed sentence. When he finished, I stood up, "Yes, Sir, Your Honor." On the way home riding with my parents, I had very little to say as I still felt very embarrassed.

I did exactly as the Judge ordered. I did go to work with Dad every day, and I did my best to stay clean. I would have a good report when we went back to court. I worked as hard as any one of his employees. With the money he paid me, I gradually began to pay off the court fine in installments.

I had just settled into a routine of going to work with Dad every day when something phenomenal happened. Dad and I were in the front yard preparing to go to work. We heard something like the sound of a monster shrieking. We looked up to the railroad track on the bluff above our house and saw the coming train had skipped the track.

The wheels of the train were literally shirring off the cross ties one by one, flinging them into the air in a perfect rainbow-shaped arch. The curve of the track right before the house, caused the train to seem like it headed directly toward Dad and me. "Dad!" I screamed. He grabbed my arm. We stood transfixed. The part of the train still on the track held it on. Cross ties fell around our house like toothpicks. Two hit the roof of our house. Dad and I watched in amazement, paralyzed. Although the train had slowed, it picked up momentum off the track.

The engine made it past our house, and past Church Road Bridge, the tail end of the box cars just cleared our house. Then on the last curve after the bridge, the train left the track completely, taking out a few houses. As the tail end of the train cleared our house, Dad and I were running down the tracks after it. After the train crashed the houses and came to a halt, we caught up to the devastation. We hoped no one had been home and no one had been injured or killed.

As we ran down the track and past all the wrecked train cars, and past Church Road Bridge, we heard the sirens of fire trucks and ambulances which were on their way. This freight train leaving the tracks had left wreckage and debris everywhere. We were quickly on the scene to see what we could do to help.

When we got to the first house, Mr. Elderberg's, Dad made me stay outside as he went into the pile of rubble. Only one room partly stood. Dad went around to the back of it and started calling out, "Mr. Elderberg. Mr. Elderberg. Can you hear me?"

Then we heard knocking. Dad motioned for me. We began to toss beams, doors, and boards until we could see him lying under what used to be a kitchen table. He had blood on his face and body and seemed barely conscious. Dad knelt over him. "Mr. Elderberg. Can you talk?" He nodded. "Do you know what happened." What he said came as totally unexpected.

"Train wreck. Like your daughter's."

Dad jerked back and stared at him. "Oh yeah. You were on the scene at Kay's train-car wreck." Mr. Elderberg had a knowing look in his eyes and nodded, but then his eyes closed. Dad turned to me, "Son, go find an ambulance. Bring them here. I'll stay with him."

I took off running down the track toward the crashed engines of the train and toward the sound of the sirens getting louder. When I saw a fireman, I shouted, "We need an ambulance." I rode with them back to Mr. Elderberg and his demolished house.

When Dad and I got home, he seemed all defeated and down-

and-out. When we had the blessing before supper, Dad prayed for Mr. Elderberg and those whose homes had been destroyed. No one else had injuries, except Mr. Elderberg who had a broken leg and a broken back. I think Dad had thought of Kay's accident all afternoon. As we sat quietly eating supper and thinking about the train wreck, the phone rang, surprising all of us.

Sam, Kay's husband, called from the hospital where he had just taken her. "She went into labor an hour ago. The baby will be here soon," he said, "So come to the hospital right away." We got ready quickly and went to the hospital. A few hours later, a seven pound ten ounce baby boy came into the world. Mom saw Kay in the delivery room, briefly. Later, we stood at the nursery window and the nurse showed us the new baby.

The next morning we went to the hospital early to visit Kay. Sam brought us into Kay's room. She sat up in bed holding her new baby whom she had named Daniel.

Everybody kept saying, "Oh, he's so cute. Look at all that hair. Oh, he's adorable."

I looked from Mom, to Dad, then to Kay and Sam to see if they really meant what they said. Daniel had a lot of black hair sticking straight up on a tiny head with a red face and squinting tiny eyes. If this qualified as cute, I would hate to see ugly. I only agreed with them. I didn't want to tell them he reminded me of a cartoon character. Here, with this little red baby, it seemed I had become an uncle.

Kay looked happy and not a bit shy when she shared with us the fact she could nurse the baby. "Momma, I can even nurse him out of my right breast, the side which was injured so badly."

They both had tears in their eyes. Kay laughed with her bright strong laugh which we had not heard for a long time. I knew she and her new family were really happy.

I had a lot to think about—all the happening of the last twenty-four hours. First there was the train wreck and on the same day a new baby came into our family. Dad and I worked together quietly every day, but today, on the way home, we talked about the past events. He talked about the baby and mentioned the train wreck less and less.

A few days later, Dad came to the hut to find me. He sat quietly down and gave me a steady look. "Son, I'm sorry to tell you this, but Uncle Sycamore died this morning."

I had been sitting on the cot, but when he said Sycamore died, I gave a start and stood up, stricken. I couldn't believe what he said. I grabbed onto his arm and studied his face, almost not believing what he had said. But when I saw the sadness in his face, I began to understand it really *had* happened. I had not seen Uncle Sycamore for a while since before I went to court. "What happened. Had he been sick?"

Dad shook his head. "It happened suddenly—a stroke," He seemed to be talking to himself and thinking about Sycamore.

I never had a relative to die and his death really affected me. Uncle Sycamore had a military funeral to honor his service in World War II. He could have worn a uniform, but all the family agreed on how to have him dressed, and if he had planned his funeral beforehand, he would have agreed with their choice. He wore new overalls and a new railroad cap like the ones he had worn every time I had ever seen him. But instead of his camouflage shirt, Daddy had him dressed in a new white, long sleeved shirt because he "was going to see the Lord."

An American flag and a very large spray of red, white, and blue carnations were draped over the casket. A display of Sycamore's army medals were arranged on an end table beside the casket. Dad knew Sycamore had given me the Purple Heart, so I brought it and laid it among the other medals on display. Everyone agreed that after the service all of his medals should go to me. "He would want you to have them," each family member told me. Some of them hugged me or patted me on the shoulder, because they all knew how much Uncle Sycamore had meant to me.

As I sat in the funeral service listening to the choir sing *How Great Thou Art* and *Amazing Grace*, I thought, the world is full of cruel and mean people. They should die, not Sycamore. I had never known Sycamore to hurt anybody. I thought about Timmy. Good people like Uncle Sycamore and Timmy should not die until they are very old.

I heard the preacher say, "Silvey Berkshire's life stood as a living example of a good neighbor, a caring family man, and a faithful Christian, and he served his country when called. Silvey, known to all as Sycamore, lived to help those around him. He served God through serving others. God has called him home, but he will be missed by all who loved him."

The entire congregation adjourned after the funeral and walked to a small cemetery, Old Macedonia, not too far from our house. There had been a church there years ago and several past members of the Berkshire family had been buried in the same cemetery—in the family plot.

Three soldiers in uniform each with a rifle fired a volley of seven shots in unison. As the twenty-one gun salute broke the air, it just about broke my composure. I felt myself shaking inside, fighting to maintain my emotions. Dad sensed how I felt and put his arm around me. On my other side, Mom put her hand on my arm. We watched the casket being lowered into the ground. I hated to leave Uncle Sycamore there in the cold grave with all the dirt thrown over the casket.

I stayed until all the flowers were placed on top of the mound and until everyone else had left. I didn't cry but my throat ached. My chest felt like it had a big rock right in the middle. I walked home by myself, deep in thought. The cold night gathered around my shoulders like an icy cloak as I walked, so I pulled my jacket tighter around me. Though I felt the freezing air on my face, I didn't hurry. I walked even slower when I got to the railroad track leading to my house. I didn't want to be inside. I remember the verses of *Amazing Grace* from the funeral. *"Amazing*

Grace/How sweet the sound/That saved a wretch like me/I once was lost/ But now I'm found/Was blind, but now I see. . . . /Through many dangers toil and snares/I have already come/ . . . ."

Well, the last line of the verse certainly applied true in my life. As I walked, I had the impression God spoke to me, "If you'll just come to Me, everything will be okay."

Yet in my mind, I rejected the thought and pushed it away—out of my mind. I knew I could never clean up my life good enough to be worthy of God accepting me. I felt like I couldn't live a life of holiness and purity and being better than everybody else. I wasn't holy; I wasn't pure. The way I had been acting and the things I had been doing were far from that.

I had learned whatever endeavors you pursue, no matter how good you are at what you are doing, something goes lacking. Usually the better you are at your endeavor the more there is that is void in the other areas of your life. If your relationship is only with yourself then you have no thoughts of others. This hurts the ones who love you. Or in my case this neglect of everyone around me—an act that spared them, an act of mercy, God would say. Except, after a while, everyone knew of my downfall.

Oh, I had relationships. The poet will say it is like one flower next to another shining in the sun for a brief time until both flowers wilt and lay sagging on the stalk then are beaten down when the first storm comes. I make the comparison of myself and my friends to a bowl of bright apples where a few rotten ones can spoil the whole bunch.

16.
Stolen Car

After the funeral, I hung around home—still expelled from school, and sad about Sycamore's passing. I spent time with my family. But at this time, I got into more trouble than I had ever been in before.

Dad suggested we go hunting next Saturday. Friday night, he came home smiling, clutching a large burlap sack tightly by the top. I remembered, like a flashback from years ago, when he brought home a duck or a kitten to entertain me. Right off I could tell something pretty big squirmed around inside the sack. I started laughing, not so much about having a surprise, but I knew with this gesture Dad was trying to cheer me up into a better mood. I took the burlap sack and pulled down the sides. I couldn't believe what jumped out.

It was a black Labrador Retriever puppy. He seemed to be all ears and legs and had big feet and a wet nose he immediately put right into my hand. The puppy started licking me, and I started laughing. I grabbed him, rolling around on the ground, roughhousing with him. It was love at first sight for both of us. We took off running toward the woods behind our house just for the sheer fun of running. Dad remained in the yard looking after us, laughing at the way the pup loped, getting in front of me almost causing me to trip over him.

When night came, I dug a small trench in front of the hut and built a fire, and the puppy ran around the fire barking at it as it blazed. After a few hours of watching the fire and petting him, I poured water on the few remaining sticks causing them to smoke. The puppy grabbed a smoking stick in his mouth and ran around the backyard. I called Mom and Dad out to see this sight. Suddenly I said to them, "Hey, I know a good name for that dog—Smoky." We all had a good laugh.

Later the same week, when the weather turned a little chilly, I built a fire in the wood burning stove in the hut and slept there with Smoky on the floor beside my cot. This puppy became a nice diversion.

Saturday morning, we were up early and took Smoky out with Dad's hounddog, Blue, to hunt a few squirrels. Blue, whom Dad had finally trained to be a fine hunting dog, seemed put-out with the pup running and playing 'til his tongue hung out, acting like he had no interest in chasing or treeing a squirrel.

I spent the next few days with Smoky, being constantly amused by his antics. He chased after sticks I threw toward the barn. When I tossed sticks up in the air, he jump higher than I thought it possible for a dog to jump. I should have been happy just hanging around home playing with Smoky, but I couldn't get my mind off the pain of losing Sycamore, and of being expelled and being illiterate. I had been off drugs for more than the three months as Judge Rourke had insisted upon. I had gone back to tell Judge Rourke and had given him a good report. But now I just wanted to escape to the great feelings drugs gave me.

About two weeks after Sycamore's funeral, Franky Frank, a kid from school, came by my house driving his Daddy's car, a Plymouth Fury 383. "Hey, want to go skating?"

I asked Dad who worked out in the barn, "Is is okay if I go skating with Franky?"

"Son, that will be fine. Be back before nine o'clock."

Franky came on out to the hut with me to get my jacket. Then he showed me what he had, some pure LSD in liquid form. We dropped some of it on blotter paper and let it dry. My heart beat faster not with the excitement of taking the drug, but with the dread I felt when I lost control. I had planned for months not to do drugs anymore. My heart beat faster because I knew I could not help myself. I acted like two different people—the one I wanted to be and who my parents had brought me up to be and the one I became when I did drugs. I reached for the blotter paper, not because I wanted to, but because I could not stop myself.

"Be careful, that's the pure stuff, LSD 25," Franky said before I put the blotter acid into my mouth.

We went into my room and called Jimmy Henderson to see if he wanted to go to the skating rink with us. "Franky told me he just came by there and saw a couple of cute girls."

Franky drove us over to Jimmy's house. He went inside to get Jimmy and he left me in the car with the engine running. About that time, I started to trip.

I had this thing in my spirit that caused me to think, I'm lost. I'll just do any damn thing I feel like doing. This came from hardening myself. When I did wrong, I knew I did wrong, but I did it anyway for some reason. What I did just didn't matter. This way of thinking proved to be very dangerous. I knew the prisons were full of people who felt like this who went against the very thing God put into them.

My heart started racing again. I knew I would steal Franky's daddy's car. I just knew it. I couldn't help myself. I slid over behind the steering wheel. Within ten seconds I had the car in reverse, and had backed out in the road. I drove around until the gas ran low. Then I stopped at a service station on Bankhead Highway. I told the service station attendant, "Fill it up, wash the windshield, and check the oil."

"The oil's a little low," he said. I told him to add a quart. He didn't catch on to this fourteen year old who had stolen the car. I waited until he got the nozzle out of the gas opening and put the cap back on, then I lit up the tires. I looked in the rear view mirror and couldn't stop laughing.

I didn't expect what happened next. He dropped the gas hose, pulled a pistol out of his jacket pocket, aimed it, and shot right at me as I went down the highway. *Pow, pow, pow.* He shot at me over seven dollars worth of gas. I took a deep breath and pressed the accelerator.

The acid surged through my body. The road rose up, parts of it twisting. I had thought drugs set you free. Drugs don't set me free. Right then, I felt like I existed in total madness. As I drove around I thought, I'm in so much trouble, but I didn't care. Nothing mattered to me. I remember the speedometer hitting ninety, then one hundred. Maybe I had a death wish and wanted to kill myself.

I cruised back through Oakdale, and lo and behold, there were Johnny and Billy Hatchett, two troublemakers from Kentwood, hitchhiking. The two redheaded brothers were from a neighborhood about a mile away. I thought, I'll pick up these boys and scare the living hell out of them. My actions showed just out and out meanness, but like everything else that night, I didn't care. I pulled off the road and parked on the curb in front of them while they ran to get into the car. When they saw me Johnny asked, "Hey, where'd you get this car?"

I didn't say a thing. I just opened the door and motioned for them to get in. Billy, the younger one, got in the front with me and Johnny got in the back seat. Billy asked, "What's going on Brother? Is everything all right tonight?"

Instead of answering, I floor-boarded the car. We were going so fast it felt like we were flying.

"Berkshire! Berkshire! Slow down! Watch out!" We went into a neighborhood and took out a few trash cans. Billy, the little boy, couldn't help being funny or stupid, but I liked him. He had freckles all over his face and had curly red hair. Johnny, the bigger, stronger looking brother came close to being a real redneck. How can you not like two guys like that? When I got to the crossroads at the stop sign, I just pressed my foot on the gas and held it to the floor heading toward a big open field.

I could hear the two boys screaming, "Berkshire! Berkshire! We're going to die!"

The impact of going across the ditch slammed me into the roof of the car, then slammed me back into the floor board. Before I could get up, Johnny opened the back door of the car and jumped out screaming, "I'm scared!"

As I managed to get myself straight in the seat and press against the gas pedal again, I could hear him flipping and rolling in the grass as I sped away. I headed down a big slope.

Billy waited too long to jump. The motor roared wide open when the car hit another ditch and did a dip, throwing us both to the floor of the car again. *Blam! Crash!* The motor raced, while glass shattered all over me. I fell against the accelerator. We went speeding deep into the woods and hit a pine tree, the branches crashing into the windshield. If we had been sitting up, we would have been killed because the branches came right into the car exactly where Billy and I had been sitting.

Billy and I lay still in the front floor of the car. I lay motionless as Billy began to crawl out of the car underneath the branches filling the front seat. Johnny, who ran after the car, caught up, now, to the wrecked car. "Are you okay?" He pulled on Billy trying to help him out. "Berkshire?"

"He must be dead." I heard Billy say.

Johnny came around to the driver's side and cut the motor off. They pulled me out and laid me on the grass. My hallucinations made my blood look like ice, and all the broken glass on me and around me seemed to move like floating ice cubes. I had scratches all over me.

"We getting the hell back to Kentwood." Johnny said.

After they left, I managed to get up. As I walked through the woods, the trees appeared as if they were waving and dipping. My knees buckled a few times, and I fell to the ground but then managed to get back up. I found a service station and called Franky Frank to tell him what I had done to his Dad's car, but no one answered. I decided to go back to the car to see how badly the wreck had damaged it.

As I walked down the road back to the field, I saw a wrecker go by, and when I got near the car, I realized it was totaled. It looked like an accordion—crushed in on the front, and it looked as if a tree grew out the front window. I stood there thinking about Franky Frank and his daddy and feeling sick about what I had done to his car when a policeman, I had not noticed on the scene, came up to me.

"You're Brad Berkshire?"

"Yes. Are you going to whoop my ass?"

"No, but I'd like to take you and get you some help. What kind of drugs are you doing? What's wrong with your eyes?"

I remember telling him I took LSD, but I don't remember much more except he took me to the hospital. I had minor cuts and bruises and a swollen ankle. Even though they pumped my stomach, I passed out for twenty-four hours regaining consciousness only long enough to see my Mom's face wet with tears. I remembered hearing Dad's voice as he prayed over me while I lay there in the hospital bed.

The next day after I went home, my parents took me to an appointment to meet with Judge Rourke. I give my lame excuse. I felt disheartened and embarrassed. When I thought about saying, "I don't know why I do these things," I just dropped my head. Charges were made and a date to appear in court came a month later.

At home, I stayed around the house, hung out in the hut, and played with Smoky and Blue. I thought about what I had done. Everyone had a right to be angry with me, and they were. One of my parents had to be at home with me at all times. They didn't trust me to be left alone. Outwardly, they acted the same toward me as they always had, but I caught each of them looking at me as though they did not know me, or understand me, or trust me anymore.

Even Rooster came out to the hut and told me, "Man, you are in trouble. My parents told me this is the last time I can come over here to see you. They know about your being expelled and know about your wrecking Mr. Frank's car." He sat down on the cot and petted Smoky who had his chin on Rooster's knee. "Everybody in Oakdale is talking about you living through a wreck like that one. I went to see the car. You're lucky to be alive." I don't think anyone knew Billy and Johnny Hatchett were with me. I didn't even tell Rooster. I knew Billy and Johnny would not tell their parents. They would have really gotten into trouble, even though they didn't know I had stolen the car or that I had taken drugs before they had gotten into the car.

I got really depressed. By this time, all my relatives knew about me stealing a car and wrecking it. Kell came over. "My Dad sent me over to talk a little sense into you." He really laughed at what he said. I thought to myself, little does his Dad know Kell is the one who first gave me drugs, who got me started taking them.

"Damn Brad. You're toast. I went by to see Mr. Frank's Plymouth. It didn't look like a car. It's a squashed pile of metal." He really rubbed it in. "Wished I'd seen the crash. Had to be some action, man." He laughed harder. "I bet you do some time for this stunt." Right then I hated Kell.

The dreaded day arrived for me to face Judge Rourke again. I gave my lame talk as best as I could, but I knew I had deep trouble. He let me talk before he had his say. I tried to paint a pretty picture and say what everyone wanted to hear, but also what I really felt.

"Sir, I don't know why I did those things." I said referring to the motorcycle wreck, the marijuana charges, being on LSD, then stealing a car and wrecking it.

"When I'm on drugs, I just don't know what I'm doing, but I feel like I can't stay off the drugs. I crave them. I try to stay off, and I do for a while, but then I take something else. I know I need help."

I told him the truth—the way I felt.

No one knew what I had done in Marietta at the apartments, nor did anyone know the part I played in the theft ring in the Cumberland community. Of course, I tried to forget about these experiences and never mentioned them to anyone.

Judge Rourke listened to everything I had to say. I think he admired me for being able to speak for myself, and for some reason, I think the judge liked me. He put me on probation, and I had to attend counseling sessions.

Dad drove me to a one hour counseling session once a week for six weeks. As Dad drove me to the first counseling session, I sat quietly in the car, not knowing what to expect. "Are you nervous, Son?"

"Yeah, I hope they can do something to help me. I want to change."

"I hope they can help you, son." He put his hand on my shoulder.

At the first session, a middle-age psychologist, Mrs. Marty, said I had to work on my attitude and behavior. She told me my actions and my choices had gotten me into this trouble, and I had exhibited behavior totally out of control. The next week she told me I needed to see the good side of being good and following rules at home, at school, and to not break the law, ever again. I had to set high standards and use appropriate behavior.

After several weeks, I began to open up about my frustration at not being able to get off drugs. Toward the end of the six weeks, I finally admitted part of my reason in wanting to escape into the world of drugs might be because of my frustrations and feelings of inadequacy in school. "I just want to be a good student. I want to learn. Everything I do at home—I'm happy and successful. Everything I do at school is a disaster. I want to feel the same way at school as I do at home—accepted and like I belong—like I'm as good as anyone else. Students have made fun of me since I tried to read in the third grade."

Mrs. Marty's eyes brightened when I told her this. She had solved my problem and announced to herself and me my problems stemmed from low self-esteem.

At the next session, she kept asking, "Brad why do you take these drugs knowing what happens when you do?"

I studied her face for a long time. She didn't have a clue about addictions. "Mrs. Marty," I said, "It's not a matter of deciding. It's like I am two people—my real self—then this addicted person who has no will of my own. I can't stop doing drugs even though I know I've hurt my parents so many times. I've disappointed them. They are good parents and don't deserve to have a son like I've become. I'm always in trouble. Now I have more problems. Other parents are telling their kids not to come around me. The Judge thinks I am a danger to others and to myself. I don't know what to do."

I gave her a searching look wanting her to give me an answer. She stared back at me, then she got up and got the schedule book to set up my next appointment. I left the office knowing she didn't have any answers and would be of no help to me.

At the last session, she said, "You need to appreciate what you have—good parents, and a good home. You need to apologize to your parents for what you have put them through."

I knew she had gotten this one thing right, but after the sessions ended, I did not feel I could deal with my problems or be any more prepared to resist drugs than I had been, though I did apologize to my parents as she suggested. Counseling sessions had gotten me to talk about myself and to see the hopelessness of my situation. But nothing had changed. I remained addicted, but for small amounts of time, I tried to fool myself into thinking I would try to stay away from drugs.

That summer I worked construction with my Dad, so I always had money which I saved. He never asked what I did with the money he paid me. I guess he thought as long as I worked around him I would do better. It stayed in control except for the weekends. I always took chances on the weekends.

A few months after I had started working for Dad and after I had been on probation, I went to Dave's Pizza Parlor and enjoyed a large pizza and a pitcher of beer. Who would ever believe Burt Treats, my probation officer, would walk right in off the street?

How he and I came to be in the same place while I had beer sitting on the table, I'll never know. I sat right up front at a table by the window not back in a dimly lit corner. No way to miss me. I came in here often with a group of Dad's construction guys to have pizza. When Dad didn't come with us, the guys would order a pitcher of beer, so I would just help myself and none of them said anything to me about being underage. I guess the manager did not want to rile me, either. So when I went in alone and ordered, he didn't hesitate to serve me.

There were quite a few situations in my life where people just turned away and didn't want to get involved in matters concerning me. I guess people who liked and respected my Dad felt so sorry his son ran wild on drugs, so they just shook their heads and turned a blind eye.

Burt came right over and sat down beside me. He had, by this time, learned how to be tactful in handling me. He said, "Look Brad, I've got another parole officer with me. I just can't let you get by with drinking. You're only fifteen. What do you think I should do?"

He knew if he didn't handle me just right, I would bolt and run, maybe even go through the glass window if I thought it necessary, to get away. He studied me, searchingly not knowing what to do. I just kept eating my pizza. "Just let me finish my beer," I said.

After I finished my meal, I went back to the office with Burt for counseling and to be written up for breaking parole as a fifteen year old who should not be drinking beer.

Drinking out in public showed a blatant disregard for authority he said. As far as I knew, the manager of Dave's Pizza Parlor never got into trouble for serving beer to a minor.

My Dad read in the Bible, "Raise up a child in the way he should go and he will not depart from it." He watched me and prayed for me. I knew this and sometimes I tried my best, but at other times, I plowed headlong into the destructions that seemed to be waiting for me.

17.
A Riot in High School

My school days were about to come to an end for a long time. At the beginning of the school year, I started the ninth grade at Stoneybrook High School, the local public school about five miles from Oakdale. The school system socially promoted me to the ninth grade even though, I had missed an entire six months of the eighth grade. They would never consider holding a fifteen year old back in Middle School. My height and age made that impossible.

I had been clean most of the summer while I worked with Dad. I had only done drugs a few times on the weekend, but when school started, drugs were all around me. There were two things I especially liked about high school. I'd never seen a place with so many drugs and so many good looking girls, everywhere. Everyone did drugs, or at least the people I knew. On most days, by noon, many in the crowd I moved in were stoned. Acid and THC flowed as prevalent as water at the water fountain.

I had all the money I needed for drugs as I had saved money all summer when I worked with Dad. I could get drugs in the hallways or out back of the school in the parking lot. I stayed high on pot. Several times I laid out of school and stayed up in the woods watching the school from a distance just to feel cool about it.

The drug culture that had moved into the communities now

invaded the schools. Most of the students here who did not do drugs knew what went on, but stayed away from those of us who did. All of the teachers were realizing this problem. I think most of the parents were like mine. They were unaware until their children were addicted and then they didn't know what to do or where to turn for help.

Mrs. Payton, the school counselor, tried to do something with me. She saw me in the hallway, stoned, and pulled me into her office. "Brad, you're so stoned you can't even stand up. Here, sit in my office until it's time to go home."

Mrs. Payton talked to me. She tried to keep me in school and tried to keep me from being expelled. Her concern reminded me of what Mrs. Kontz tried to do for me back in the seventh grade. It's nice when people, like teachers, really care what happens to you.

Although Mrs. Payton, a likeable person, did her best to keep me out of trouble, I stayed as miserable as I could be. I felt like a ball of static electricity rolling down the hill with sparks and fire coming out of it. I felt uncontrollable and that my life was not worth living.

One morning during the week of mid-term tests, I laid up in the woods, taking the day off, doing barbiturates. I had a mayonnaise jar lid and five yellow barbiturates. I dissolved the barbs in a little water, put them in a syringe, and thought I could run them up all at one time. I wasn't aware I might really be trying to kill myself. Maybe with this act I reached out for help. I put the needle in my vein and immediately got the death rush. I had more barbs, and knew if I took any more I would overdose, so I tossed them down through the woods. In doing this, I made one last conscious effort in trying not to overdose.

The next thing I knew, I stood in front of Mr. Upson smoking a cigarette and cursing him out. I glanced to my left and there stood Mrs. Payton staring at me. Dennis Brown, a big guy on the football team, stood beside her looking tough. They obviously had called him to handle me if

I got out of control. Dennis sold hundred of hits of drugs there at school, but Mr. Upson didn't know about his drug activity.

Mr. Upson said, "Dennis, get him out of here."

Because of the drugs surging through my body, I hit the floor before he could grab me. When he leaned over to help me up, I hit him in the face. He backed off. I got up and took off, staggered through the lunch room. I staggered through the parking lot and fell, hitting my ribs on the curb.

As I tried to stand, a maintenance worker tackled me. Mr. Upson caught up with me and helped the maintenance worker hold me down. I quit resisting as my ribs were hurting badly, so I just lay there thinking what to do. I knew I needed a chance to run. I wanted to run.

A policeman arrived on the scene, handcuffed me, and put me into the back of his patrol car parked beside the school parking lot.

The school bell rang and the students started coming to the outside area where they went to smoke during their break. Soon, this area filled with students. Some of my drug buddies come over to the car to help me out. They opened the door, and I got out. I thought I could get away, but I couldn't stand up to run. If I hadn't been high, I could have bolted and ran like a rabbit. The cop put me back in the car, but before he could drive off, some of the kids opened the door again.

The word had gotten around the school, and my friends and lots of other kids were really mad about the cop trying to take me away. This young rookie cop didn't think to call for backup. He got the doors locked, but before he could drive away about fifty to seventy-five students came running out and started to riot. They started shaking the car and rocking it. Some rocked the patrol car and others got in front of it so we couldn't leave. They started chanting, "Let Brad out, let Brad out!" I felt like crying. Ashamed, I glanced at my friends, thinking, my life is so full of trouble. Are the drugs worth it? I could understand why people on drugs wanted to commit suicide when they were as involved in drugs as I had been.

The teachers and principal gathered around, trying to control the crowd. As the principal cleared the drive for the patrol car to leave, I glimpsed Mrs. Payton standing close by on the sidewalk. She had tears in her eyes. As I looked at all the students, I clenched my fists and clinched my jaws in anger. I knew many of these students were doing drugs too and even selling them. They were as guilty as me, but I had gotten arrested.

As we finally drove away, I raised my hand slightly as if to say, "Sorry, thank you, but good-bye." Mrs. Payton waved back slowly. She lowered her head and gave me a weak smile.

The patrol car headed down Oakdale Road. All the time I wondered how could I get out of the car and run. The rookie cop smoked a cigarette, so I said, "Give me a cigarette."

"I'm not giving you a cigarette."

I started kicking the back of the seat and the doors. "Give me a damn cigarette! Give me a damn cigarette!" Finally, he pulled the patrol car over and gave me a one. I took it and said, "Where are we going?"

"Fulton General Hospital."

"Put my handcuffs in front of me."

He made a smart move when he took one of the handcuffs and hooked it to the window grid between us, freeing my other hand. I started feeling an overdose coming over me. "Why don't you go faster? Why don't you turn on the blue light?" I fell over onto the seat, as stoned as I could be and yet still conscious. I had a plan. I held the cigarette in my mouth so the end of it touched the upholstery.

He stopped the car and came back there. "Are you all right? Are you all right?"

I purposefully held my breath to make him think I'd passed out. Holding my breath also kept me from inhaling the smoke coming from the burning seat covers. The policeman got on the radio and called in,

"This is an emergency. I have an overdose. I am in route to Fulton General Hospital. Arrival time approximately five minutes." He turned on his blue light and siren and sped toward the hospital.

When he turned in the emergency lane, I sat up and said, "Rock and roll man. You were giving it hell." He looked at me like he could kill me. He knew he'd been had. Two ambulance attendants were waiting for me at the emergency entrance. They put me on a gurney, and ran with me to the emergency room to check for vital signs. They gave me ipecac to clear my stomach of the drugs. This straightened me up somewhat.

They then put me in a private room with an old, old security guard. Here I am—a strapping, young buck full of hell, piss, and vinegar and this old man intended to guard me? He started to lock the door. "Don't you lock that door," I demanded. "I can't take the confinement." I felt like a wild animal. I guess I had been acting like a wild animal.

After the attendants got me into the bed, the guard locked the door anyway. I got a chair and started beating the hell out of the door. The door opened. "Please don't make my day any harder," he said. "If I leave the door open, do you promise not to run?"

"Yes." I fell asleep.

When Dad got home from work, the counselor at school called and told him they had tried to reach him all day. She told him I been arrested and taken to the hospital. He and Mom came and one of them stayed with me until I woke up—two days later.

When I awoke, a doctor checked my blood pressure. "Your blood pressure's finally coming down," He said. "You might make it after all." I immediately began a plan to escape. Dad stayed a while, then left for work. I slept until they served my lunch. I finished with my tray, went into the rest room, dressed, and went into the hallway when the old guard wasn't looking. I pushed my food cart down the hallway pretending to be hospital worker in charge of picking up the trays. I pushed the cart to the door of the stairway and then went down three flights of stairs and out through the woods near the hospital. I hitched a ride to Oakdale before anyone missed me.

When I got to Oakdale though, I didn't go home. Being on the run, I went to the Old Macedonia Cemetery to Uncle Sycamore grave. I knew the cops would never think to look there for me. I sat in the cemetery in the quiet next to the Sycamore's tombstone for hours. Strangely enough it gave me some comfort to sit there and remember Sycamore and his kindness to me in the past. I thought about the drugs and all the trouble I had caused and what I had done to those who loved me. I did some heavy contemplating and reflecting.

I had been so focused on myself and my problems, I felt like there could be nothing else or no one else in the world. I didn't know what to do to stop. No matter what happened, I always wanted more drugs. My life since age nine had been centered around doing drugs and getting high, to suppress my feelings, and to try and cover up the pain.

I left the cemetery and began running down the railroad tracks toward home. The wind blew my hair and a light rain started falling, mixing with the tears already on my face. I asked God to help me, but I didn't feel worthy of Him even hearing me. Dusk came and I looked up at the sky as the wind picked up. I had the impression that God told me, "If you'll just come to Me, everything will be okay."

But how could I go to God with all the things I had done and the trouble I had been in? I did not understand how He would ever accept and forgive me.

When I went into the house, Dad had gotten ready to leave for the hospital. No one from the hospital had called today to tell him I had escaped, so he looked surprised when I opened the back door and stepped into the kitchen. He came to me, put his hand on my shoulder, and said, "Come, let's sit at the kitchen table and talk."

I guess he could tell by the looks of me I had been through a lot this afternoon. I sat down, and put my head in my hands. He didn't say anything, but put on a pot of coffee. I could feel him glancing at me. Maybe he thought about what to say to me or how to help me or maybe he prayed for me. When he did sit down, he said gently, "Son, what are you going to do?"

He didn't tell me what I should do. He didn't reprimand me or scold me. I felt relieved Mom wasn't home now because I just needed to think.

Dad and I talked for an hour. I told him how badly I felt about my behavior and my mistakes and how I didn't seem to have any willpower over the drugs. I told him about my frustration and about not knowing what to do with myself.

"What's the right thing to do now?" Dad asked. "Well, I guess I need to call the authorities and turn myself in."

I called Burt Treats and told him Dad would bring me in to be booked at eight o'clock, after supper. Mom came in and we told her what had happened. She went into the bedroom and cried for an hour while Dad fixed supper for us.

When Dad called us to supper, Mom dried her tears, and we sat down. Dad said a prayer and we ate. Mom didn't say much.

After dinner, Dad took me in to be booked. They charged me for being on drugs at school and for running away from the hospital. They set a hearing date for two months later.

Pleasure. That had been mine, for a while. Sometimes pleasure is a sin; sometimes sin is a pleasure. There is a kind of pleasure I knew to be wrong, but I did it anyway savoring each moment. I had pushed the fear of consequence so far back into my mind I found it astounding when I had to pay the price.

18.
Concert

With being home every day now, I don't know what to do with myself. The Fulton County School System decided to dismiss me permanently. I would never be allowed to return to school. The day of my arrest when the patrol car took me away from high school became my last day to attend public school. This day, my education ended. Since I stayed home with Mom and Dad I vowed I would try to stay out of trouble. I almost succeeded.

Then I went to a party next door at the Walker's house. When I went in, Mrs. Walker gave me a warning look. I remembered the day I walked down the street toward my house when she had gone inside, and locked the door. Tonight, Mrs. Walker came over to me, "Brad, I don't trust you as far as I could throw you. I've heard a lot of bad things about you. But since you are home with your parents now and not allowed to go to school, I hope you will turn yourself around and do better. You can stay at this party for my girls, but I'll be watching you." She turned and walked away before I could answer.

The Walker's lived in a nice brick house with a full basement that had a pool table in the center of the very large room. This was a perfect place for a party. After Deputy Sheriff Walker had divorced his wife, he left her this house to raise their two daughters, Teresa and Renee. Mrs.

Walker stayed upstairs, but came down occasionally to bring trays of food. I knew she checked on us at the same time.

She did not see the tub filled with iced-down beer Teresa had hidden behind the sofa next to the wall. She had no idea the kids had any beer. Some danced to very loud music, but mostly we just hung out and talked. Everything remained pretty calm.

Then Jimmy Henderson and Franky Frank came walking through the door. I went over to see if Franky would even talk to me. "Sorry about your Dad's car. I guess I shouldn't have taken the LSD 25. It really blew my brains." He studied me like he didn't quite know what to say.

Jimmy remarked, "Brad Berkshire, you are a dangerous character." We all laughed at this. Jimmy told Franky, "The last time I saw this guy he had me on the back of his motorcycle going ninety-mile-an-hour and a cop was shooting at me." We laughed again.

Franky replied, "The last time I saw him, he drove my Daddy's car right out of the driveway, went on a joy ride, wrecked it, and now it's at the dump—ruined."

We three were quiet for a second, then I said "What about a beer?" We each got one from the tub hidden behind the sofa. After that we lightened up. Everybody there drank beer, talked about beer, and got drunk. Most of the kids at the party were fifteen as Jimmy, Franky and I were, and they had never drank beer. So we made a big deal of going around putting salt in their beer telling them it tasted better with salt. They each agreed.

As the party progressed, we began to smoke marijuana and listen to Led Zeppelin on the record player. Franky and Jimmy got so drunk they couldn't stand up, so we started giggling at them. Then we sat down in front of the television. Mrs. Walker came down and saw us all watching the Midnight Special on TV. She said, "I heard all of you laughing. I guess you are having a good time?" She looked doubtful. When she went back upstairs, I looked at Franky's orange-red hair and the million freckles on his face.

"What are you looking at?" He demanded.

I started laughing and couldn't stop. I almost lost my breath I laughed so hard. "Jimmy, look at Franky. His freckles are all twirling around like sparkles."

We started calling him 'Franky Farkles.' I'm not sure he liked us laughing at him.

"Brad, your laugh sounds just like your Daddy's laugh." Jimmy said. "I could tell you were here when I came in the driveway. I could hear you laughing all the way out there."

By the end of the party there were no hard feelings from Freddy about his Daddy's car. "I know you were high, man, and you didn't know what you were doing."

"Let's go to the Led Zeppelin concert tomorrow night," Jimmy suggested. We agreed.

The next night, Saturday, I started out to a concert, but Mom wanted to keep me home. She had gotten desperate to keep me straight. I got ready to go out of the house, and she told me I couldn't go. I left anyway.

Mom ran into the yard after me trying to reason with me not to go. I ignored her and kept on walking. "Come back here. Don't you leave this yard," she demanded. I laughed at her. "Don't you laugh at me. You come back here."

"My life is so bloody miserable, I've got to laugh." She ran halfway of the yard toward me and stopped. She listened to what I said. "Laughing eases my pain. I'm in a living hell. I can't read. I'm expelled. I'm addicted to drugs. I've got to go to the concert. That's all there is for me." I felt a lot of anger and again started walking out of the yard. When I got to our bridge, I caught a glimpse of something flying past my head and heard a thud. She had picked up a rock and had thrown it, just missing my head. As I turned around, the next rock hit me square in the mouth. As I wiped away the blood, all of a sudden I saw things her way.

"Bradley Elijah Berkshire, I'm not letting you go to a concert where there will be drugs. You'll get into trouble again."

"Yes Ma'am," I said and followed her back into the house.

Later that night, I raised my window, slipped out, and went with my friends to the concert at the Atlanta Stadium. I felt guilty going against my Mom and disobeying her. I knew I might regret it, but I planned on getting high. I couldn't help myself.

When we went to a concert, you couldn't buy from the crowd since the police watched everyone, so we had to take our own drugs. The cops checked people randomly. So each time a different one of us carried the drugs. Sometimes none of us carried anything, so when the police stopped all of us and searched, they found nothing. I surely didn't want to get caught with a lot of drugs on me this time, being on probation already. So tonight I concealed what I had. I put my drugs in the corner of a small sandwich bag, sealed it by burning the edges with my cigarette lighter and put this corner of the bag into my ear canal. Then I pulled my long hair down over it. If I had been searched, the police would never have thought to look in my ear.

We had general admission tickets and held our position up against the gate. Time went by quickly as we were just trying to keep standing on our feet. I decided to take my acid, a purple microdot, right then. A brother standing in line saw me, "Hey man, you didn't take the whole thing did you?"

"Yea," I growled back, already feeling the effects of the drugs.

He sounded shocked, "That's a four way hit. You took enough for four people."

I had some liquor hidden in my jacket, and I swallowed some. I knew better than to do this, but with the crowd and the heat of the moment, I chose to do the wrong thing. Immediately, I threw up—a good way to get a little room in the crowd. There were so many people pressed up against the gate it couldn't open. Sheer madness, and sheer chaos ran through the crowd. Finally the gates opened. I had my ticket. I went over the top of the turnstile and just did get the ticket to the man taking them.

When the gates opened and everyone ran to get front row seats, the acid I had taken made everything appear to be moving. I saw things that weren't even there. I saw designs and patterns. I really tripped. I got hotter and hotter. I got higher and higher. I saw the stadium appear to roll and melt. I couldn't believe I had gotten to this point trippin'. People were running and knocking against me. I need to move away, I thought. My high made moving people blur into streaks. All kinds of sounds ran together. It didn't make sense. People appeared to be monsters from outer space. I've got scrambled eggs for brains, I thought. I learned later sixty thousand people were in attendance at this concert.

The next thing I knew I stood at the top of the stadium. I looked toward the city of Atlanta beyond. The skyscrapers waved backward. Buildings were deformed and flowed down like melting candles. My heart beat with the thud of the drums when the opening band, Deep Purple, started playing. Then Led Zeppelin started with "Stairway to Heaven."

I thought I had another hallucination when I looked down toward the stage and saw white objects rising up, flying higher and higher toward the in a night sky. The stage, the audience, and the sky was filling with a haze. I wondered what this could be as I stood there confused. The music and lyrics washed over me. Later found out hundreds of doves were released and flew upward in smoke blowing from the stage.

Afterward, I don't remember any of the concert, any of the music. I woke up in a stolen car driven by a stranger stoned out of his head. I managed to tell him Oakdale and he managed to drive there. He let me out somewhere close to Oakdale. I got home, somehow, and eased up my bedroom window without waking my parents. Then I fell into my bed and passed out.

The hippies were under an illusion with their idea of "peace and love." This idea became a farce as there could have been nothing farther from the truth. With drugs, there could be no peace and love but only meanness and a whole lot of hell to go through. Since I had started drugs, I'd become a slave to the habit and I'd lost my freedom. Drugs became first in my life and everything else became second—my friends, my family, and now, even my life.

19.
Prodigal Son

The next day, I decided I needed to leave town, to leave my parents, and to leave everyone I knew. I started hitching north on I-75. One day later, I found myself in Lexington, Kentucky.

I walked the streets until dark then I became lost and thought I might be mugged. I headed for a park I saw up ahead. I found a secluded area and lay down behind a high wall. Though the weather chilled me to the bone and I had to sleep on the ground, I fell right to sleep. At two a.m., I awoke with an awful conviction telling me I should not be there. This is wrong. Here I've left my parents, and they don't know where I am, I thought to myself.

I felt condemned. I sat up and put my head in my hands. I sat like this a few minutes. A strong power started coming over me to go back home. I started walking back toward the interstate in the middle of the night. I had an overwhelming desire to call my parents, so I found a pay phone. Dad surprised me when he answered on the first ring. "Dad I'm in Lexington, Kentucky. I'm sleeping in a park. I don't know where to go."

"Son, you need to come home."

I started hitching, but I didn't make it home until the next night. When I came into the house, Dad sat at the table like he had been waiting for me. He stood up and put his arm around me and said, "The Prodigal

Son has returned."

I hugged him and as I sat down at the table I said, "I don't know anything about a Prodigal Son, but I hope he felt as happy as I do to get home. Tears welled up in his eyes, and he asked, "Are you hungry, Son?"

As I filled my plate with left-overs from supper, he said, " I don't have but this one biscuit left, but you can have it," he said as he put it on my plate. Then he said, "The Prodigal Son is a story in the Bible about a wayward son who goes away from his father and gets into a lot of trouble for a long time. Then he returns and the father rejoices."

Then he began to talk about what happened when he found I had left. "Last night, late, I went out to the big rock there in the backyard and sat down at the picnic table and prayed for God to show me where you were—to let me hear from you. I cried and prayed and cried and prayed. I came back to the house and then went back to the big rock and prayed again. I came back in and that's when the phone rang. That's when you called and said you were coming home."

As I ate and listened, I realized that at two a.m. when I awakened and had the overwhelming desire to go home and to call home is exactly when Dad sat on the big rock out back praying for me. I thought about what Dad said about the Prodigal Son from the Bible. I guess I must be a type of Prodigal Son.

After I had been home only a few days, Rooster came over. Rooster knew I had ran away as Dad had called him looking for me. I hadn't seen Rooster in quite a while since his Dad had told him he couldn't come over after I had been expelled. It felt good to see him. Rooster had grown up quite a bit and had put on a lot of weight. He had let his brown hair grow to the top of his collar, but it wasn't nearly as long as mine. He didn't look the part of a hippie as I did. I missed not riding our motorcycles together like we did for a while.

Then we went to one of our secret hangouts at Dead Horse Road down by Split Rock Creek. The stillness lay peaceful as the babbling of the water ran over the rocks in the creek in this secluded place. We lay back on the high, granite rocks there and smoked pot and got high. We sat there for hours. I looked up at the cold, sparkling, night sky. The stars were clear and bright. I felt insignificant when I studied the sky and felt as small as a grain of sand.

I had a worried mind turning the same old thoughts over and over. As a small boy in church, I had been taught, "*Be ye perfect as I am perfect.*" The church members talked about holiness and purity. I knew in my heart, I wasn't holy or pure. I felt like I couldn't live up to the standards of the church—I couldn't be better than everybody else like the church goers taught. God said the ten commandments were the rule, and if you broke one commandment, then you were guilty of breaking all of them. Well, I saw no way out.

"What are you doing? Contemplating life?" Rooster asked.

His question shocked me. I didn't think Rooster ran that deep. "Yeah. I was thinking about what would happen to me if I don't quit drugs."

"I've thought about quitting myself," Rooster said. He stood up and began pacing back and forth as he talked. "I don't take drugs like you do—not nearly as much. My Dad is always on me, watching me. I've never had the money for drugs like you have had—working with your Dad like you did last summer. I know I'm not addicted like you are. I figure I will get all I can and enjoy it while I'm young." He started to strut and to brag. "When I grow up, I'm going to trade school and then get a good job. Then I'll quit doing drugs—after I'm on my own."

"Rooster, I hope you *can* quit when you make that decision. I feel like I'm an old man, but I'm just fifteen. Rooster, I don't know what to do." We walked back, slowly. The night turned cold and rainy. As we walked, I wondered if God rolled the dice in my life. I knew better. I knew

I had made wrong decisions and had only myself to blame. Sin takes you further than you want to go. It robs you of your happiness. When we got to my house, I told Rooster to come over more often.

He left and I went into the house about supper time. I could smell roast cooking. Mom stood in the kitchen dishing up the food. "Son, I fixed smashed potatoes, macaroni and cheese, roast, and homemade yeast rolls." She said. "You are going to eat aren't you?"

I walked past her and went into my room. I forgot to close the door because I had done drugs earlier with Rooster and hadn't come down. In a second, I had the syringe out shooting up when I heard someone say, "Brad, what are you doing?"

I glanced up. Dad stood there watching me. I pushed the syringe down and missed my vein. The drugs went into my arm, making a knot. I grabbed the three or four pills on my night stand and popped them into my mouth.

"I'm leaving, Dad," I said.

"No, you're not." Dad tried to keep me from going out the door, but at only five-seven and a hundred and fifty pounds he could not stop me. He tried to hold me back, but couldn't. I pushed right past him. He ran after me and grabbed me by the arm. We struggled in the yard. I didn't want to hurt him. I pulled away. He ran after me. "If I can't handle you, I know who can," he yelled. When I got to the bridge, he called after me, "Don't cross that bridge!"

I didn't look back, but I knew he went down on his knees.

I staggered up the road. A cold, drizzling rain started to fall. I don't remember much but was told later what happened. Dad went next door to Mrs. Walker's house. She called her husband, the deputy sheriff, and he notified the police. Within a short time a search party of about fifty people started looking for me. Mr. Goodson from the Busy Bee, and Rex and Jed from Pac-A-Sac's Groceries came out to join the search party.

Rooster had gotten Tophat off work at the Tastee Freeze and both of them joined the group. Almost everyone in Oakdale joined the search. They were concerned about me taking an overdose.

In just a few minutes, Deputy Walker had police cars with their blue lights flashing, swarming everywhere. Patrolmen and volunteers canvassed every house within Oakdale area to ask if anyone had seen me. They went down every street in town, in every back alley, and through any store, still open. Every patron in the store began to search.

By this time, the temperature had fallen to thirty-five degrees and the rain really came down which made it tough for the search party. Mr. Goodson from Busy Bee General Store searched the playground of Fitzgerald Elementary School with Mayor Mortimer who followed on his three wheel scooter. "Brad! wh'r ar' ya?" He kept calling out into the cold night. They didn't find anything. Everyone got cold, wet, and tired and about ten o'clock, everyone came together to decide whether to continue looking for me.

Mr. Goodson heard someone call through the darkness, "The search has been called off." Mortimer said, "Can't leave. Find Brad or he w'l die. I look again." As the two of them walked back by the concession stand again, Mortimer stopped and put his hand up and said, "I h'r cofin'."

Mr. Goodson listened, "I hear someone coughing, too."

They couldn't tell where the sound came from, but when they walked around the back of the concession stand they heard me cough again. Mortimer ran ahead and found me lying behind the concession stand in such a way the rain coming off the roof ran right into my mouth and ever so often, I coughed. If my neck had been at a different angle, the rain would not have gone into my mouth. I would not have coughed, and he would not have heard me in time. When Mr. Goodson called out, several people came and pulled at me and sat me up.

That's when I quit breathing. Someone did CPR, and the ambulance came immediately. The deputy rode with me to the hospital. At the hospital, the doctor gave me ipecac to drink. At first I resisted.

"If you don't drink this, we'll have to pump your stomach."

"Let me have it," I said.

They gave me a pan, and I threw up like nobody's business. I came to for a few minutes, then I hovered at the point of unconsciousness. The hospital admitted me. When Dad arrived shortly afterward, the doctor told him if Mr. Goodson and Mortimer had not found me when they did, and I would probably have died. I guess Dad got the kind of help he asked for, help from the Lord.

I stayed for about twenty-four hours, and when the nurse left the room, I took off out the door. I went into the night. A couple of hours later, I walked out of town hitchhiking to Marietta when my sister, Kay, pulled off the curb in front of me to give me a ride. She had been driving around, on this, another cold, rainy winter night, looking for me. When I did not run to her car and get in, she got out and came to me as I walked down the road passed her car. "Brad, I'm here to give you a ride. This weather is terrible. You don't need to be out in it." I just continued to walk, ignoring her. I didn't want to go home and face everybody. "Brad, come with me. You can come to my house. Where are you going?"

I hollered back to her, "I just can't go back with you, Sis."

I walked faster and kept thumbing. A car pulled over and I got in and rode with this stranger. I glanced back and saw Kay standing there, looking dismayed. I made it to the Marietta apartment where I had lived on the weekends three years ago when I had been just twelve—the summer before my seventh grade. When I walked in, none of the guys noticed. I saw Fat Jack sleeping in the corner, and there were a few new guys. I didn't see Don Pace. All of them were stoned as usual. I found an old mattress on the floor in the back bedroom and slept it off for several days.

After a few days, I woke up feeling weak and very hungry. I called the house. Mom answered, "Oh Brad. We didn't know what happened to you. Where have you been? Are you okay? Why didn't you come home with Kay?"

"Can you pick me up in Marietta? I want to come home." I met her within the hour and she drove me home. After a while I knew what I had to do. I dialed my probation officer. Burt Treats answered, "Well I'm ready to give myself up." We talked for a few minutes. He told me to come to his office the next morning. They added another drug possession charge to my offenses and reminded me my court date came up in one month.

I thought, I'm a lost child causing suffering, pain, and misery not only for myself but for everyone involved. I hate this horrible way I live. I realized there was nothing nice about me now really. Love? No one loved me. Maybe my parents, but they surely were angry and didn't know what to do with me. Maybe God still loved me. My mind had been clouded so long with drugs, I didn't want to know what God thought about me. What happened the next week changed my life forever.

20.
Girl of my Dreams

After I came home, I tried to recover from the physical and mental exhaustion I suffered during the drug overdose and from staying at the Marietta apartment "sleeping" it off. When Jimmy Henderson invited me to a party at his house, I refused. Later he called again insisting. I almost didn't go. But the way things turned out, my life changed for the better after the party.

I walked in late. Everyone turned to look when I came into the room. I suddenly stopped when I saw the most beautiful girl I had ever seen. There she stood—the girl of my dreams. It happened just like that. She looked at me for a lingering second, but then lowered her eyes. I wasn't expecting shyness. Or does mean she's not interested? I thought, I don't think so. Her look would not have lingered. This girl was intriguing. I had never been around a shy girl. I thought this new age of free love, sex, and rock and roll had affected every young person.

I moved around the crowd to get a better look at her. What a knockout! She had a small, slender, shapely body that just wouldn't quit. She wore jeans, and a black low-cut, sequined blouse. Her silver chain necklace had one black teardrop stone laying close to the crease between her full breasts. Her black hair flowed down her back like silk and fell across her breast when she tilted her head forward. She had soft brown eyes that were interested in me, but for some reason, guarded. I couldn't take my eyes off her.

A guy walked over to her and said, "Hi, Baby," and smiled at her. He moved in close, too close, and I watched to see her reaction.

She took a step back and said firmly but not unkindly, "I'm not your Baby. I'm not anybody's Baby." Then she turned her back and walked away toward some friends she had come with. Wow! I thought to myself. Independent. And not a pushover. She definitely had my interest. I had to know more before I approached her. I didn't want her to walk away from me. I found out her name—Julie Wallace. She had just turned eighteen and had already graduated from high school. Someone told me she played hard to get. I'd turn sixteen in a few months, but I hoped I appeared to be older, so, I thought, maybe I would have a chance with her.

She kept glancing my way. I knew she knew I watched her. I made my way over to her and said, "Hi, I'm Brad. How are you?"

She smiled. "I'm Julie and I'm fine."

"Yes, you are," I said in a slow observant way. She smiled again. My heart flipped. She had clear skin, a broad face and fascinating dimples appearing and disappearing when she smiled or talked. I felt spellbound.

She continued to gaze up at me. I could feel the attraction between us. I found it hard to think of something to talk about because I just kept staring at her, memorizing her. I took her over to get some punch. I motioned to the sofa and we sat down together. I asked her where she lived, how she came to be at the party, and if she knew anyone here. At first she answered just what I asked. "I'm a friend of Jimmy's brother," she said. "I'm from Marietta, and I came with some girlfriends."

"And you're not very talkative." She really smiled then. "What do you like—what do you like to do?" Her eyes brightened at this question. "Oh. I love animals—any animal. And I love to ride horses."

"Do you have a horse?"

"Oh no. I ride my grandaddy's horse. Grandaddy has a farm and I go there." She really opened up after that, telling me about herself. She told me she had a job as a secretary and had an apartment and a car. This girl seemed to have higher standards than any of the other girls I had been around lately. She walked with dignity and acted more like a respectful young lady.

We started slow dancing. I didn't hold her close to me, as I didn't want to scare her off by coming on too strongly. But I could feel the chemistry. When we finished dancing, we went back to the sofa and talked about many things.

Later, there were a few couples at the party doing reefer who also had a few beer too many and were talking loudly and having a little too good of time. She glanced toward them, "I don't like to hear vulgar talk. I don't think people should act that way."

This one night, I did not do any drugs. "I would like to see you again if you would give me your phone number," I said as I studied her. She wrote her phone number down on a piece of paper she got from her purse. Then she tucked the folded note into my shirt pocket, slowly and seductively, while she gazed at me. I think she blushed slightly, as she lowered her head. Then she did the unexpected. "I like your hair." She reached out and stroked my long hair and let her fingers linger on my neck for a moment. My heart really did a flip.

I called her the next morning—Saturday. She said she would pick me up in Oakdale at Daniel's Grocery where I waited out front for her. I paced in front of Daniel's hoping nothing would go wrong and she would come. Then she drove up in her Chevrolet Malibu. On the clear, late winter day, we drove to Kennesaw Mountain Battlefield Park, north of Marietta. At the park, we found a picnic table out in the sun and had lunch. I spread a blanket on the early green grass, and we sat in the warm sunshine and talked all afternoon. We sat on the blanket close enough that I could smell her perfume. She wore jeans, a low cut, black cotton blouse with a ruffle around the top and a black, lace choker around her neck. I kept thinking, she is a "living doll." That's what she reminded me of—a doll on a shelf. She took off her sun glasses. Then I could see those soft brown eyes.

We drank some wine and talked about life. I wanted her so badly I couldn't stand it, but I played it cool. She flirted with me, but I didn't want to move too fast. She really stirred my blood when she took a long blade of grass and ran it slowly across my face and neck. The seductive look in her eyes told me she felt the same as I did.

I reached out and pulled her into my arms giving her a long, warm embrace. She lay her head on my shoulder momentarily. I tilted her chin up and kissed her lips lingeringly, thoroughly. We went back to her apartment and had an afternoon of passion I won't forget. My earlier experience with women caused me to be confident that I could be a good lover. I know she never guessed I was just fifteen. I felt like I had fallen totally and madly in love.

Every day afterward, we talked on the phone and made plans for the weekend. I worked with Dad during the week and saved money to take Julie out each weekend. We ate at the Pizza Parlor in Oakdale several times. We stayed at her apartment some, and she cooked for me.

One weekend we went to the North Georgia National Forrest and drove aimlessly, four or five miles down a winding mountain path. We found a grassy knoll, spread a blanket and made love. Peace and beauty spread all around us. We began to plan to be together. We couldn't stay apart. I couldn't think of anything else but Julie. I even forgot about drugs.

I told Mom and Dad about having a girlfriend. We dated for several months, then I took Julie to meet my parents. Dad's eyes brightened when he saw Julie come into the kitchen with me. He said, "Well, Bradley, you're right, she is very beautiful." She smiled sweetly as she took Dad's hand. He broke into a broad smile and looked smitten. When Mom came into the kitchen, she greeted Julie, "How are you?" Then she gave Dad a glance as he was still smiling from ear to ear. Dad offered Julie a seat at the kitchen table, then some apple pie topped with vanilla ice cream. Mom joined us and started asking questions. She seemed impressed Julie had already graduated and had a good job. Mom continued to be polite, but I think she might have been a little jealous that I had another woman in my life beside herself.

Then Julie invited me to meet her parents, Wilson and Jewell Wallace, at their home close to Kennesaw Mountain. We pulled up to a very nice ranch style house on five acres. Daffodils and azalea bushes in full bloom covered the immediate area around the house. As we went to the side door, Julie said, "Mom does all this. She gardens more than she stays inside." As we opened the door, I saw her Dad leaning back in a recliner in the den with his eyes closed listening to the stereo where Patsy Cline belted out, *I Fall to Pieces*. As Julie ran to the stereo to turn the volume down, she explained her Dad had the music very loud because he had been almost deaf all of his adult life. He had not even heard us come into the house.

Right then, Julie's Mom came in the door just behind us, fussing. "I have to stay outside in my garden. I can't stand the stereo playing so loudly. He loves his Patsy Cline. He plays it over and over."

Wilson opened his eyes when Julie turned off the stereo. As he stood, I saw his back was curved so much it caused him to stoop, severely. He had the stature of someone appearing to be looking at something on a low table. He tilted his head upward and studied me as he extended his hand. I shook hands with him. "So you're Brad. Our Julie is so crazy about you, and I'm glad to meet you." He pumped my hand as he talked.

"Here, have a seat." He indicated the sofa.

He began telling me about himself and about his past. He explained why he was so stooped. He told me his spine had been gradually stooping more and more for ten years. I learned he lost his hearing as a child when he had an ear infection that went untreated. He began to tell me about his past, and about where he lived in the mountains. "We didn't have doctors and if we had of, my family couldn't have afforded one. We were poor then." He told me about his accomplishments in the military and of being a supervisor over a hundred men, building airplanes. I had real admiration for this man. He seemed genuine and friendly. Wilson and Jewell had been married twenty-five years and had three children older than Julie who were already married and had children of their own. He talked cordially and friendly.

Jewell came in with a pitcher of iced tea and some homemade cookies. From the first instant I saw her I knew her to be a totally different, howdy-do person than I had ever met. This five-foot-two-hundred-pound woman had a pistol-packed personality. She wanted to know all the goings and comings of everything. She asked so many point blank questions, she came across as almost rude. Julie tried to show me off to her parents. Wilson accepted me, but I could tell already Jewell didn't know what to think of me. She asked, "Do you go to school?"

"Well, no Ma'am. I'm finished with school."

"Do you work?"

"Yes, Ma'am, I work with my Dad at his business."

"Are you one of those hippies we see on television? You look like one of them with your hair growing long."

"Well I guess I do look like them." After we finished our tea and cookies, Julie stood up and said we had to go. Somehow I could tell Jewell picked up on how my life had been and didn't trust me. Soon she would have a reason not to like me at all.

The next day, I called Julie to make plans for the weekend, but she said she couldn't talk. She told me she couldn't see me that weekend.

I felt confused. "Julie, are you mad? Have I hurt you?" Right then I wondered if Jewell disapproved of me so much that she had convinced Julie not to see me again. "But Julie, tell me why you can't see me."

"I just can't see you. I'm not feeling well. I'm staying in bed. I'm not in a good mood."

I had a brief happiness. Why did I think I deserved for it to continue? I had only done a little marijuana, once, since I had met Julie. I had felt hopeful, for the first time in a long time, that I could change. I would do it for her. Was she through with me? I stayed home in my room on Saturday. I felt stunned. Julie had acted like she loved me. I knew I loved her.

Kell called and said he had his Dad's car and wanted me to go riding with him. When I got into his Dad's car, I had a feeling I shouldn't go with Kell, and that I would regret it later.

21.
Upside Down in the Kudzu

I knew I had free will, but many times since the third grade, I had hung out with Kell and followed him and did what he did. I had steadily paid the consequences for my actions. Tonight, I followed Kell for the last time.

I told Kell about this beautiful Julie I had met. "Kell, I'm falling in love with her."

He really laughed at me. You're too young for that. I didn't tell him we had made love. I kept thinking about her as we started the night smoking THC. I got into a utopia-like state, but at the same time I felt a deadness, a numbness. This even seemed better than the pain I felt thinking I had lost Julie after such a short time.

We were really stoned in the wee hours of the morning when we got the idea to go fishing at West Point Lake in west Georgia. Kell drove his dad's Impala which was jacked up with air shocks, had slotted mag wheels, four in the floor, and a four-barreled carburetor. Man, this car looked hot. We felt as if we were invincible.

We headed out by way of the Atlanta Federal Penitentiary going around ninety in this hot rod with wide tires. I saw a twenty-five mile an hour S-curve sign fly by the passenger window. Kell stared straight ahead unflinching, as if he were frozen with his hands on the steering wheel and his foot on the accelerator. I heard a squall of tires as we hit the curve.

I saw a street light do a three-hundred-sixty-degree turn. I dove for the floorboard. Too late. I became airborne.

The car flew into the air, off a steep embankment and flipped. The car came to a stop two hundred feet down the side of an embankment, facing up the hill the way we had been going. When things got still, I realized we were upside down with the car on its roof in a kudzu patch. Green vines were all around us. I had burst out the dome light in the ceiling of the car with my chest. I felt like all the air had been pushed right out of my lungs.

My first thoughts were the police were coming, so I started to kicked out the windshield so I could run, but the windshield lay up against the ground. I crawled out the window on the passenger's side chunking beer cans out of the broken windows into the kudzu as I gazed up at the Federal Penitentiary knowing the guards had to be on their way. I tried to take a breath. I gasped. My chest felt like fire, but I managed to take in a breath.

I couldn't see Kell anywhere, so I crawled back into the car.

"Kell, Kell where are you?" We were so close to the Federal Pen I dared not call out as the guards might hear me.

I heard a moan from the back of the car. Kell had almost gone out the rear window. His head and upper body were lodged between the top of the rear window and the top of the back seat. He lay stretched out as if he were suspended in the air. I grabbed his feet and pulled him free. He gained consciousness.

We left the car and climbed the hill back up to the road. Even with the street lights and security lights from the Pen, when I looked back down the embankment, I could not see the car. The overgrowth of the thick green foliage of the kudzu covered everything including the car. No police or guards came from the Federal Pen. No one seemed to have heard the wreck or knew we were even there.

I realized Kell and I could have been killed and without the car being visible from the road it would have been a long time before our bodies would have ever been found.

Now Kell had a brilliant idea. "You think if we could flip the car over, we could drive it out?"

I didn't answer. I looked at him like he must be crazy and started walking back north toward Atlanta. The faint light of a rosy dawn lay all around the horizon and illuminated the skyscrapers of Atlanta in the distance. There were very few cars on the road. All the same, we didn't try to hitch a ride. We just walked. We were too bloody and banged up to be thumbing. If someone had picked us up, they would find out we had been in a wreck and would have reported us.

Finally, we came into a housing project, one of Atlanta's finest if you know what I mean. Here we were, two white boys at dawn knocking on doors. A black lady peered down at our white faces shining in the street light.

"We need help. We need a wrecker," I shouted up to her.

She said she would call one for us. We sat on the curb for an hour, but the wrecker never came. Then we found a pay phone and called for a wrecker ourselves.

Slim, a tall, curly haired laid back, out-of-place-for Atlanta looking guy picked us up, and we rode with him back out to the Federal Pen. When he pulled on the car, the front end of the wrecker came off the ground. He had to call for a bigger wrecker with a dolly. When this wrecker hoisted up on the Impala, we saw it had a flat top and all four tires were blown out. We rode with Slim in the larger wrecker to leave the car at the junkyard, then he gave us a lift back to Oakdale.

Back in Oakdale, I headed down Hill Street toward home. I don't want to be around Kell and his parents when they found out about the car and when all hell broke loose. I eased the kitchen door open. When I went into the kitchen at eight o'clock, my parents were having breakfast and gave me the eye when I came in. I said nothing about the events of the night.

"Son, where have you been? You know we are supposed to be in court at nine."

"Oh, I spent the night with Kell. Can I have some breakfast before we go?"

Mom served me biscuits and sausage and Dad went outside to the barn while Mom finished getting ready. I didn't tell them I had just been in a serious wreck and my chest still burned like fire.

When I showered, I saw abrasions, bruises, and cuts on my chest. I knew I had brought this on myself—my own doings and didn't wish anyone to know about last night. I put band-aids over the cuts on my chest and slipped into an undershirt. Then I dressed quickly in my white long-sleeved shirt and suit Mom had laid on my bed, earlier. We were in court on time.

My charges were for drug possession when I overdosed and for leaving police custody at the hospital. Mom and Dad sat in the Fulton County Courtroom on the second row behind me. I sat up front with my probation officer, Burt Treats, thinking about all of my offenses and wondering what would happen to me today. I saw a little blood seep through my white undershirt under my dress shirt and suit coat and hoped no one would notice.

Things had been going so fast for me lately. I thought about Julie and about our time together. Lately I had been so happy with her, happier than I could ever remember. I wanted to leave drugs behind and be with her. Then I go and do something so stupid—get high on THC and get myself in a wreck were I could have been killed.

I thought about Kell. Why did I get high with him? Why couldn't I stay away from him and other bad influences? How long would it take for me to understand he became my bad news every time I got around him. I had known this for a long time. Why had I gone off with him again? I shifted uncomfortably in the chair as my chest really hurt.

I thought about the wreck again. I felt shook up about the happenings last night. Kell and I could have been killed and with the car hidden in the kudzu like that, no one would have ever found our bodies. I wondered why I had not been killed. I thought of Timmy Mitchell. Why did he slide off the hood of the car and die? How could I have gone through this horrendous crash and be able to walk away? It didn't make sense why Timmy died and why God let me live.

I thought about Mom and Dad and Julie and how my death would have affected them. "Bradley Elijah Berkshire," I abruptly came back to reality when the court clerk called my name.

I stood up as I had talked Burt into letting me represent myself as I had before. I started to talk my usual talk. The judge had always listened to me. This time he said, "Brad, be quiet and sit down." Right then I knew this had gotten serious. "Brad, let's just pretend I'm not wearing this robe up here, that I'm not a judge." He studied me over his half-glasses, took a deep sigh and said, "You've got all these offenses—seventeen of them."

He began to shuffle all the paperwork in front of him, and then he held up my juvenile record. All of a sudden, Judge Rourke stood up. This shocked me and those in the courtroom, and all, collectively, uttered a faint gasp.

He threw the pages toward the floor. Obviously these were printed on connecting pages of paper. These records reached from his hands where he stood up there on the podium all the way down to the floor. I guess there were about seventeen sheets of paper—my records, one for each of the seventeen offenses. The bottom papers lay on the floor.

"You have one of the longest records in Fulton County history for anyone who's not been turned over to the Youth Delinquent Program," Judge Rourke remarked sternly. He peered down from the podium toward me with those stern black eyes. "Every inch of me wants to believe you're a good person, and I still do. But I've tried everything—parental custody, counseling, and probation. I could try other things, but I'm not going to be lenient any longer. I'm going to commit you to the Youth Delinquent Program at Macon, Georgia."

Burt Treats, who sat beside me, jumped up and said, "Your Honor, we are willing to take whatever you give us."

Where did you get that idea from, Burt? I wondered. I knew this meant juvenile prison, where the hard core criminals went—the rapists, robbers, and murders. I felt like I had only committed Mickey Mouse crimes compared to what these people had done. Most of the harm I'd done, I'd done to myself. I felt embarrassed to see the Judge standing there with my long written record of offenses literally stretched out hitting the floor.

From just behind me, I could hear Mom crying softly. I turned and made eye contact with Dad. I saw him grit his teeth, take a deep breath, and drop his head. I know this hurt him to the core. I didn't go home this time. They locked behind bars.

Frantically I thought, what can I do? I didn't want to go to youth prison. What can I do? I called Burt Treats. He came into the jail cell. "You've got to do something. I'm not going. I can't be locked up. Go tell the judge I want different representations and I want to appeal to someone. Do something." Burt seemed skeptical, then left. The next day, the guard unlocked the barred door and a guy in a suit walked in and introduced himself as my court appointed counselor, Buddy Barnesby. I knew then I have a chance. I started hitting the drug problem. I told him how I took responsibility for my actions. He agreed with me and said he would talk to the judge and see if he would agree to sent me <u>*anywhere*</u> but the YDP.

I sat in the jail cell for five days seeing no one and talking to no one but the guard. On Saturday, I sat there in the jail and realized today I turned sixteen. Mom and Dad came by the jail for a few minutes in the afternoon for the once-a-week visitation.

They smiled but looked so sad. Mom kept quiet and only said, "This is a shame and disgrace." She hugged and kissed me when she left.

"Keep your chin up Son. Maybe you won't go to YDP," Dad hugged me and left.

On Monday, I went back into the courtroom. Judge Rourke studied me like he had to pull patience from somewhere deep inside him to the surface. "Brad, I'll give you one more chance to straighten out your drug habit. I'll sent you to a one year program at the Rehabilitation Center in Atlanta. This is a place for the worst drug offenders. If they can't straighten you out, then you'll go automatically to the Youth Delinquent Program in Macon.

I could only have visitors on Saturday, so Mom and Dad came by two more Saturdays before I left for the Rehab center. I called Julie only once, but did not tell her what had happened. She asked questions, but I told her I could not talk and would call her later.

22.
Rehabilitation Center

Two weeks later, a deputy took me to the Rehabilitation Center on Peachtree Street in Atlanta. I stepped out of the patrol car and walked up the broad steps to an old red brick dormitory-type building, not knowing what to expect. The deputy took me inside the door and left. I had my teeth gritted and my jaw set in determination that I would be able to take whatever they had to dish out. I stood six-two and weighed two-twenty-five. I acted cocky and mean as hell. The first thing, they got rid of the long hair hanging down my back. They didn't just cut it—they shaved my head.

I learned the hard way how they break a person down physically and mentally. They strip away all the hippie facade and the crap until they get down to just you, just the inner "gold" as they called it. They get you to where you have no "attitude" left.

They sat me in a straight chair that the legs had been sawed off. I sat there with my legs straight out in front of me for seventeen hours a day starting at six a.m, an hour before everyone else got up. They only allowed me to leave the chair an hour after everyone got into bed, about eleven p.m. I had restroom breaks, and my meals were brought to the chair. I ate sitting on the floor in this straight chair with my legs straight out in front of me.

In front of the chair, written in bold capital letter, they placed a sign. I figured I would have to read it sooner or later, so I asked one of the inmates to read it for me. He replied: "DON'T BLOW THIS LAST CHANCE."

I found out many of the guards were exjunkies who had gotten straight in this very program and had come back to take some of their meanness out on the new inmates. We were to call them, expediter. The one they called Expediter Zadar Slick came by me and screamed into my ear like a drill sergeant, "READ THIS SIGN, DOPE FIEND!" Relieved I could answer, I screamed back, "DON'T BLOW THIS LAST CHANCE!"

I sat in the straight chair for three days. At eleven p.m. each night, a guard took me to a cell with only one drab, small cot. I lay down until the guard left, and then I got up and silently ran in place to get my circulation going. I did sit-ups and push-ups on the floor for about half an hour before I went to the cot and fell asleep.

They set a goal to teach each inmate honesty, humility, and get them off drugs. We also had one-to-one counseling, therapy, and group meetings. They kept me busy—constantly giving me things to do. If they ran out of something for me to do, I cleaned. When I mopped the floor, if left one tiny particle, they screamed, "You're doing a sloppy, half-ass job. I'm going to pull you up, brother, so you'll be up to speed." They called this technique a "pull up." Pull up lectures sometimes lasted fifteen minutes. Then I'd have to mop the entire floor again, not just one spot. They watched my every move hoping to make me blow my temper.

I kept my cool for three of the twelve months treatment. I had survived the shocker treatment of the chair, but I knew I couldn't last the rest of the year, maybe six months or even nine months, but I knew I would blow sooner or later, so I made the decision to leave and save myself months of abuse.

After three months the inmates could have a visitor as well as the privilege of sleeping in a dormitory rather than a cell.

Once I got into the dormitory, I devised a plan to leave. I had been told I could call and arrange for my visitor. I wanted to see Julie so badly, but I just called her instead and explained I had been in a rehabilitation center which sounded better than being in jail. She never knew I had been in jail for three weeks prior to coming here. I felt too embarrassed to tell her. We talked for a while then I called Mom and Dad. I knew I owed it to them to have them visit, but we just talked and I didn't ask them to visit either.

I called Kell and asked him to come see me and bring drugs. He told me after he flipped his Dad's car at the Atlanta Pen and after I left for the Rehab Center his Dad said he would not allow Kell to hang around with me. His Dad called me a bad influence. I hung up, and felt anger rising in me. Talk about bad influence. Kell had gotten me started on drugs and here I am in a Rehab Center and his Dad won't allow him to associate with me? Whenever did Kell do just what his Dad allowed? I couldn't spend any time thinking about Kell. I had to get out of this place.

I called Rooster and told him to bring me some drugs. He came on a Sunday afternoon and slipped me six seconalds. These were small, and I hid them in the cuff of my uniform. "Man, how are you doing in here?" Rooster looked skeptical.

"I'm getting by." We shot the breeze for a while. I couldn't tell Rooster I had plans to get out of this place. If anyone questioned him later, it seemed better for him not to know anything.

After Rooster left, I bribed one of the Korean cooks. "I'll give you these three seconald, if you leave the kitchen door unlocked on Monday night when you leave." I got the drugs from my cuff and handed them to him. "You understand?" He nodded. "I will leave three more wrapped on foil in the sugar canister on Monday night." He nodded and slipped the drugs into his shirt pocket as he looked around the mess hall to make sure no one watched us. He had been serving my tray as I talked to him about the plan. I knew after he got high on the first three drugs, he would want more and would come through for me.

On Monday night, I slept in my clothes and waited until about two a.m. I pulled the covers back, got up, walked down the two flights of stairs very quietly, and went to the kitchen door. They kept the door to the main dormitories locked at all times as it lead to the kitchen, and the kitchen had a door leading to the outside. Sure enough, I found the kitchen door unlocked. I went inside the kitchen, pulled the door closed behind me, and locked it. No one would ever think to blame the cook, I thought. I put the three seconald, wrapped in foil, into the sugar canister as promised. Then I checked the kitchen door and found it unlocked.

I opened the outside door, locked it behind me, and ran into the brightly lit streets of Atlanta. I walked to the entrance ramp of I-285 north, leading away from Atlanta, away from Oakdale. The streets were almost deserted at this time of night. The summer smells of smog, traffic exhaust, and freshly cut grass along the edge of the interstate were stronger than usual to me as I had not been out in the open for three months. I walked along he interstate for an hour then came to the outskirts of Atlanta. Here someone gave ma a ride.

I ended up in Duluth about six a.m. where I walked for a couple of hours looking for work. I finally saw a construction crew and approached the foreman. I told this foreman I needed work and about my experience building houses with my Dad. He looked at me with suspicion but talked favorably since he saw me as a strong, young, worker. At one point in the conversation he grabbed me by the arm and led me over to the construction. He had tested to see if my arms were muscular. After talking to him a few minutes, he introduced himself as Joe Austin, the head foreman, and gave me a job on a trial basis.

At the end of the day, Joe saw I proved to be a good worker. After he questioned me, I had to admit the authorities might be looking for me and admitted I didn't have any money for food or a place to stay. Joe said he would take care of me and took me to a low-rent motel room and paid for a weeks lodging and gave me enough money for food for the week. I went to a second hand shop and bought a couple of changes of clothes and another pair of boots.

The second week, Joe asked me to sell drugs for him. How ironic. I realized I had ended up with seedy underworld people. I just couldn't get away from trouble—even in a new place, with new people. I found myself still stuck in illegal activity. I told him no. I needed to get out of town.

No one knew where I had gone, not my parents nor my probation officer. I had literally disappeared from the Rehabilitation Center. No one saw me leave. I had not even taken my clothes. I knew my parents had to be worried sick. Here I am in the same old rut, but this time I'm alone. I don't see my parents, Julie, or any of my friends. I don't know what to do. If I went home, I will be found out and have to go back to court and then to the Youth Delinquent Program, or I could stay and do what Joe had for me.

Because I told Joe about being on the run, he took me to Lakeland, Tennessee, and set me up to live with an older couple, Ed and Mae Austin who lived in a middle-class, quiet neighborhood. Ed, a thin guy about sixty years old, had blood shot eyes, and was bald except for a few hairs standing straight up on top of his head. Mae looked like a typical middle age lady who had gray hair, too tight a perm, wore house dresses, low shoes, and a full-length apron all day.

Joe told me Ed Austin was his uncle whom he helped out sometimes, I guess financially. There I had a small bedroom I kept neat and Mae Austin cooked good meal for me three times a day. Mae and Ed were civil but not friendly. Several times, I caught each of them eyeing me, suspiciously. Joe got a job for me, painting with Ed who laid out most of the time because he rather lay up in bed drinking beer than go paint a house all day. He had to be an out-and-out alcoholic because he drank from early until late some days. Mae just stayed around the house cleaning, cooking, and watching to see what happened next.

After two weeks, Joe came back up to Lakeland to check on me. He brought a motorcycle for me and rode back with a buddy who had come up with him. When Joe left, he gave me a 38 revolver. He had placed me here for my protection, but I had a feeling he had something in mind for me to do later. I knew he had plans for me. I knew in a matter of time, Joe would appear and cash in on helping me—in giving me the motorcycle, a job, and a place to stay. I dreaded finding out the reason he gave me a gun. I dreaded the thought of seeing him again. It would be like him to just show up and require I commit some crime for him. I stayed confused as to whether to stay or leave, but I couldn't go home. I would be arrested and sent to YDP.

Joe also had my address back home where to contact my parents for any reason.

After a few paychecks, I bought myself some decent clothes and began to save money for what—I didn't know. I had so much time on my hands, I didn't know what to do with myself.

I worked myself into a state. I couldn't believe the boredom here at Lakeland—just peace, quiet, and work. I had led the wild life—partying, drugs, and women. I only escaped from the boredom when I drank a few beers after work. I had been at Lakeland since the first of August. Now it was the end of October. I had been here three months and felt like I couldn't stand it here any longer, not another minute.

I sat at the kitchen table one night and noticed a prescription bottle. The old man had quaalude —714, called "gorilla biscuits." Taking one of these would feel like taking a six pack of beer in a tablet. I thought, I'm not going to do this to Ed—steal his drugs.

I went to my room and lay on the bed thinking about Julie. I missed her so much. I called to ask her if she would come up and live with me—to be on the run with me. "Julie I'm so miserable without you. I need to see you. Why don't you come up here and live with me?"

"Bradley Berkshire, you must be crazy. That's no life. I could never live like that. I love you, but you've got to straighten yourself out." She told me, "If you're in trouble, you have to work it out. I can't quit my job and come up there."

I hung up, disappointed. The radio played touching lyrics, *"Please Come to Boston in the Springtime."* Even the lyrics told me to go home. I had a few beers and then I grabbed the prescription bottle of gorilla biscuits, and downed three of the old man's quaaludes. I got my things together, got my revolver, and went out to my motorcycle. Mae just stood in the kitchen door watching me leave, saying nothing. I think she felt relieved when I left. Ed didn't know. He had passed out on the sofa earlier. I headed for the interstate, south toward Atlanta.

I'm living dangerously—speeding down the interstate in the middle of the night, stoned, feeling numb, carrying drugs, and a revolver. As stoned as I felt, I thought about the craziness and potential danger of my situation.

I got to my mom and dad's house about five in the morning. When I turned onto Hill Street, I cut off the motorcycle and coasted down the hill. At the bottom, I lay the motorcycle down in some tall dry grass and weeds in the front pasture to hide it temporarily. I whistled lightly for Smoky and Blue and after a few minutes, a wary Smoky with his head lowered, sniffing, came whimpering to me, wagging his tail. The ol' hounddog dragged up a few minutes later sniffing and wagging his tail slowly too sleepy to know me at first. I knew if I had gone into the yard unannounced, they would have barked and howled thinking me to be a trespasser and would have awaken Mom and Dad.

I grabbed the two dogs, hugging and petting them. I felt so glad to see them and to be home. I quietly made my way, in the dark by half moonlight, toward the backyard with the two dogs trailing me. We found the big granite rock where I sat down and petted Smoky, rubbing his head and ears, waiting for daylight to come. Ol' Blue went back to sleep on the ground at my feet.

As the sun came up, I looked around at the signs of a glorious autumn: the red oak leaves in the towering trees overhead, the blazing sumac in the edge of the woods, and the goldenrods growing in plumes out behind the barn. Then I glanced at the sleeping livestock—the cows lying down and the horses standing— in the closest pasture just behind the barn. I saw the creek flowed low from lack of rain. Just then the rooster crowed its announcement of daybreak and the chickens in the barnyard begin to stir. I waited for the seven a.m. train to come by the house, hoping the clatter and noise of the train would cover the sound when I eased my bedroom window up and let myself into my room.

I lay on my bed quietly until I heard Mom and Dad stir. Then I called out to them that I had come home. When I walked down the hallway from my room, they looked up with such a happy surprised look on their faces, it almost caused me to cry. "Son, I'm so glad to see you, Dad said as I grabbed onto Mom. "Bradley, where have you been. We haven't seen you or heard anything about you for six months," Mom said crying and hugging and hanging on to me.

I held her in my arms for a few minutes. Dad stood by wiping his eyes, waiting his turn to hug me and said, "Son, the guards from the Rehabilitation Center came here looking for you then the deputy sheriff came then the probation officer came here to question us several times. Many people have been looking for you." I released Mom who wiped her eyes with a napkin and sat down at the kitchen table like she felt overwhelmed. I put my arm around Dad as I told them about working construction and then living in Tennessee, painting. In the six months I had not seen them, I had spent three months at Rehabilitation House and three months in Tennessee.

Mom said, “Bradley, every time the phone rang we thought it might be the deputy calling to say you were dead. You have really put us through a lot of anxiety and misery. I love you, and wish I could do something to help you. You have gotten yourself into a shameful mess.”

Dad said, “Son, I think you have hit rock bottom. I pray for you all the time. God will work this out. Just trust in him.” We had breakfast, then I helped Dad with chores while we talked. I stayed around the house thinking what to do next.

That afternoon, my construction job boss, Joe, paid me a visit. Dad and I saw him come up in the yard as we stood out by the barn. I went out to meet him. Dad stayed at the barn and watched. Joe’s anger showed as he threatened me, tried to intimidate me, and asked if I had killed anyone with the gun. I told him I had fired the gun twice when I did target practicing in the backyard earlier in the day. Being the adult in this encounter, he took the gun from me and held it as he threatened me, but I could see he feared me. He stood up close to me, within my striking distance. I could have kicked his ass and taken the gun away from him, and he knew it.

I glanced at Mom standing in the kitchen door glaring at Joe and saw Dad still stood close to the barn, watching us. I told Mom, “You go inside. Everything is okay here.” I left Joe standing there and went up to the front pasture, got the motorcycle, and brought it to the backyard to him. He scowled at me as he checked it for dents. Then he took the gun and the motorcycle and left. Dad said to me, “Son, I think you were in a very dangerous situation having anything to do with that man.” I had told

Mom earlier to go back inside because I knew she was probably thinking about going out to tell Joe just what she thought about him.

Later that day I said to Dad, "I'm ready to call Buddy Barnsley. I'm ready to go to the Youth Delinquent Program." I had known from the time I went to the Rehabilitation Center that if I did not get straight there, I would automatically do time at YDP. Buddy Barnsley told me to report to the diagnostic center in Macon on Monday morning at nine a.m.

I called Julie and she laid out of work to be with me all day. We had a short but wonderful day together. She said, "Brad I can't condone what you've done. You need to pay your dues and serve your time. I love you and will miss you when you're at YDP but you've got to straighten up so you can be clear of all this trouble and be with me."

When I left Julie, I went to a party and got very stoned. I know it was a crazy thing to do, but I had not seen any of my friends or had a good time for half a year. Rooster and I had a few beers, did a little marijuana, had a lot of laughs, and I talked about how much I dreaded going to YDP. Then Rooster told me about Tophat. He had moved with his mom to Cobb County where she had an apartment. I got Tophat's phone number and called him when I got home.

"Hey, Buddy, how you doing?" Tophat seemed glad I called. Soon he told me, "I'm finished with drugs—forever. I'm in high school and doing pretty good. I work after school—I have to help Mom, to make ends meet she says." When he asked, "What's going on with you?"

I felt ashamed to admit I had not been able to overcome doing drugs and on Monday my parents were taking me to YDP. He remained quiet for a moment, then said, "That's a bummer. I'm sorry to hear that. Good luck, Brad."

"Tophat, I admire you and envy you for being off drugs. I wish I could have overcome drugs. I would not be in this predicament."

23.
Youth Delinquent Program

Sunday night at home, after we ate supper, the air inside the house echoed with Mom's ranting and raving. Dad and I still sat at the table as she got up to do the dishes. My own thoughts of what might happen to me filled my head, and I heard only fragments of what she said, "I told you so," and "Nothing like this has ever happened to our family." The clunk of dishes in the sink brought me back, "Everyone in my family will be spreading this around." That meant gossip. She washed the skillet with more force than needed, "Our family is disgraced. How can we ever hold up our heads again?" Dad sat with his head down as if he studied the table cloth as he sipped his coffee. At least he stayed to ride out her anger with her and didn't take off to the barn as he had on so many occasions when things got touchy. I felt worse and worse, listening to her.

I got up and put my arms around her and hugged her to me. "Mom, I'm sorry. It will be okay, I promise you." She allowed me to hold her only a few seconds then pushed me away and finished cleaning the kitchen. "You've been gone six months. I missed you. I like having you here." She looked at me angrily, "But because of what you've done in the past, on Monday we'll be taking you to *jail*."

I think Mom felt at fault and blamed herself indirectly for my bad behavior because she could not control me, even when I was a child.

She just couldn't understand why the whippings she gave me when I had been very small had not stopped my bad behavior. "If I had been able to stay home with you and not had to work . . ." Then for a few hours she blamed her diabetes. "Well, I've just not been well in a long time."

I thought about all the times Mom had tried to discipline me. When I had misbehaved as a child, she had made me well acquainted with the hickory switch. When I got older, I graduated to a belt beating. Sometimes when I knew she intended to whip me, I hid the belt. Later on, I got big enough to pull away from her, but she would chase me through the house and beat the fool out of me when she caught me in a corner. One day I just took the belt away from her. "You're not going to whip me. I'm too big. I'm leaving." She was so frustrated and did not know what to do that she called out angrily, "You'll go to hell for that."

She tried everything to discipline me. She tried slapping. There were times my jaw would go slack, she slapped me so hard, trying to knock some sense into me. Once when I got into trouble, she hit me with the broom handle. I just laughed at her, picked her up, and put her in the closet laughing all the while at her protest. Then I remembered the time she threw the rock, hitting me in the mouth trying to stop me from attending a concert.

I knew my Mom loved me and wanted to help me but didn't know how. All those whippings were done in utter frustration and in fear of how I lived my life and of what could happen to me. I felt badly for all the grief I had caused Mom and Dad and my extended family.

Late on Sunday night before I went to bed, Dad came into my room. "Son, I'm glad you're going to see this through and pay your dues. This is the right thing to do. Serving time these next few months will be tough but just keep in mind these months should wipe the slate clean. There's still hope you can do well after you get out of YDP and can led a normal productive life." He patted me on the shoulder, lowered his head, and left my room.

On Monday, we left early for the long drive south to Macon to the Youth Delinquent Program. Mom sat with her mouth clinched in an angry, tight line all the way there. All the things she didn't say hurt me even more. Dad drove silently. I knew he prayed while he drove and also concentrated on the interstate and the turns. I sat in the back seat studying the passing landscape, wondering what I would encounter there.

We arrived to rolling green lawns, neat shrubbery, and a lake. But the lush green landscape and the flowering shrubs along the driveway could not apologize sufficiently for the worn-out brown, brick buildings where the front windows sagged like sad eyes knowing too many unhappy stories. The three of us walked through a sagging door marked "admissions" and into a drab foyer with long curtains that had hung there too many years. The old carpet had been cleaned too many times with Pine cleaner as the whole place smelled heavily of the Pine scent.

We walked up to a stern looking receptionist who sat behind a second-hand-store desk. The receptionist wore dark framed glasses and had her straggly, brown hair in a pony tail. She looked up at us like we were intruders. "I'm Bradley Berkshire and I'm here to check in and to serve my time."

She thrust a large book toward me and told me to sign-in. When I did, she said, "You have to tell your parents good-bye now, and I have to take you up to the third floor. I hugged both my parents. Mom just wiped at her eyes and gave me a hurt look like I had done all this to hurt her. Dad said, "Son, I hope all this turns out okay for you. May the Lord be with you."

As they left, the receptionist took me up two long flights of old stairs to the diagnostic center. The counselors there gave me a series of tests and evaluations for the next three days. They were evaluating me to see what kind of problems I had and how long I would need to stay at the facility.

On the fourth day, Mr. Williams, our director, gave me a sentence of seven months. They said I needed to be off drugs for seven months to have time to reform my behavior. I felt like they had thrown an iron cloak about my shoulders. How could I stand staying here for seven months? I vowed right then to do whatever it took to be out early. I had heard of being released early for good behavior. I had to be smart about this situation and I had to have a plan.

Next they had me dress in loose fitting gray pants, a button-up gray shirt, and black brogan boots. Then they assigned me to a cell block according to my size. The cell blocks were like barracks housing fifty other big guys like myself. Each inmate dressed in the same gray work-looking uniform. The chow hall served three meals a day. There were no concession places to get snacks or cigarettes. We had to get these items from someone on the outside. The once-a-month Sunday visitors usually brought a supply to each inmate. We could get these items from someone on the inside who had them smuggled in, but most were too stingy to share what they had stored in their locker or under their mattress.

All the inmates here were ages thirteen to sixteen years old. Some of these boys had committed murder, some had killed more than one person, and some were sex offenders who had raped children and the elderly. The low life scum of the earth resided here, and the guards put me in there with them. No matter what they had done, they were kept here until they turned seventeen and many were scheduled to go on to Alto State Penitentiary or Reidsville—both maximum security prisons. I knew I had to find a way to get through this situation.

From the beginning of my stay here, I realized there were unbelievable racial tensions. The first day I dared to ask questions, I learned there were about four hundred inmates—three hundred blacks and one hundred whites.

I studied each of the inmates closest around me. Freight Train who looked to be about my weight, stood a little shorter. He had long black hair, unshaven facial hair, and walked like an animal on the prowl, looking to the left and right as though he expected trouble. He got his name because of the large amount of drugs he had bought and sold. He looked as though he wanted to kill someone, anyone would do, anyone crossing him. I had the luck of sleeping on the bunk below him.

I studied those around me. Steve Dawson and Danny Pollard were white guys who bunked next to Freight Train and me. Steve must have fried his brain as he acted like a crazy person. Pollard seemed to try to be invisible, kinda like he tired to not be there. I became particularly cautious of a big tough-looking white guy in our section. The whispers around me told me Jerry Johnston had murdered someone. Every sentence Jerry said had the word sh— in it.

The blacks bunked in the next section. I knew the leaders there were two tough looking guys named Graves and Laster. Graves must have lifted weights at some recent point in his life. His had the largest upper arm biceps I had ever seen. Laster, a dyed-in-the-wool, black racist, let everyone know he lived to kill a white guy.

At the end of their section were the queer guys. There, a big kid nicknamed French seemed to be their leader and seemed the most threatening.

Then I learned the guards had assistants from among the inmates called "dog boys." These hand picked young criminals went around in sets of two assisting the guards, carrying out orders, and many times setting up their own rules. I tried to stay clear of everybody and just watch out for myself, glancing around wherever I went.

Mr. Phelps, the guard in my section, had slicked-back black hair and a black handlebar mustache dropping down on the sides. He wore jeans, a jeans jacket with the sleeves cut out, and dingo boots. Hanging from his belt loops were a great amount of keys, a pair of handcuffs, and a large flashlight which all together gave a metallic jangle with every step he took. You could tell when Phelps came around by the jingle-jangle sound. He had a night stick swinging next to the gun he wore, strapped at his side.

The first day, trouble was brewing when I walked into the dorm. I came right into the middle of it, but dared not ask what had happened. I had to play things cool until I knew what was happening. I already knew each inmate could have six cigarette breaks a day. I figured out Freight Train, had done something causing one of the breaks to be taken away from everybody. I could feel the tension. Freight Train lay in the bunk above me, and he kept leaning over saying things to me and to others trying to provoke a fight.

I leaned out of my bunk and warned him. "If you don't shut up, I'll show you what being in outer space feels like," Well, he kept mouthing off and would not hush. I kept quiet and finally he got quiet. When I knew for sure he had fallen asleep—when I heard him snoring, I put both my feet on the underside of his bunk about where his hips and waistline met. I gave a powerful thrust with both feet, and he came off the bunk, went a few feet into the air, and crashed to the floor. He came up swinging and fighting the air, hitting at nobody. I just kept laying in my bunk. Mr. Phelps came when he heard the commotion, "What happened?!" He glared at me.

"I have no idea. I've been sleeping," I replied as sleepily as I could. I heard a few muffled laughs, then everyone else pretended they were asleep also. As Freight Train turned to climb back up to his top bunk, he muttered to me under his breath, "Damn you. I'll get you for that."

After things were quiet for only a few minutes, I heard a shuffle of feet coming toward me. I thought several of the guys were out to beat me up. There were six of them, but they reached for Freight Train, dragged him off the bunk above me, and gave him a beating, bad, right in the aisle beside my bed. I turned over, so I would not be a witness to what happened in the dark. As they kicked and punched Freight Train, he screamed and hollered. Phelps came again, but not before the six disappeared back into their bunks. The guard glared at me, grabbed me up out of my bunk. "You did this."

I shook my head. "I've been asleep. I don't know what happened. I heard him holler, but I turned over and tried to go back to sleep."

Two dog boys carried Freight Train out of the dorm and an ambulance carried him to the hospital. At the chow hall the next morning, I learned Freight Train had a broken nose, several broken ribs, and a punctured lung. At the diagnostic center the next day, Mr. Phelps came up to me with the same dog boys and said, "This is Brad Berkshire." The big guys grabbed me, twisted my arms behind me, handcuffed me, and put shackles on my ankles. I tried to resist, "What in the hell's going on?"

"I'll let the boys beat the hell out of you if you don't go along easily," Phelps said as one of the boys cursed me for trying to resist. They carried me to solitary confinement. While Phelps stood outside the cell, the boys took me inside and removed the shackles and handcuffs. Then they went out. As I stood there stunned, I thought, I've been at YDP for four days, most of which I've spent in the diagnostic center, and here I've already ended up in solitary confinement.

I glanced around at the solitary confinement space. I stood in the middle of a cold, damp six by ten foot cell with concrete block walls and one dim light recessed in the ceiling. A little light came through ten holes the size of pencil sharpener holes arranged in a grid pattern on the door. A small window at the top of the door in the hallway let in very little outside light. On one wall a platform of concrete blocks, three high, four deep and seven long, were cemented into the floor. This is where I would sleep.

I glanced back at Phelps, feeling resentful and wanting out of this tiny, cold space. Phelps stood there observing me. I knew if I raised a commotion I would get more time. On one end of the concrete bed platform, I saw a piece of steel bar bent like a horseshoe with each end anchored into cement. I dared to ask him, "What's that?"

"If you don't act right," he said, "We'll make you act right. I'll let my dog boys come back and have their way with you. They'll make a believer out of you. I will just take a little walk around the square outside the cell until they're done." I knew an inmate could be handcuffed to the curved bar. As Phelps pulled the barred door closed and began to lock it, I realized I had been blamed entirely for Freight Train's beating. I hadn't laid a hand on him, but I had kicked him out of his bunk. "I'm in here because somebody thinks I beat up Freight Train," I said.

He clicked the lock and withdrew the key as he observed me. "Well, of course." He had a sly kind of grin on his face.

"I kick him out of the bunk when he wouldn't quit bugging me, but that's all I did. I didn't get a chance to beat him up. Six other guys came in the dark and did that. I had no part in the beating," I insisted.

He grinned with even more cunning. I think he liked my saying, "I didn't get a chance to beat him up." He gave me a peculiar look for a second, then left. I had the feeling he believed me and noticed I didn't hesitate to admit what I had done—that I had kicked him out of the bunk.

I sat down on the floor and leaned up against the side of the concrete bed. I had to figure out how to handle all this time with nothing to do. I felt like a caged animal. I never could stand being closed in. I felt like I could go wild locked up in this place. The first two hours I ran in place, did push-ups, sit-ups, and kicked off the wall. After I wore myself out, I sat down with my back up against the wall and my feet out in front of me.

After a while, I began to count the squares of tile on the dingy, putty-colored floor. After the fifth hour, I couldn't stand it. I lay down on my back on the bare floor. I couldn't do anything but think. I hated to think. After several hours passed, my thoughts got around to school—I remembered my fourth grade teacher, Mrs. Betts. "Well, Mrs. Betts, your predictions were wrong. I'm not a ditch-digger. I've turned out worse. I've turned out to be a dope fiend in solitary confinement." I realized I had ironically spoken this out loud, but to myself.

I lay there stretched out on the floor trying not to think, then I turned my head to the side and about eye-level came a big roach crawling out from the cracks straight toward me. Mr.-Fat-and-Nasty twitched his antenna at me. "Hey, what ya' looking at?" I asked. "What did you do to get in here? How long before you get out? I must have lost my damn mind to be talking to a roach! This is insane!" I jumped up and went to squash him with my boot, but he scurried back to wherever he had come from. I got so angry that, without thinking, I ran over and banged hard on the door and called to the guard. "I gotta have something to do. I'm going crazy."

Phelps came and gave me a bad look. "What ya' want boy?" he growled impatiently.

"I need something to do—a magazine or something."

"Say, kid, how old are you?"

"Sixteen."

I put out my hand to take the magazine he held out to me but pulled my hand back quickly when I saw he handed me a religious magazine with a cross on the front. That's all I need now is to be reminded of how bad I am, I thought. "I don't want that," I scoffed.

"I'll get you something else," he said nearly slamming the door on me.

Late in the day Phelps opened the door and flung something

across the rough floor toward me. It lay there. I glanced away, but then I looked back at it. He had thrown me a black leather-bound Bible. I wasn't going to say I couldn't read, so I let it lie there for the rest of the day.

Two dog boys brought the evening meal. After about five minutes, they came back for the tray. They were trying to provoke me. After a couple of unfinished meals, I learned to drink all my drink fast and scoop the food with a spoon and eat as fast as I could. I hid the roll to eat after the dog boys left.

At ten o'clock, two dog boys threw a mattress and a pillow through the doorway locking the door behind them. I placed the mattress and pillow on the bed platform. They left no blanket even though it was November. The dim, recessed light in the ceiling stayed on all night.

The next morning a full stream of light came from the outside window into the cell. This light fell on the Bible still on the floor. I slowly reached for it, wanting to read it, but knowing I would only be able to read a few words. I wanted to know what the verses said. Maybe, I thought, this could be a source of help. Maybe I could get help from just holding the Bible. My Dad so valued this Book, and I guess I had always been curious.

The Bible had always been a mystery to me. I picked it up and turned the pages. In Genesis, I read all the little words I knew: a, and, the, thou. Then I sounded out some of the words like Mrs. Bennett had taught me in the fifth grade. The light from the overhead bulb gave off too little light to read by, so all afternoon I slid across the floor to stay in the sun's thin ray as it streamed into the cell. In a short period of time, I found I could sound out words and even whole sentences. In Psalms 18, I found I could read, "The Lord is my rock, and my fortress, and my deliverer;" I sounded out "for-tress" and "de-liv-er-er."

I sat there amazed. Up to now, I had thought I couldn't learn and I had something wrong with me. I had always felt dumb and stupid because of my experiences in trying to learn. But now, I read better than I'd ever have been able to, and on my own. Maybe I had just never gotten still and really tried before. I thought, it's a shame to have to come to this—being in a hole to come to this realization. I hadn't tried in a very long time to read without being stoned or falling asleep.

For three days, I pored over the words. I read some and even recognized the same words when I saw them again in another verse. I felt hopeful maybe I could learn. But being in prison, how could I ever have a real opportunity?

After four days in solitary confinement, I woke to a loud metal click. The door opened. "You're going back to the barracks." As I got up to follow Phelps, I left the Bible on the floor where I had been sitting the night before. I joined my group from barrack number nine where they were getting ready to go to the chow hall, marching two by two. Afterward, we went to a work detail.

The scariest time of being in the barracks came at night. The barracks were one big room, two stories high. The bunks were on the first floor and the guards were above us looking down. The lights were turned low, and only one armed guard watched fifty inmates. He sat in what we called the nest, a platform coming out over and above the room. He had a pistol and a rifle he aimed right toward anyone who moved or caused trouble.

I learned the guards wanted an excuse to turn the dog boys loose on us. Dog boys were young thugs with authority. If the dog boys got a job done for the guard, then they got the freedom to do what they wanted to do in the prison. I learned from the other inmates who had been here for a while that the dog boys were rumored to have beaten one inmate to death down by the river. The dog boys were the cream of the crop—the worst of the worst. If a person tried to escape, they'd go in and make a believer out of him. They made this place even more dangerous.

About a week after I got out of solitary confinement, Phelps came and got me to assist one of the dog boys to put another guy in solitary confinement. I had a feeling Phelps thought he could trust me. This was my chance to become one of the dog boys. I thought, it might be better to be with them than against them. I remembered all too well how little, blond haired Timmy had been picked on in school. I remembered how Kell had beaten on me. I also remembered how Don Pace showed me how to fight while I lived with the guys at the Marietta apartments.

Just because of my size, I began to assist the maximum security guards as a dog boy on a regular basis every night. I tried to stay out of the way and not get involved in trouble and survive the best I could.

One of the dog boys told me, "Bruise them but don't make them bleed."

When a prisoner left maximum security to go to the bathroom, I made sure he stayed under control coming out of the bathroom and going back into his cell. When he tried to run, I grabbed a handful of hair on the back of his head and smashed my elbow into his face, busting a few teeth. I moved so quickly, that after the first week, I became known as "Grasshopper," an association to the TV show, Kung Fu, about a martial arts guy who stamped out evil in the name of good.

Then I saw Steve Dawson, go crazy. He had slowly declined while there in the barracks. I woke up one morning, and saw Steve who seemed to be talking to someone outside the window. I looked out the window and saw nobody there. Another week later, I woke up and saw him standing between the bunks again talking to thin air. I moved closer to listen and realized he thought he spoke to Mr. Williams, our director, but Mr. Williams wasn't there.

Steve said, "Mr. Williams, I'm going to get out in three or four months and get a school bus and come back to get all of you, and we'll go to Stone Mountain to the lake."

He ran to one end of the building then came back into the barracks. He went over to where Danny Pollard slept on the lower bunk, and jumped hard right on top of him and started singing. "Coca Cola. It's the real thing. It's the real thing."

Danny pushed him off and Mr. Phelps came running. The other dog boys put him in shackles, and carried him up to Central State Mental Hospital.

I assisted dog boys several times to take other inmates to the mental hospital. I went along and made sure they got there without any trouble. If trouble started, I helped control it.

Four weeks after I got to YDP, the once-a-month visitation came around. At the first visitation, Mom and Dad and Julie came, and we had a picnic out on the grounds. While Mom and Dad were laying out the food, I spread a blanket, and Julie and I sat down on the blanket. We started caressing and kissing.

One of the guards, who watched us sent two dog boys over. "If you don't get up off the ground and get back over to where your parents are, your visit is over." We got up and went to eat the picnic lunch. Mom, Dad, and Julie stayed for an hour, and we talked. Mom cried some and hugged me. Dad put his hand on my shoulder and said, "Son, I'm praying all day long for you, every day."

Mom had brought a case of potato chips and boxes of candy, so I would have plenty of snacks. Because I had asked her, she also brought two cartons of cigarettes. I had requested Marlboros—as the white guys smoked these and referred to them as "Cowboys." The blacks here smoked Cools and referred to those as "Cadillacs."

Neither Mom nor I had any way of knowing what she brought me would end up saving my life.

Phelps locked up most of the things Mom brought, but I kept a few items in my locker and carried some with me to the barracks. We had a few minutes before lights-out, so I started talking to Jerry Johnston, who strutted around like he wanted to pick a fight. I had heard him say more than a few times, "Hey, man. What you want to do, man? You want a piece of me?"

Unless his victim walked away, Jerry would shove him around. Then he would grab his victim by the back of the neck or grab a handful of hair with his left hand and take his elbow and smash it into his face once or twice before he hit the ground. Sometimes he broke his victim's nose. Sometimes he knocked the victim's teeth out.

This common fighting technique, one I had used earlier, could stop an opponent without permanent injury, but the bloodier Jerry left them, the better. I realized it would just be a matter of time before I tangled with Jerry.

On Sunday night after my visitors left, I tucked some of the cigarettes under my mattress. When I sat on the top bunk, I asked Jerry, "Hey Man, what did you do to get in here?"

I guess he just felt like talking because he sat up on the side of the bed and bragged, "My girlfriend kept talking sh— I didn't like. I told her to shut up. She just kept giving me sh—. So I took out a gun and shot her right between the eyes."

I gave him a strange and surprised look. I didn't show any fear, just disbelief.

"I got thirty-three years and one day," he said.

"One day? What does that mean—thirty-three years and <u>one day</u>?"

"When they add the one day, that means no parole," he replied.

Before I could comment, the "lights-out" call sounded.

"Hey, you want some Cowboys?" I asked instead.

He grunted, "Yeah." The lights went out, and I tossed him two packs of cigarettes.

I lay there in disbelief. I thought about Jerry and about his girlfriend with the bullet hole between her eyes. Somehow I had to live through this YDP experience and get out of here. I figured giving Jerry the cigarettes might be a way to get on his good side. I surely didn't want to be one of his enemies.

The next day I asked Phelps what Jerry had done to be sentenced to YDP, and he collaborated the story Jerry had told me. Apparently, he'd shot the girl for no reason. She had died instantly.

One Saturday after I had been a dog boy for a month, I learned a lesson some things happen for no reason. My first trouble with the blacks came that morning, unexpectedly. I had never thought that the racial tension might be because of jealousy. By serving as a dog boy, I had earned certain privileges. I earned the right to watch TV on Saturday. Maybe someone wanted my spot as dog boy enough to try and kill me. Trouble started as I sat in the TV room with only a few guys around. I sat in a big overstuffed chair with my back to the door. Suddenly Graves, a leader of the blacks, grabbed me around my neck, from behind. He placed an arm around my upper shoulders and held my neck in the crook of his elbow.

The choker hold took all the air out of me. I couldn't breathe. I struggled to pull his arm away. I knew he intended to break my neck. He had me firm in his grip and applied pressure to my windpipe. In desperation, I balled up my right hand into a fist and threw a backward punch over my head. I whopped him right in his eyes. By sheer luck I hit him in the eyes when I couldn't even see his face. He weakened his hold somewhat but he refused to let go. I slipped my hands under his arm and broke free hollering, "You damn nigger, I'll kill you." Just as I said this, twenty black guys appeared behind him. I couldn't have said anything worse to them than the word, "Nigger."

"I'm going to bust me a cap on a cracker," Graves threatened.

I knew bust meant kill, cap meant head, and cracker meant a white guy—me. Phelps came running around the corner when he heard the commotion. Graves began to back up. "That's okay, man. I'm just playing." He walked backward. I ignored Phelps and walked toward him, saying, "I'll whip your ass, you nigger! I'll kick your ass so hard it'll knock you into next week! You almost made me pass out!"

My neck hurt and I felt the anger rising in me. Phelps gave me a warning look. I had surprised Graves, getting out of that choker hold.

That night when about thirty of us went into the shower area to get ready for bed, I saw a guard I didn't know, lock us in. That had never happen before. I became keenly aware of every movement around me. Some guys were showering, some shaving, and some were in the toilet area. We each had a locker with several uniforms inside. I stood in front of my locker to take off my shirt, then I loosened my belt. I let my pants fall down around my ankles and bent over to take my pants off when I heard someone running.

I turned around and saw Graves running from across the room as fast as he could toward me. I didn't have time to react. When he got to me, he hit me full force as hard as he could with his fist right on the jaw beside my ear. I had been "sucker punched." I went numb and fell into the inside of my locker. He had knocked me about senseless. I knew I had to stay on my feet or I would be killed. I came out of my locker, weaving, stunned, hurting, and dizzy. All of a sudden, Laster came at me from the back right side. Laster meant to kill a cracker, which again meant me. Laster carried a "shank," a piece of metal shaped into a knife.

Jerry Johnston came from nowhere and treated Laster to his machine gun rapid elbow hits right in the face. Blood splattered over the lockers and on the floor. Laster fell backward, dropping the shank.

Jerry's intervention bought me some time to recover as I threatened, "You want to fight me? Just let me get my pants up. You think you are a bad ass? Well if you want to fight..."

Graves said to us, "He ain't going to do nothin.' He can't even bust a grape, right now."

By this time, I had my pants up and buttoned. When Graves tried to kick me, I grabbed his foot and tried to put his heel above his head, so he'd lose balance and fall backward. But he got loose. Then I got close enough to him, so I drilled him, hitting him right between the eyes.

He took off running. I, like a fool, chased him down the hallway. The queer guy, French, grabbed me from behind with a full nelson hold, putting his hands under my arms and locking his fingers behind my neck. My arms were pulled back and he pushed my neck down. So, I ran backward and smashed him into the wall. He kicked me behind the knees, and I fell backward on to him.

"Graves, Graves, come back, I've get him down," he called out. About this time Phelps came and Jerry caught up with us. French took off, and Graves ran in another direction.

Later, in the barracks that night, I thanked Jerry. He shrugged it off. My neck still hurt and my jaw burned like fire. I lay stunned. I could have been choked to death, or raped or had my jaw broken. I thought about Jerry. I knew things were bad when a murderer became my friend. I thought about why Jerry had saved me. The two packs of cigarettes had bought the allegiance and caused him to come to my rescue. That one gesture a couple of nights back saved my life. I lay in my bunk and did a lot of thinking.

I thought about the Bible verse I had memorized. I said this to myself, "The Lord is my rock, and my fortress, and my deliverer." I vowed to repeat this verse every day and often. This affirmation seemed to have put a shield over me today. A plan on how to survive slowly started forming in my mind.

I would simply be manipulative and buy allegiance as I had with

Jerry. The next day I picked out the biggest and roughest guys I could find in my barracks. At lunch I spoke to one of them and gave him a candy bar. The next day, I gave another guy a pack of cigarettes. As long as my snacks and cigarettes held out, I could buy loyalty and protection in my circle of criminal friends. I had to move quickly, because it would be two weeks until Mom came to visit and to replenish my supplies of snacks and cigarettes. It amazed me nothing had been stolen from my unlocked locker or taken from under my mattress, but later I realized, you just don't steal from a dog boy.

Within a few weeks, I had formed a group of nine white guys who protected each other. We stuck close together. We ate together and stayed in a group when we were on work detail, in the chow hall, or in the shower area, or in our bunks at night. I became known as the group leader, "Grasshopper." Several smaller guys bought into our group for their protection.

I saw things happen I could not do anything about. As a dog boy on duty with the guard Expediter Ledford, I had to watch a beating. This guard intimidated just in the way he looked. He weighed 450 pounds and had not one ounce of kindness in him. I knew he didn't like a certain inmate, Shaw. While I took Shaw out of his cell to the restroom, the guard rolled up a joint of marijuana and hid it in his cell. When I came back with Shaw, the guard had his cell searched. I stood out in the hallway on watch. They tore up the cell and gave the inmate a beating he would not forget. If I had tried to stop the set up and the beating, the three of them would have turned on me.

I called out during the beating, "Remember bruise them, but don't make them bleed."

The two dog boys and Expediter Ledford turned and gave me a sudden, sharp look. But the dog boys let up some on Shaw and gave him a shove landing him on his bunk.

As the three of them came out of the cell and past me, the Expediter gave me a crooked grin and said, "Well aren't you learning fast."

I tried to look cool and tough standing there. Later I learned Shaw got 30 days more for having marijuana in his possession—in the cell.

When I went to dump the waste can, I thought I wasn't being watched and had the chance to run and wanted to run. I took off and ran 25 yards. As I ran I thought, what if I'm apprehended and brought back here? I stopped, turned around, and ran the 25 yards back to the trash can. I glanced up and saw Expediter Ledford standing ten yards away watching me.

"Grasshopper, what are you doing?"

I replied, "I thought I saw some trash out there." He had a smirk on his face.

In my job of assisting the maximum security guards, I chased down and brought back anyone who bolted out of line and ran. Once when an inmate escaped, I chased him through the woods. When I got close enough where he could hear me, I called out, "Slow down and act like you are hitting me with a stick. I will fall down and say you got away." He slowed down, grabbed a really big stick, and clobbered the daylights out of me. I lay there stunned. I had no trouble convincing the guards why he got away.

After serving as a dog boy for two months, I started learning my way around. When I worked out in the gym, I could press two hundred pounds. I pressed one-eighty-five with one arm over my head. When I first picked up this weight, the bar on the barbells curved under the weight. I earned the privilege of going swimming once or twice a week. In the chow line, a worker told me I could have all the milk I could drink, so I got extra pints.

When Mom, Dad, and Julie came to visit me at the end of the second month, it was during Christmas week. Mom brought my supply of cigarettes, candy, and snack food. Julie gave me a leather jacket. I asked the guard if I could keep it and he said he would keep it locked up. I could only wear it during visitation times. Later after my family left, one dog boy, known as a murderer, offered me $50 for the leather jacket. I told him my girlfriend had brought this jacket for me and it wasn't for sale at any price.

About three weeks later, right before the "lights-out" call, I noticed Jerry Johnston sat quietly on his bunk and had not spoken much lately. I sat on the top bunk next to his. Then he said, "I turned seventeen today. I'll be leaving tomorrow. I'm going to Alto." No one said or did anything to celebrate. I guess no one knew.

I knew going to Alto meant hard time, no parole, and maximum security. What could I say to him? Happy Birthday? As I lay in my bunk I thought, maybe Jerry is finding out really what's it like to be a murderer. I could tell he, just now, had started to feel regret and had about thirty-two and a half more years more to feel regret.

In the time I stayed at YDP, I found I had the ability to learn to read. I found strength in repeating Bible verses and felt repeating these verses put a shield of protection around me in many situations. I worked toward my goal to be released early for good behavior.

But during my time at YDP, I got a basic education of survival from other criminals. I put my size and my ability to fight to good use in a way I never expected. I prevented and even stopped some of the meanness and tried to help some of the inmates during my time there.

24.

Bliss ?

I had originally been sentenced to seven months, but my release came early—given for good behavior. I had served only three and a half months and earned my release for the middle of February. The Sunday came for me to go home. I dressed in my street clothes and my leather jacket. Mom and Dad were in the waiting room when I came out. When they hugged me, they said Julie waited outside. I had never been so glad to walk through a door. I felt good to be free. I had these three people who loved me more than anything. And Julie and I were in love. Several times, Julie and I had talked on the phone. Today, when I stepped through the door, she threw herself at me. Both her arms came around my neck and her feet came off the ground. I swung her around once or twice. We both laughed. We had plans. Serious plans.

Julie Wallace and I were married one month after my seventeenth birthday. I had stayed clean, worked for Dad, and dated Julie while we made our plans. We planned to live at her apartment in Marietta, and I had a job lined up. Even though I had just turned seventeen, still under age, we could wait no longer.

Mom went with us to Wallahalla, South Carolina so she could sign and give me permission to marry. Julie was twenty. Before we left, Dad asked, "Son, is this what you really want to do?"

"Yes," I replied, being very serious.

"Well, I wish you luck, and you two have my blessings. I hope you'll be happy."

When we got to the Magistrate's office, Julie and I were very excited. She wore a white lace and taffeta dress and had a veil just the length of her dark hair. She made a lovely bride and her big brown eyes sparkled with happiness. Mom had bought a new dark suit for me for the occasion. At the Magistrate's office, we met a cornball Justice of the Peace who wore a plaid sports coat, had a flat-top haircut, and spoke in a monotone voice. He greeted us then he asked me, "Son, I guess you have slept on this." I nodded, but I didn't understand why he asked this. "Yes Sir, I have."

We repeated our vows in a short ceremony, by promising to "love, honor, and obey, until death do us part." My heart pounded as I repeated these vows. Julie squeezed my hand. We then exchanged simple gold bands and I kissed my bride in a lingering, loving kiss and held her for a lingering second in a warm embrace. As we started to leave with my Mom, Judge Cornball gave us a complementary package containing condoms, Kotex, washing powder, dishwashing liquid, soap, and toothpaste then we were on our way home to make our new life together.

I married Julie for two reasons. First, I loved her. Also I wanted to be out on my own away from my parents. They had tried to led a gentle, God-fearing life and didn't deserve to be put through the hell and torment I had caused them. My stormy youth could make my parents old before their time. They were beginning to look worn down. Like everybody else involved, I thought this would straighten me out.

Julie and I and moved into her apartment right away. We were in heaven. Relatives gave us everything else we needed in a family bridal shower given at our apartment the next Sunday afternoon.

Jewell and Wilson Wallace and came in her white Cadillac. She worn a velvet blazer and a black, velvet derby hat. Of course, she knew about me doing time at YDP. The way she glared at me, I could tell she was not happy with Julie marrying an under age youth who had done time and had been on drugs. The look she gave me told me she meant to keep me straight. When Julie told me of the family's Native American heritage, I glanced at Jewell again. I could imagine she stood ready to go on a war path any minute and come at me. While at the shower, Jewell came off to everyone as friendly and even gave us a cookware set. As Julie opened the package, she exclaimed, "Oh how nice. I will love using this."

Jewell said in a low voice as she picked up the wrapping paper and turned her back to the guests, "If you stay together long enough to use it." Then our eyes met. I realized she meant for only me to hear what she said. Here again, she indicated she watched to see me mess-up.

Wilson, a nice guy and a regular fellow, enjoyed seeing his daughter happy, but he had taken so much arthritis pain medication he fell asleep in the corner chair during the refreshment time. I felt I could get along with him better than I could with Jewell.

We began our first week together. Julie went to her job as a secretary in Marietta. I went to my new job at a sheet metal company working ten hours a day. After a month I got a promotion to head the spray paint department. After several weeks, the fumes got to me. I would blow my nose and the Kleenex would be the color of the paint I had been spraying.

I had to get out of the paint department, so on my lunch hour, I got a worker to show me how to weld. I practiced for several weeks on my lunch break, and then I got someone else to show me how to read blueprints. Once I accidentally burned up a whole section of blue prints. A extra copy turned up, so no one ever knew.

When a welding job came open, I convinced the boss I could do the job. But being outside in the winter weather proved to be very difficult. When I would have to wash down the big saw, my hands felt like they were freezing. At the same time, I felt like I stood in fire when I handled the welding torch. My skin burned. Because I did not know fractions, I kept everything I did plumbed or squared. In a couple of months, I transferred to aluminum welding. The work ethics my dad had taught me were paying off. I felt proud of my progress.

I rode my motorcycle to work as a temporary measure until we could save the money to buy a second car. So one night after working ten hours and riding twenty miles home in the cold winter air, I felt beaten up and half frozen and very glad to get home.

When I entered the apartment, I knew immediately things weren't the same. Julie's car sat in the driveway, but no lights were on in the apartment. No aromas came from the kitchen where dinner was usually cooking on the stove and the kitchen lights were out. I found Julie in the bedroom crying. I could not console her, nor could I find out what had gone wrong.

"You never spend any time with me," she said. "We never have any fun. I always have to do the cooking and cleaning." She put her head back down on the pillow and started crying again. I sat down beside her and rubbed her back. "I'm sorry, Honey. I'm sorry you feel that way." She just pushed my hand away. I fixed a sandwich and slept on the sofa that night, totally confused.

The next few weeks at home were hell, and I couldn't figure out why. I went into the apartment one night after work and had to dodge a plate she threw at me when I opened the door. The plate crashed to the floor and shattered. "I hate you," she screamed.

I grabbed her in an embrace not only to keep her from throwing another plate she reached for but because I didn't know what else to do. "Just tell me what's bothering you," I said. "Tell me what you want me to do. Tell me what I've done wrong."

She squirmed out of my arms. "You don't understand."

We had sandwiches again. While we ate, Julie didn't speak. She went to bed early and slammed the bedroom door. Once again, I decided to leave her alone and slept on the sofa.

When I got up early to go to work, she stayed in the bedroom. I could hear her moving around, but I did not bother her. I did not want to risk another confrontation so early in the morning and start the work day on the wrong foot. I just eased out the kitchen door without saying good bye.

At night, I went home after work not knowing what to expect. But when I went inside, things were different. We were like the newlyweds we really were. Julie met me at the door with a passionate embrace and kiss. She had dinner ready, and remained sweet and loving all evening. This totally baffled me. We made love, and afterward, I held her all night while she slept.

Life soon became a strange unpredictable up and down pattern, the pattern of a roller coaster. Some days were so good, I felt like I lived in an unbelievable dream, and some days were completely baffling. I could never figure what happened differently making things so wrong to upset Julie so much. She turned from a princess to an evil woman, in a short time, and I never knew which one to expect or what controlled the change.

One Saturday Julie went shopping, and I stayed home to clean the apartment. I thought this would make her happy. I carried out the garbage, washed dishes, and washed clothes. I had the rooms in good order, but when she came in she didn't notice anything. I told her what I had done, thinking she would be happy, but she glanced at the end table, ran her finger over the dust and said, "You call this clean?" She locked me out of the bedroom, and I went drinking to get away form the problem I didn't understand.

I added to our new pattern of ups and downs. When the downs came, I left the apartment and met Rooster and some old buddies to drink. I realized I had reverted back to the same behavior I had before my marriage.

When I rode my motorcycle home late that night, I had a flashback to another time. The wind blew my long hair underneath my helmet. My hair had grown long since I had not had it cut from the time I spent in the Rehabilitation Center. That had been over a year ago. This night I also had smoked a little marijuana with Rooster. When I went in, Julie had a real reason to scream and throw things at me. I came in late, and from the looks of me, she knew I had done drugs and gotten stoned.

She got out the new china and begin throwing and things began crashing. "Are you crazy? You're acting like you did before I met you. Are you going back on drugs? My Mom said you would." She went into the bedroom slamming the door.

I had no argument nor a chance to argue. I passed out on the sofa. The next afternoon I wondered what I would get when I went in—flying tea cups, a lecture, or a warm embrace. This seemed to be good mood day. I played it cool. I sat ready to fight or to make love. But I grew tired of being confused. After a few good weeks then a few rocky ones, Julie set up an appointment with a marriage counselor in Marietta.

On the day of the appointment, I drove my Oldsmobile 98, a used car we had finally been able to purchase, toward Marietta to meet Julie. Rooster came with me. We were on THC chasing it with malt liquor. This action gave me courage to face what would come, blame. By doing the drugs and liquor I had given Julie more reason to blame me. I felt numb and rubbery. I had taken this road several times before to cut through to Marietta, but I realized too late the area had become a subdivision, and the road had been turned into a cul-de-sac.

When I realized the road ended, I slammed on my brakes and spun the car around. A man, wearing an army shirt, stood in the nearest driveway, watching. He shouted, "You better watch what you're doing." I threw him a bird as I drove off, screeching and smoking the tires. Rooster and I laughed.

Five miles down the road Rooster said, "There's a guy driving an Electra 225 with a gun on the steering wheel pointed right at you." I glanced in the rearview mirror and saw the guy in the army shirt, the same guy we had seen at the cul-de-sac. He pushed up toward us, the front of his car, about one foot from my bumper.

I decided to go toward the police station, so maybe a policeman would see this guy had a gun pointed at me. As I drove past the station, I slowed down, rolled the car window down, and called out while waving, trying to find someone to get their attention. Every policeman must have been inside. We had to drive right on by. I didn't dare stop. I thought, this guy behind me would shoot at any minute. I had a bigger motor in my car, so my next option could only be to lose him. But the guy stayed right on my bumper, so I knew I had to outrun him.

I stepped on it at Kennesaw Avenue, went off and left him. I hit one-hundred-twenty then a car pulled out in front of me and stopped. The woman driving the car saw me coming and just froze caddy-corner in the road. I had a choice to hit her or to take the bridge embankment adjacent to her. I knew if I hit her car, she would be killed.

I tried going around her car to miss it. I went broadside, and when the car hit the bridge, it hit so hard it took out a six foot concrete section of the bridge. Yet this didn't stop the car. We hit the utility pole next to the bridge leaving the top of the pole dangling downward by the lines. The car flew over the creek and plowed up into the muddy side of the opposite bank.

I jumped out and ran despite a great amount of pain shooting down my legs. I saw part of the motor had gone through the windshield, and Rooster had been thrown out of the car. I fell down and covered up in pine straw to hide. All the while I lay there, I thought about the man with the gun chasing us. Later I hear the police talking, and I could tell the Georgia Power Company men had come to look at the damage done to the pole. Finally I managed to get up and run. I saw a low frame house and knocked on the door. When a lady opened the door, I said, "Ma'am, would you call an ambulance for me?" Before she could speak, two policemen grabbed me from behind.

They took me to the hospital where x-rays showed I had a dislocated hip. Rooster had been picked up and brought to the hospital also. His x-rays were done at the same time. He had a broken collar bone and lacerations on his face.

As I lay there on the gurney at the hospital, one of the cops said, "Boy, someone bigger than you or I rode in that car with you. I don't know how either of you survived."

I let out a curse word then said, "Where were you when I went by the police station needing help? A guy with the gun chased me." The guy in the army shirt who had been chasing me walked into the hospital room.

"Boy, if you had of run over one of my children, I would have shot you," he said.

"Who in the hell are you?" I demanded.

"I'm Officer Stone with the Cobb County Police Department."

I came off the table at him, "You SOB," I said as I lunged for him. "You had a gun pointed at me like you were going to kill me. I drove fast to get away from you." About four or five people restrained me from him: the nurse, doctor, and a couple of orderlies. One of them said, "Just take him to jail."

Even though extreme pain shot through my hip, my treatment ended right then. After I had been strapped down to the hospital gurney and had been rolled down the hallway toward the ambulance to be taken to jail, a nurse handed me a large bottle of pain pills. She said, "You're going to need these for your hip."

Julie came to the Cobb County jail and got me out on bond but didn't speak to me. Her face turned red with anger as she held her mouth in a tight thin line. As she drove us home in her Malibu, she let the cork out. She told me she waited at the counselor's office for two hours. Then she told me about going home and waiting by the phone. Finally she called the police station. That's when she found I had been in an accident, taken to the hospital, then taken to jail. "I should have just called the jail first and saved myself a lot of time," she screamed at me. "I should have known you were in jail. That where you always end up." She trembled with anger.

I just added a couple of heavy pain pills to the THC I had taken earlier that day and passed out for a few days. I never told Julie what happened and she never asked. I lay around home in pain. We each stayed to ourselves until the court date came a couple of weeks later. I took sick leave from my work.

Then I appeared before the judge in Cobb County not knowing what would happen. The lady in the car who had stopped in front of me appeared in my defense. She told the judge I had chosen to hit the bridge instead of hitting her car. She said, "I would have been killed if he had hit my car, and he knew that and made the split second decision saving my life."

She looked straight at me and added, "Thank you for that."

Again in my destruction, my treatment in court came off as a near hero. I had to pay the fine, pay for the utility pole and the slabs of cement it took to fix the bridge. It seemed strange to me the policeman in the army shirt who had chased me did not appear in court that day. No one mentioned him. I never knew if anyone took into consideration that the policeman in an unmarked car, not wearing a uniform, chased me with a gun pointed at me. What choice did I have but to run? But at the time, everyone saw a teen looking for trouble, and I had found more trouble than I could handle.

After court, Julie came off all sugar and honey. "Brad, I didn't understand you saved a woman's life. I explained how I came to be speeding. She forgave me. My hip gave me pain for several months. Finally as a last resort before surgery, I saw a chiropractor in DeKalb County, Dr. Culberson. After several visits, he had my hip put back into place, and I avoided surgery.

This escapade when I hit the bridge did nothing for my marriage and my relationship with Julie. Even though she forgave me, I felt I walked on egg shells each day when I went home.

One night when I came in, Julie said she wanted to go shopping for paint. She had bought new white curtains with little blue flowers for the kitchen. "We've got to paint," she proclaimed. I looked at the new curtains she had just finished hanging then I looked at the off white walls. Both seemed like they matched pretty good. "Now?" I exclaimed. This being a weeknight meant I had just put in a ten hour day and only wanted rest. I had also gone back to riding my motorcycle in the cold, to work and back as my car had been totaled. I felt exhausted. But what did I know? I could not reason with her about the off-white walls matched just fine with the stark white curtains.

"No," she said, "It just won't do. They've got to match. The walls are dingy. They need to look clean and new like the curtains."

Rather than have another upheaval, I went along with her. We went to the hardware store, and searched through the paint sample cards to select a color. Julie had the curtains with her to match the shade of white. "Brad the color snowdrift matches exactly. Get a gallon of "Snowdrift."

I headed toward the stack of paint knowing I couldn't read the word "Snowdrift." What could I do? Julie didn't know I couldn't read, and I didn't want her to find out, not tonight anyway. I glanced back at her as she waited at the counter watching me. Just as I reached down to look at the first can of paint, a clerk said, "Sir, can I help you?"

"Yes, we need one gallon of Snowdrift." He selected a base and told me he would have to mix it, so I headed down the aisle to buy brushes and a ladder. I felt relief Julie didn't have to find out about my reading problem tonight. As I loaded the supplies I felt perplexed enough. If this could have waited until Saturday, I could have used Dad's supplies and not had to buy brushes and a ladder, and stay up half the night to paint the kitchen.

We were home by seven, and after we had a quick supper, I started painting by nine. I finished and had everything moved back into the kitchen at one o'clock the next morning, five hours before I had to get up and get ready for work.

Being a young man I didn't know much about women. My sister, Kay, had a lot of reasons to be a troubled person, but she seemed like a happy, determined, thankful person. She actually worried more about other people than she did herself. I never heard her complain about life even when she had been through her terrible tragedy and even when her husband had left her and her first house had burned.

But as time went by, I listened to guys at work during lunch and never heard any stories like what happened in my marriage. I never told anybody how Julie's moods changed. I really didn't understand completely how much of the problems were mine and how much of our problems were her fault alone. One day, I told one of the older welders I thought I could trust, "Well I hope my wife has supper ready and will be in a good mood when I get home." He looked at me curiously. "Brad, you're a newly-wed. Things have to be good now. How can they go downhill later if they're downhill now." He let out a whopping laugh and hit me on the back. I didn't expect his response. I think he had just tactfully told me these should be mine and Julie's good years.

The next week, as I left to go home, I saw one of the young welders in the parking lot. I said the same thing, "Well, I hope my wife has supper ready and will be in a good mood when I get home." This young welder jerked his head around and said, "Well how are you going to act? Are you going out drinking and doing drugs like I heard you did." I just shrugged my shoulders and left. How did this new person know about my background? Maybe our problems all stemmed from my behavior. I know things got worse when I went out with the boys. But I only left to go drinking when things were so bad at home. I could not understand why Julie's moods changes were so severe. She told me my actions frustrated her causing her to live, daily, with the fear of what I might do or what might happen to me.

I went to work and worked hard to get ahead. I gave Julie my paycheck, and told her to manage the finances. I never got involved in reading a bill, filling out any application or writing a check. When I needed to read something, I just made up an excuse. I used, "My eyes are watering," or "I must need glasses, or I can't read the fine print, or "I have dust in my eyes. You read it." Julie never caught on I had a problem reading.

About a year into our marriage, Julie stayed out of work for a week and didn't leave the apartment once. When I came home each day, she would still be in her pajamas. I checked the sink for dirty dishes and found it clean. I knew she had not eaten all day. She would not talk to me. She only said, "I can't go on like this. "

I called Julie's mom, Jewell. "You've got to help Julie, I don't know what to do." I explained the situation. She screamed at me over the phone that Julie should never have married me. She said angrily, "Julie had a little problem before, but since she married you, she has only gone down hill." I felt almost relieved to hear Jewell admit Julie had a "little problem" before she met me. That meant it wasn't all my fault.

"She needs to see a doctor," I said. "I will go with you and Julie, but you need to talk to your daughter and decide what kind of doctor she needs."

I handed the phone to Julie. After a moment, Julie turned to me, "You'll have to leave the room. I have to talk to my mother. I went into the kitchen but could hear Julie crying. She called me back to the phone and we all agreed for her to see a clinical psychologists.

Julie's doctor diagnosed her with clinical depression and put her on antidepressants. After the three of us came from the doctor's office, Jewell left and Julie took a nap in the bedroom. About an hour later, Jewell opened the front door and came in with her suitcase and announced to the air in the living room, without even looking at me, "I'm staying here until Julie is better. I need to look after my daughter so she won't be left alone and not cared for. Her husband is always out at night instead of being home with her. I will just sleep on the sofa until Julie gets better." Jewell treated me like I had become a big, horrible monster. She blamed me for all of Julie's problems. Things were very cold during supper. I grew angry with Jewell for taking over.

After a unusually bad scene, it seemed like a good time to get out of town. After Julie went to bed, I packed my bag, called Rooster and left the apartment. Without a word to Julie, I left. Rooster and I went on a little vacation to Mobile, Alabama just to get away and go to the beach. We hung out in Mobile going to bars and to the beach. We were gone a week. I felt free and good there.

After a few days, I wanted to see the loving, good Julie, and thought about calling. But I decided to give her a few more days. Maybe she would miss me enough to be glad to see me when I did go home. I dreaded going home. I dreaded to find out things were the same as when I left. Julie had not seen me for almost a week, and I left without telling her I would be going on a trip. The more I thought about it, the more I knew I had made a mistake in taking off without telling her where I planned to go.

As we neared the apartment, I didn't know what to expect. Would

Julie be better? Would Jewell still be living in he apartment with us? I saw Jewell's, white Cadillac in the parking lot out front of the apartment. When I went in, I felt like an intruder as both women glared at me as if their eyes were shooting darts and hoping the darts went through my heart. Julie looked like her old self. She wore a new outfit, had her hair fixed nice, and wore makeup. Jewell wore her derby hat and velvet blazer. They had been shopping and were going through what they had bought. I wanted to go over and hug Julie. I had missed her. I wanted to explain where I had been and tell Julie I loved her.

Before I could move or speak, two angry women were shouting at me. We all had an ugly scene. They gave me hell. "Brad, where have you been? I didn't know if you were laying in a ditch somewhere dead. I'm having trouble with depression, then you disappear for a week. Where were you?"

"I took a little vacation to let you and your Mom be on your own since the two of you were always mad at me." I knew even as I spoke how lame this sounded.

"You abandoned your wife is what you did!" Jewell screamed at me. She seemed madder with me than Julie seemed to be. Julie actually seemed glad to see me. Of course, I left. What else can a man do with two women screaming at him? Later I went back to the apartment and found it had been stripped, leaving only the mattress. They had even taken the toilet tissue from the bathroom.

I stayed at the apartment and went to work everyday. I called Julie's parents' house, but no one there would let me talk to Julie. Two weeks later, I received a court document where Julie had filed for a divorce.

I hit rock bottom. I rode my motorcycle fast, and went back to drugs and drinking. For a while I managed to work. Then one day, I just didn't get out of bed. I got so stoned for a couple of days I didn't realize

I had even missed work. When I sobered and realized I had let my good job go, it just didn't really seem to matter.

I had married to escape my problems and had done very well, for a while. But my mistake came back to haunt me. I had married a person who had as many problems as I had. Our marriage had not survived, would I? So far, in my life, I had failed at everything I had ever tried: getting an education, coming off drugs, and now I could add marriage to the list.

25.
Raccoon Mountain

I didn't know what to do. I felt lost. Since we had already paid for a month's rent in advance, I stayed at mine and Julie's empty apartment, sleeping on the bare mattress in a sleeping bag. Four weeks after the divorce papers came, I signed and mailed them. We had been married almost a year. I felt broken. I went into Atlanta to pick up my drug fix for the week and then went into a bar. I sat at the bar sipping a beer thinking about what I could do. I noticed a girl sitting two seats down from me who kept looking my way. I glanced up at her a couple of times then went back to my thoughts and my beer. "You sure seem lost in thought," brought me back. She had moved to the stool next to me. "I'm Gail," she extended her hand.

I took her hand but didn't shake it. I just held it for a brief second and said, "I'm Brad," and looked back down at my beer.

"Can I buy you another beer?" I nodded. Gail was probably five foot, eight inches tall, and a large young lady—not fat just big boned and filled out. She had a full lovely face, blue sparkling eyes with a hint of mischief playing about them. Her long dark curly hair framed her face, and she dressed with sophistication like a lawyer or an executive. "You seem pretty lost in thought. You want to talk?"

"I don't have anything to say that anyone would want to listen to. My life's a mess."

"Oh, try me. I'm a good listener." She sat patiently and listened attentively for half an hour as I unloaded all my problems. "Say, why don't we get out of here. I have an apartment not far from here, and I could fix you something to eat." I glanced up at her hesitantly. I had been so absorbed in reliving the past events I really had forgotten she sat there.

I got up from the bar stool and followed her. She had a nice car and drove me about two blocks to an upscale apartment building. A doorman greeted her when we went through large swinging glass doors. Even with the appearance of the building, I did not expect such a nicely furnished and decorated apartment when we entered the large living room. "Make yourself at home," she indicated a plush sofa. "You like scrambled eggs, sausage, and pancakes? Coffee?" I nodded and said, "Yes, please."

I sat down, and studied the living room. Then I walked to the window of the fifth floor apartment and looked out at the glittering grid of city lights in the traffic on the interstate beyond, then out at the taller lighted city buildings on the horizon. "Nice view," I said.

Gail called out to me when she had the meal ready. I ate without saying much. I started to think. What am I doing here? What does this girl want? After we ate, we sat on the terrace, and I finished telling her about my miserable disappointing life and about all my failures. I also told her I couldn't go back to the apartment after tomorrow because we had only paid the rent through the end of the month and I didn't want to go to my parent's house to live.

Gail insisted I stay the night. "Brad, I have an extra bedroom. Stay there tonight. There's no strings attached. You can leave tomorrow or whenever you find a place."

I had a couple of quaaludes in my pocket. I took those and went to bed alone in her extra bedroom. The next morning she left without waking me. I got up and fixed myself a sandwich and cola and sat on the terrace until she came home. She took me back to mine and Julie's apartment, so I could get a few clothes and things I had there until I could decide what to do. Then we went back to Gail's apartment. I told Gail I would only stay temporarily.

When I told Gail about my divorce, I told her how broken-hearted I felt. "I don't want a serious relationship. I'm not over my marriage. I still love Julie," But in a few weeks after moving in with her, she told me she had fallen madly in love with me. You might say I used Gail. I never made the decision to stay, I just didn't leave. I stayed high most of the time, laying around her apartment, or at the swimming pool. She said I didn't have to work, but she wanted me there when she got home from work. Her life centered around me and she supported me. She also paid for my drug habit. When I ran out of what drugs and money I had, I said, "Say I need a couple of bucks."

The next morning after she left for work, I found a hundred dollar bill on the kitchen table with a note, "Brad I know you are going through a hard time. This is to help you with whatever you need."

Of course, I spent it all on drugs. After a few weeks, we fell into a routine. I spent time with her every evening, took the drugs late at night, and stayed stoned until she came home the next night. She began to leave money on the table for me once a week. I'm not sure she knew I spent it all on drugs and I stayed stoned until she came home. I think she knew but didn't admit it to herself.

After a few weeks, Gail began to seduce me. She began with hugging and kissing. We were both lonely and she provided for me, so I pretended to care for her more than I really did. After a month or so, I stayed high even when Gail came home. I stayed in a stupor most of the time, dreaming of Julie. I couldn't get her off my mind. When I made love to Gail, I pretended I made love to Julie. I grieved for my marriage. I saw this as yet another failure I had brought on myself because of my addictions. This life-style weighed heavily on my conscience. After a while, Gail could see my downward spiral and tried to talk me into changing. "Honey, you shouldn't take so many drugs. I want you to change. Will you try to get off drugs for me? I can afford to take you to a rehab clinic. I found "The Rehabilitation Center" close to here on Peachtree Street. Brad, let me do this for you. Let me put you in this program."

I just shook my head. I didn't tell her I had stayed there for three months a couple of years ago and that I couldn't take it there and had escaped.

After a few more weeks, I stayed too high to even have a conversation with her about my addiction. I didn't call or see my parents for a long time. I guess they called my old apartment to try and find me. I don't know what they thought when they never got an answer. I lived like this for almost a year.

The guys I got my drugs from were not hippies. They were scum bags, and I felt like a hell cat, trying to bust hell wide open. I hated them. I hated drugs. I hated myself.

When I started coming down off a high, I could see my death before my eyes. I could smell death. I could feel it, and I could taste it. Death tastes like muddy water with old cigar ashes dissolved in it. It smelled like a rotten carcass. I kept seeing my body laying on the ground like from above myself like a bird's-eye view. Sometimes I would be bleeding. Sometimes my body would be broken.

At my lowest, I saw scenes before my eyes too horrible to even think about. I tried to stop those thoughts by getting high again. When I wasn't numb or unconscious, I tingled all over in a pain of withdrawal that only more drugs would stop. I knew I had to come off drugs or die.

Once again, the music on the radio described my life. Lynard Skynard seemed to sing about what was happening to me. How ironic. I knew I had to get hold of myself. When you are on cocaine for a long time, you get paranoid. You think someone is out to get you. I had to get away. I felt like I needed to go into hiding.

I thought, I've got to clean up my act and then God will help me. I promised myself to try and quit smoking pot and doing cocaine and to quit drinking beer. I would do better, somehow. I told Gail I had to leave. She cried, "Brad, don't go. I love you. Stay with me. When I didn't respond, she said. "I'll buy you the jeep you like so much—if you'll stay."

"Gail, I can't keep living like this." She cried even more. "Honey, I'm not trying to get away from you. I'm trying to get away from doing drugs. I know you are doing what I want when you give me money to buy drugs, but that is not helping me come off drugs. Somehow, I've got to get a grip and help myself. It broke her heart when I left. She lay on the bed sobbing as I pulled the door closed behind me.

I left Atlanta and went to the north Georgia mountains. I had no destination, I just hitched and went where the driver headed—north. Eventually, I got out of a car at the Raccoon Mountain Lodge.

I walked into the lodge office, glanced around quickly, then went into the restaurant and bar area and spoke to a muscular guy behind the counter. He seemed friendly. He appeared to be in his fifties, and had a broad, wrinkled, tanned face. He had a narrow red bandana around his head and a long black braid of hair down his back. When he introduced himself as Indian Joe, his appearance made sense to me then. "How's it going?" he questioned giving me the once-over. "It'd be going better if I had a job and a place to stay," I replied. "I can do odd jobs, building, cleaning up. I'm willing to do whatever work you have."

I sat down at the table and ordered a barbecue plate and a pitcher of beer. When he brought the meal, he asked, "Where you from?"

As I ate, he straddled a chair across from me. There were no customers in the restaurant or the bar at three o'clock in the afternoon. "I've been living in Atlanta with a girlfriend, but I need a change if you know what I mean. There comes a time, you just have to get away." He nodded and sat thoughtful for a minute. I'll give you lodging and three meals a day in exchange for being available to work ten hour a day, six days a week parking cars, sweeping, cleaning up, and doing whatever is needed. We can't have you doing drugs, or getting too friendly with the customers.

About 8 o'clock when the bar scene picked up, Indian Joe also said I could have as much beer as I wanted. I glanced around at the honky tonk bar and saw the exact same life style I meant to try and avoid. A continual party went on here with women, alcohol, and drugs—all available for the asking, anytime. I called this the Devil's last throw to me and decided right then not be a part of what went on here. If I did become a part of this scene, this would be the place I would die.

For five days, I resisted the drugs and drinking. I could have easily become a part of it, but I just worked and talked to Indian Joe every afternoon before the crowds came.

Then early one morning on my first day off, I went up the mountain, sat on a one-thousand foot cliff, and thought about jumping into the ravine below. I sat on the boulder projecting far out above the valley. I had such a turmoil inside. I leaned back and closed my eyes. I pictured going over the cliff and landing in the small creek running through the valley below. I imagined I could hear the thud of my body crashing into the creek below, and I imagined the pain I would feel when I hit. I looked below imagining my body sprawled there, broken and bleeding. I pictured the water in the creek running over me.

I leaned back against the mountainside and tried some deep breathing. I focused on the sound of the waterfall splashing down the adjacent cliff nearby. I listened to a bird chirp, felt the warm breeze blow around me, and stared at the purple haze beyond the mountains.

In these still moments, I had the overwhelming feeling God knew

I sat there looking upward. I knew He loved me in spite of how I lived. I felt His voice not through my ears but deep somewhere inside me. Or His voice came from somewhere between the spilling waterfall, the distant bird, or maybe it came from behind or above the distant haze, but I felt it. It vibrated to my inner core. He said, "If you will just come to me, I'll make everything okay. Things will be different."

I didn't leave the peace I found there above the valley until my eyes and ears were filled with the sounds and the view. I watched clouds and the shadows the clouds made on the valley. I watched the sun travel from my left shoulder to my right shoulder. I guess I remained in a state of meditation and prayer all day.

I came down the mountain trail about dusk. I climbed down to the creek, surprised at the whiteness and the fragrance of a mountain laurel hidden in thick growth where wet moss lay in the shadows. I watched the moving wetness trickle on the dark rocks. By the time I saw the rooftop of the lodge, I knew I had gained enough strength to go back to Atlanta, and turn my life around.

I packed up and told Indian Joe, "Thanks for the job and lodging. I'm going back home and do right." Joe wished me luck, but I saw doubt in his eyes. Even though I had only known Indian Joe for six days, he knew my kind. I had become the kind who always failed even when I tried to do better, but this time I felt different on the inside.

I decided to go home to see my parents. I hadn't been in touch with any of my family for almost a year because I didn't want them to know my life had turned out so badly. I'm sure they probably had talked to Julie and she had told them we were divorced.

When Dad opened the door he looked shocked when he saw me. But I stood there not believing what I saw. Dad sat in a wheelchair. I knelt down and embraced him and held on to him as I asked, "Dad, what happened to you?"

"Well, I had a stroke," he said slowly and quietly almost like he talked to himself. "I can't see out of my right eye and my right arm is affected." He studied his right arm, moving it slightly. I saw his arm hanging limply in his lap.

Mom came from the bedroom, wearing a cotton housedress, her hair rumpled as if she had been laying down. I couldn't believe how old and tired she looked as she limped and leaned on a cane with each step she took. She threw her arms around me, sobbing, "Bradley, where have you been? We have missed you so much." I held on to her for a few moments and kissed her forehead.

I felt devastated to find both my parents' health had declined markedly. I felt guilty I had not been there for them. When Mom sat down on the sofa to tell me what had happened to her, she seemed frail and weak. She said, "Bradley, I've been in and out of the hospital every few weeks. I keep going into diabetic comas. I have sores on my feet that will not heal." She took off her shoes and socks and loosened the bandages to show me how badly her feet had been damaged. "The doctors want to take my right foot off and the toes of my left foot. I'm not going to let them do that. I'm tired of this, and I'm ready to go on," Mom said, her voice soft but determined.

"Mom, don't talk like that. We'll take care of you," I said. But as I said this, I'm sure it seemed obvious to them, as it was especially obvious to myself I had not been here when they needed me. I regretted spending a year away from my parents—a year I had been in a constant drugged state. I had missed a year of their lives. I ached inside at my loss and what I could have been doing for them.

Dad called Kay and she came by after work with Daniel who was now five years old and a regular little kid running around. When she came in, she grabbed me in a hug and said, "Wow, I am glad to see you."

After we ate a small supper, Dad fell asleep in his wheelchair and

Mom went to bed by eight. As Kay put away the dishes, she said, "I think if Dad had gone to physical therapy he would have recovered sooner, but he has just dragged himself around. He's learned to feed himself with his left hand, but the right arm and leg will never be the same. I have done what I could to look after them. I've taken them to the doctor and to the hospital when they needed to go and I cook for them when I can."

Kay told me she had called Julie's parents and found out we were divorced but she had not told Mom and Dad. She also told me she couldn't find out how to reach me.

"Sis, I'm sorry I wasn't here for them and for you. I know you could have used my help with all they've been through."

Then Kay told me, "Uncle James died of throat cancer several months ago. Lilly is really lost. She needs help since both of her children live in Mississippi now. Her eyesight is not good enough to drive even just to get groceries or to go to the doctor. Some of the ladies from church come by for her on Sunday for church. A few times they have taken her to the grocery store. But she calls on me to take her to the doctor. I'm just worn out trying to take care of Mom and Dad and now Aunt Lilly."

I decided I had better stay around and help Kay with all she had to do with taking care of my parents and of Aunt Lilly. I told Mom and Dad about my divorce from Julie, but I didn't tell them I had gone back to drugs after the marriage ended.

The only person who didn't seem glad I had come back home to stay, was Aunt Lilly. After I was home a few days, she opened the kitchen door and came right in talking and looked at me like she did when I had been a teen on drugs. "When I heard you were home again, I came down here to see what you look like. I see you still have long hair. I hope you don't give your parents grief this time like you did before." She didn't stay long. When she had enough information to gossip about me, she left.

Mom helped me when I started looking for a job by filling out a master list I could copy when filling out an application. Soon, I found a good job close to their house working in an air condition plant, *Scientific Welding*. While I took care of my parents and worked, I tapered off the heavy drugs, doing only a little pot and drinking a beer every now and then. I tried to quit both as I had promised myself at Raccoon Mountain. After a few months, one Sunday morning when Dad felt good and got up early, I said, "How 'bout we go to church today?"

His eyes brightened and filled with tears as he studied me. He had to wait a minute to answer to keep from crying. "Oh, yes, Son that would we great." I looked at Mom to see if she might be interested in going, "Mom?"

"No, Son. I'm not able to go. You go on with your Dad and I will take a nap." This is what she had said so many times when I had been a child.

I lifted Dad into Mom's car and put his wheelchair in the trunk. When we went into church, Lilly saw us coming down the aisle and her mouth fell open. I also had my long hair pulled back with a rubber band on it and had it tucked inside my shirt collar, so it appeared as if I had short hair. This meant she had to revise her gossip. "Good morning, Aunt Lilly," I said giving her a grin. Her mouth still hung open as I rolled Dad on by passed her. We both laughed at Lilly's expression. This time I spent with Dad meant so much to both of us. I prayed a lot. I think just being around Dad helped me, even though he never lectured me. We went to church each Sunday morning and I began to look forward to going.

Dad improved somewhat in the use of his hand. When he cleaned and bandaged the sores on Mom's feet twice a day, he looked at her with so much love. It took him a long time to change the bandages with only partial use of his right hand, but she enjoyed the attention from him in the time it took him do this. He struggled to take care of himself and struggled to get around in the wheelchair inside the house.

At my new job, I worked my way up and after a while, I became certified to do nuclear welding by the American Welding Society. I built things to send to a reactor site to be part of the underwater setup. If I had paperwork to fill out, I asked Mom to help me at night. After I stayed at Mom and Dad's house for about six months, I became free of both drugs and alcohol, totally. I had been driving Dad's pickup to work, but after I became successful at work and had some savings, I bought a new Kawasaki KZ1000 motorcycle.

One afternoon at work at *Scientific Welding*, I got a call from Dad. "Son we're at Kennesaw Hospital. I had to call an ambulance to get us here. I found Lila unconscious, on the floor in her bedroom. I thought she was in there taking a nap after we ate lunch. Then I found her sprawled out. Bradley, things look badly for her."

I ran from the plant crying. I got on my motorcycle and headed toward I-285 going about one hundred miles an hour, still crying. I pulled over on the side of the interstate to collect myself. I had always tried to be a hard ass. Now that I had gotten religion, I guess I tried to be a religious hard ass, but I could not be so tough when it came to my mother.

When I reached the hospital, the doctors already had her in intensive care and had started her on a dialysis machine. Her diagnosis: a massive stroke and kidney failure. Only two family members were allowed in the room at a time. Together with Kay and her husband, Sam, we began an around the clock vigil. Kay stayed with Mom during the day, and I stayed every night. Sam came when he could and helped out by bringing Dad for a while each day then taking him home as he was too weak and disabled he couldn't stay at the hospital all day.

One night I sat in the lounge chair by Mom's bed, praying. I listened to the steady tempo of the oxygen machine and the dialysis machine and thought about life. I couldn't take it if Mom died. I thought about Julie. She liked my Mom. She should know. I wanted to call her, but what if she rejected me again? I felt like I needed to see her, to hear her voice. I needed her comfort, but what if she spoke angrily and cut me down. I felt as if I couldn't take any negativity right now. My hands shook as I dialed Julie's parents' phone number. I prayed Julie would answer. She did. "Julie, this is Brad. I need to talk to you."

"Well I thought I'd never hear from you." Her voice sounded warm and soft, but questioning.

"Mom's gravely ill. She's in intensive care at Kennesaw. I feel like I need to see you."

"Oh. Brad. I'm sorry. I don't know if I can come."

Then I blurted out. "This is not right. We were married, and we should have stayed married. We belong together. Please let's try again. I need you."

Julie said, "I have a job in Florida. I'm moving there—leaving tomorrow. I'll try to come by the hospital before I leave." We hung up.

I felt letdown. I had loved hearing Julie's voice. She had been kind. The next day I sat in the hospital recliner watching Mom and listening to the oxygen machine pumping when I glanced up and saw Julie standing by the bed. I jumped up from the chair and grabbed her in a hug. She hugged me and we kissed, passionately. She held my hand when she went over to talk to Mom who awoke to smile at Julie and squeeze her hand. I propped Mom up on a pillow, and Julie held a straw in a cup of juice for her to sip. Julie brushed the sides and top of Mom's hair, and Mom turned her head so Julie could brush the back, but she did not raise her head off the pillow, being too weak. Then she fell back to sleep, exhausted.

Julie held my hand and had tears in her eyes. "I thought about what you said on the phone last night—about us belonging together and that marriage should be for our whole life, for better or for worse. I'm not moving. I'm staying here to help you take care of your mom. We need to talk about getting back together." Julie stayed at the hospital with me day and night.

The next few days, Mom began making a strange gargling sound like she needed to clear her throat. She still responded when I put a straw filled with liquid into her mouth, but I felt something had changed She seemed close to being unconscious, though she still swallowed the liquid.

The nurses said the gargling in her throat was called the death rattle, and it would not be long now. I never left her side except to go home to change clothes and eat and to get Dad and bring him to the hospital to stay with her for a few hours. Julie took breaks also but planned to be there when I came back. She sat close to me holding my hand. I don't think I could have taken it if Julie had not been there. My stomach did flip-flops. I stayed in constant dread that Mom would pass away. I tried so hard to be there every moment. I didn't want to be going home or coming back and not be by her side when she passed. At the same time, I dared to be happy that Julie stayed by my side. Could we really be getting back together? It seemed too much to hope. My mixed emotions had me in a turmoil.

Every night as I got Dad ready to go home, he had me take him by the chapel in the hospital to pray. Instead of waiting outside like I would have done in the past, I went in and knelt beside him. We both did some mighty hard praying.

We stayed around the clock for five days and nights. I hated the sterile white environment that smelled as if everything had been washed down with alcohol. On the sixth morning the doctors asked for the family to meet together with them in Mom's room. "Mrs. Berkshire is technically brain dead. There's nothing else we can do. The family has to make a decision to take her off the machines." As he said, "family," he nodded toward Kay, Dad and myself. The doctors checked Mom one last time and quietly left the hospital room.

Kay brought me out into the hospital hallway, "I can't make the decision. You and Dad have to decide without me." She walked away from me down the long highly-polished tiled hallway toward the reception area. I stood transfixed only listening to the squeak of her shoes as she walked away. I went back into the hospital room and over to Dad who sat beside Mom holding her hand. I looked at him questioningly. "Son, it's up to you to decide when to take her off the life supports." He shook his head as tears streamed down his face.

I felt Mom's hands. They were cold. I lifted her eyelids and saw her eyes were dilated. I realized the doctors were right. Mom was already gone, only the machines were making her breathe. I left Julie sitting with Kay and shook my head when she started to follow me. I went outside the hospital and sat in the night air in a little park on the hospital campus. I cried and prayed and cried and prayed. I went back into the hospital and met with the doctor. I nodded to the doctor and told him to go ahead and take Mom off all the machines. The nurse disconnected all the tubes. The oxygen machine slowed it pumping, then stopped cold and silent.

I could hear Kay in the hallway crying, hard. Dad sat in his wheelchair next to the bed holding Mom's hand crying softly, and saying, "Lila. Oh, my Lila." I sat on the sofa and held onto Julie. We heard a whisper of air expel from Mom's lungs, then another, and another. She lay still. I rushed over to the opposite side of the bed from Dad and held onto her other hand as the warmth of her body slowly left her hands. When her hands grew cold, I let go.

I bolted for the door, leaving the room and the hospital. In a few moments, I rode my motorcycle speeding away. I didn't just cry, I bellowed. Only the sound of the motor disguised my sorrow.

Over the next two days, friends and family gathered at the local funeral home. Flowers were brought in by the baskets. Aunt Lilly and her family came. She stayed every possible moment and fussed over every detail, of cards and flowers and guests, but I never saw her crying. Mom lay in a blue silk suit, her face pulled in a slight smile causing her to appear twenty years younger. A lace handkerchief covered her hands and she held two red rosebuds to signify her two children—Kay and me.

Mom was buried in the family plot at the Grace Memorial Cemetery on a warm late spring day. I pushed Dad's wheelchair down the hill to the graveside. Julie sat with Dad, Kay, Sam, and me and Aunt Lilly and other family members were around us. This area around the cemetery was made up of older homes and industries. Within a half mile of the cemetery was the electric power plant. The plant's smokestack towered over the entire area, and seemed to me like a marker for her grave. Later, anytime I drove on the interstate near the area, the towering smokestack reminded me Mom lay buried only a half mile from its base. She had just turned sixty-three.

The loss of my Mom lay heavy on my heart, and I vowed to look after Dad and help him through this difficult time. Being with Julie again eased the pain a little.

I had overcome the drugs, gained Julie back, had a wonderful but short time looking after my parents, but after only six months, I had lost my mother, forever. I would always regret the lost year I stayed high on drugs instead of being with Mom, Dad, and Julie—the ones I loved.

26.
Time Together

Two weeks after Mom's death, Julie and I talked about getting married again. I told her I had been off all drugs and alcohol since I had come back to live with Mom and Dad. She told me she did not have the mood swings as she had gone on antidepressants recently which helped her tremendously. "Brad, I'm never depressed or moody any more. Let's get married again. We should never have divorced. You were right when you asked me to come to the hospital when you said, "We belong together."

I had been one day away from losing Julie, forever, and I wasn't going to let her go this time. If I had not called her when I did, she would have taken a job in Florida and moved there the next day. But she stayed at the same job, and we talked on the phone or saw each other every day after work while we made plans for our future.

Two months after Mom died, Julie and I were married at the Baptist Tabernacle before a preacher. This wedding seemed more sacred and official than when we had gone to South Carolina to be married the first time. One of Julie's friends stood with her as her maid-of-honor. I asked Dad to be my best man. Julie wore her hair up and wore a cream colored suit with a long skirt. She looked lovely, happy, and relieved to be with me again. Kay and her husband, Sam, and their little boy, Daniel, came to the wedding, also. Jewell, Julie's mom, refused to come to the wedding. "They've already done that one time," she said.

After the wedding, I moved into Julie's new apartment with her, and we were like newlyweds again. I turned twenty-one, Julie was twenty-four. About two weeks later, Julie and I decided we needed to take a trip as part of our fresh start. Kay said she would look after Dad while we were gone. When I first mentioned getting away, Julie had pleaded excitedly, "Oh Brad, take me to see Granny Almeda and Papa Lel. They live on a farm in northern Alabama. I would love to ride their old horse, Pet, again." Julie almost jumped up and down with excitement at the prospect. I was looking forward to meeting her grandparents.

On an early summer morning, we went to DeSoto Falls and Cloudland Canyon just over the Georgia border into northern Alabama on the tail end of the Appalachian mountains. The mild weather and post-card-picture scenery made for a wonderful trip. We stayed there a couple of days, hiking the park trails around the canyon and enjoying the most gorgeous views.

After we left DeSoto Falls, we took a short trip to Mentone, Alabama to visit Julie's grandparents, Almeda and Leldon Shankles. As we drove a dusty winding road to their farm, Julie told me her grandmother would not marry until her prospective husband built a new house for her back in 1920. He did, and they were married. When we found them, some sixty years later, they were sitting on the same porch of the same house, surrounded by huge oak trees. Maybe Julie and I could learn some secret for staying married so long from her grandparents.

The minute Julie and I stepped onto the porch, Julie began hugging and making over her grandparents. Granny Almeda gave me "the eye."

"Are you one of those longhaired hippies we see on TV?"

I sat down in the swing beside her and took her hand. "Yes, Ma'am. I guess I am."

Still holding onto my big hand, she came back at me quickly.

"Well, when I saw you get out of the car with that long hair, I thought you were a girl. But I never saw a girl as big as you. I saw a bear that big once."

We all laughed, and when she heard my big booming laugh, she said, "Well, I guess if you're good enough for Julie, you're good enough for us." She patted my shoulder.

Papa Leldon got up and started pumping my hand and patting my shoulder, too. "So you're our Julie's husband. You had better take good care of her."

"Yes sir. I will."

We sat there for a moment, and I brought up the only subject I knew about them. "Julie tells me you have always lived here."

Almeda perked up as she began to tell the family story. "We're living on the original forty acres owned by the Shankles' family for two generations. When Leldon asked me to be his bride back in 1920, I told him when he finished building me a house then I would say, 'yes'. So when he finished it, we got married and have always lived here. This is where we raised our five children."

Julie asked, "Papa Leldon, do you remember singing to the grandkids—that song about the 'simmon tree? You bounced us on your knee and sang: 'Possum up the 'simmon tree, coon on the ground. Coon said to the possum, 'Shake those 'simmons down.'"

Julie and Papa Leldon laughed and hugged again. "Yes, I've bounced a lot of kids in my day. We have, how many is it, Almeda?"

Leldon's inquiring expression seemed as though he had asked her the question just to hear her tell the story again. "We have five children, twelve grandchildren and six great-grandchildren," Almeda replied, pride showing in her voice.

The more we talked, the more Julie's eyes sparkled. I'll bet she hugged Papa Leldon fifty times during the weekend. The longer we stayed and the more we ate, the more I learned about the Shankles family: the tall tales, the kids, and the family history. Granny Almeda started talking directly after supper. "You know my grand-momma was an Indian baby."

I opened my mouth to say I did not know that, but she went on before I could reply. "Her momma carried her in her arms as long as she could on that Trail of Tears. You know, when the Indians were driven from the south to the foothills of North Carolina. We don't know what happened to her parents. I guess they died some way or another. Starved or frozen or maybe killed by soldiers. There's no tellin' what happened."

She talked for another half hour then said, "That's enough of my stories for tonight. It time to go to bed."

Julie and I could not believe they were going to bed at nine o'clock. We sat on the porch for an hour listening to the tree frogs and other night sounds and watching the fireflies flicker about the summer night.

The night turned cool, and we soon went inside and slept in an upstairs bedroom. We kept the windows open and slept on an ancient brass bed with a feather mattress. Julie spread a handmade quilt on the bed for us to sleep under. Outside, a huge oak tree had grown right up to the window, filling it with leaves. It appeared the branches hugged the house.

I awoke the next morning with Julie in my arms. I lay there thinking about this family. I thought about my parents and about the long-ago Berkshires who settled the area around Oakdale. I thought about my life. I felt ashamed of who I had been until the time I came back home to live with Mom and Dad. I felt that now, as a grown-up, I wanted to be better than I had been.

We went downstairs to a warm, bright kitchen where wonderful smells came from the stove. Granny Almeda had tied on her apron and cooked bacon in an iron skillet. In another skillet, she whipped up a stack of strawberry pancakes. She served Leldon a plate of pancakes and began telling us about truck farming. "Oh we worked hard on this farm. We sold vegetables and strawberries all our lives. When Jewel—she's the oldest—was about twelve, we loaded all the produce onto our wagon early in the morning. We picked the vegetables and strawberries late in the cool evening and left everything in the barn overnight. We got up before daybreak and got everything ready. Jewell watched after our younger children, Jo, Essie, Aaron, and Mattie, the baby, and I went off to Mentone to sell to the big hotels there.

"I got so tired and many times fell sick from working so hard and having so many babies to care for, I would just lay down on the buggy seat and go to sleep. Daisy, our old horse, knew the way back, and I trusted her to get me home.

"I worked hard all my life. We always had a half acre in strawberries. We didn't grow the great ol' big ones, but the medium ones that are real sweet. These are the kind we grow."

Leldon ate his pancakes and we listened to her stories. Then she sat a bowl of fresh strawberries in the middle of the table. They had been chilled and each sat with the point up and had little mountains of white sugar on top. Then she served Julie and me a plate of hot pancakes. We had a choice of toppings: whipped cream, maple syrup, or more strawberries that had been warmed with sugar into a glaze.

After breakfast Julie and I went for a walk. We walked arm-in-arm, just listening to the oak trees stirring above us. When we went into the barn, I could smell the hay and the animals, warm and musky, different from any other smells except those that had been caught up in the barn for fifty or sixty years. About this time Papa Leldon and Granny Almeda caught up to us.

"Ma wants to bend your ear a little more," Leldon joked. She lowered her head a little, raised her eyes to him, and gave him a slight smile.

Julie went over to the barn to see the horses. “I love old Pet,” she said as she rubbed the old brown horse on the nose. “Papa Leldon, can I ride Pet? Is she too old? Please, please, can I?” Julie hung onto his arm pleading, and acting like the eight-year-old she had been once.

“Well, I think she is good for at least one more ride. Just don’t ride her too long or too hard like you used to.” He left us, went into the barn, and came back in a minute with a saddle, blanket, and bridle and began helping Julie saddle up the old horse.

Almeda and I sat in lawn chairs under a couple of big oak trees next to the pasture. When Julie rode Pet into the pasture, Papa Leldon joined us. Together we watched Julie ride several times around the pasture. As I watched her jolting up and down, her long dark hair blowing back from her face and streaming behind her, I thought, this is what happiness feels like.

I could feel my love for Julie filling up my heart. I watched with interest as Papa Leldon and Granny Almeda watched Julie ride Pet around the pasture in a big circle. They didn’t look away from the horse and rider for as long as Julie rode. They had loved Julie for her whole life. That’s what I wanted to do, love her for the rest of her life.

After Julie and Pet were both tired, we met them at the barn. Papa Leldon took care of the horse then joined us. He squinted up at the sun and said, “It’s about eleven o’clock, but we can get in at least one hour of fishing at the crick before lunchtime.” Mine and Julie’s eyes met when Papa Lel said “crick,” and I raised my eyebrows questioning in a silly way.

She giggled and said, “When you’re this far up in the north Alabama mountains, crick means creek. We all laughed at this remark and then gathered up some fishing poles, dug some worms, and walked along the path to where the crick widened into a circle of a pond.

When Papa caught a small trout, and I caught a larger one, we decided we had enough for a good lunch. "While you men folk clean the fish, I will pick a few squash, green beans, and tomatoes," Almeda said starting for the garden. After we cleaned the fish, Papa Lel gathered and prepared a few ears of corn straight from the garden. Julie swung in the rope swing hanging from the biggest limb in the backyard. After a great lunch, Julie and I took a blanket and went down by the crick again and spent the afternoon together while Granny and Papa rested inside.

That night after supper, Granny came into the sitting room where Julie and I were. She held a local newspaper, *The Groundhog*, that contained history of the area. "Read this," she said. "It tells about what happened to my Indians ancestors." She read the headlines, *Granny Dolly, Last of the Cherokees* and then handed me the paper. I glanced at the picture of a very old American Indian woman and handed the article to Julie, and said, "My eyes are watering. You read it to me."

Julie still didn't know I couldn't read. Since we had been back together, it just never seemed the right time to tell her. I leaned back in the recliner and closed my eyes as she read the article. "After the Indian Removal Act of 1838 was passed, the Cherokee and Creek Indians were gathered up and held at Fort Payne then were herded up and driven out like cattle.

"A few managed to hide in caves behind DeSoto Falls near Valley Head in the mountains near Fort Payne. This group sold their possessions and goods and gathered all the funds they could to sustain themselves over the years.

"To protect their future they lived together as a group. One of these ancestors, Granny Dolly, age 89, a full-blooded Cherokee, still lives in Mentone. She was a descendent of those who escaped the cruel whip if the soldiers, the freezing winter, and the hardship of walking hundreds of miles to a dry underdeveloped area of Oklahoma."

After Julie finished the article I kept lying there thinking about what Julie had read, and about the Native Americans who had been taken from this area and that Julie's great great-grandmother had been among them. Almeda came back into the sitting room and told us she had been to see Granny Dolly before she died. Dolly said her oral family history told of a baby named Watrichta who had been taken on the Trail of Tears.

Julie and I glanced up at Almeda when she said this name. She stood there and glowed with great pride and said, "That great-grand-momma of mine, that baby grew up with the name Watrichta. Her daughter, my mother, came back here to live and this area where I was born. I think Granny Dolly is part of our ancestry line.

Julie and I were amazed at the story: how a baby had been taken away, how her daughter came back to the same area to live and how the granddaughter, Almeda, had found her ancestors. Jewell was the fourth generation from the Trail of Tears. It seemed difficult to comprehend and amazing at the same time.

That night as a cool breeze came in through the open, upstairs window, I pulled the handmade quilt over Julie and me again and dreamed of soldiers with whips and long lines of oppressed people. I dreamed of Julie riding horseback away from them with her long hair reaching way back into the wind, blowing away from her bare body. Her legs were wrapped tightly around the saddle blanket and as she looked back at the long lines of her distant ancestors, I woke up.

Outside, a light rain fell, wetting and rustling the leaves filling the window from the oak tree. I turned to Julie and watched her sleep. I prayed we could make it together. I really loved her so much.

On Sunday the mood and atmosphere stepped up somewhat when Jewel arrived "to see what we were up to." She drove up in her big Oldsmobile, stepped out of the car wearing a sun dress and straw hat and demanded to know why we were all so laid back while she had been down in Atlanta working.

She watched me for a few minutes, and finally said, "I don't know why Julie wanted to marry you again. We all know you'll never give up those drugs. She did better without you."

Julie squeezed my hand. We both knew Jewell would try to cause an uproar and that she tested me to see if I could keep my cool. I let her words pass over me and did not show any reaction.

After a glass of iced tea and a whole lot of fussing, Jewell began to tell how hard life really had been up there in the mountains. "I cut timber with Papa Lel here when I was twelve years old," she said. "I did a man's work, but I had to do it."

"Let's get some more tea," Julie whispered to me. We left the front porch where Jewell told her story so enthusiastically she didn't notice we had left. We made our way through the kitchen and out the back door.

We walked down the country road for about two miles. As we walked, we stirred up a fine red powder, from the dry dust on the road, coloring my shoes and Julie's sandals and her toes. The day turned hot and I listened to the July-flies making their high-pitched shrill sounds high in the trees lining the roadside. We gazed at the peaceful, green countryside as we walked slowly. Julie said wistfully, "I wish this day would never end, I want it to always be like this."

I thought about us as we walked there on the hot country, dirt path. When my mind flashed to the past, I immediately brought myself back to the present. When I thought about the future and my apprehension, I immediately brought myself back to this country road and focused on Julie. For a split second, I thought about Julie's depression. Since we had been back together, she had been fine. I hoped her moodiness from the past would not return. I, like Julie, wanted our relationship to always be as close as it was this weekend.

We turned into a path leading to a deserted, summer house with an old tin roof and faded blue shutters. The old house had a screened-in porch on the side closest to us, and the yard had grown up with grass a foot high. This house belonged to one of Almeda and Leldon's friends. They had watched after it for several decades each time their friends were away.

Julie carefully and quietly opened the screen door to the porch. She showed me the secret hiding place for the key. Even though we knew no one would be there, we quietly let ourselves inside. We stayed for a couple of hours, laughing, talking, and enjoying just being together. After an hour, it began to rain. The rain picked up, drumming its raindrops on the tin roof making a kind of sound-cloak around us causing everything else to seem far away. We leaned back on the old worn sofa, and I hugged Julie to me. I liked being here and hoped the rain would last for a while as I wanted this feeling we had at the moment to last as long as it could. I felt reluctant to leave here and reluctant to leave the farm. I guess I felt a little afraid our happiness might not last when we went home and had a go at our marriage again.

I decided this might be a good time to have a talk with Julie and tell her about my illiteracy. This honesty might be what the marriage needed. I had kept it from her the year we had been married before the divorce, and I wanted to start fresh with no secrets.

"Julie, I've got something important to tell you." She regarded me with attentive questioning eyes. "I've never been able to read very well."

"Oh Brad, I didn't know you had trouble reading. I'll help you learn, Honey." She stroked my hair. "I love you. I'll help you with anything that will make you happy."

As we sat there listening to the thunder and lightning, I told Julie about some of my disappointments and failures in school. She stroked my face as she listened. I held her in my arms until the storm let up. Then we walked the two miles back to the house. The weather had gotten cooler and sent a slight breeze.

We arrived just as Almeda and Jewell spread lunch at the picnic table on the front porch. After lunch, we packed up and as we said our good-bys, there were many more hugs and promises, except between Jewell and me. We each stayed as far from the other as we could, and still be civil.

As we drove back to Atlanta, I realized what a laid back lifestyle her grandparents had now but how hard they had worked all of their lives. I hoped Julie and I could remain married for as long a time as Almeda and Leldon had been married. I admired them for their closeness all those years. That weekend became one of our favorite times to remember. Whenever I thought of them, I pictured Papa Leldon fishing at the crick and Granny Almeda in the kitchen preparing some strawberry dish. I thought I understood Jewel better, but that didn't help me know how to deal with her. To me she still remained the mother-in-law from hell. I guess to her, I remained the son-in-law from hell. I hoped that would change. I hoped to improve her opinion regarding me.

During this time together, I learned Julie and I could live together in peace if Julie could keep her moods and depression under control and if I never went back to my addictions. Since we had been back together, Julie had been happy and not depressed at all. I knew we both had to work at making a go at our marriage.

I knew I had to trust in the Lord. We had started a better life together than what we had before and hoped that meant Julie and I were going to be together for a long time. I had a taste of how good life could be if we could go back home and live like we had been with each other that weekend.

Part III–Losing Myself, Finding Myself

27.
Supervisor

Julie and I returned from our vacation to northern Alabama rested and optimistic about our future together. We were happy about getting married the second time. We had a new lease on life. I went to apply at American Fabrication. When the secretary handed me the application, I took it home and Julie helped me complete all the blanks. I went back the next day and had an interview. They called me on Monday and said I could start to work immediately. From then on when I had things to fill out, I just took all the forms home, so Julie could help be.

I had my new motorcycle and rode it to work each day eager to learn and to advance so I could make a successful financial future for us. I came home each day thinking of the Julie she had been on our vacation.

The antidepressant the doctor had prescribed for Julie while we were divorced had helped her tremendously. It brought her to the level of being in a smooth, even temperament without depression or temper tantrums. Each night, Julie met me at the door of our apartment, bright eyed. She always embraced me and said, "I love you, Honey." She always had dinner for me and had our evening together planned. Often we just lay around the apartment. Sometimes we went for a walk in a nearby park. I felt happier than I had been in a long time.

Then out of the blue Julie declared, “I don’t need these pills. I’m just fine now. Anyway they give me headaches, and I’m starting to gain weight. I think they cause water retention, so I’m coming off them.”

“Julie the pills are helping you. You have been doing great. Please don’t come off them,” I insisted. But she had made up her mind to discontinue taking the antidepressants and told her mother she could not stand the side affects they were causing. The rocky road of hills and valleys started again. A few days later when I got up to go to work, Julie just stayed in bed. “I can’t take my life anymore,” she said.

She didn’t go to work, in fact, she didn’t get out of bed for three days. I tried to persuade her to start the same antidepressants again. She did for a week, but it was not enough time to get into her system to help before she quit again. So I took her to a general practitioner, then a specialist. I had to pull her up out of bed, coaxing her to go to the doctor. “Julie, the appointment is in an hour. You need to get dressed.” I went to the closet and got slacks and a pullover sweater for her. She still refused to get dressed. “If you go to this doctor, maybe things will get better for you.”

“I hate you. Leave me alone. I just want to lay here. I have no reason to live.” I practically dressed her and stood her up and helped her into the car. At the specialist Julie barely answered his questions. Finally he said she needed counseling. So every Monday night, I took her to counseling sessions, but this did not seem to help her. We saw another specialist who said Julie had a spiritual problem.

She started doing a little better, I think, because of all the attention I gave her. Each time we went to the doctor, I took her out for lunch or supper or for a milk shake. Then I found yet another specialist who said Julie had a hormone imbalance. He gave her a book he had written and a shot of yam extract— a progesterone he had a lab develop for him. The next day Julie broke out in hives all over, and became severely depressed.

When she went back to his office, she slammed the book down on his desk, and snapped, "Your sweet potato shot did *not* work. I am worse than ever." She turned and walked out.

I tried to help her by learning all I could about depression and antidepressants and by talking to each doctor. She tried another antidepressant but it caused stomach cramps and dizziness. On the third antidepressant, Julie went into a sinking spell. Her depression went the deepest I had ever seen it. "I should end it all," she cried. "I'm no good to you or to myself or to anybody else. Life is too much trouble. My legs feel heavy. I feel better when I don't move."

She didn't eat and would not get dressed or get out of bed. On the third day of this I got up to get ready for work. She turned over and went back to sleep. I fixed her some oatmeal and got her to eat a few spoonfuls and some toast. I took these latest pills away from her and called the doctor. He said she should come off them gradually and not all at once. I disagreed and said she would never take this kind of antidepressant again. I took off work and stayed with her for five days. I figured it would take about a week to get all of the drug out of her system.

Over the weekend, she told me she had been planning her suicide. "I could not decide whether to use razor blades on my wrists and get into a filled bathtub or connect an exhaust pipe to my car window."

When we saw the doctor on Monday, he said the drug had caused an adverse reaction. I tried to understand, but we left the office and did not go back there. I felt alone in this. I couldn't burden Dad as he had problems of his own. Kay had to care for her family. Jewell would be the last person I would ask for help. She would only make the situation worse. She would also find someway to blame me.

I knew I couldn't be happy without Julie, but living with her, caused me to stay in a state of great turmoil. After two weeks, Julie recovered from the deep depression, became somewhat functional, and went back to work, but each day when I came home, I didn't know what to expect.

Would her depression return since she took no medication at this time?

I felt like I rode on a rocky roller coaster again, and that I got flung out occasionally. When Julie started screaming and throwing things again, I would either go back to smoking pot and drinking beer or would leave. Many times, I just left a note and went on a trip for a few days. I could find peace and quiet better in the mountains of north Georgia.

But I realized a terrible thing: When I stayed alone in the mountains, I got strength and always bucked up to come back and try again. Then when I went to my old habits, Julie's depression got worse. My lifestyle became something she could not condone or accept. She hammered me to do better because she cared and because she grew afraid something would happen to me. And it did.

I had a terrible motorcycle wreck. I stopped at the intersection at Kings Springs going home from work. The light changed, and I punched it. A seventeen year old, who had been driving only one month and had his momma in the car, turned left in front of me on a yellow light. My motorcycle hit his rear tire; my head hit the roof of the car; and the gas tank of the motorcycle flew off and hit me in the stomach. I flipped and flew fifty feet through the air. Wearing a helmet is all that saved me. I blacked out for a moment. When I opened my eyes, the kid stood over me. I would have hit him if I could have gotten to him. I blacked out again.

More trouble and loss for me. I went into surgery for repair on my lip, gums, and the roof of my mouth. The kid who hit me didn't have insurance. Both of us were at fault, so no one had to pay. My motorcycle days were over since my Kawasaki KZ1000 was now a smashed pile of metal in the junkyard.

For a few weeks, I recovered at home, and became as depressed as Julie, so I went to visit Dad. For a long time after Mom died, Dad just sat around, lost. Lila had been the light of his life. She had given him reason to get up in the morning, to see what he could do for her.

He still had the effects of the stroke, being paralysed on one side and blind in one eye, but he tried to be functional. He showed me he could wiggle one toe then he got out of the wheelchair and dragged himself along. A few weeks later when I went by to see him, he walked on his own, just dragging one foot. He kept trying to move his arm. Soon it moved slightly, so he just kept trying to use it. After about two months, he regained some use. Soon he could do everything he normally did but always favored his hand a little.

Dad still had a contract on the apartments being built around Oakland. Kevin, his nephew, ran things for him. His crew collected garbage, cleaned stairwells and laundry rooms, and did all repairs and painting. Dad employed several men and Kevin saw that everything ran smoothly. Kevin drove him to each site to inspect the work.

At American Fabrication, when my supervisor got a promotion to became the company's vice president, I received a promotion, his job. I was to become the supervisor, over twelve men.

I went to work everyday in constant dread someone would find out I could not read or write. Thelma Ivy, my secretary, never suspected me to be anything but an educated person. Thelma, a middle-age neat lady who dressed in business suits, had her hair pulled back into a bun and wore dark rimed glasses became the "in charge" person. Her expert secretarial skills and overly diligent aptitude for having everything in ship-shape, kept everything running smoothly. She made it very easy for me to be the boss.

"Thelma, read the incoming letters to me while I put all the shipping receipts in order," I told her each morning, as I pretended to sort the receipts. I listened intensely as she read each letter then I told her how to answer each one while she took notes. "When you finish typing, just send someone to the warehouse to get me. I will come back and sign them before I go home." I learned to read the work orders well enough to check off what I had for the men to do. I put one man in charge of ordering materials and in charge of receiving.

At home things could still go from "honey-sugar" to uncivil in a span of time from morning to evening. Occasionally things would be fine. On the good weekends Julie and I went camping and backpacking a few times. Many times we went with friends.

On a snowy winter weekend, we drove into the Cahutta National Forest early in the morning. By nightfall we were deep in the wilderness on an icy dirt road. The woods on either side of us were pristine and covered in snow. Suddenly I heard Julie exclaim, "What's that?" Our car headlights shined on what appeared to be a herd of large dogs, but it was about a dozen very small deer. Our headlights caused them turn and run up the side of the mountain. We continued to drive and in several hours were back to blacktop roads and the main road leaving the park.

"I just love looking at the woods covered in the snow. It looks like a Christmas card here." Julie told me when we cuddled up on the big sofa in front of a wide fireplace roaring with warmth at the vacation lodge.

That night we made passionate love. Julie awoke early, opened the heavy drapes and looked out watching the snow fall in the forest which surrounded the three story lodge. At breakfast in the restaurant downstairs, we sat by the window for a snowy view.

"Oh Brad, let's stay for another night," Julie pleaded. "Oh please, please." They way she pleaded reminded me of when she had begged her Grandfather Lel to let her ride old Pet. I got a glimpse of that same little girl from long ago. This weekend turned out to be as good for us as our vacation with her grandparents, and I also wanted it to last. Could I dare to hope that Julie would stay in this good mood? This would be so wonderful. I wanted to hang onto this hope, so we stayed another night.

But what you least expect, happens. When we went back home, things stayed good for a while. Julie had the pictures of our vacation developed.

She framed one for her desk at work and one for an end table in the living room. We talked about our trip and were planning a summer vacation.

I felt proud of my work where I made good money and had benefits for Julie and myself. We lived in a nice apartment and had adequate furniture, but Julie wanted a new living room suite and a new kitchen table and chairs. But instead, after I wrecked my motorcycle, I had to have a vehicle to go to work. So, I bought a new Dodge pickup, had it insured, and mapped out the vacation we planned. Then she got strange on me again.

It all started when Julie wrecked her car. She overshot a parking spot and hit a post, crushing the right front fender. This shook her up a bit, but we had the fender repaired.

When we got the car back, she kept saying, "This car doesn't drive the same. Something's wrong. It doesn't sound right. Hear that roar? I think the frame is warped." Then she got really strange. "Brad, that truck belongs to me. That extra money should have bought my new furniture. You just did what you wanted and didn't tell me you were buying a truck. It's mine and I will have it."

I knew trouble brewed. I had to be ready for whatever she planned to do. Every day for several weeks when I got to work, I would take the coil wire off the engine and use a logging chain to hook the truck to an I-beam cemented into the ground in the parking lot. One day at work, I heard someone say, "There's a wrecker out in the parking lot."

I went out and asked the guy, "Can I help you?"

"I'm here to get a dark blue, Dodge pickup," he replied.

"That's my truck," I said. He glanced up at me as I asked, "How do you feel?"

He looked like he did not quite know what to say, but replied, "I feel fine. How do you feel?"

"That's not the point," I said. "Do you want to remain feeling fine? If you do you'll leave." He stepped back and said nervously, "Wait a minute.

I don't want any trouble." He left in a big hurry.

I called Julie, and she became irate. I tried to reason with her. She continued to be adamant about the truck being hers. She said she had gotten a ride to work with a neighbor until I came back to give her the truck. "I'm not driving a car that has been wrecked."

This did not make sense. If I went home, let her drive my new pickup, and I took the car, I would be giving into her moods. I came up with another solution. "Get off work early," I said. "We'll go trade your car for a used one. You pick it out, and when I get off work, I'll meet you at the car lot."

"No, I'm not going to do that. I'm going to have what is mine."

I could not reason with her. We hung up and I didn't go home. I just couldn't stand having a storm every time I talked to Julie and every night when I went home.

I usually went over every afternoon to help Dad around his house. That afternoon, after I helped him, I just stayed. My afternoon visits meant so much to him, and, really, he needed me. Without Mom, Dad felt lost. His life was a great empty void. So I decided to stay with him for the next two weeks and give Julie time to be alone and get her thinking straightened out.

Julie called me later to say she had a used car and hoped I was happy that I had her truck.

I wanted a smooth peaceful life and never had that with Julie. I found I could stay off drugs and drinking much easier without her. Now that I lived with Dad, I planned to stay clean.

28.
Sad Times

I moved in permanently with Dad and focused on my job and on taking care of him. I waited until I knew Julie had left for work and would not be back at the apartment for a couple of hour then I went there and got my clothes and things. I moved into my old room at Dad's where I settled into a peaceful routine. Dad began to perk up and even improved physically. Every night when I came home, I found him in the kitchen moving round in his wheelchair trying to get a little supper ready for us.

Blue and Smoky were happy that they had me back on the farm, too. They greeted me every night. Smoky became my constant shadow when I did chores. Dad had kept only one horse and one cow, I guess for old time sake. I pushed him in his wheelchair out to the barn each afternoon, and as he managed to milk the cow, I opened up the stall for the horse and filled its trough.

The next day, we decided to clean out the barn. I pushed Dad out and positioned his chair where he could see most of the barn. He got up and dragged around doing chores, but soon sat back in the wheelchair and gave me instructions. First I shoveled out the stalls and rearranged some of the buckets and tools on a low table where he could have easier access. As I worked, Dad began to talk about God. "He never gives up on us son, and I never give up on my prayers. Sometimes things take a long time to turn around, but you just have to keep the faith. Keep the joy in your heart and mind like your prayers have already been answered, then one day you will look up and see the results." I turned around and made eye contact with him when he said this and we had a big laugh. I knew he meant he had prayed for me for a long time to see this moment.

Dad and I were up early the next morning getting ready to go to church. We talked about old times, the ones that were good memories. I liked filling up my weekends as I had done this weekend, so I would not want to go drinking or out with the boys. After we got to church I listened to the preacher and the singing, but I still felt like an outsider. The church members were friendly, but I knew they were nice to me for Dad's sake and because they remembered me as a young boy. I also knew many of them remembered my past. They thought of me still as the "wild one who had done drugs." They had a certain look in their eyes when they shook hands with me. Many of them knew I had married, yet I'm sure they were thinking, Why isn't his wife with him? But no one asked.

After Mom died, Aunt Lilly came down to the house and took some of Mom's clothes. Being Mom's identical twin, when Lilly wore these clothes it felt so eerie to me like when she wore Mom's beige coat with the small brown mink collar. Dad let her have the bird vase also. She said in almost a gloating way, "Now I have a matching set." She focused on what she wanted more than on the loss of her twin sister. Aunt Lilly had her own way of looking at things.

The next Sunday when Dad and I got to church, Lilly stood there wearing Mom's beige coat watching me push Dad in his wheelchair across the parking lot. When I made eye contact and spoke to her, she tilted her chin up slightly as we passed her. I knew her well enough to tell she thought to herself, You might fool everybody but you're not fooling me. But then the next day, she asked me to take her to the doctor. Since Uncle James died, she had asked Dad to help her until he had a stroke.

She started relying on me more and more to do things for her. Though

I didn't like Aunt Lilly mainly because she didn't like or trust me, I had to do things for her since she was part of our family. The next time Aunt Lilly called she said, "Brad, I need to go see an eye doctor. I can't see to read. Anyway it's been years since I had my glasses changed. I want you to come over here and take me."

When I took her back home, she started complaining about her house. "I need the door fixed on the screened-in porch. It won't close all the way and flies come in on the porch then they get in the house. A front step is broken and it's a wonder I don't fall when I try to go down those steps."

I went to the shed out back and found Uncle James' tools. His things were still in the same place he left them. I made these repairs for her. A week later Aunt Lilly called with another complaint, so I went back to fix the hot water heater. Aunt Lilly regarded me and remarked, "I never thought you'd be the one to take care of me in my old age." She seemed as surprised as anyone that I had straighten out.

I thought about Julie all the time. I missed the loving, good Julie, but I gave up on ever living with her. I felt happier living with Dad, and I knew Julie got along better without me.

My Dad and I lived like this for about a year and a half when one morning I went out back of the house and sat on the big rock sipping coffee. I thought about all those years in the hut and about all the bad things my friends and I had done as kids. It was amazing that we had gotten away with so much. The hut had been torn down long ago, but the swing still hung there for Kay's boy, Daniel. The big logging chain we used when we killed a hog still hung from the oak tree back behind the barn.

Every morning before I left for work, I checked on Dad. On this particular morning, I did not hear him moving around in his room. He must still be in bed, I thought. I eased the door open slowly, so as not to wake him. I was shocked to see that his left arm was hanging off the bed in a grotesque way like it had become dead weight. My heart jumped.

I rushed over to him and found him pale and unconscious. I called an ambulance right away. When the ambulance came, I helped load him and followed them to the hospital where the emergency room doctor said Dad had suffered another stroke. I stayed by his side and called Kay who came immediately.

I really felt alone. I wanted Julie. It had been almost two years since I left her. I dialed the phone to tell her about Dad. When she answered, and heard my voice, I detected a tone in her voice indicating she was glad to talk to me. Could it be that she would come like she had done when I called to tell her about Mom being in the hospital?

Julie did come to the hospital to help me with Dad. Because of his weakness, Dad could not stand, so I carried him in my arms to the bathroom. My heart broke to see him so helpless as he had always been such a strong, able man. Then the next day, he had another stroke, and in spite of what the doctors did, Dad died later that day. Julie stayed at my side and became a comfort.

We held the funeral at Dad's church. The members there really came and supported Kay and me in our grief. One elder in the church came to me before the service and asked, "Brad, are you going to continue to come to church now that your Dad had passed?" As I shook his hand, I thought about what he asked. It seemed obvious that I had been coming just for Dad's sake. I looked him in the eyes and said, "You pray for me that I will be strong enough to continue without him." The old man nodded in understanding and left me.

We laid Dad to rest at Grace Memorial Cemetery beside Mom, under the shadow of the electric power plant smokestack tower. Mom had been gone almost three years. Dad would have been seventy-nine on his next birthday.

Julie came to the funeral and acted civil when she sat with me, but after the funeral, she went back to her apartment, and I went back to Dad's empty house. Julie told me on the phone that night, "I don't want you back because your Dad died. If we go back together it has to be because we are ready and because we have changed." She, once again, closed the door on our relationship. Somehow I felt if she could not support me, love me, and help me through this sadness, I would be better off not to try, at this time, to get her back. I could not take any more storms. I felt upheaval enough at this point.

The next Sunday after the funeral, I went to Dad's church. It felt strange to go without him. I mainly went to thank everyone for their kindnesses and for the flowers the church sent. But I felt lost without him there. I felt almost like an intruder.

A week later when Kay and I went to the Fulton County Courthouse to have the will probated, we found Dad had appointed me the executor of the estate. In Kay's emotional state, she wanted me to handle everything but also insisted we start putting a price on everything, for an auction.

Kay had no idea of my difficulty in reading or the extent of the trouble I had been in when I was younger. Instead, she said, "I have confidence in you, baby brother." But later, she questioned everything I did. And there were other problems.

Dad had paid monthly on a nice tombstone. When he died he thought he had paid the total, but when we went to bury him, there had been no record of him buying a tombstone. Later we realized the clerk at the cemetery had pocketed his money.

Then I discovered Dad had no life insurance to cover the burial expenses or to pay the outstanding doctor bills. I found Dad's retirement benefits had included monthly checks and health insurance, but not life insurance. When I contacted the company Dad had worked for, they explained that Dad missed getting life insurance benefits for himself by one month. If he had worked one more month, we would not be in this financial crisis. They had really done him dirty offering a mandatory retirement before he was eligible for life insurance. I would never know if Dad had realized he did not have life insurance. If he did know, then I understood why he had continued to carry the apartment jobs and why he had worked so hard even when he became disabled and partly blind.

With Dad gone, I now had to pay a small mortgage on the house, pay seven doctors, and pay all the hospital bills that his insurance did not cover. I felt overwhelmed. He had left me the executor of the estate, but I had no idea what needed to be done. I paced through the empty house not knowing where to turn then I decided I needed a lawyer.

I called Chuck Burton, a lawyer friend, who drove a black Ferrari, smoked cigars, wore black cowboy boots, and a black cowboy hat. He got drunk every day by nightfall, but looked like a preacher going to work the next day. After I told him all my problems, he said in his rough voice, "I'll take care of it," and slammed the phone down. I called Chuck back and asked him what he planned to do. He said he would send me a copy of the letter and slammed the phone receiver down again. I called him back again. This was the third call in five minutes, but I had to have answers. I asked, "What's this going to cost me?" He replied, "There's no charge for you."

Two days later my phone rang, and when I answered, I heard Kay say, "Damn your ass. I hope you burn in hell for this, you son of a bitch."

"What are you talking about?" I replied, shocked.

"Chuck Burton sent me a letter saying not to set foot on Dad's property and not to touch anything or we would be arrested," she replied angrily.

I had only seen or heard Kay angry a few times in my life, but never this angry. I tried to make her understand I didn't tell him to write that letter, but she would not listen to me and hung up on me. I felt her angry words hit me right in the heart. I felt hurt with her and angry at Chuck. I needed someone to help me, but Dad had left me in charge.

When I received my copy of the letter, I called Chuck. "Hey, Chuck, the letter you sent my sister is a little harsh. She can come on the property, and we are going to sort out Mom and Dad's belongings. She's not going to be arrested, and I want you to send her a letter straightening this out."

"Brad, that's just a standard letter I send to family members."

Chuck agreed to send Kay a revised letter. In the meantime, I called Kay and told her how Chuck had overreacted. "I'm doing the best I can. You've got to understand." She said she knew I had a lot on me and that she did also. "It's a sad time for both of us."

I put Dad's house up for sale and stayed there to clear it out. I went to work every day, but every night and on the weekends, I cleaned, cleared, and boxed my parent's belongings. I packed everything I wanted to keep. Then I stacked up what we were going to sell at the auction. The hardest part came when I cleared out Dad's barn. There were things I would never use and had no place for, but I could not let them go.

It had been a month since I attended Dad's church. I thought it might help me feel better if I went again. When I stepped inside the double doors, the organist played the prelude as the church filled. Several older members who had been friends of Dad's looked around and greeted me. One came and shook my hand and said, "Well we haven't seen you in a while." I stayed and listened to the preacher and enjoyed the music more than anything, but when I left, I felt relief that I would not get anymore of those "you're a backslider" looks.

On Monday Kay came and we started dividing Mom and Dad's things. "Now you take all of the kitchen utensils and what furniture you want," I told Kay. "I have no use for them as I don't have a house." Kay took Mom's piano, organ, and accordion since she also played. She boxed up all the sheet music and hymnals.

After she left, I passed through Mom and Dad's room, and went over to the dresser. I pulled out a dresser drawer. There lay Mom's gold compact with the gold roses, each having a rhinestone in the center. I remembered that day long ago when I had been four and watched her powder her face and apply lipstick. She had kissed me and left a smudge on my cheek and laughed at me trying to wipe it off. I remembered how beautiful she looked and how close I felt to her.

I pulled out the other dresser drawer and there, wrapped in her scarf, lay her hair brush. I took her comb and cleaned the hair off and started toward the trash can. Then I stopped. A faint fragrance of her shampoo still lingered. I sat down on a stool in front of her dresser, put the hair back on the brush, and gently packed the brush into a box. I felt like my heart was breaking. Then in the drawer, I found a tissue she had used to blot her lips. I unfolded it and could see the little lines of her lips—her lip shape, in red lipstick. By this time, I sat there sobbing into my hands.

On the weekend of the auction, Kay came early on Saturday morning to help. Then I called Julie, "We're clearing out Mom and Dad's house. Do you want anything of Mom's?" There came only silence on the line. I continued, "I've put the house up for sale." She replied, "I don't care what you do. You always do what you want anyway." I sighed, "Julie, I'm having a hard time right now. How about give me a break?"

"I don't want to come over there. It's too sad. If you're having a hard time, go get high. That's what you always do."

"I've been off drugs and alcohol for a long time. I started coming off way before Mom died," I insisted.

"Oh. Yeah? How long will it last this time? I just don't feel like being around you now. I've got problems of my own."

With that, she hung up on me. I just sat there, feeling rejected. I could not believe she could be so hostile to me with what I had to face. At this low point in my life, I really needed someone who cared about me. Well. It might be better that I didn't have Julie's contention. We might have ended up in a fight and that would have caused me more pain.

After the auction, I continued to live in the house waiting for it to sell. Six months went by and I went through the lowest time in my life. The boxes of things were packed to move, and I had everything else cleared out of the house but the bare necessities. I continued to work each day and went home to an empty house. On the weekend, I rambled around not knowing what to do with myself. My thoughts of the past rose up around me. Depression fell on me like a dark cloud I could not shake.

I sat on the front porch one Friday afternoon just relaxing after work when a Bronco came barreling down Hill Street right across the bridge and into the yard. It screeched to a halt close to where I sat. It was Don Pace, one of the guys I roomed with in Marietta the summer I was twelve. He was the last person I would ever want to see. As he stepped out of the Bronco, I could see he was so stoned he could hardly get to the porch. He wanted me to go into Atlanta to buy drugs with him. I told him, "I don't do drugs any more. Don, you need to leave."

"Hey, Man, that's a mighty high bluff." He gestured to the steep bank beside the house where the railroad tracks ran above the house. "You think I could make it to the top in my Bronco?" I felt ticked-off at him coming around and growled back to him, "I don't care what you do."

I just watched as he gunned the vehicle up the thirty percent grade. The tires were spinning and the motor was winding. He was up to the tracks before I could decide this was a potential dangerous situation. Sure enough, the front tires bounced over the tracks, and the Bronco stalled. He started the motor again and as he let off the brakes to ease back down, the front bumper of his Bronco hooked on the tracks. It was stuck.

I came up out of my chair realizing the last train had come by at three o'clock that afternoon. Another train was due at five o'clock. I checked my wrist watch and saw it was four thirty. If we did not get the Bronco off the track in half an hour, a fast-moving train would tear it apart. Don ran down to me in a frantic fit wanting a crowbar.

I ran to Dad's barn and managed to find the crowbar. Thank goodness I had not sold it at the auction.

Now we had twenty minutes left to free the vehicle. We were both big guys, but could not apply enough force to free the front bumper. I went back to the barn twice and brought up a concrete block each time to use as a lever. I got into the Bronco, put it in reverse, and gunned it as Don applied force on the crowbar. With him prying the bumper upward, I shot his vehicle backward down the bluff and sure rattled it around before coming to a full stop just short of the bridge.

We had both just walked back to the porch when a passenger train came speeding by, shaking the house. I was angry at the trouble this drug addict had caused. Don Pace kept mouthing off, and again, I asked him to leave. He got out of control and was ranting and raving about how he could have been killed. He stood under a tree just beyond the porch when he said, "This house is too close to the tracks, I think I'll burn it down."

I went in, grabbed Dad's shot gun, took it to the porch, and pointed it at him. He began to shake and back up. I took the gun to my shoulder. Don called out, "Man don't do that. I'm not going to burn your house down. I was just having a few laughs."

I aimed the gun just above his head and shot the limb off the tree above him. The gun's firing and the limb falling across his head convinced him it was time to leave, in a big hurry. He was in his Bronco in a split second, turned it around, and sped away.

No sooner had he left than the phone rang. It was Aunt Lilly, "What in the world is going on down there? I heard a gun shot." I patiently replied, "I just shot at a rabbit running through the yard."

"Well who was that taking off so fast from your house?" she asked as though she did not believe me about the rabbit. "That was someone who didn't know the street dead-ended." She hung up.

I went in shaken over the ordeal. I was so thankful that the part of my life dealing with scumbags, like the one who just left, was over.

The next morning I awoke to the coldest day of the winter. About four o'clock in the afternoon, a light freezing rain began to fall. By dusk, the snow covered the ground and stuck, which is rare for the South. Smoky and Blue were in a pen out back. Smoky came out of the doghouse and began to howl, matching the feelings I had inside.

We had always kept our animals in the barn, or in a pen, or running loose, but never in the house. I glanced out the kitchen window. The whole backyard had turned white. Blue hid in the doghouse, but I could see Smoky's black outline as he sat outside the doghouse howling in protest of the cold. His white breath came out like steam in the air with every howl. This struck me as funny but sad. So I let the two dogs inside to lay in front of the fireplace on two old blankets.

After they were settled, Blue got up and went over to Dad's big blue corduroy recliner and kept sniffing around. I wondered, What's wrong with him. Why's he sniffing like that? Then I realized he searched for Dad. Dad had sat in that chair for years every evening reading the Bible before he went to bed. I guess Blue picked up Dad's scent lingering there.

That night I slept on the living room sofa to be near the fireplace and near the dogs in case they needed to go outside. The next morning, Smoky awakened me by laying his chin on my chest, whining. "Hey, Boy." I rubbed his head and lay there with my eyes closed for a few minutes. Smoky whined some more, and I sat up.

Then I noticed Blue had not moved. He seemed to be too still. Oh no, I thought. I went over to the ol' dog. He was dead. "Well, Blue." I said out loud. "I guess you have found a way to go find Dad, your buddy." Blue had been in about as bad a shape as Dad had been before he died. Old age had put grey hairs on his face and clouded his eyes with cataracts. The old injury from being shot in the foot had caused arthritis which had made it difficult for him to walk. I rolled Blue in the blanket he lay on and took him to the barn and put him on a shelf until I could bury him.

Later in the day when some of the snow melted and when the temperature went up to about forty degrees, I took the shovel from the barn. Smoky ran alongside me as I went out to a high hill above the railroad bridge where I had spent so many hours as a boy throwing rocks into the creek below. I dug a hole deep and wide enough for Blue.

Smoky and I walked back through the pasture toward the backyard. I surveyed the place as though I saw it for the last time. The snow had melted except in the shaded areas. My boots were muddy, and as I walked I used the shovel as a walking stick, making a "thunk" on the ground with each step. I reflected some on the immediate past.

I took Smoky, went inside, built a fire in the fireplace and sat for a few minutes until I got warm. Then I left Smoky in the house and went back to bury Blue. I covered his grave with big rocks then I walked back to the house and sat in Dad's recliner again. "Well Smoky. It's just you and me now."

I reflected on all my sadness but found a little humor when I thought of my life like the lyrics of a country-western song: My wife's gone, my parents died, now my dog has died, and I'm all alone. I had to smile. I fell asleep in the recliner with Smoky at my feet.

One week later, the house sold. Kay and I went to the lawyer's office, then paid the doctor bills and hospital bills, and divided what we had left. We each got five thousand dollars.

When I went shopping for a new home in Cobb County, I used my share of the money to put a down payment on a small ranch-style house and some acreage. I immediately began to build a barn for Dad's things. I had plans to build a new life and to find new reasons to live.

29.
Work Farm

I transferred within my company to a high risk job as a millwright, working along side a crane, welding. With this high risk job, I really brought in the money. I did welding on the floodgate project for the Richard B. Russell Dam. I didn't have any trouble understanding blueprints and faked my way through by bringing any written material home and studying at night. When I found a word I could not figure out, I would tell a co-worker that my blueprint had gotten smudged or wet, and asked him to read the word from his corresponding blueprint. Then I would laugh it off, so he would not suspect I had low reading skills.

With a new home and a good job, I didn't have time to think about doing drugs or drinking.

I called my sister to see how things were with her and to tell her about my house. She told me that with Dad's inheritance she did not have to have renters in her house any more. She planned on moving upstairs to live. She had lived in the basement of her house and rented out the two upstairs floors for ten years. So on the weekend of the move, I helped her and Sam and Daniel move all their furniture upstairs. I felt happy for them and felt reluctant to go home when we finished. Kay, Sam and little Daniel were my only family now except for Aunt Lilly.

When Dad's house sold, Aunt Lilly had no one in her family living close, so I kept driving back trying to help her out. As her health failed, she needed help daily, more and more. Finally after I made several trips back to Oakdale in one week, she looked at me and said, "I need my children. I need to move to Mississippi." I helped her make the arrangements and she called her family. After her son came for her, I soon had her house cleared out and boarded up. In Mississippi Aunt Lilly went into a nursing home close to where both her children lived.

Now with my great house and high-paying job, I made a good life for myself. But I could not forget about Julie. I needed her. I had a plan to get her back. I waited for several months to call her to make sure I stayed clean and to make sure I remained strong enough to not go back to drugs if things got rough between us again. I tried to have everything right before I called. I felt nervous. What if she were as unfriendly as she had been when I invited her to come by Dad's house before the auction. I wanted her to come live with me. We were still married, but she might be reluctant to try again. I took a deep breath and dialed her number. When she answered, I plunged into the conversation by blurting out, "I have a house. Would you like to see it?"

"Hello Brad." She seemed hesitant to speak. It sounded like she hated to give up a bad mood just to be happy and cheerful. She asked cautiously like she would not like the answer, "Where is the house?"

"It's a ranch style in Cobb County. I have five acres, and I've built a barn for Dad's things. It has a big kitchen and a big den," I said.

"How many bedrooms does it have?" She asked, sounding a little interested.

I smiled. "It has three bedrooms, one and a half baths, and a big flower bed out front."

She got caught up in the discussion of the house and forgot to be cold and distant when she said, "It will be spring soon, and I could plant some bulbs."

Wow. I thought, I haven't asked her to come back, but she is rightly assuming I want her here by talking about plans for a flower garden. "You want to see it tomorrow tonight?"

When she agreed, I felt excited and full of anticipation all the next day. I picked her up after work and drove her to see the new house. When we came in the driveway, she looked around amazed, "Brad, all this is yours? This is a lovely house. You built that barn? I didn't think it would be so big. I parked and as we got out and started toward the house Julie excitedly remarked, "Oh, there's a porch on the front!" Then we went inside the house and through every room.

As she looked at everything, I talked. "Julie would you come here and live with me? I bought this house with you in mind. I've been off drugs and alcohol since before Mom died. I've got a really good paying job. You could quit your job." This really had her interest now.

"Oh, Brad." Then she hugged me to her, "I'd love to live here with you. There is so much I could do to the house."

"We can buy the furniture you've always wanted." When I said this, it seemed to finalize her decision. She stayed with me in the new house that night. I felt so happy. We were finally back together.

The next afternoon we went shopping and bought enough furniture to fill up every room. I paid for it all with a check as I had opened my first checking account when I moved into my house. I had been saving for this day.

Julie quit her job, stayed home, and began to decorate our new home. Another chance for happiness? Did I dare hope we could finally be happy? All the things were in place for a normal life. We had every young couple's dream, our first house. Julie seemed happy in her surroundings and her days were filled with work and plans.

I became immersed in my job, putting all my energy and thought into it. Even at night, I thought about what I had done all day. We did some awesome things involving crane work, like roofing a shopping center. I also did welding on a four story furnace, used in making aluminum.

Then I went to a job working up on a huge conveyor belt, seventy feet in the air. I worked with another aluminum worker, Lenny. The crane operator nearby lifted sheet metal onto the seventy foot ledge several yards away for us. Then Lenny and I welded this sheet metal onto the conveyor belt. We had been working ten hours a day for seven days a week to meet a deadline. When we both took a short break just standing there, I drank from my water jug. "Man, this is good money, but dangerous work. Last night I dreamed I floated seventy foot in the air," I told Lenny.

"Yeah. The money's good, but I haven't seen my wife and kids but a few minutes a day for several weeks now," he replied. "It would be nice to have a day off once in a while. But we've got to finish this job in the next two weeks."

Late in the afternoon when the crane operator lifted the last batch of metal up to the ledge, he accidentally let his foot off the pedal on the crane, something you just don't do. The boom fell toward us. Lenny, who stood next to me, saw the boom coming and yelled, "Look out!" He lunged toward the ledge like he intended to jump.

Out of the corner of my eye, I caught a glimpse of it coming, and threw myself flat grabbing Lenny as I went down. We hit the surface, that we had been standing on, just as the boom swept over us, missing us by three feet. It had swung by exactly where we had been standing about four feet in the air. It would have hit both of us in the chest had we still been standing. It appeared as if the crane operator had tried to bowl us off the ledge, like the boom was a bowling ball and we were the pins.

This had been an accident, but one that would have cost two men their lives, so the crane operator got fired on the spot. The supervisor told Lenny and me to go ahead and leave, to take the rest of the day off. This happened about four o'clock, so we took off an hour early, and I headed home, still shaking on the inside because of this close call. I knew both of us could be dead right now, if we had not ducked down at the exact second that we had.

On the way home, I stopped off at a local bar close to the interstate for a few beers to calm my nerves down. After a few beers, I felt better, felt calm, and my hands had quit shaking. I got back into my Dodge truck and headed toward the interstate. A patrol car sitting close to the ramp, flipped on the blue lights. I knew this meant trouble for me. Sure enough, the patrol car pulled me over and the patrolman checked my license and asked me to step out of the car. "Sir, I only had a couple of beers. I needed them. I almost got killed this afternoon." Everything I said made things worse because the patrolman thought I lied trying to make an excuse. I figured he would give me a ticket. But instead, he gave me a sobriety test—one I failed by one point over the limit. The patrolman arrested me for DUI. I went straight to the county jail.

I felt stunned. This all happened so fast. One minute I'm on a seventy foot ledge nearly getting killed, then I have a few beers, and now I'm on my way to jail? How very ironic. I felt slapped down. When the State Patrol office pulled up my record, nothing showed regarding all the trouble I had been in as a teenager. I was now twenty-five years old and had no prior convictions or arrests in the last nine years.

I could not understand why I didn't just get a ticket, but I kept quiet. If I started pleading for a lighter sentence, things might get worse. I knew I had a lucky break when none of the trouble I had been in showed up on my record.

I overheard another man talking to a patrolman. "Why am I going to jail? This is my first offence." Just beyond the two men was a poster on the wall. Written in large letters: *Stamp out a problem before it becomes a crime.* This was the motto that had just gotten Sheriff Larry Lee elected. I remembered now hearing about his campaign and what a landslide election this tough-talking guy had won.

But I couldn't stand not saying anything, so I told one patrolman, "Sir, this is my first offense for a DUI." He talked to another patrolmen and came back with, "Okay instead of jail, you're going to the work farm." I didn't know what that meant, but I kept quiet hoping a work farm would be a better environment than jail.

As I rode in the patrol car to the work farm, I thought of all the things I had done and had gotten away with as a youth and as an adult. The year I stayed high and laid up at the apartment with Gail, I had never been arrested or caught with drugs. It really hurt that just when Julie and I were back together and I had done the best I had ever done, I got busted. Julie and I were happier than we had ever been. I had more income, a home, and had been off my addictions for a long time. I guess I thought by staying clean for so long my slate had been wiped clean, and God had forgiven all. But it seems I had not earned exemption from trouble even when I had cleaned up my act.

I called Julie from the work farm after I was admitted and the paper work was signed. When Julie came to visit me the next day, she turned livid that I had let this happen. "You son of a bitch. You told me you had changed. And I believed you. It would be better if I had not come back to you. Now I'm sitting home alone." She turned pale and started shaking and barely heard what I said when I tried to explain the situation and why I had stopped for a beer. She got so angry, I think she started to lash out and hit me, but then she tried to control her anger there in a public place with the deputies close by in the adjacent interview room.

When we had moved to our house in Cobb County, Julie had quit her job as I made big money then and we did not need her income. For the time I spent at the work farm, Julie made no attempt to get a job and did not come to visit me again or call, though the work farm was in the same county and only about fifteen miles away. The only contact I had with her was when I called her. Then she was barely civil to me.

At the work farm, I made up my mind to become a model prisoner, so I could get out as soon as I could like I had done when I was a sixteen-year-old at YDC. So, I volunteered to work as a trustee on a cleanup detail.

A month after I went to the work farm, a devastating tornado hit the area. When the sky turned black and the wind hit sixty miles per hour, the trustees and other inmates were put back in their cells that morning. Orders came over the intercom for each inmate to go to the corner of his cell, to kneel down, and to cover his head. It got as dark as night. The winds howled, and I heard hail and rain pelting the roof. Strangely enough the bars on my cell seemed like protection. But any real damage to the individuals would come if the roofs were blown off or caved in on us. I felt like a trapped mouse in a little box. Soon the storm subsided.

Later in the recreation room, we watched the news on television and learned about the devastation the tornado had caused when winds had hit one-hundred-sixty miles an hour. The entire west side of the county, around the work farm got hardest hit. The tornado twisted a church into a pile of rubble. One guy on a small farm nearby went to check on his cow and found it dead. The barn had blown apart and a board had hit the cow on the head. The news crew filmed the devastation in his yard as the farmer called a butcher to come and butcher the cow for the meat.

The roads were blocked off, and residents were unable to go home from work until the power company could check for downed lines and leaking gas lines. As a trustee, I became a part of a crew sent out to clean up the debris. Six trucks loaded with five men each went from the jail to the closest neighborhood and started putting tree limbs on truck beds and into shredders. There were yards so strewn with branches and boards that I could not put my foot flat on the lawn to take one step without stepping on a pile of branches.

The second afternoon, I scraped my arm rather badly when I picked up a tree trunk to put into the truck. Another inmate had the other end of the tree trunk and shifted all the weight on my arm as he threw his end on the truck bed.

That night I went to the infirmary handcuffed and shackled to another inmate who also had an injury on his hand. This customary way to move prisoners put me in too close of contact with the other inmate. I noticed his skin had turned the color of a lemon, even the whites of his eyes were yellow. "What's wrong with you?" I asked. He knew I wasn't talking about the little cut.

"I have hepatitis B," he replied.

The worker at the infirmary bandaged my arm and also bandaged the inmate's cut on his arm, then we went back to the work farm. The next day, as part of the crew, I went back out to clean up debris. I never saw the yellow guy again.

After I had the cut on my arm, I became sick and weak but I did not tell anyone. I still went out as a trustee each day because I knew this would count toward early release.

I also began to attend night literacy classes two nights a week. A tutor came in and worked with each inmate and gave each of us a diagnostic test to find what level of reading we were on, then he assigned us a book to fit our reading level. I reviewed phonics and began to sound out letters and words. There were times in the classroom that I felt dizzy. I thought I might have been trying too hard. One night, I kept rubbing my forehead, not knowing the tutor watched me. "Brad, are you alright?"

"Oh. I guess I'm just tired. I stayed on the work crew all day, then I came in and took a shower before class. I didn't have time to eat." I made up this excuse because I didn't want anything to go wrong with my coming to class. I really had eaten. I didn't understand why I felt dizzy. The tutor nodded that he understood and walked away. I tried to concentrate and focus. I remembered some things I had learned in school but as I struggled, I learned a great deal. I had picked up quite a few words when I had struggled on my own to read the blueprints when I worked as a millwright. I looked forward to the classes and even took some of the handouts to study at night in my cell. I felt positive and made some progress. I didn't tell anyone that I didn't feel well.

Since I became a model prisoner, working as a trustee during the day and going to reading classes two nights a week, my five months sentence came down to three months. Needless to say, while I had been at the work farm, I lost my good job. I felt really low when I got home.

I prayed, God, I have failed, and I never thought I would end up at a work farm. God, please help me. You will have to help me get my life back together.

30.
A Door Opens

When I got home, I found that my dog, Smoky, had taken sick. If fact, Julie said he hadn't eaten well for the three months I had been gone. Now he refused to eat at all. I took him to Dr. Henderson, a local veterinarian.

I liked Dr. Henderson immediately. He stood about five foot seven, had a red-faced completion and watery, blue eyes and white hair piled up right on the top of his head then swirl on one side reminding me of a swirl on an ice cream cone. He had a dynamic, friendly personality. He gave Smoky a through examinations and told me some sad news, "Your Labrador Retriever has heart worms, and there's nothing I can do. It's in the advanced stages and my only suggestion is that I put him to sleep."

I spent a few last minutes with Smoky, rubbing his head, talking to him, and remembering the past. Then the vet took him in the back of the clinic. After a while, I bundled Smoky up in a blanket to take him home to bury him.

As I left, I talked to Dr. Henderson, who listened to me talk briefly about my life. Right off he seemed interested in me and in helping me with my problems. He invited me to come back by the office and talk.

On the way home, I felt as if one door had closed and another one had opened. Smoky was my last link with Dad and that link had vanished with his death. I felt sad to lose Smoky, yet I felt optimistic about this vet guy I had just meet. I surely needed someone to confide in and this person seemed interested in me and in what I had to say.

When I got home, I buried Smoky in the backyard out by the new barn I had built.

The next week, I went in to talk to Dr. Henderson, whom I began to call Big Dog. When he spoke about God, I replied angrily, "I'm fed up with God. I'm fed up with trying to live right." I ran wild for years and made my life and everybody else's life around me hell. It took me years to come off my addictions. When I worked hard to make my life the greatest it had ever been, I slipped, and now I have lost my job, and my marriage is on the rocks again."

I told Dr. Henderson about my life and some of the times I had been in trouble. I told him about Julie's mood swing problem. I told him how she had taken some antidepressant drugs several times, for a while, but usually stopped because of bizarre side effects. I told him how when she got upset, she could be irritable and even angry without me understanding why.

"Now that I'm home, she still barely talks to me. In the time I served at the work farm, she has gone into herself and appears to have gotten very low self-esteem. When she came back to me, I made big bucks. Now that I have a jail record and couldn't find a job, she won't look for work," I shared with him. "Big Dog, I can see her gradually changing for the worse, every day. I don't know what to do.

He listened but would not be judgmental, just sympathetic and only asked a few questions. Then he reached up and patted me on the shoulder, "Hang in there, Big Guy." Before I left he calmly read scriptures to me and invited me to attend church with him to hear the teachings of Dr. Charles Stanley at the Atlanta First Baptist Church. I became skeptical. For one thing, I didn't want to attend another church, get my hopes up, and be disappointed again.

I soon learned Dr. "Big Dog" Henderson had a heart even bigger than his wallet. He gave away money to people who were temporarily in need, but mostly he loaned money to people who would pay it back. He also spent his life doing many good things, anonymously.

Big Dog had a big booming voice, a loud laugh, and drove fast—the biggest and most expensive pickup you could buy. With his magnetic, entertaining personality, he helped many people, and I could see I had become one of his main projects.

Big Dog believed if he didn't go to bed by eight o'clock, the next day a dog could die. He had to get a good night's sleep in order to be in top shape and be in his operating room at the clinic by six o'clock in the morning. I went in one morning to find him in surgery. "Come on in. Help yourself to some coffee," he called out. I walked into the operating room where he had one assistant who had put five dogs under anesthesia, ready to be neutered. Big Dog laughed and talked to me and went by snipping each one. He finished within a few minutes then the assistant took over. He and I went into the reception area to talk.

As I got up and out of the house everyday, Julie started looking for a job also. But then she found a nice diversion. She had always wanted to work with animals, so she went into the volunteer internship program at the Atlanta Zoo in the Hoof Barn. At least two days a week, she cleaned out stalls, set out food and sometimes fed the animals apples and other fruit by hand and petted them. Rosie, a rhinoceros, became instrumental, in an indirect way, in bringing up Julie's self-esteem. After Julie had worked in and around the rhinoceros pen for a couple of weeks, Rosie would perk up her ears when she heard Julie's voice, and come to the iron bars for Julie to pet her. When Rosie sat on her tail and broke it, Julie assisted the zoo veterinarian when he bandaged the tail and put duct tape around it to keep the tail straight and dry as Rosie liked to sit in her water trough.

When a film crew came to document a story on the Atlanta Zoo, the head of the volunteers asked Julie to appear in the film rubbing Rosie's soft, pointed nose. Julie had begun to dress up and wear make-up again, and I knew she had been chosen to be in the film because of her attractiveness. I think she felt this too and it improved her self-image.

Every afternoon Julie came in the door excitedly telling stories of the animals. She came over to me and sat in my lap, "Brad, there's a two ton rhino who walks around his food all day like he is guarding it and every now and then he takes a bite. When he butted the iron bars of his stall it sounded like a car wrecking."

When I went with her to the zoo, I had never seen her happier as I watched her interact with the animals. When she fed the giraffes, she climbed a ladder and put a special blend of hay on a platform for three of them. Her face became flushed with excitement as she acted as a tour guide showing me the animals. "Tommy, the Gazelle broke off one of his long horns. This afternoon, I had to put Spot, the Zebra, out in the cold while I cleaned his stall. Then I heard three knocks coming from the outside. I knew Spot kicked the door, wanting back into the stall because it was so cold outside." When she said Spot the Zebra, she really giggled. I had an enjoyable day at the zoo watching her with the animals.

Everything seemed to be going well, and I became hopeful things would turn around for her now that she seemed happy again and had something to do to fill her days. Life had finally leveled off, so I took off a day from looking for a job to go fishing on Big Dog's property.

While I fished at a stream, I sat on a high bank over the rushing creek studying the water and wondering what would happen to me. I had just listened to a tape Big Dog loaned me where Dr. Charles Stanley talked about God's unconditional love. Could it be that He loved me after all I had done to mess up my life? I wondered, What am I going to do with myself. I have a jail record and no job. Then I heard a voice in my head or maybe a thought came so strong it sounded like a voice. But clear as could be it said, "Go back to school." I sat there stunned. Where? I had attended literacy classes in jail and had made quite a bit of progress in reading. But maybe I could find someone to teach me on a regular basis.

I did some calling around and found a local reading group which offered one-to-one instruction. So I joined this group and met with my first tutor, Mrs. Jones, who was a retired teacher and volunteer. We met in a small private room at the local library. Mrs. Jones was a tall, slender, middle-age lady with brown hair, blue eyes, a kind voice, and a lot of energy. She let me know right away she felt strongly about tutoring reading. Man, she knew how to hammer phonics. When I left our one hour sessions each week, I felt wrung out like a sledge hammer had been taping on my head all evening. She also gave me reading assignments to do and flash cards to practice each night at home.

Julie and I were having dinner one night when the phone rang. I answered. Julie's Dad, Wilson said, "Brad. I've got something really awful to tell you, and I want you to break the news to Julie as gently as you can when we hang up." I pulled the phone cord around the kitchen door into the living room, trying to keep Julie from hearing my end of thc conversation.

When I hung up and went back into the kitchen Julie sat at the table as of she were frozen, not eating but staring at me with big eyes. "Somebody died," she said just like she had made the statement to herself, as she looked at me to deny this, but when I looked at her with compassion, she asked in a breathless way, "Who is it?"

I replied as gently as I could, "Your grandfather."

She cried out, "Not my Papa Lel." She ran and grabbed on to me. After she cried for a while, she asked, "Was it a stroke or a heart attack?" I held her, gently stroking her hair, and told her it had been a tractor accident. "Wilson told me Papa Lel drove the tractor on the side of a hill reaping hay when the tractor tipped over, pinning him underneath. After several hours when he did not come home, Granny Almeda sent a neighbor to look for him. They discovered him under the tractor on the hillside hours later. The coroner said he had died instantly."

Julie sobbed some more then said. "If he had to die, then I'm glad it happened quickly. I'm glad he didn't lay there in agony for hours before they found him."

Within an hour we were on our way to Mentone to join a grieving family. When we arrived at the Shankles' house, Julie ran to her Grandmother Almeda and put her arms around her and hugged her and they both cried. "Oh, Grandmother, I'm so sorry. We will all miss him."

"You were his favorite grandchild. I know you will miss him," she comforted Julie. Then Almeda shook her head and said, "I told that old man he shouldn't be out on the tractor. He'd just turned seventy-nine." She seemed more angry with her husband for not listening to her than she was upset about him dying. But I knew it felt easier to focus on the cause of the accident than think about the fact she would be alone for the first time in more than sixty-five years.

Jewell took the death and funeral so hard. She remained inconsolable. The death happened as a result of an untimely tragedy and the funeral could not have been anything but sad for everyone who loved Leldon. But the way Jewell carried on crying and wailing became an embarrassment. "What will I ever do without my Daddy. I want to die right now to be with him. I can't stand to live another minute." Then she went into wailing and moaning. Wilson, Jewell's dear, stooped husband, couldn't handle her. No one could stop the wailing. Julie just held on to me. Whatever Jewell came into the same room we were in, Julie and I would leave and go into another room. Then one of the family members called the local doctor who came to the house and gave Jewell a sedative to calm her down.

On the way back home after the funeral, Julie said, "If Grandaddy could have seen and heard my mother today, he would of slapped her and told her to shut up." She sat pale and quiet, then after a while, she fell asleep and slept the rest of the way home. When we got home, I put her to bed.

Julie's devastation about her grandfather's death went so deep that she became dysfunctional, even her pills didn't help her. She didn't stay in bed as she had done before when depression had gotten to her, but this time, she just wandered around the house aimlessly.

She cancelled her volunteer work with the animals at the Atlanta Zoo. This broke my heart because I knew what a positive experience that had been for her. I thought about how much enjoyment she had gotten from the animals and how much she loved them.

Julie stayed away from her mother too, and barely talked to her on the phone. Instead, she tried to cope with her own feelings in her own way.

For the first time, Julie kept her mother at a distance. Jewell would never again be Julie's consort against me if things did not go as well as Julie thought they should.

31.
Cement Block, Full Force

I continued to search for a job, and each Tuesday night I went to my tutoring sessions with Mrs. Jones. In between our meetings, I did the homework assignments she gave me.

During this time I became sicker. I felt like I had the flu. My joints ached, and I became nauseated several times a day. This went on for a few weeks. One day when I filled out an application for a job, by copying from a master list Julie had made for me, I noticed I became so weak I had difficulty pushing and pulling the pencil to write.

I went to see the local doctor in Cobb County, Dr. Derek Slater. "Well, I don't know," he said. "Your blood pressure is elevated. I think we will do some tests."

A week later, Dr. Slater called and told me I needed to come into his office for the results. I felt a little concerned when he would not tell me the findings over the phone but wanted to talk to me in the office. When he told me the results, I felt as if a load of cement blocks had fallen off a building and hit me on the head, full force.

"Brad, you've got hepatitis B and C".

I felt the room sway, and I felt my heart jump up into my throat. My mouth got dry, and I blurted out, "How did I get that?"

"Hepatitis is a virus transferred from an affected person through the blood. This virus causes inflammation to the liver. Do you know anyone who has hepatitis?" Dr. Slater asked.

"No, no, no." I sat across from his desk in a big chair. I put my head in my hands for a few moments then I remembered the other prisoner at the work farm, the "yellow man" who went to the infirmary with me and who said he had hepatitis B. I leaned forward in my chair and looked the doctor in the eyes. "Doctor Slater, how serious is this? Give it to me straight."

He didn't mince his words, "The hepatitis B is curable. But the C. . . . He paused and remained thoughtful for a moment. "One of three things will happen," he finally said. "You will die, or you will have a liver transplant, or you will live long enough for a cure to be found—maybe in eight to ten years from now. There are some experimental drugs in the works already."

I told Dr. Slater about being handcuffed to an injured, prisoner and having an open wound on my arm.

"There's no doubt," he said. "That's where you got your hepatitis B. But you could have been infected with hepatitis C for as long as ten years. Your getting the hepatitis B could be a blessing because that's what made you feel badly enough to come and see me. Hepatitis C virus can lay dormant in a person's body for a long time. Some people carry the virus for thirty years and don't know it until it's too late. "Have you ever had any blood transfusions or injected drugs as a teenager?"

I told him I had not had any blood transfusions, but I had been into drugs at a very young age. I was so young I had been afraid of the needle and had allowed someone else to inject me. I got very quiet and had a flashback of Jon Pace injecting me with heroin when I had been twelve years old. He had probably used a dirty needle, or maybe when I learned to shoot up, I could have gotten a used needle. But then I remembered taking the syringes from those I picked up from the druggist for Mom when he sent her a dozen syringes at a time. I always used her new syringes. I guessed I would never know for sure which had led to my predicament.

When I told Julie, I didn't know if she could take it. At first she didn't understand how serious the threat of this disease could be. "You can get over this." She said. "You said there are experimental drugs."

I told her exactly what Dr. Slater had said. "Julie, Dr. Slater said I could have a liver transplant, or in five or ten years a cure might be found, or I could die."

When I told her the third option, she began to wring her hands and cry. "I don't know what I would do if you died." She began to cry and hug me. "If you die, I'll kill myself."

Still later, Julie ask, "How contagious is this hepatitis? Can I catch it from you? Can we still make love?"

"I don't know the answers, but we'll find out everything we can about this disease and manage it as well as we can."

Then Julie got angry with me and blamed me for getting this disease. "It's the kind of life you've lived. This's what you get. You probably used a dirty needle when you were doing drugs."

She could have been right on this point. It wouldn't have hurt me so badly if I had not come out of my addictions. I guess I had thought God had given me a chance to live a normal life after screwing up for so long.

I thought, I had made my peace with God and had started living a clean life. Then I get this bad news. I felt like this had became my punishment for all my wrongdoings, but how ironic, that I found this out when my life had really started turning around, again.

I began treatment for the hepatitis B immediately. After several weeks, further tests showed the treatments cleared me of the hepatitis B. When Dr. Slaker diagnosed me with hepatitis C, he examined me physically and found my liver greatly enlarged. He put me on a low fat, low sodium diet plan, and said walking could be very good for me. I followed his instructions on the diet, and walked at least five miles a day at a nature reserve.

In order to evaluate the liver damage, several months later, I had a liver biopsy. The physician made a small incision between two of my ribs, inserted a needle and took a small piece of my liver. The results showed my liver enzymes to be extremely elevated. I had the battle of my life ahead of me. As I recovered from the surgery, I applied for Social Security Insurance. Six months later, I became a recipient of this disability insurance.

While I recovered, I felt too weak to attend my literacy sessions with Mrs. Jones. I did all I could to remain functional and manage my hepatitis C. I walked five miles a day and took drugs the doctor provided. Then Dr. Slater told me of a new treatment. "Brad, it's brutal, but some people have been treated and cured on this drug."

This new drug, Interferon, was scheduled to be released to the public on my birthday. I took this as a sign that I should try it. Julie told me I should do anything that had a remote chance of giving me back my health, so I agreed to become a guinea pig.

When Dr. Slater acquired the Interferon, I met with him for the instructions. I left the doctor's office loaded down with vials of Interferon and syringes and pills. This new Interferon treatment would work better to eliminate the hepatitis C virus if it were continued for one year. I picked up a month's supply at a time. Because of my weight and height, I had to take a double dose of what most people would have been given. Three times a week I gave myself a shot in the top of my leg every morning at six and followed it up with three pills in the afternoon. The medicine made me weak, shaky, and nauseated.

On my trips to hike at the nature reserve, I hiked less and less. Some days I could hike a few miles. The next time I could only hike a mile, then only a half mile. Finally I gave up and didn't go to the nature reserve at all.

Each month I took the Interferon I became a little sicker. I began to ache like I had to flu then I began to run a fever. Then I started vomiting. There were times I couldn't even keep the pills down. I not only threw up the pills, but also anything I tried to eat. I stayed home, mostly in bed. Depression became the worst side affect of Interferon. I learned the suicide rate for hepatitis patients on Interferon, remained extremely high, and I fell prey to this suicide tendency.

One day after I had been on the Interferon for nine months, I took a short ride to get out of the house. As I drove toward home in my pickup, I thought I heard my tire going flat. I pulled over on the shoulder of the road, got out, and walked around my pickup to check the tire. When I started back around the front of my pickup to the driver's side, a tractor-trailer came toward me on my side of the road. I froze. I had the overwhelming desire to step out in front of that huge vehicle. I knew I would be killed. My heart pounded. I held my breath. I knew I could do it. I wanted to do it.

At the last split second, when the tractor-trailer came to only a few feet from me, I looked up at the driver. He gave me a puzzled frown like he knew what I planned to do.

I thought, *I can't do this to that man. He's an ordinary guy trying to make a living. He might be blamed for my death.* I just stood still as the huge truck passed, close enough for me to feel the rush of air on my face and body.

When I got back into my pickup, I shook all over and became nauseous because I had almost stepped out in front of the oncoming vehicle. I also shook because I knew I had two choices: one, to stay on the Interferon and inevitably, commit suicide, or, two, to come off the medicine and not ever have a cure, which meant eventually my liver would become so inflamed I would die.

I went home and packed up all the left-over Interferon and pills and returned them to Dr. Slater. "I can't continue to take these. I almost stepped out in front of a tractor-trailer today. I changed my mind in the last split second."

Dr. Slater told me, "Brad, the last time I checked your blood, the virus count per units of blood had reduced down to zero. In other words, there is no sign of the virus and if you come off the medication three months early, the virus could return."

"You don't understand Dr. Slater, if I stay on the Interferon, you won't know if my virus count is up or down, because I will be dead somewhere under a truck or at the base of a bridge." I left the medication with him and went home. I knew I had made the right decision.

Taking the Interferon had bought me some time. Dr. Slater said it would take several years for the virus to multiply to what it had been nine months ago when I started treatment.

32.
Servant's Attitude

I stayed home for a few more weeks until my strength returned then I went into the vet's office to visit Big Dog. We talked for a while, then he finally convinced me to go to the Atlanta First Baptist Church with him. He promised to buy my lunch afterward, so the next Sunday, I went with him into Atlanta to his church.

When Big Dog turned off the interstate in Atlanta, we saw the massive church complex stretching out in a panoramic view before us. As we parked, I noticed the tall graceful water fountains shooting upward in a fan shape, and the tall flowering white crepe myrtle trees lining the drive from the entrance. Big Dog explained this structure had been the Avon building before renovations turned it into this beautiful church. We entered the church walking among droves of people headed toward several sets of large double doors.

The inside massiveness set a grand scale for the thousand people attending that Sunday. We sat in theater type seats where I studied the lovely gold and blue interior. I looked up to the choir loft to see the one hundred member choir in blue robes with white scarves. I sat captivated when a small but wonderful orchestra played the prelude. I leaned over to Big Dog and asked, "What are they playing." He glanced at the program and answered, "Aaron Copeland's Appalachian Spring." I studied the program and silently spelled out the composer's name and prelude title, to myself. The music was uplifting to me as I felt my spirit stir with inspiration. We sat close enough to have a good view of Dr. Stanley, but there were two large screens—one to the left and one to the right—above him for the audience in the back to get a better view. In this televised service, Dr. Stanley talked about having a servant's attitude. "*If you serve one, ye serve me. When you lose yourself, you find yourself.*"

"When you trust God, you become a servant, dying of your old selfish ways," Dr. Stanley said. "Turn away from your old self. Life will be fruitful. Almighty God will honor us. He created us for himself. He owns us to serve him. He will provide for you. We cannot serve God and ourselves at the same time. It's not what you are but how obedient you are. He will exalt you in due time. The more successful you are in serving yourself, the more disastrous it will become."

I sat there in church listening to the sermon and thinking about my past. As I left the church with Big Dog, I felt hopeful. I had enjoyed the beautiful church, hearing the glorious music, being among the throngs of worshipers, and seeing and hearing Dr. Stanley in person. I wanted to hear more, so I told Big Dog I wanted to attend church with him every Sunday.

Being around Big Dog became an altogether positive experience. In church, he sang loudly in his booming voice, found all the scriptures in the Bible during the sermon, and talked about the sermon as he drove us away from the church. "Brad, that's true about the servant's attitude. There's nothing like it. I've tried to put it into practice in my life. When you help people, you forget about yourself. When you make people happy by helping them, you are happy too. I thought about what Big Dog said and about Dr. Stanley's sermon. That might become something I would like to do. I might think about finding someone I could help, one day.

After church, we went to a nice cafeteria and ate heartily. Both of us. I had southern fried chicken, turnip greens, fried green tomatoes, cornbread, and blackberry cobbler for desert. On the way home, I thought more about Big Dog. I had never known a more genuine person. He worked hard, spoke with great animation, had a great sense of humor, and put everything he had into life. He also lived a good example. He put into practice what he believed.

The same week I first went to church with Big Dog, I called my literacy tutor, Mrs. Jones, and arranged to continue my one night a week class with her. She gave me assignments for homework, and I always had them ready when I returned the next week.

Over the next months, I steadily improved in reading. When I could read on the sixth grade level, I started reading the Bible and the newspaper more and more with Mrs. Jones's help on some of the words. She helped me with these words, but then wrote them down in my vocabulary notebook. I had to know these words for the following session in addition to my usual work.

As I read the newspaper each day, I became interested in local politics. I had always kept up with the national and state governments by watching news broadcasts on television, but now that I could read the newspaper, I pored over the national, state, and local happenings each day. I felt like, after a lifetime of trying, my pursuit of an education had finally begun to pay off.

I felt so much better and my attitude changed to one of optimism because of my trips to church on Sunday with Big Dog and because of the confidence I gained in being able to read so much better.

Julie began to get better, I think because I had gotten better. She found a job as a secretary at the Atlanta Capitol Building in downtown Atlanta. She dressed well and looked nice as she left for work each morning. She seemed interested in her job and in spending her money on new curtains and on things around the house.

As I felt better physically and gained confidence being around Big Dog, I got up the courage to answer an ad for delivering flowers at

"Eilene's Florist." During the interview, I met the owner, Eilene Howard, a pleasant, petite, middle-aged, woman. She needed someone to deliver flowers and set up at weddings and funerals. "I want to tell you the truth about me from the start," I said. "A while back I had only one DUI, but because of it I served three months at a work farm. I assure you if you see fit to hire me, I will never drink while I'm on a job."

"I like your honesty and your enthusiasm," she said. "Let's give it a try. Can you start tomorrow morning at eight?"

When I went into Eilene's Florist shop the next morning, I immediately liked the atmosphere. The smell of bacon, eggs, and biscuits drifted over the shop from where they were being cooked in the kitchen toward the back. Soft music played and there were flowers and plants everywhere and friendly people came in all day. I met the main flower arranger, a gay guy named Mac. I hoped I could tolerate being around a gay person, since I had bad memories from the Youth Delinquent Program, but I put this out of my mind. I became the main delivery person, and Mac gave me instructions on how to set up the large sprays and baskets at weddings and at funerals. All in all this became a pleasant part time job. Eilene and I developed a good work relationship and became friends. I looked forward each day to going into the shop.

Julie came by Eilene's and met everyone. She liked the place and the people and bought several green plant arrangements for our house. I had been telling her about how I enjoyed working there and how nice the people were. This gave her a chance, first hand, to know them.

I met Eilene's family—her husband, Mr. Howard, and their only child, Cindy, a cute blond who had just gotten married. I learned Eilene had season tickets to the Atlanta Falcon Football games and never missed a game. Mr. Howard didn't share her enthusiasm for sports.

Toward late summer, after I got to know Mr. Howard he asked me, "Eilene told me you liked football?" I nodded wondering where he could be going with this. "Well you see, I've just retired and I've just become committed to laying on the sofa watching TV. How about you consider taking Eilene to her games. She'll pay for your ticket. Also ask your wife. Make sure that's alright with her."

When I explained to Julie, she didn't object. She had met Eilene and liked her. So it seemed, I would be taking Eilene to all the games.

When the night of the first Atlanta Falcon's game finally arrived, I took Eilene to the Atlanta Stadium for the game. I looked around the stadium, remembering. This is where I had attended the Led Zepplin concert, so long ago. Thinking back, I felt like that had been another person in another life.

Eilene's idea of fun was acting like a kid—so she did. She had smuggled in a large amount of candy because she loved candy and because she didn't want to pay the stadium prices. She also carried in ten or twelve packs of gum and chewed a stick until the flavor had gone, spit it into a napkin, then got another piece. As she watched the plays, she screamed as loudly as she could, and screamed so much I thought she was going to have a stroke. I laughed at her the entire game. She entertained me and those around us who watched her as much as they watched the game.

Several weeks after the first game, I noticed Eilene kept to herself and stayed unusually quiet. I kept looking at her behind the counter. When I asked questions, she just lowered her head and gave me quick, short answers. I went behind the counter, stood close to her and said, "Eilene is there a problem?"

She turned her head from me and sobbed, "Brad, I've got Lou Gehrig's Disease."

"Oh no." I put my hand on her shoulder as she sobbed into her hands. "I'm so sorry to hear that." I didn't know what to say, but I felt so sad for her. "Eilene, you tell me what I can do to help. I guess you're under a doctor's care?" She nodded as she wiped the tears away.

Over the next months, Eilene gradually began to lose the muscle control in her arms and legs, and her speech became slurred. I took her to Emory University Hospital for her breathing to be monitored to show if there had been loss of breath capacity. We also picked up her weekly medications. Mac and I took over for Eilene. I answered the phone, and took orders. Mac continued to make the arrangements. I continued to deliver and set up at large events.

Mac and I got along fine especially after Eilene got sick. One day when there were just the two of us in the shop Mac remarked, "When I saw you the first day, I thought, That big country boy will one day kill my ass." We laughed. He had picked up on the fact I didn't like gay guys. I never said anything about my past at YDP where I had been attacked. Again, this seemed like something that had happened to someone else in another life.

About the time Mac and I were learning to run everything smoothly, Eilene got much worse. When she came to the shop, she couldn't talk. She just grunted and nodded her head or wrote down what she wanted to say. I began to look after her more than her daughter did. Cindy was pregnant now and having some difficulty. Mr. Howard thanked me for being there to help. At Emory, Eilene got shots and pills and each week took a breathing test to measure her breathing capacity. After a few months, the doctor's test results showed the medications had done little to help her. But maybe while she took the medicine, it had given her a little hope.

One day at the shop, I remembered Dr. Stanley's message. I felt amazed to realized I had the servant attitude in helping Eilene without even realizing it until then. I wanted to continue in having a servant's attitude in helping anyone I could. Since I had been so busy at the flower shop and so busy taking care of Eilene, I had not one time condemned myself for my past, nor had I the time to think about my hepatitis C.

A couple of weeks later, Eilene wrote down on a note pad, "Oh,

Brad, I really wish I could see one more game, but you know I'm too weak to go."

I knew she wanted me to take her, so I had a plan. When the night of the game arrived, I literally picked her up and put her into the car. When we got to the stadium, I parked in the handicapped space, picked her up out of the car, and carried her into the stadium. An attendant found a wheelchair for her, and we took the elevator, but when we got to the stadium steps, I lifted her out of the wheelchair and carried her down the steps to our seats.

She laughed and shook her head. I knew she wanted to say, "Don't drop me." Everyone who saw me carrying her down the steep steps, made way for us. She sat all during the game and managed to clap her hands together a few times. She smiled from ear to ear and laughed, though no sound came. I guess she laughed silently on the inside too.

She got so excited about one play, she forgot herself and somehow found the strength to stand. Then she immediately sat down. "Eilene, are you all right?" I asked in a teasing tone though I felt concerned. She nodded and gave me a weak smile before she slumped down into her seat until the next play.

A few weeks later, I took her to a game when the Atlanta Falcons played the San Francisco 49ers. I made arrangements with an Atlanta TV news announcer and the Atlanta Falcon football coach to allow me to bring Eilene down to the VIP section of the playing field to meet the coach and all the players and have her picture taken with them. She looked at me with surprise and delight. She couldn't speak, but smiled broadly until her eyes sparkled.

When she started to cry, I told her, "Now don't cry." She held back the tears, and I think she hugged everybody at least twice. Later when she got home she put the VIP pass and the pictures in a scrapbook.

Eilene had been so happy at the game, but her health declined markedly after that, so much so, that if the game had been one week later, she would have been too weak to sit up in the stadium seat. I felt good about that last day she attended the game. I knew I would always remember how happy she had been and how she had laughed silently and patted my shoulder as I carried her.

Eilene became too weak to move or to write, then her family took her to the hospital. Earlier in the week, she had written a note to me asking that she be put on life support until her grandchild was born. When I related her wishes to her family, they said she had suffered so much they didn't want her on life support for the next two months until the baby came. I really think they doubted she would live two months even with life support.

When I went to the hospital to visit the next morning, I didn't find Eilene in her bed. The room had been vacated. I hurried out to the nurses' desk to ask what happened.

"Eilene passed away during the night," the nurse replied.

I felt shocked that she had passed so soon and that I had not been there to squeeze her hand one last time. I felt surprised and hurt that the family did not think to call me. I had been allowed to be one of the family while I helped, but when it came to being by her bed when she died, the family didn't consider me one of them. I had been at the flower shop for over a year. From the time she had been diagnosed, she had lived only seven months and during that time, I had cared for her daily, in some way.

I left the hospital and went immediately to the flower shop to tell Mac. When I pulled into the parking lot and went bursting into the front door, Mac look up suddenly.

By the looks of me, he said, "She's gone isn't she?" I nodded. I held back my grief. We glanced around at all the flowers and plants.

I said, "We'll find out when the funeral will be held, and we might as well deliver all the flowers in the shop. This place will be closed up and sold after the funeral."

I felt her loss as if she had been a sister. I went to the bank of the Chattahoochee River, where I had fished as a child and sat there and cried.

On the day of the funeral Julie got off work and came to the church, but Mac and I did as planned. We delivered truck loads of flowers. When we went by the casket, Mac broke down. I put my hand on his shoulder, and we both had to wipe our eyes. He said, "I have never known any finer lady." I could only nod in agreement. Julie went with us to the cemetery and helped put all the sprays of flowers around the grave side. "Brad, this is a gracious thing you and Mac did for Eilene." Julie felt sad with me. We went home, had a light supper, and Julie held me in her arms that night as I fell asleep.

After Eilene died, I didn't know what to do or where to go. I had no job as Eilene's family sold the business, and I didn't feel like starting something new. I felt emotionally wrung out and physically exhausted and just lay around the house.

Then I decided to track down some of my old buddies. I called Tophat Taylor and see what had become of him. I had not heard from him since he started high school in the suburbs. I found his number in the phone book and called him. A much deeper voice than I expected answered. When he recognized my voice, he really flipped out. "Brad, how's it going, Man?" Tophat said. "Hey remember those old days in Oakdale? We really had some wild times didn't we? It's a wonder we lived to become an adult."

He told me he had married and had two boys. He talked about them for several minutes. I could tell he had great pride in being a husband and father.

"What are you doing now?" I asked.

"I'm a electrician at Lockheed Aircraft Corporation. I took the two year course and everything—been there eight years."

I said, "It sounds like everything is going well for you."

"Brad, did you ever go straight and give up drugs completely? I heard you got married?" Then he referred to the conversation we had right before I left for YDP. I told him about my time at YDP and about being a dog boy. Then I told him about marrying Julie and about having hepatitis C and about my medical problems and even about going to the work farm. It felt good to talk to an old friend. "My childhood really got out of control and I'm still paying the price for bad mistakes," I told Tophat.

"Brad, I hate to tell you about Rooster Roberts. He contracted hepatitis C also, like you did. After years of abusing drugs, he is still fighting abuse. He got so bad he couldn't continue his job as a machinist at Lockheed where he worked along side me for many years. But Lockheed kept him on there as a custodian, sweeping and cleaning up. He married a nice girl, but after a few years, she divorced him because of the drug abuse.

"Right now, Rooster's under the care of a methadone clinic. That's where a drug abuser goes into a clinic every day and is given a small amount of drugs. The abuser is monitored—their urine is tested to make sure they are not taking any other drugs in the meantime. This treatment helps wean the person off drugs. I sure hope it helps Rooster."

The news about Rooster hit me hard. I really hated to hear that this old childhood friend had such a hard time. Tophat and I talked a few more minutes. I told him about Big Dog and about going to church. I told him about my literacy classes and about learning to read. We laughed about old times and promised to keep in touch.

When we started to hang up Tophat added, "Hey, you can't call me Tophat anymore; my hat's not there. I'm practically bald. I guess you'll have to call me Baldy."

We had a good laugh and hung up promising to keep in contact. It felt good to hear from Tophat. I felt so happy for him that he had come off drugs, finished high school, and got good training for a job. I felt really happy about him having a family.

I sat there thinking about Rooster, feeling so sorry to hear that he had hepatitis C. Guilt hit me in the gut. I remembered the night I took blotter acid over to him when he ate too much cabbage and we watched his stomach swell and he had his first experience of trippin'.

I had always blamed Kell for getting me started on drugs. But I had done the same in giving Rooster drugs. I hoped the methadone treatment helped get him off drugs. I remembered how we had gone from marijuana to blotter acid to shooting up. I wondered if Rooster had used a dirty needle the same time I did or if he had gotten the disease after I knew him. I felt badly that he one day would probably have to go through the Interferon treatments as I had. I hoped he could finish out the one year plan and be cured. I made a mental note to call him one day. I had to think about it. I would do it later.

As young kids, we all acted like taking drugs would be a temporary entertainment and never realized the far reaching consequences. Some things take a long time to come to fruition. But sooner or later our endeavors or lack of endeavors comes home to each of us.

33.
East Cowpen Mountain

I continued to attend church with Big Dog each Sunday. I still studied with Mrs. Jones and daily, I read the newspaper and the Bible. I grew stronger physically and began walking at the nature reserve again. Then I decided to begin lifting weights. I checked with Dr. Slater and he thought that would be a good idea. I walked in the mornings and lifted weights about four o'clock every afternoon right before Julie came home. All in all things were going well.

Julie seemed proud I had interest in body building. Every afternoon, I shared what I could do. Then one afternoon, she didn't want to come out to the barn where I had my weights and did my exercises. "Brad. I'm tired. I put in eight hours today and drove to Atlanta and back. Now I have to cook dinner."

I went on out and worked through my routine. But Julie's mood made the evening strained as she remained huffy while we ate. "Brad, you lay around the house all day. You should have dinner ready for me when I come home. You should find a part time job again. You said yourself that Dr. Slater said you were doing well."

So one night, I fixed chili and had it ready when Julie came home. Another time I made hotdogs. Then Julie wanted me to help her more with the housework. Each day I focused on walking five miles, reading for at least two hours, and then doing my exercise. Sometimes, I just got busy reading and forgot the time. Then I started getting pains in my stomach. I went back to Dr. Slater and he found I had a hernia and had to have abdominal surgery to repair the hernia. Everything went well. Julie seemed sympathetic and supportive.

Dr. Slater said, "No more walking or lifting weights for six weeks. You are to lay around the house, take it easy, and take this pain medication until your incision has healed."

I followed the doctor's orders and while I lay around, I doubled up on reading the newspaper and the Bible. I bought a concordance and began serious study.

I continued the pain medication because the incision still throbbed, but this medication also acted as a sedative causing me to sleep. Many afternoons when Julie came home, she found me asleep. She seemed jealous of my time doing nothing and fussed about what I had not done in the house. Occasionally she got on to me about taking the sedative. "You are going to get addicted again. I know it."

Then she hit the hepatitis C. "Your bad habits got you where you are today. You would have never gotten that disease if you had listened to your good parents and not done drugs and used a dirty needle."

I felt like this water had flowed under the bridge long ago. Now I tried to live my life the best I could. I had no power to erase the past but that did not stop her anger with me. I just ignored her and continued to do what the doctor told me.

I didn't make the trip into Atlanta with Big Dog on Sunday, and soon I became spiritually low because of not going. After five weeks my incision still throbbed, and I knew I still had to take it easy. I felt sorry for myself. I had a fatal disease, could only work part time, had not felt like looking for a job, just lost a good friend—when Eilene died, and just had surgery to repair a hernia, and now my wife chewed on me all the time.

After five weeks of laying around the house listening to Julie fuss at me, I could not take it any more. She could become an irate woman on the drop of a dime for no reason. I had just read in Proverbs: "It is better to dwell in the wilderness, than with a contentious and angry woman." I also read how the Lord provided for Moses and the Israelites when they wandered in the wilderness. I lay on the bed thinking about these scriptures. I thought, "God, is this word true or is this junk? Would He take care of me if I were in the wilderness?"

Sometimes a little knowledge of a subject can be a dangerous thing, and with a little knowledge of Bible verses, I decided to put God to the test. I had a yearning to get completely away for a while, so I decided I would go into the wilderness and see if God would provide for my needs, out there alone. Would He passed the test or would I die?

I made my plans, packed my backpack, and supplies ready to leave. Since we had to put Julie's car in the shop the day before, I had driven her to work that morning. When I drove my truck to picked her up from her job at the capitol building, I headed toward the north Georgia mountains without telling her. The horrendous Friday afternoon traffic on the interstate allowed us to move only at a snail's pace. I felt calm and hopeful about the trip. She chewed on me pretty good as I drove and didn't notice for a while that we were not driving home.

"Brad, where in the hell are you going?" She asked, finally noticing where we were.

I never replied. She kept on bitching, telling me what I should do and shouldn't do. "The life you've led put you where you are today. You're taking too many sedatives. That's what's wrong with you."

I never replied. I glanced at Julie in the passenger seat. Everything about her irritated me from the way her leg muscles were clenched under her slacks, the sweat that beaded on her upper lip, the one strand of hair that had worked itself loose from her ponytail. I glanced from the road back to that one strand of hair. It waved loose, whipping across her clenched jaw. That strand frantically whipping seemed to manifest itself from her anger. A modern day Medusa, even her hair seemed angry. I rolled the window down further hoping to free another strand. I wanted to see how far I could go. This is why I wanted to go—to test myself, test her, test our marriage, my life, even test God.

I needed answers. I needed to get back to nature and God. Julie's constant nagging became white noise like television static blocking all signals from any higher power trying to get through to me. "You must have lost you mind. You are not thinking right. Where are we going?"

Julie spoke again. "Bradley, I...." I waved my hand to silence her. Even the way she said my name raised my hackles. She must have sensed my irritation because she sat back against the seat in quiet indignation, clenching and unclenching her jaw and narrowing her eyes in protest.

The miles rolled by. It seemed the further we rode from Atlanta, the hotter it got. After an hour, Julie had stopped clenching her jaw. Her legs had relaxed, and she leaned her head against the side window. Her forehead furrowed with worry. The strand of hair had even quieted. It hung sweaty, limp, and wind blown. Julie appeared exhausted. I guess it took a lot of energy to be a bitch. I felt exhilarated. As the odometer counted off the miles my heart shed the worry and weight. Julie seemed more and more pulled down. I felt more and more free.

I could make out the dark silhouette of the rolling hills of north Georgia wrapped in the purple haze of twilight. The stars above the mountain seemed close enough and large enough to touch. I felt clean and free for the first time in as long as I could remember. Even the sweat rolling down my back and dripping down my neck felt cleansing.

Yet still, in the back of my mind there remained a dark shadow of doubt. With every throb of my incision scar, a voice seemed to whisper, "You're not strong enough. What are you doing? You know you don't have enough food. You could get lost. You did not think this out. The pain medicine could be clouding my judgment."

As these thoughts repeated over and over in my head, I took a deep breath and clenched the steering wheel in silent resolve. I thought about all the positive things I had been doing to improve my relationship with God. I had started going to church. I read the Bible. I sought God. I had tried to make amends for my past. I deserved for God to take care of me now. "God will provide," I sighed.

I didn't realize I had said this out loud. Julie jumped, startled. This was the first time I had spoken since we had left Atlanta almost two hours ago and now her eyes filled with tears. But she didn't speak. I thought, well, miracles are happening already. She is silent for once.

I suppose I should have felt more compassion for her, but I really didn't care. She owed me. She owed me for all the hell she had put me through. All the fighting and yelling. God owed me. He owed me for the way my life had turned out. I really felt this trip would get both of their attention.

We were now on I-75 headed toward the Appalachian Trails near the Blue Ridge Mountains. High mountains captivated the view and lush green valleys plunged at the road's edge. Occasionally we traveled beside a mountain stream for miles. I turned into the Cohutta wilderness area that adjoined the Tennessee National Forest and found the entrance to the trail over East Cowpen Mountain.

I stopped, got out of the car, grabbed my backpack and flashlight, and walked off into the dark down the trail.

Julie called after me, "Brad, where are you going?

I turned toward her where she stood outside the car and called back, "Pick me up in five days at the north entrance to the East Cowpen Mountain.

"I don't know how to get to the north entrance."

"You'll figure it out. Or if you don't figure it out and find me, who cares anyway." I walked off into the dark and down the trail.

I could hear her calling, "Brad, come back. Come back. I love you." I just kept walking and did not look back. She repeated a couple more times, "Brad! Brad, come back. I love you."

As I walked almost out of earshot, I thought I heard a sound like her crying. Soon I could only hear the crunch of my boots on the trail, the sound of a million tree frogs, and the occasional sound of a whip-o-will in the distance.

I walked for about two miles down the trail. About midnight, I decided I needed to cut off my flashlight to save the batteries. I set up camp for the night by making a lean-to from a tarp I had brought. Then I collected some sticks and small logs and built a fire. Even in June, the nights in the mountains were cool. I threw out my sleeping bag, laid out my backpack, drank the last of my Gatorade, and stuck my machete in the ground beside me. Then I went to sleep.

I didn't wake up until late morning when I heard water running in a stream not too far away. I searched my backpack and realized immediately I had not brought enough food. I had a couple packets of instant oatmeal, a metal cup, cheese cloth, two cans of tuna fish, a can opener, my Bible, an old map of the area, and the empty Gatorade bottle. I realized then I had not exercised good judgment in packing my food and really in even coming on this trip. But I had no choice now—being alone. There could be no turning back now. Anyway I didn't give a damn. Nothing bothered me.

After I built a small fire, heated water from the creek and ate my oatmeal, I studied the map. I had already made a drastic mistake when I found I had not followed the right trail. To get to East Cowpen Mountain's north entrance, I had to cross over a four thousand foot mountain and get on the trail to Panther Creek Falls. Following the trail marked with white arrows would be of great importance. If I made a mistake, I could end up in the Tennessee mountains. I could get lost or hurt, and no one would ever find me.

Before the hernia surgery, I had the strength of a damn monster when I worked out, lifted weights, and walked five miles easily. Now, here I am a man just getting over surgery. The incision had not fully healed nor had I recovered my strength. I knew the hike would be tough, and I would have to pace myself.

Before I broke camp, I got out my Bible. I thumbed through Genesis and Exodus. "Okay, God, you took care of Moses when he led the Israelites in the wilderness. You prepared a table for them in the wilderness. Here I am, without much food and water, and if you're real, you'll take care of me, or this promise is all a bunch of crap." Then I packed my gear and headed up the trail.

As I walked, I prayed, "Lord, I have faith. I know you will take care of me. Here I am in the woods, alone and my food is going to run out tomorrow." I stopped to eat one can of tuna fish at lunch and drank several gallons of water.

Toward the end of the day I picked a camping spot between two rising forest covered mountains where the valley creek widened into a river. I crossed over this river to a spring as clear as an iridescent mirror. I could see trout swimming, but I had brought nothing to catch fish. The area stretched before me so green and peaceful. I walked on spongy, wet moss. Even moss covered the rocks.

I got out my cheesecloth and strained the water as I dipped my Gatorade bottle into the creek, and as I came back across the river from the spring to my camping spot, I saw something on a large log jutting out from the woods. I went over to investigate. There sat three cans of Beanie Weenies. I threw back my head and let out a big booming laugh that echoed back to me. Manna for the Israelites, three cans of Beanie Weenies with a pop top just for me. God did provide like he promised in the Bible.

As I ate one can of the blessed weenies and beans from Heaven, I surveyed the area. This place showed a lot of activity. The ground appeared to be torn up as if someone had plowed it for a garden. I knew wild hogs had rooted for grubs or roots, or even bears could have been here clawing and pawing. I moved my camp away from the river as I knew many of the trails around there were animal's trails where they came to get water from the creek.

As I gathered wood for a fire, I contemplated just how dangerous my situation could be. If I weren't eaten by a bear during the night, I could become lost on the trail tomorrow. This might well be the last fire I would build. Many trails crossed the one I followed, and I had to take the right one. I had grown physically too weak to use up any strength getting lost. I had to follow the white markers on the trees and posts along the way. If I took a wrong turn it might be months or longer until another hiker traveled the same route.

I collected branches and logs and built a fire. I put extra logs beside my head, so I could just reach for one and lay it on the fire during the night to keep the fire going.

I lay down early, before dusk, and studied the sheer beauty of this area between the two mountains. I could not believe the magnificence of the greenery of my surroundings. A white, misty fog collected over the crevice of the creek as it cut through the valley. The smell of the mountain laurel came strong and fragrant. I could make out the faint rush of water in the distance from the creek where I had stopped to drink.

I fell asleep early and awoke hours later when a log of firewood hit me on the head. I opened my eyes but didn't move. My fire had died out, and the moon did not show brightly enough for me to see anything. The pitch black darkness filled my eyes. I felt something heavy and hard rubbing across my hair. Fear rose on my skin like a physical wave. I lay there afraid to move wondering how a log had hit me and what dragged it across my head. The rough bark on the log caught a strand of my hair and jerked it out.

I jumped up grabbing the injured place on my head with one hand and my flashlight with the other. I expected to find myself face to face with a bear. I shined my light toward the noise and saw the biggest beaver I had ever seen. It waddled away like a big hog, dragging its wide tail with its ears back. Its hair shined wet, glistening in the light of my flashlight while it waddled away with a log from my firewood. I ran toward the river to get a better look as it dove in carrying the log.

Suddenly my flashlight went out. I heard a tremendous noise from the spring across the river, a sound between a snort and a growl. My hair stood on end. Goose bumps rose all over me. Whatever it could be, I heard it moving slowly up the mountain, taking its time. I pictured a large, lumbering animal, maybe a bear, or a wild hog. I shook and beat on the flashlight until it flickered back on revealing only the beaver taking a leisurely swim.

I stood there listening to the night sounds: tree frogs, the beaver splashing, and whatever-it-was still climbing the mountain. I shined my light up the mountain and saw only the bushes moving. A distant owl shrieked, and I went back to my camp, built up my fire again, and went back to sleep. The next time I awoke, daylight had broken. I decided to get the hell out of this place.

I realized my route became critical at this point. I estimated I had three to four hours travel to Panther Creek Falls. I came to several intersections in the trail marked with blue and yellow markers. I had to make the right decision when it came to choosing the trail, crossing the river, or the creek. If I took the wrong turn, it could be days before I could retrace and find the white markers.

The rushing roaring stream beside the trail made such a noise a bear could have walked up on me. In this lovely but dangerous place, a person should not be alone. I glanced at the ground, wet from the spray of the stream beside me. Tiny, white wheels on the wet ground surrounded my feet. They were everywhere. I glanced up and saw they were the tiny petals from the mountain laurel blossoms. I could not fully enjoy the beauty of the area because I watched for danger. I tried to be cautious looking for whatever large animal had torn up the ground I had seen earlier.

I saw the next white marker ahead and entered a dark, shaded, mountain trail ascending straight upward. Despite the bright sun, the trees were so thick and the trail so shaded, it seemed like I walked into a dark room. I saw more signs of animals' digging and rooting as I climbed.

As I started up the mountain, I heard a breaking, popping sound to my left. I went to investigate the noise, but thick mountain laurel obscured my view. I got closer and closer to the sounds. The thought came into my mind that this might be the last backpacker who had passed this way, being eaten. It sounded like bones popping. A sour smell like something from a bear or hog filled the air. I didn't really want to know more. I retreated back to the trail as fast as I could.

From there I entered into a rock-strewn boulder field. There were so many big rocks and stones that I lost the trail marker. I sweated profusely and decided to rest and eat the last can of tuna fish and one can of Beanie Weenies. As I surveyed the area, I knew I had come about half way up the mountain, and I did not know which way to go from here.

I said a prayer out loud, "Okay, God, You brought me this far and you're going to lose me?" I sat for about half an hour while I rationed my water, rested, and prayed. As I glanced up, way up to the top of the mountain, I saw what appeared to be white smoke rising into the sky. But it wasn't smoke. This had to be Panther Creek Falls. The water fell from an overhang protruding out from the top of the mountain. These falls were not accessible from where I stood on the mountain.

As I sat there looking around, resting, I noticed a faded-out white marker painted on a tree across the boulder field from me. From here the trail got steeper and steeper. I made it to the white marker, and I saw another one further up ahead. Relieved, I pressed on, wiping my forehead on my handkerchief occasionally. I didn't drink my water as I noticed I had very little left.

As I continued climbing, I heard voices up ahead. I looked up. Three guys were busy throwing rocks off the falls. I hadn't seen anyone in two days and now the first people I meet are throwing rocks blindly off the falls in my direction. I supposed they were just throwing the rocks for the fun of it and hadn't seen me. They were about one hundred yards above me and the baseball-sized rocks were hitting within ten feet of me. "Hey, stop that," I yelled up to them. I couldn't understand what they yelled back, but they stopped throwing the rocks.

I made my way up the trail toward the falls and saw the same kind of large boulders and rocks I had seen earlier, but this time there were crevices, a good place for snakes to hide. However, the real danger stood at the top of the falls.

I finally make it over to where the rocks became flat and level. Here the wide creek sprayed curtain-like water off a huge high rock into the most spectacular waterfall. I had the urge to look over to see more of the magnificent waterfall, falling like a lure of danger down the rocks, down the mountainside.

The three guys I had seen from below were waiting for me. The first one appeared to be college age, a preppie-type, clean cut, and dressed in white shorts and a tee shirt as though he were on vacation at a resort rather than a rugged hike. The second guy wore army fatigues and thick glasses. The third guy had long hair, wore camouflage, and an army cap. Hanging from his belt were several stainless steel knives, a throwing star, a hatchet, and a numb chuck. Anyone with a numb chuck usually knows how to use this chain with a stick at each end. One stick fits into your hand and you swing the chain around and use the other stick as a weapon. A numb chuck is very dangerous. The way he scowled at me, I would have rather faced a bear.

I knew I wasn't making a favorable impression on them either. I was dirty, exhausted, and soaking wet with sweat. "Is this the last water before you go to the end of this trail and on to East Cowpen Mountain?" I asked. I took off my backpack and filled my water bottle.

"Yeah, it is. Where'd you come from?" the guy with the weapons asked.

"I came in from Cohutta. I started about two days ago. Man, these mountains are really steep," I replied. "Well, it couldn't be all that steep," he sneered. "I had a beaver and maybe a bear come around me last night," I said.

They laughed like they didn't believe me. The guy with the weapons flipped his lit cigarette off the falls and said, "We ain't seen no bears. We'll be going down tomorrow about three o'clock. How far is it down to the bottom?"

"It's a couple of hours climb. It's really rugged. A person could easily get lost. You also have to cross a river and several trails."

The guy with the weapons, I started thinking of as Numb Chuck said, "Surely, it can't be that far."

Numb Chuck pulled out marijuana cigarettes. The other two regarded me and said nothing as they each took the marijuana he offered them. "Want one?" Numb Chuck asked.

I noticed the barrel of an AR 15, a major military weapon, with the distinctive sight on the end of the barrel sticking out of the back of his pack. "Yes." I replied.

I decided it might be better to smoke than not, and better to socialize, than to turn them down.

I took the joint, leaned back against a rock and ran a scenario through my mind: throwing Preppie over the cliff and hitting Sarge in the mouth. I figured Numb Chuck would cut me at least once with one of those knives or get me with the throwing star before I took him out. I wasn't sure I could handle the three of them, but I might be forced to try.

"Well, man, far out, I feel better when I'm stoned." Everybody laughed and I laughed with them. Numb Chuck mocked me, "Well, man, I feel better when I'm stoned." I ignored him and said, "I'm going to set up camp and get firewood for tonight."

Then they turned and went further up the trail to their camp. I decided they had come from the entrance of the park of East Cowpen Mountain down to the falls.

I stayed at the falls to rest and enjoy the scenery before picking out a camping spot for the night. I also did some thinking. Here I'm on a wilderness mission to test the Lord, I thought. He provides for me when I doubt, and the next thing I'm doing is smoking a joint. I thought of the allegory of Jesus in the wilderness for forty days and nights when Satan tempted him. I tried not to feel guilty and instead wondered just how much these guys might have in common with Satan.

After a while they came back down the trail with a girl. She had the appearance of a party girl even though her brown hair was pulled back casually, and she wore shorts and hiking boots. She had on loose clothing, but I could tell she had a slender figure and large breasts. She seemed to belong to Numb Chuck. I thought about Julie back at work in Atlanta. Would I ever make it back home to see her?

They passed me and went down the trail I had just come up. As they went down the mountain, I went up to their camp about a fourth a mile up from the falls. There, I saw a large tent and a monstrosity of a rig in the trees. Between four trees hung an army-green, hammock like a sleeping bag suspended about twelve feet in the air by cables. I knew this is where Numb Chuck slept, so bears couldn't get him once he climbed up into the hammock and zipped up in the sleeping bag. If anyone came into the camp at night and didn't see him up there, he could drop on them out of the trees like a ninja.

I walked further up the trail and found they had lied to me about the water. A small spring flowed down from their camp. I also thought it a little strange that Numby had insisted that they had not seen any bears, but he had prepared to be sleeping safely in his rig if one came along.

I knew they would be back soon, so I left their site. On my way back down from the falls I found another small stream I followed until I came to a good, level place to pitch my tent. This spot had a gorgeous view, a place to get water, and I could see the boulder field and the trail back down the mountain if I needed to make a run for it. I sat outside my tent and watched a red-streaked sunset.

The three guys and the girl were gone only about ninety minutes, but when they came by my camp, they were exhausted, sweaty, and dirty. As they walked past, they must have known I had been by their camp. Numb Chuck regarded me coldly and growled, "Well, you get around, don't you?"

"We hadn't realized how steep that trail got," Preppie said to me "You were right."

I did not understand who these people were and if they were merely camping or were they criminals hiding out. Why did Numb Chuck have an attitude with me? What were all those weapons about. I didn't feel good about their presence there on the side of the mountain with me. They could be a threat to me and want to harm me just for sport. I might have to defend myself before morning came. They knew they could get away with whatever they wanted to do, since they outnumbered me.

I had fashioned my tarp into a tent. As night came, I built a fire outside and got inside the tent. I read a little in my Bible. "Fret not yourself because of evil doers." David, in Psalms, had said over and over, "If God is for me, who can be against me?" Then I realized if they came by, they would be able to they see me sitting in my tent, so I got out of my tent and closed the front with a piece of string. My hands were shaking from nervousness. When I cut the string with my knife, I accidentally cut my finger. A drop of blood fell from my finger, and I repeated to myself what I had just read from Psalms. "Fret not yourself because of evil doers. If God is for me, who can be against me?"

I let my fire die down, hid behind a large boulder, and piled up a good amount of large stones. Then I climbed up onto the hidden boulder and brought the large rocks up there one at a time and stacked them up in front of me. I sat watching a billion stars come out around a half moon. The stars were brilliant on this clear night. I studied the faint wisp of a white cloud that streaked the length of the sky. I thought to myself, I wonder how this night will turn out? Will there be an incident? Will I survive?

A few hours later, I saw the three guys coming down through the woods. They were having a hard time walking, stumbling around as they were not on the trail. The way they were walking and the way they were acting made me think they might be high on something. As they neared my tent, they hooted like screech owls. My fire had died down to embers and gave off only a minimal amount of light. Next the group started making growling sounds and throwing baseball sized rocks. I gave them about fifteen minutes to have fun. This whole situation had started to piss me off, but I had prepared for them. I threw a big rock behind them. "What's that!" I heard one of them exclaim. I threw another large rock to the other side, closer this time. That scared them and they ran like jack rabbits. I stayed put. "God, can I trust you or not? Can I go in the tent and go to bed?"

From far away, real owls hooted. The night filled with lonesome sounds. I could hear animals stirring and walking, coming down to drink at the creek. "Okay, Buddy," I said to myself. "You've had enough of this wilderness experience. I'm getting out of here."

I went back to my tent but slept very little. About dawn I packed up, filled my water bottle, and walked up the trail toward the other camp. "God, you did take care of me, and I thank you for it, but I have to go through the enemy's camp."

As I walked up the trail by their camp, the party girl came out of the tent. She had on only pajama bottoms, naked from the waist up. Her long hair hung around her shoulders and she appeared to just have awoken. Uh-oh, I thought. Seeing her like that is enough reason for them to want to hurt me.

She saw me just then and said, "Hello," in a sweet, seductive way. "Good morning," I said as I continued up the trail, walking quickly.

Soon I reached the highest part of the mountain then walked for several hours down the other side. When I got to the end of the Panther Creek Falls dirt road, there stood a sign: "fifteen miles to Blue Ridge, twenty miles to Ellijay." If I turned left that would take me to Tennessee. I turned right, and headed toward East Cowpen.

The day grew hot. Mountain flowers bloomed and yellow jackets buzz everywhere. I could hear a low buzzing that sounded like a million bees, enough bees to sting you to death. I stopped short, glanced down, and could not believe what I saw. I stood in a mass of miniature grasshoppers, smaller than flies. There appeared to be a million or so. When I took a step, they jumped forward with each step. Their movements sounded like rain.

I moved away from the grasshoppers and continued to walk the rest of the day. The dirt road had turned to dry red dust, and soon my boots were covered in this red dust. As I walked, I still talked to God. I concluded that my challenge was to have more faith and trust in God and to go on from there. I had drunk the last of the water and had only one pack of oatmeal which I could not eat without water or a fire to warm the water. I still carried an eighty-five pound backpack, and happened to be two days early for Julie to come and meet me. I didn't know what to do.

I stepped out of the woods onto Forest Service Road. Five minutes later, a green forest service truck with a rolling swirl of red dust billowing behind it pulled up beside me. As the ranger put on the brakes, the old truck let out a screech and came to a halt. The ranger in uniform leaned out the window and said, "Hey, Buddy, what are you doing out here?"

"I'm headed toward the north entrance to East Cowpen Mountain," I said. "But I'm out of the woods two days early."

"East Cowpen's about fifteen miles north of here. I'll give you a lift. I'm headed that way anyway. We might as well eat lunch first." He pulled his truck off the road into a shaded spot under an oak and asked if I would like to join him for lunch.

"My wife packed way too much lunch for me. She packed two of everything. It's more than I can eat," he said. He gave me his extra sandwich, fruit, and candy, plus a quart of water. I wondered if God sent this skinny, old mountain man in the green uniform. It did seem co-incidental that out of the thousand of acres, the minute I step onto a road, a ranger comes driving down the road in my direction. People could walk on such a road and not see anyone for twelve hours or more. As we ate, he talked. "It gets pretty lonesome up here in the mountains."

"I've been in the mountains three days, and I must have traveled about fifteen miles. I'm ready to go home," I said as I ate. Suddenly, I realized, he had a radio. "Can you call my wife?" I asked.

"No, but I can call someone who can call her."

"Have them call Julie Berkshire." I gave him the phone number. "Tell her that her husband is ready to come out of the wilderness and will meet her at the north entrance of East Cowpen."

Once we got to the ranger station, I lay in a big chase lounge on the front porch and slept all afternoon. I had not realized just how tired and weak I had become until I closed my eyes. Julie arrived that night, and ran up to the porch to find me asleep. "Bradley!" She called out as she approached. "Are you alright? Honey." I sat up then stood up as she grabbed me. "I've been afraid I would never see you again. I thought you might be lost and not find your way out. Did your incision break open? I've been so scared that it would. You could have fallen and broken your leg, and I wouldn't have known where you were."

"I had some tough times, but I'm fine. Are you ready to go home?" I drove us through the mountains and stopped at a Mom and Pop barbecue restaurant and we talked as we ate. "Julie, I made a mistake leaving you and coming on this trip alone, and without enough food. I should have never done so much walking and mountain climbing after surgery. I'm sorry I worried you. I'm also sorry I didn't explain things as we drove here."

She said she forgave me but to never do anything like that to her again. We left the restaurant with our arms around each other.

After we were back home, I noticed Julie lightened up on me and everything settled down, everything went smooth for a while. I stayed home and tried to recover from both the hernia operation and from the trip. In two weeks I went back to Dr. Slater for him to check my incision and make sure I had not injured myself further. He said I had healed in spite of my strenuous trip and he also checked the status of my hepatitis C. Good news: my viral count still remained at zero.

Because of my hasty and irresponsible trip to East Cowpen Mountain, I found that God took care of me no matter how foolishly I had acted. I also learned the lesson of being more cautious with issues of my health. Maybe I learned to be more patient with Julie.

34.
Milestones

Julie continued to work in Atlanta at the Capitol Building, but after two years, she grew tired of the commute and got a job locally as a secretary.

As time passed, I continued my reading sessions with the literacy group. When my reading skills were on the twelfth grade level, I began to study to pass three of the five part GED test, the three reading sections.

After a year of preparation, I took the Science, Social Studies, and Literature tests and made ninety to one-hundred points higher on each test than the requirements needed to pass.

My health improved steadily, but I remained on disability because the welding jobs I qualified for were beyond me physically. I continued to pray everyday for guidance. I read the Bible and continued attending the First Baptist Church with Big Dog. I spent time with Big Dog, attending the Braves games at the Atlanta Stadium since he had time on his hands after leaving his veterinarian office every evening.

My literacy tutor told me since I passed all the reading sections of the GED, the next part of my education should be to pass the Language Arts Writing and the Math section. She advised me to go to the local Adult Education classes for help with these subjects. The closest classes were taught at the local technical college.

The night I went to enroll in the Piedmont Technical College Adult

Education program, I felt very intimidated. I pulled up to the campus where four large three story buildings stretched out in front of me. I followed the signs for the adult education department, found the right room, and took the diagnostic test. I felt nervous when the instructor interviewed me for placement. This interviewing instructor seemed impressed that I had already passed parts of the GED. "Your math and language arts scores are very low, though. Were you having a bad night or did you lose your place or forget your glasses?"

"No," I replied. "I have very little skills in these subjects."

This instructor seemed surprised at my reply. "Well you surely made high scores on the reading test." She assigned me to a class which met four afternoons a week.

The teacher in the classroom seemed nice and kept telling me I could do it. Like the first instructor, she seemed very impressed at my reading level, but she didn't understand why I had missed my basic skills in math and language arts. I didn't even know how to divide or to punctuate a sentence.

When she told me to write a paragraph, I couldn't think of anything to write. When I did write a few sentences, I could not spell many of the words. The teacher put red marks all over my paper and corrected all the errors. I felt so inferior and intimidated.

She gave me assignments to complete, but I felt too embarrassed to ask for help and didn't want anyone to know I couldn't do some of the most basic things. Teenagers who had just dropped out of school filled the room. They were talking and clowning around. I didn't remember my multiplication tables if I ever did know them. The next morning I dreaded going back. So I didn't. I dropped out. No one ever called to see why I didn't come back.

Maybe I could learn math on my own or perhaps get Julie to help me, I thought. So I asked her to help me with division. She showed me quickly and told me how simple the steps were. But when I tried and got stuck, she had no patience with me. "Brad, you just divide, multiply the numbers back, then subtract, then bring down the next number and do the same thing again." Again, she showed me quickly and couldn't understand why I didn't catch on.

I felt ashamed to even tell her I didn't know the multiplication tables. My teacher had given me several sheets of basic math, so when Julie went to work, I brought out the multiplication sheet and started by trying to memorize the sevens table.

My desire for an education seemed almost tangible. I wanted it so badly. My self-esteem had improved so much after attending the literacy tutoring group and after passing three of the five sections of the GED battery of tests. I still read about two hours a day, every day, still mostly the Bible and the newspaper.

By now, Julie realized she would always be the main bread winner of our household. She had known that she needed a professional skill if she planned to advance to a higher paying job. So, she set her goal to get an accounting degree.

Right after I dropped out of Piedmont Technical College, Julie enrolled there at the same technical college. She kept her job as a secretary and attended classes at night. Once again at home alone, I felt lost. If I tried to work, it could be only part time like I had done at the flower shop, or I would lose what little I did make on my Social Security Insurance.

After Julie attended classes for a year and a half, she graduated with a 3.8 GPA and earned an associate's degree in accounting. She received the honor of being placed on the President's Honor Roll, and got an award for academic achievement.

As Julie achieved her goal, I felt an invisible wedge build up between us. She became so confident and self-assured, which I felt glad to see, but she seemed to lord her education over me. Maybe I imagined this or maybe I envied her the education I could not get. I had come so far. But that was part of the problem. I now knew how it felt to succeed and to learn. Without telling Julie, I worked up enough courage and enrolled at the college, again. If I failed, I wasn't going to share it with her.

I enrolled in Adult Education at the Piedmont Technical College one more time, and this time, I hoped I would find the teacher who could understand me and help me. My new class met four mornings a week.

On the first day I attended class, Mrs. Laney, a tiny lady with long brown hair and a very kind smile, walked into the classroom. I could tell she meant business, and she meant for each student to succeed. She stood barely taller than me when I sat down at the desk and she stood in front of the class. She only talked when she had something important to say, and she kept the room quiet so the students could concentrate on their assignments.

When she looked at me, it seemed like she focused on only me. I noticed she did that with each student she interviewed and gave assignments. We each had a folder showing our academic level in reading, math, and language arts. As she quietly did the interviews, she studied the diagnostic scores and the data in each folder. From the beginning, I made her aware of my low skills. She looked me straight in the eyes, and asked me if I was serious about getting an education and if I could come to class every day. When I told her how much I wanted to learn and that I would be there every day, she said, "Well, we're going to be able to do this then."

I immediately felt hopeful and lifted up. I noticed she had said, 'We're going to be able to do this, meaning she was in this with me. Mrs. Laney told me she believed in using positive reinforcement meaning verbal reinforcement for work done well and discouraging anything negative, especially a negative attitude or a negative comment. Mrs. Laney told us the worst thing we could do, other than skip class was to not ask for help when we needed it.

While all the other students worked on their assignments, Mrs. Laney left the aide, Miss Joyce, in charge of the class and took me into a small open area of the conference room where instructors came through. This area was quiet and away from the other students. Here she tutored me one-to-one for a few minutes, each day. This second floor room with glass petitions across the length and width of one wall, looked out over the green lawn of the campus where I could see a gazebo and the flowering shrubs and flower beds.

Mrs. Laney patiently and calmly went over the method of division. She taught me as if it were a game and gave me an easy way to learn by association. "Think of the division as a family—**D**addy, **M**other, ***S***ister, **B**rother, stands for **D**ivide, **M**ultiply, ***S***ubtract, **B**ring down. Now start back with **D**addy—**D**ivide and do it all again. It seemed easy the way she explained it when she drew the large capital letters, **DMSB,** vertical down the left side of the page for me to follow. After I learned to do a couple of problems without her help, she left me there to complete the page of work. My size and the fact I had such low skills did not seem to intimidate her or bother her at all.

Every morning she set me up in this conference room, gave me instructions, made sure I could do the work, and left me there to work undisturbed. I spent the first part of every morning working here and made tremendous progress. Mrs. Laney and Miss Joyce helped me one-to-one, and checked on me often even though they had a full class.

Then I went back into the classroom to what Mrs. Laney called peer tutoring—students on the same subject and approximately the same abilities—helping each other in small groups. The first week, I finished multiplication since I had studied at home. Then the second week, I finished the division section in the text book. In the next two weeks I covered fractions and decimals. I recognized what I should have known when I worked for Scientific Welding. Mrs. Laney told me men were usually good at math because of skills they had used on their jobs.

I could not wait to go to class each day, but I tried my teacher's patience about one thing. During peer tutoring, I took a big breath and said where everyone heard me, "Man, this math is too tough for a dumb guy like me." The other students giggled and some nodded that they felt it was tough also. "I can't seem to get it," I remarked. I guess I said this to make an excuse in front of other students who had figured out that I started with learning the basics.

In reply, Mrs. Laney said nicely but firmly, "Don't say 'I can't' in front of me. Leave the 'I can't' outside the door when you come into this classroom."

A few of days later when I had been sitting a couple of hours studying in the classroom, I leaned back in my chair, stretched my arms out behind my head and heard the plastic chair I was sitting in—crack. "Oh no. Mrs. Laney, I broke the chair." She told me to not worry about it as several chairs had broken recently and they had already placed an order for new ones.

One kid remarked on my size, "How big are you anyway?"

I told him, "Six-two, two-eighty. I'm not only the biggest one in here, I'm the dumbest." When I said this I remembered Mrs. Laney had warned me about being negative. I glanced toward her to see if she heard me.

She cut her eyes at me and said loud enough for the entire class to hear, "I'm going to get a great big gong. You know, like they had on that game show, and every time you say, I am dumb, or I am stupid, or I can't, I'm going to hit the gong really loud."

Everybody in the class laughed, and I laughed the most in my big booming voice. Somehow after that moment, I felt free of the negative past when it came to learning. Later she said my picturing her hitting the gong was visual imagery, and when I had envisioned the gong, that made an impression on me to leave the negative thoughts behind.

I continued to study math every morning and in a month, I started studying percents. A few months later I had moved to geometry and algebra. I asked Mrs. Laney if I could also attend the afternoon class and she agreed. So, from eight thirty until twelve, I studied math. Then I went to the student center and ate a sack lunch, I had brought from home.

In the afternoon, from one o'clock until four, I studied language arts. I went home and read the Bible for an hour before Julie got in from her new job as an accountant with a local Certified Public Accounting office.

At times Julie and I did fine, but there were times she still seemed disagreeable or moody. She thought I should have dinner for her and I did many times but not every night. She didn't seem too happy with me putting so much time into class. "You could still get a part time job, you know like you had at the florist shop. You could work and go to school at the same time. I did that for a year and a half," she reminded me.

But I continued school full time. Each afternoon I studied Language Arts, and when it came to writing a paragraph, Mrs. Laney said, " Don't worry about spelling. I can figure out what you wrote. Just get some thoughts down on paper, and we can learn to spell later."

I stood there looking down at her, amazed. I could not believe I had found a teacher who could encourage me like she did. This way of teaching—the "write now, spell later" came as a great relief to me. No one had ever said, "Don't worry about spelling."

Wow. Maybe I can do this, I thought. She also told me to write about fishing after she found out what I liked to do.

I wrote an essay about fishing in the mountain streams. Mrs. Laney gave me a top score, knocking off only one point for my handwriting, not my spelling. She told me to improve my handwriting and gave me ample opportunity by giving me a journal to write in every day. As I practiced writing essays about many different topics, I got better and better at creative writing.

Mrs. Laney also gave me a notebook where I could keep my list of misspelled words. I had to write each word I misspelled, twelve times each. She wrote the first one correctly for me, and I wrote the others in columns underneath. I didn't have to go floundering in the dictionary to find a word I didn't know how to spell.

I passed the GED language and essay section. By sheer coincidence the randomly given essay topic was similar to the ones I had practiced in the classroom. I think my essay score brought my language score up and helped me pass this section. When I shared my success with Julie, she just looked at me and listened to my excitement on doing well. Then she said, "Well no wonder you passed. It took you a year of studying." I didn't let her burst my bubble of happiness. In class, I shared the fact I passed the GED language and essay test with Mrs. Laney and with the other classmates. They were all very happy for me and understood how much I had worked to pass.

One of my fellow classmates seemed upset at the end of class and told Mrs. Laney she had to drop out because her husband's truck broke down and he needed her car to get to work, so she had no transportation to get to class. I talked to her, found out where she lived, and started giving her a ride to class. Later I picked up another lady. I gave them both a ride for over a year.

During my classroom time, the hepatitis C returned. I had pains shooting throughout my liver and abdominal area so badly that I had to go back on the pain medication. I took just enough to mask the pain in class and still be able to drive to school and function during class. I waited until I got home to take the required dose to stop the pain. "Brad are you alright?" I glanced up to see Mrs. Laney standing there with a concerned look on her face. "Your face is red and you have beads of sweat on your forehead." She had spoken quietly so the other students did not overhear her when she questioned me.

"Can I talk to you during the lunch break?" She nodded that she knew I wanted to talk privately.

When the class went to lunch, she and I stayed behind. I had been coming to class for almost a year and decided I should tell Mrs. Laney about my problem especially since she noticed and asked. So, I told her I had hepatitis C. She did not judge me or condemn me. "Bradley, is there anything I need to know or do to help you?" I told her if I ever had to be out, she could save the assignments for me. Later she said she could tell when my pain came over me. I didn't think any of the students realized I had these bad days.

I made up my mind to continue class and not let anything stop me from passing the last section—the math test. I continued doing percents, decimals, geometry, and algebra and added graph and chart study. On the math practice tests the problems were word problems only. I came so close on the needed score on the practice tests, but I had such a long way to go. I continued to be diligent and faithful in my attendance.

Each morning, I read the Bible before I left home. In Proverbs I read: A good name is rather to be had than great riches. Around campus, I certainly had a better name than I had back in Oakdale. Each morning, I also had a prayer time before I left for school. On the way to school, I picked up the other two students and still arrived early. I knew my persistence would one day pay off.

35.
A Celebrity at Graduation

When a Workforce Development Forum was held at the Piedmont Technical College to discuss ideas to improve Georgia's workforce, a former governor along with local dignitaries, local politicians, senators, and state representative were invited to attend. Mrs. Laney asked me to be the student speaker on behalf of the Workforce that could benefit from education. This meeting of dignitaries, for lunch and speeches, was held in the large conference room at the college.

On a September day, I sat at a long banquet table next to Georgia's former Governor, Zell Miller and his wife, Mrs. Shirley Miller. I opened the program, saw my name, Bradley Berkshire, and the name above mine, Zell Miller, now a senator.

I surveyed the audience of about three hundred, and saw Julie's new accounting boss, but not Julie. I guessed Julie had chickened out, or just hadn't wanted to come. I felt almost glad she wasn't there. She might have had a negative attitude I would pick up on that could affect my concentration when I gave my speech. She had been through so many bad times with me, but somehow she didn't seem to want any part of my successes. I wondered if she might be threatened by my success in some way. Maybe she didn't have the confidence in me that I could get up and speak. After I told her about speaking at the forum, she had said to me, "Brad, your being a student speaker to the big wigs—the dignitaries and politicians is pretty top notch stuff." Maybe if she were here, she would be proud of me. I could not think about her now.

I heard the governor's stomach growl like a rhinoceros coming through a cane break. I chuckled to myself. He took a couple of drinks of ice water and started to sneeze. Mrs. Miller handed him an extra napkin. Suddenly I didn't feel so intimidated. I smiled to myself.

I would get up there and bare my soul, but I couldn't tell everything. I had experience speaking in front of people. At twelve years old, I had represented myself in court in front of a judge. I thought about those years only briefly then pushed those thought aside. I felt my face grow red and felt a sweat breaking out on my forehead, but I wasn't nervous. The pains from my hepatitis C had started to shoot through my side about the time lunch begun. But no one would know about this part of my life and how I came to have this virus. I had gotten good at suppressing pain. With a big laugh like mine, no one would ever guess. My laugh had become part of what kept me going and what had such an affect on people.

With lunch finished, the governor stood and gave his speech and gave statistics on unemployment and problems of the state workforce.

Then I heard my name called, "Bradley Berkshire." As I stepped up on the portable stage, I felt the platform give slightly under my six foot two, two-hundred-eighty pound frame. Damn, I thought what an entrance to just fall through, but the platform held. I laid the speech Mrs. Laney had typed from my handwriting out in front of me and studied the audience, glancing from my left to my right.

I began, "I'm a student here in adult education. I came here to get my GED, but first I went to a tutor for many years to learn to read. This is very hard for me to say—to admit." I paused. The audience got very quiet and still. Three hundred pair of eyes were on me and no one moved.

"Most of my life I could not read a sign on a billboard unless there was a picture and then I could guess the words. If there were a picture of a coke bottle, then I knew it was an advertisement for Coca Cola.

"My fourth grade teacher asked what each student wanted to be. When she got to me, I told her I wanted to be a truck driver because that's what the kid in front of me had just said, and I thought it sounded pretty good. She replied, 'People like you will dig ditches all your life.' That's when my self-esteem plummeted, and I hated school. I became truant and always in trouble. I left school as soon as I could.

"I had good work ethics and worked my way up without an education. When I became a supervisor over twelve men, I went to work every day afraid someone would find out I couldn't read or write and had only minimal math skills. I learned to delegate really well and had a secretary who never guessed I was illiterate. I gave her a great amount of verbal instructions, and she followed through for me.

"When my company moved to another state, I didn't go, but went out looking for a job. I couldn't even fill out an application and told the employer I was in a hurry and would fill out the application at home. At home I would get my wife to fill it out for me." I ended my speech by looking at the Governor. "Send us back to school, not to the unemployment lines." I folded my speech and heard the audience began to applaud.

I turned to the Governor. He rose to shake my hand. "Son you just topped everything that was said. What was presented earlier today was nothing compared to your speech. What a great message." I thanked him and went toward my seat, where I shook hands with Mrs. Miller.

I could hear the audience applauding as I started thinking about leaving. Then I turned and saw a wall of people who all stood, applauding. They were giving me a standing ovation. People crowded around me. Suddenly the newspaper photographers snapped pictures of the Governor and me. Then the president of the college came to get into the next photograph with us. Then the state representative came forward. All the local dignitaries gathered round to get in the picture.

I managed to introduce my teacher, Mrs. Laney, to the governor, but she didn't get in the picture. She just shook her head and smiled when I motioned to her. She said later she didn't need the honor—her reward came in seeing my success. She enjoyed the amazing moment with me. Little did she or anyone here this day know of really how amazing it was for me to be here with the former governor and dignitaries telling my story, at least the part I was willing to share.

After that day I became a celebrity. My picture appeared in the local newspaper many times over the next few years. I was invited to the capital to meet the new governor, Roy Barnes, and to hear the legislature in session. The following year, I spoke at the Legislative Luncheon to honor the Georgia Legislators.

As a part of a statewide made-for-television documentary, I gave a brief testimony and told what education had done for me. They had me reenact scenes from when I worked at the welding plant where I had been a supervisor. They had scenes of me catching a bus to look for a job and then leave because I could not fill out the application. The filming took three days, but they used only three minutes of the tape. This video was broadcast all over Georgia and in some other states. These were the highest accomplishments I had ever had.

At the house, the phone rang off the hook. Family members I had not heard from in years called. Many told me they had given up on me when I had gotten into trouble as a child. Most of them never knew I had gone to YDP, but all were happy for my accomplishments, now.

Kell, my cousin and old drug buddy from Oakdale, called. When I picked up the phone and recognized his voice, I felt shocked to hear from him. I hadn't seen or talked to him in fifteen years. I knew through Aunt Lilly that he had graduated from high school and had gone to college. But that was the last I had heard.

He had seen my documentary on television and called to congratulate me. He said he never knew I couldn't read. At first, I felt that his call was a gesture of kindness, but it came across as condescending. "I'm Dr. Kelly Berkshire," he informed me, "and pastor of one of Birmingham's largest churches. We have five hundred in attendance on Sunday," he boasted.

"Kell, when did you become a minister?"

"I went to seminary and then got an appointment in Birmingham. I've been here ten years."

Then I told him about my attending the First Baptist Church in Atlanta each Sunday to hear Dr. Charles Stanley and how much his sermons had changed my life.

"Our services are televised each Sunday and we have a fifty member choir."

He started in on trying to impress me thinking I compared Dr. Stanley's church to what he had or didn't have, so I changed the subject. Then I said, "Man, I guess you mended your ways?" I referred to the drugs we did as kids and let out a hardy laugh. "We really had some wild times back when we were kids. You remember some of those drugs we used to take?"

His tone changed. "Don't ever bring up any of that stuff we used to do." I thought I detected a hint of fear in his voice. "We don't talk about that any more."

I think he feared his congregation might find out what their exemplary preacher had done in his youth. I think it would be something he could have shared with his congregation to show what God had done for him in overcoming the drugs like I had done. But before I could tell him what I thought on the matter he suddenly had to hang up. He wouldn't even admit to being any part of the drug culture. This burned me up. He wasn't just a part, his influence was instrumental in getting me started on marijuana at nine years old. But what happened to me afterward was no one's fault except my own. I let it drop and put it out of my mind.

I sat at home looking at the newspaper articles telling of my accomplishments and putting a scrapbook together when Kay, my sister, called. Excitement filled her voice, "Oh Brad. I saw your documentary for literacy. You looked so good. And were so impressive. I'm telling everyone I know about my brother being on television. You told me several weeks ago about your filming the documentary, but I didn't really understand how successful you had become.

She continued, "Last night I laid in bed watching late night television and had almost fallen asleep when I heard your voice and thought, somehow, you were in the room. I jerked upright, looked around the room for you, and then saw you on television. I am so proud of you, Baby Brother."

All of the calls and all of the newspaper articles about me and all the speeches I made came in second to the pleasure I had when I continued to attend class. I looked forward to the learning each day. I had waited my whole life for this experience and I wanted it to last as long as it possibly could.

When I moaned and groaned about failing the GED math section by one point, and therefore, having to retake that section of the test again, Mrs. Laney said, "Well, all you've got to do is take the test again, get the same amount of problems correct plus a few more correct than you did before."

The way she put it was that I had not failed the math test in the way I thought I had, but I had just fallen short by one point, probably by one or two problems. After studying for a few more months, I took the math test the second time, and passed.

Passing this fifth and last of the GED tests meant I passed the GED. Two years after starting classes at Piedmont Technical College, I was graduating with a General Educational Development Diploma from the Adult Education department.

When I told Mrs. Laney I would be riding to graduation in a white stretch limousine, she replied, "Not without me."

The student I had given a ride to school for a year provided transportation to graduation. Her husband who now happened to own a limousine service picked us up at a designated place where Mrs. Laney met Julie and me. Jewell pulled up in her Oldsmobile and announced to everyone, "I used to tell Brad he should get his education. I don't know what he would have done without my help." Jewell was old enough now for me to just consider maybe she was getting into her senile years. What she said didn't bother me at all, but Julie laughed at her. Julie, Jewell, Mrs. Laney and I rode in the white stretch limo that pulled up to the conference center's huge double glass doors at the college where I was to speak in the conference room in front of six hundred students, their family members, and guest.

I wore a navy, graduation cap and gown and lined up with the other students. The tassel from my cap stuck to my cheek when I moved my head to talk to the students in line. I glanced at the program that had been handed to me. I found my name beside the words: Student Speaker—Bradley Elijah Berkshire. We marched in together, but when we got to the front of the conference center, I went to the stage with the other speakers, the dignitaries.

My speech was basically the same as I had given at the Workforce Development Forum except this time I shared my aspirations. I had plans to attend the college and major in computer technology. The speech was a success. Julie came into the large conference center, late, and sat in the back. She told me later she could not hear my speech and did not know if it was good or not. I didn't understand why she had been late coming in though the hallways were crowded, she came with me, early. I couldn't understand why she showed no enthusiasm for my success. I got no praise from her, though I did from everyone else: my teacher, friends, and fellow students. All said they were proud of me and that the speech was moving and inspirational. I had my portrait made in my cap and gown and had an extra one made to send to my sister, Kay.

After graduation, we had a quarter break and I really had time to consider Julie's mood swings. She had acted very stand-offish for a couple of months and had not reacted well to my happiness at graduation. I became worried about her and insisted she go for a checkup. I went with her. After an examination and x-rays, the diagnosis showed Julie had a tumor the size of a golf ball on her right breast. She had surgery within a week. The tumor was benign. But because of a family history of breast cancer, she was put on Tamoxifen as a precaution.

Julie spent several weeks convalescing at home in bed. "Honey, are you recovering from the surgery like you should be? Are you feeling alright?"

"The doctor said it would take a few weeks. Right now I just feel washed out." I held her and stroked her hair, then I actually made soup and sandwiches and brought them on a tray to her bedside table. She managed a sweet smile as I pulled up a chair and sat close to her as she ate.

We were about to celebrated our fifteenth anniversary. To cheer her up, I bought her a honey colored, Palomino colt with a blond mane and tail, and a blond streak down its nose. Julie had never been happier with a gift. She immediately named her colt, "Shadow." We boarded Shadow at a stable close to the college that I attended and to Julie's job where she had worked as a CPA for the last year. Every afternoon we went to the stables to see Shadow. Though Julie had reason to be happy, something still did not seem right with her.

When the summer quarter came, I started my core classes at the college, and Mrs. Laney nominated me to represent adult education in a statewide Student of the Year contest. I won. I went to the CNN Conference Center in Atlanta to the Georgia State Literacy Conference to receive the award. Doc Henderson, Big Dog, went with me to the banquet as my guest, but Julie was unable to attend. Mrs. Laney sat at the table with the other teachers. Big Dog and I sat with the other students who were receiving awards.

When I was announced, Big Dog went up front with me. There were about eight hundred people in the audience. This was obviously my finest moment. First they mispronounced my name, presented me with a plaque that was printed Burkshire instead of Berkshire, and then announced it had taken me five years to get my GED. I had prepared a short speech of acceptance, but they whisked me away in about thirty seconds, so the singers would have more time to perform after the awards.

I can't say I was disappointed but more less stunned. As I sat back down at the banquet table, I thought about the "five years" they had said. Five years to get a GED? People must have thought I was an idiot or retarded. Then I remembered the first test I had taken *had* been five years ago. But I hadn't worked toward my goal for the entire five years. There were so many years I had been too sick to study with my tutor, and then there were the years I enrolled, didn't get the right help, and dropped out because I was too discouraged. I folded the speech I had planned on giving and gave the plaque to Mrs. Laney who promised to have the officials correct the misspelling of my name. When the last award was given, Big Dog and I were ready to leave.

We left the banquet as soon as the last closing remark was given, so I could to go to St. Joseph's Hospital to see Julie. After she had recovered from the breast surgery, she had not felt just right, so I had taken her back for more test. She had finally been diagnosed and the problems that were found could have contributed to her mood swings and depression even for all the previous years, for maybe as many years as we had been married. She had undergone surgery on the previous day to have a full hysterectomy to remove a large tumor the size of a grapefruit from her abdominal area. She was put on a new antidepressant drug and an anti-inflammatory drug.

Julie's health improved markedly after this last surgery and the new medication. After all she had been through, she was finally able to manage her health. She was cancer free and her problems with depression were under control. Each day of her life was filled with things she liked to do. She loved her job as a CPA, and made good money. In the afternoons and on weekends, we visited Shadow. More importantly we learned how to get along with each other without fighting and disappointing each other.

During the fall quarter break, Julie took a vacation from work and we went back to Mentone, Alabama to a birthday party. Julie's dear grandmother Almeda was having her one-hundredth birthday. She still lived in the same house that her late husband, Leldon, had built for her when she had been a fifteen year old bride. She had a health care nurse staying with her, and many family members taking care of her. Julie had a weekend of mixed emotion. She felt happy to see Almeda, but still felt a great deal of sadness over losing her dear Papa Lel several years before.

When the fall quarter started at the college, I continued my core classes for Computer Information Systems and went back to Mrs. Laney for help with my advanced math. When I had entered adult education, two years before, she had taught me to divide. Now she helped me divide polynomial for my algebra class. I passed both of my core classes—the algebra and the English 101. Then I enrolled for the second quarter.

In each local newspaper there is a certain amount of space for civic news. It seemed over the next few years, I became the person to fill these newspaper columns. Mrs. Laney nominated me for the Literacy Advisory Board and named me the student representative for adult education to be a part of the CHSI organization, Community Help with Social Issues where I became a spokesperson on the board representing community issues. I appeared on the video of the local town-hall meeting.

After a year, I became a member on the Board of Trustees for CHSI and from there I became a representative for my district in Georgia Family Improvements, a state level social reform program. This was an appointed, paid position on a part-time basis. In other words, I was paid to attend meetings and give my input.

I attended meetings in Atlanta, Savannah, Macon, and was invited to the Chicago meeting. At the Atlanta Freight Depot, an Atlanta restaurant, the CEO of the Georgia Family Improvements told me she was looking forward to working with me.

My achievements had exceeded my expectations: I was attending the Piedmont Technical College taking college core classes, and I was getting paid for attending meetings and giving advice on how to help people. I had become a valued member of Georgia Family Improvements where I was not afraid of speaking candidly about the issues. I knew firsthand some of the trials and needs of people. Many of the members at this state level social program were well-to-do people with a degree in sociology or human resources. My degree was in human suffering. I didn't necessarily speak of my own hardships, but I let everyone know I had experience with people who were down and out.

Quite often I gave inspirational talks to youth groups about drug abuse and to adult education classes and teachers about what education had done for me. I also spoke to hepatitis C support groups, telling them about the latest treatments for this epidemic proportioned virus.

When I spoke at Georgia State University about adult literacy, I met educators who talked about dyslexia. I told them about my experiences trying to learn when I was young. I told them that sometimes the letters were backward to me. When I did memorize something, then the next day I couldn't remember what I had memorized. They said I probably had undiagnosed dyslexia and to come by and be tested. If I were dyslexic, I would be eligible for a series of special classes.

When I took this test for dyslexia, it showed I definitely had dyslexia and was therefore eligible for their program. I was stunned. All these years I had difficulty in learning, I never knew there was a name for it and that other people had the same problems. I attended their clinic and started taking training. But I had to drop out and didn't complete the first eight weeks of classes. My hepatitis viral count had increased to where I couldn't manage to function because of the pain and weakness.

I also had to drop out of the college core classes. I had only completed one year toward my degree. The saddest day came when I went and withdrew. As I left the student services office, I walked through the campus to leave. Since I had made many friends and had become well known and popular by this time, several students greeted me, "Hey, Brad." I just nodded and didn't stop to talk as I usually did. I felt like crying. I had come so far.

The more I had learned the more I realized I didn't know. I loved learning. I loved being a part of the classes and a part of the college. It gave me pride. Something inside me all those early years had felt so empty and incomplete. Learning and education filled up this empty part of me. Knowledge and learning is what I missed in my youth. I had been doing what I had longed to do so many years ago. My spirit felt uplifted here. I left and went home with a heavier feeling than I had experienced since I had enrolled there several years ago.

I continued speaking engagements on a part time basis. When I spoke at Georgia State University in the fall to college recruits, I encouraged them to work hard and stay in school. At least I could encourage those young college students to do what I was physically unable to do.

"I would like to say it is an honor and privilege to be here today. I would like to share some things I have learned in life, and I hope you can learn these things the easy way and not the hard way as I have.

"The first idea I would like to share with you is that I have

learned the longer I live, the more I realize the impact of attitude on life. Your attitude will make you or break you. I am convinced that life is ten percent of what happens to you and ninety percent of how you react to it. The remarkable thing is we have a choice regarding the attitude we embrace for each day.

"Thomas Jefferson said, 'Nothing can stop the man with the right mental attitude from achieving his goal. Nothing on earth can help the man with the wrong mental attitude.'

"So I believe it is the way you see yourself. You have got to tell yourself that you can do what you want to do. If you see yourself as a success, you will become successful.

"Have a positive, upbeat outlook. Be polite. Be responsible. Be a team player. Learn to delegate work. . . .

"Consider pride. Consider humility. It is said, 'Pride goeth before a fall.' There is a good pride, and there is a bad pride, and you have to be able to distinguish between the two. If Arrogance and Humility faced off, who do you think would win. Not all people, but most people, like a person who is down to earth or humble.

"What about discrimination? I would hope that if you think you are going to be discriminated against that you would be prepared. If you know something is coming down the pipe, be ready. Do not let it rock your world.

"And what about luck? Do you believe your life could be dictated by luck? I am a great believer in luck, and I find the harder I work the better luck I have.

"My Dad taught me to have strong work ethics. I would not have made it in life except for knowing not to be afraid of work and to be proud of my accomplishments.

"I hope this advice will help you on your way in life. You all are about to go on your journey in life, and I hope it includes higher educa-

tion. Education is so important. It is estimated today that a person with a four year college degree will make one million dollars more in a lifetime than a person who does not have a degree.

"With the Lord's help, I have overcome many problems in my life. For you to really know who I am, I have to tell you I believe God brought me through many trials so I can say with courage, faith and hard work, and His help you can overcome anything life has dealt you.

"Emerson said, "Hitch your wagon to a star."

"So, settle for no less than your dream. Work hard. Keep the faith. Have the right attitude, and don't be afraid of work."

36.
Full Circle

The Quarterly State Meeting of Family Advisors to Georgia Family Improvements was held on the tenth floor of the Equitable Building in Atlanta. I had arrived early and sat in my car on the parking deck preparing my notes and spelling key words, for the meeting.

During these weekly sessions, I was instrumental on committees implementing family assistance by collecting demographics, writing a resource books, and writing the booklet, "When People Need Help." This entailed making services available to those who did not know how to find what was available. Included were: senior services, block grants, immunization for children, meeting children's medical needs, after school programs, new mother's programs at the hospital level, training first time parents, and making food available for low income families with children under the age of six. I also helped pass local funding to build a half-way house for runaway youth.

During the morning break when everyone had coffee and donuts, I walked to the window and slowly surveyed the panoramic view of Atlanta from the tenth floor. Our meeting room just happened to be facing the northwest view of Atlanta. I glanced out of the window and was immediately transported in my mind to another place and another time.

There in the distance, standing like a narrow pencil on the horizon was the old smokestack of the electric power plant, so close to the Grace

Memorial Cemetery where my parents were buried. The smokestack tower had always seemed like a special marker to me because their graves seemed almost close enough to be under the shadow of it. I felt as if my heartstrings were being stretched all the many miles back to their grave sites. I could see the whole area in my mind: the headstones, the writing on the headstones, the green grass, and the rain-splattered plastic flowers. All the love I had for my parents flooded back to me at that moment.

I glanced up to the clouds above the Equitable Building. Lazy and white the large cumulus clouds drifted in the August sun. I had the strange feeling that Lila and Frank—Mom and Dad—knew I had overcome so much and was now successful. They knew that, finally, all their prayers had been answered.

I turned my back on the window and looked at the board members in the conference room. My future was here; my past was behind me. But I realized my past had made me who I had become. I realized that I wanted to visit Oakdale again and see if I could remember exactly what had been, and how things had happened to bring me to this point today.

After the meeting, I drove away from the Equitable Building in a somber mood, drove down I-285 and passed the old smokestack tower, and back to Oakdale to visit the scenes of my youth.

All the way back there, I thought back to my childhood and to all of the things that had happened to me. When I walked over the places of early memories, I continued to think about those people who had been a part of my life, and what they were doing now.

Kay, my sister, eventually sold her house and property to the State Department of Transportation. The D.O.T. put the I-285 east-west connector through her property. They paid her in six figures; she now lives in a modern new home. She and Sam have a good marriage and Daniel is grown and in school. Kay suffers from constant pain as the result of the train-car accident when she was sixteen, but she refuses to indulge in excessive pain medications. She spends her days in faith with prayer and meditation to get through the pain one day at a time.

For a year, I took care of Aunt Lilly after her husband, James, died. Lilly reluctantly closed up her home and moved to a nursing home in Mississippi to be close to her children and grandchildren. Fifteen years later a development company bought the tiny house and property also for six figures. The parking lot of the shopping mall takes up most of Hill Street. Aunt Lilly still lives in the nursing home in Mississippi. She is eighty-eight years old.

Frank and Lila Berkshire's house stands empty but in good repair. The yard and cornfield have long overgrown right up to the bluff where the railroad tracks have been made into the Silver Comet Walking Trail.

I thought about my parents again and knew they would be proud and happy to know that their prayers for me were finally answered. I remembered the time when Dad talked to me about God when we were out in the barn and he sat in his wheelchair. I thought about his words, 'Sometimes it takes a long time to turn things around. Keep the joy in your mind like your prayers have already been answered then one day you will look up and see the results. Don't give up on yourself or on praying. God never gives up on us.'

Decisions made in my youth, even my childhood, took me a lifetime to overcome. I overcame illiteracy. I overcame my addictions. I stuck by my wife throughout her undiagnosed health problems until she finally received the right help. I have a close relationship with God after I learned, even at my lowest point, I *was* worthy to ask Him for help.

"Ask, and it will be given to you; seek, and you will find; knock, and the door will be opened to you."

www.ingramcontent.com/pod-product-compliance
Lightning Source LLC
LaVergne TN
LVHW050923080826
845145LV00001B/183

* 9 7 8 0 9 6 2 8 0 2 3 8 6 *